Jessie flew into Tommy's arms.

'It's all over. Drop your weapons, son,' a voice commanded.

Tommy looked up to find he and Jessie were surrounded by police, all with truncheons drawn.

Tommy gazed round him. There were Black Marias at either end of Linton Street, while the street itself was overrun with bobbies.

He brought his attention back to Jessie, who was clinging to him as though she would never let him go.

'I love you,' he whispered.

'And I love you.'

A flashbulb popped. It was Fraser Tulloch taking their picture.

Arm in arm, Jessie and Tommy were led to the nearest Black Maria. Ragged cheer after cheer from the Boyd Street Boys still standing followed their progress.

'Who are they?' John Cameron asked one of the boys.

'That's Tommy McBride, our leader, and undisputed King of the Glasgow Teds.'

'King of the Glasgow Teds!' John Cameron breathed, already visualizing the words in print . . .

Emma Blair

JESSIE GRAY

timewarner
paperbacks

A *Time Warner* Paperback

First published in Great Britain
in 1986 by Arrow Books Limited
This edition published by Warner Books in 1997
Reprinted 2001 (twice)
Reprinted by Time Warner Paperbacks in 2002

A CIP catalogue record for this book
is available from the British Library.

ISBN 0 7515 1665 1

Printed and bound in Great Britain by
Clays Ltd, St Ives plc

Time Warner Paperbacks
An imprint of
Time Warner Books UK
Brettenham House
Lancaster Place
London WC2E 7EN

www.TimeWarnerBooks.co.uk

PART ONE

Star
1947–48

1

The first time she laid eyes on Tommy McBride was in mid-November, 1947. Miss Parrot was in charge of the assembly where classes 2A, hers, and 3B, Tommy's, were to practise their dancing for the forthcoming Christmas 'do'.

'Gentlemen, take your partners please,' Miss Parrot instructed, and the boys who'd been lining one wall moved towards the girls lining the wall opposite, a few of whom were sniggering and giggling.

Suddenly he was there in front of her, mumbling the appropriate words while looking at some spot in the cleft of her neck. His own neck was flushed. He clearly found asking a lassie up on to the floor acutely embarrassing, which amused her.

'Thank you,' she replied demurely, thinking to herself that she'd never noticed him before.

'A waltz,' Miss Parrot announced, and bent to the old phonograph on which a record had already been placed.

She went into his arms, and then they were off to the somewhat scratchy music. He was a terrible dancer, stumbling over his own feet and hers. Halfway through the dance it felt as though a ton weight had been dropped on her left big toe.

'Sorry,' he muttered.

'Don't worry about it, I've nine others,' she answered testily, but immediately wished she hadn't when she saw how her reply had hurt him. 'We all have to learn, and polish up our techniques, that's the purpose of these assemblies,' she added, giving him a smile.

For a brief second their eyes met, then he quickly glanced away, his entire face colouring.

This one really is shy, she thought, which she didn't

find at all unattractive. Many of the boys at Queen's Park Senior Secondary had far too big a tip for themselves, some cocky in the extreme. A shy lad made a pleasant change.

When the waltz was over Miss Parrot told them all to separate into their lines again, then proceeded to give a demonstration of the fox trot, Miss Parrot doing this with John Drumsheil who was almost as good a dancer as she was.

When the fox trot had been demonstrated to Miss Parrot's satisfaction, Miss Parrot instructed the boys to take new partners.

She wondered if the shy one would ask her up again, but he didn't, he asked Marcie Allen instead. It was Rog Hastie who presented himself in front of her, Rog who always smelled as if he never changed his vest or underpants. Reluctantly, she accepted.

She didn't see the shy lad again till the end of the week when their two classes had another dancing assembly under Miss Parrot.

'Gentlemen, take your partners for a polka, please,' Miss Parrot announced.

He materialized out of the milling boys to mutter his request in such a low voice she had to strain to hear.

'I'd be delighted,' she replied, and followed him further out on to the floor.

He didn't speak, just stood there looking everywhere but directly into her face. She noticed his neck wasn't flushed this time round, and thought that an improvement.

What hadn't improved was his dancing which was even worse than before. Within seconds he'd managed to kick her shin so hard she knew it would be black and blue before the day was out.

'Try to relax, it'll come easier to you if you do,' she said kindly.

He did his best to relax, but that was no help. She exclaimed in pain when his heel came scything down on

8

two of her toes. Muttering his apologies, he returned to being rigid again.

'Sorry for being so clumsy,' he mumbled at the end of the polka, then reluctantly left her.

She saw his reluctance, and was touched by it. When later on he asked her up again she was pleased, though apprehensive. Miraculously, she escaped this encounter unscathed.

The following Monday morning she was coming out of Latin class when she found herself beside him in the corridor. 'Hello,' she said.

He gave her a startled look, not having been aware of her. 'Oh hello.'

She said she was on her way to South Building, and he said he was too. They continued on their way together.

As they walked, and talked, she discovered he'd only been at Queen's Park a few weeks. He and his family had just recently moved into the district.

'Where from?' she asked, curious.

He hesitated fractionally before replying, 'Govanhill.'

She knew Govanhill was a rough area, quite different to Battlefield where they were now. Govanhill was lower working class; Battlefield was upper working to middle class. Or, as some folks might have put it, in Battlefield the toilets were inside the houses, not outside on the stairhead.

'How are you settling into Queen's Park then? Are you making pals?' she inquired.

He shrugged his shoulders. 'It's not that easy. I suppose it takes time.'

Lizzie Dunnachie called out to her and she waved over. Lizzie made a gesture that told her Lizzie had been round behind the bicycle shed having a fly smoke.

She brought her attention back to the shy one, and suddenly realized that she didn't know his name yet. 'I'm Star Gray, what are you called?' she said.

9

He gawped at her. 'You're what?'

'Star Gray.' Then, seeing his disbelief, explained, 'I was christened Jessie but I haven't been able to abide that since I was wee. I'm Star to my friends.'

Star! He'd never heard the like. 'I'm Tommy McBride,' he grinned.

They reached South Building and went inside. She was about to say goodbye when the idea came to her. 'When you lived in Govanhill were you in the Boys' Brigade?' she asked.

He shook his head.

'There's a church only a couple of minutes away from here called Battlefield Central. I know for a fact they've a grand B.B. Company there who meet every Friday night at a quarter to seven. Why don't you go along? They're a right friendly bunch.'

Tommy didn't fancy the B.B., or the Scouts, at all. In Govanhill they'd laughed at both lots. And those daft pillbox hats the B.B. wore! Proper nanas they looked. 'No thanks, the B.B.'s not for me.'

'Pity that. I certainly enjoy my nights there.'

She had to be taking the mickey out of him. 'They don't have girls in the B.B.,' he said.

'True enough,' she replied, eyes twinkling mischievously.

'So how can you enjoy your nights there?'

'Come along and find out,' she retorted, and, turning abruptly, strode off leaving him staring perplexedly after her.

As she went into class she wondered briefly if he would come down to the Hall, but decided he wouldn't. As it turned out, she was wrong.

Friday night at eight thirty on the dot she went through the door connecting the manse to the church, and along the narrow passageway at the rear behind the pulpit. This took her into the musty corridor that led down to the Church Hall where the B.B. meetings were held.

10

Up until the moment she entered, Tommy had considered the evening a waste of time. Well, not a complete waste, several of the lads had made friendly overtures.

Then Star walked in, and his evening was made. But what was she doing here? That was the mystery. A mystery that was soon resolved when she seated herself at the piano in the corner and started to pick out a tune.

Star had been playing piano for the B.B. since the previous year, when Mrs Lang's arthritis had got so bad she'd had to pack in playing for them.

When it was discovered that no one else in the congregation wanted the job, Star had volunteered. Although she was no older than many of the boys, her father had been delighted, declaring it a good Christian act.

The Maze Marching, for which Star played the accompanying music, was always the last item on the evening's agenda, and lasted through till nine o'clock. After that the entire Company came together to be dismissed.

Captain Bell (inevitably called Ding A Ling by the lads) strode into the Hall and barked out the command for those taking part in the Maze Marching to get, as he put it, fell into line.

'Shortest to the left, tallest to the right, single rank, size!' Ding A Ling shrieked in his best parade-ground manner, his voice so loud it made Tommy jump right up off his chair.

Seeing Tommy looking uncertain, Ding A Ling came over and told him Maze Marching wasn't compulsory. Tommy immediately replied that he'd love to take part.

Actually, he couldn't have cared less about Maze Marching, or any other sort of marching come to that. What did interest him was that Star would be playing the music for it and he didn't want to risk being sent to any of the rooms adjoining the Hall to do some other activity.

Star suddenly saw him grinning at her, and grinned in return. She was delighted he'd come, but it didn't occur to her to ask herself why.

Ding A Ling told Tommy just to follow the chap in front and he couldn't go wrong. Convoluted and complicated as Maze Marching was, only a handful of the marchers and the Staff Sergeant at the front had to memorize the various movements and patterns. Everyone else followed like sheep. But sheep who followed smartly, Ding A Ling emphasized, *very very* smartly, with bags of swank.

'By the left quick march!' Ding A Ling screamed, and Star struck up as the line moved off.

The first ten minutes were easy, and quite enjoyable, going over what had already been plotted and learned. After that, though, new moves were given and it became excruciatingly slow and tedious for everyone except the Staff Sergeant, who had to do this new piece of memorizing.

Finally the Maze Marching finished. To Tommy's disconcertment, Star immediately slipped from the Hall. He was about to follow her when the entire Company was called to order for the final proceedings which consisted of a short speech by Ding A Ling, followed by an even shorter prayer.

Then it was all over, and time to go. Picking up his things, Tommy made a beeline for the door through which Star had vanished, convinced that she'd be well gone by now and that he'd lost her.

But she hadn't gone, she was in the kitchen adjoining the Hall, washing up the officers' tea cups.

Suddenly he was shy again, completely lost for words. He made a sort of strangulated coughing sound to attract her attention. She turned, and immediately her face lit up with a smile.

'I was pleased to see you out there. Are you glad you came along?'

He looked down at his shoes. 'Oh aye. But I must say I

12

was surprised when you actually did show up. I was certain you were having me on.'

'And I was surprised to see you. I didn't think you'd come.'

Silence fell between them as she dried the cups and saucers, then began putting them away.

Tommy couldn't think of anything to say. He'd never been so taken with a lassie before. There was something different about Star. All he wanted was to be with her.

He shyly gazed at the small oval face, and the deep brown eyes and dark brown hair. She was slim, skinny some might have said, but although only fourteen, she already had a womanly body. Aye, very womanly, he thought to himself.

'Stare any harder and you'll stare holes through me,' Star said as she dried her hands on the tea cloth.

Embarrassment flooded him. Thankfully, she had no idea what had been going through his mind. He made a gesture that encompassed the entire building. 'What's your connection with this place?' he asked abruptly. 'You must have one.'

'My father's the minister here.' Her eyes twinkled as she went on with mock solemnity, 'The Reverend Kenneth Gray.'

He was momentarily stunned. That was the last thing he'd expected to hear. Her father a minister! Bloody hell!

Star couldn't help smiling at his stricken expression. It was one she was used to seeing when she announced what her father did. 'The manse is attached to the other side of the church. That's where I live.'

There were voices in the corridor as a contingent of the boys went through the door that led to the outside. Their voices were replaced by others which Tommy recognized as belonging to several of the officers.

'Everyone's leaving. I suppose I'd better get on my way, too,' he said, reluctance in his voice.

She was about to make a crack about his marching being an awful lot better than his dancing, then decided

13

against it. She already understood that he could be easily hurt. As her mother would have said, he was a sensitive lad.

'Listen,' she said, suddenly inspired. 'I usually go round to the Fives Cafe in Battlefield Road after this. A few of us get together for a cup of coffee and a bit of a natter. Would you care to come?'

'Sounds smashing,' he instantly replied, leaping at the opportunity to be with her longer.

'Whereabouts round here is it you live?' Star asked as they headed for the Fives.

'Millbrae Crescent. Do you know it?'

Star nodded, slightly puzzled. Millbrae Crescent was one of the poshest streets in the district. It surprised her that Tommy's family should have a house there. Govanhill to Millbrae Crescent — a big jump indeed, she thought. It was the difference between fish and chips and fillet steak. Not that she had any first hand knowledge of fillet steak, with the war only two years over and the country still heavily rationed.

On arriving at the Fives, Tommy saw why it had been given that name. Its address was 555 Battlefield Road. On entering the cosy cafe, they were immediately hailed by Lizzie Dunnachie, who was sitting at a table with another girl Tommy recognized from Queen's Park, and a lad from the B.B. There were about a dozen members of the B.B. in all scattered round the various tables.

Star introduced Tommy to Lizzie and Catherine, while James Ledingham said that he and Tommy had already met at the B.B. meeting.

Tommy ordered coffee for Star and himself from the short, fat man who came to take their order.

'Talking about dead boring places,' sighed Lizzie. 'Isn't that just Glasgow on a Friday night?'

'There's the cafes and that's about it,' agreed Catherine.

Lizzie lit a cigarette, blowing out a long thin stream of smoke, in a way she thought was *très sophisticated*, and certainly better than Glasgow deserved.

14

Catherine asked Tommy where he'd moved from. As soon as she heard he was from Govanhill, Catherine lost interest in him. As far as she was concerned only neds came from there; neds, hooligans and roughs. It was clear from her expression that anyone from Govanhill was unsavoury and inferior.

Noticing Catherine's disdainful attitude, Star became angry. She could tell from the veil that had descended over Tommy's eyes that he'd caught it also.

Lizzie prattled on that there was only one really decent entertainment available in Glasgow at the weekend, and that was the dancing in the town. She'd have been there like a shot, she said, if her Dad would allow her. But the old man wouldn't entertain the idea, not until her seventeenth birthday when he'd told her he'd allow her to go to the wee dance halls over at Shawlands Cross. She'd have to wait till eighteen before being allowed to attend the town dancing.

'There are always church activities, you could try getting involved in some of those,' Star said innocently, knowing fine well that Lizzie would be the last person to get involved in such.

Lizzie knew she was being teased. Star was always doing it to her. 'You do the only activity I'd be interested in, if I could play the piano that is,' Lizzie retorted.

'You'll come to a bad end one day if you're not careful Lizzie Dunnachie,' jibed Star.

'I live in hope,' said Lizzie, raising her eyes to heaven, and making everyone laugh.

Things were just relaxing when Star glanced at the clock and said she had to get back. Tommy jumped to his feet. 'I'll walk you,' he offered. Adding as the perfect excuse, 'I have to go that way anyway.'

'Will you be going back to the B.B. next week?' Star asked Tommy as they arrived in front of the manse. It was a squat, Gothic building that looked like some cancerous growth on the side of the church.

15

'I'll be there all right,' Tommy said quickly. Wild horses wouldn't keep him away.

She touched him lightly on the shoulder, sending a shiver through him. 'I'm glad. Good night, then.'

'Good night.'

She flew up the gravel path to the manse's medieval-style wood and metal door, opening it with her own key. She waved to Tommy, then the heavy door thudded closed and she was gone.

As Tommy continued towards Millbrae Crescent his walking became a march, and he began whistling one of the tunes she'd played earlier.

The next Friday night Tommy bolted his tea, then polished his shoes for the B.B. meeting. Jeannie, his mother, remarked drily that if the B.B. could get him to polish his shoes with such enthusiasm after only one attendance then the age of miracles was indeed not past.

Tommy duly presented himself at the Church Hall wearing his highly polished shoes, gleaming brass and leather belt, and daft wee pillbox hat. From that point onwards, the evening went interminably slowly as he waited for the Maze Marching — and Star.

When she finally arrived he caught her eyes as soon as he could, and smiled. Her smile back made his stomach turn over.

Later, at the end of the prayer, he hurried from the Hall to the kitchen where he found her washing the officers' tea cups and saucers just like before.

He entered the kitchen as nonchalantly as he was able. 'I thought we might go to the Fives again, what do you say?' he asked.

'I was on my way there anyway, so we might as well go together,' she agreed.

He wasn't exactly chuffed with the phrasing of her acceptance. But she *was* going with him, that was the main thing.

16

On arriving at the Fives they were again hailed by Lizzie Dunnachie. Catherine was sitting beside Lizzie, and beside Catherine was a chap whose face Tommy had seen around school. Star introduced him as Alec Muir.

'How was the Scripture Union class?' Star asked Alec as soon as she'd sat down.

Glancing at the lapel of Alec's jacket Tommy saw a green and gold S.U. badge there. He listened while Alec eagerly expounded to Star all that had taken place in that evening's class.

After a while Star glanced over at Tommy. She could see he was clearly bored by this conversation, but he was also wearing a peculiar, intense expression whose meaning she couldn't fathom. Then Alec claimed her attention once more, and Tommy's strange expression evaporated from her mind.

Eventually Tommy started to chat to Lizzie. When he tried to speak to Catherine she only replied in mono-syllables; it didn't take a genius to realize he wasn't quoted there.

Alec waxed long and passionately about the S.U. class. Religion intrigued him, and he was seriously considering the idea of becoming a minister himself. He was almost convinced that he had 'the calling'.

Alex bent down under the table to lift four fat tomes off the floor which he placed beside his now empty coffee cup. 'These are the books I borrowed from your father the other week,' he said to Star. 'I thought I might return them tonight.'

Tommy's ears immediately pricked up. It would spoil everything if this Alec tagged along when he took Star home.

Lizzie Dunnachie leaned across to glance at the title of the top book. She pulled a face. 'Yuch!' she said.

Tommy reached over and picked it up: *The Life of St. Paul*.

'He had a fascinating life. Quite fascinating,' Alec said to Tommy, mistaking his curiosity for interest.

17

Tommy could see that Alec was in deadly earnest. 'I prefer Edgar Rice Burroughs myself,' he replied in a friendly tone.

Lizzie made a gargling noise at the back of her throat. 'Naked men cavorting about the jungle. Lovely!' she hissed, eyes agleam.

Alec was the first to laugh. He might be religious, but he wasn't without a sense of humour.

'You'd better come on then if you want to give those to Dad,' Star said to Alec, starting to rise. To Tommy, starting to rise also, she added. 'I'll see you next week at school, no doubt.'

Tommy had already risen several inches off his hard wooden chair, he now slowly sank back into it again. He managed a weak grin. 'No doubt,' he echoed, pleased that the words didn't come out strangulated as he'd feared they would.

He watched jealously as they headed for the door, Alec bowed under the weight of the books.

'God Squad,' Lizzie said to Tommy after Star and Alec had left, and winked.

The Reverend Kenneth Gray was most distinguished in appearance, every inch a right and proper minister. His face was finely boned, his hair a glossy silver which he wore extremely short and parted at the side. He was a little more than average height for a Glaswegian, and walked with a stiff and upright carriage as though at one time he'd been in the Army, which he hadn't.

The Reverend was sitting in his favourite leather arm-chair in front of the small fire burning in the grate. He'd just sat down again, after going to the bookcase to get some more books for Alec to borrow and replacing the ones Alec had returned.

Jessie was seeing Alec to the front door. The Reverend Kenneth Gray liked Alec. He was such a nice lad that. And he came from a terribly good background, even though his parents had no money. The family were minor Scottish gentry who'd been fairly wealthy up until the late twenties, when Alec's grandfather had lost nearly everything speculating on commodities.

He glanced over at the settee on which Alec and Jessie had been sitting, and wondered for the hundredth time if anything was ever going to come of that relationship. They would certainly have his approval if it did. He considered Alec a fine catch for his lass. A union between the Muirs and Grays would be a step up for the Grays, no doubt about it.

'You're looking gey pensive dear,' Alison Gray broke into her husband's reverie. She was knitting herself a new winter cardy from some excellent unpicked wool she'd managed to buy at the church's last jumble sale.

Before the Reverend could answer, Star came bursting back into the room. She went directly to the fire, squatting and holding out her hands to the flames. 'It's bitter outside, I wouldn't be at all surprised if we had snow before morning,' she said.

'I was just about to say to your mother what a grand couple you and Alec Muir make,' the Reverend said.

Star smiled into the fire. She was only too well aware that her father had hopes for her and Alec. Snob that he was, she knew why he fostered that hope.

'Aye, Alec's a fine lad, there's no disputing that,' said Alison. 'And what about that new boy from the school? Did he turn up at the B.B. again tonight? The one you were trying to help make friends?'

Star turned to look at her mother. 'He did. I think he's taken to the B.B.'

This was the first the Reverend had heard about Tommy McBride. A question to Star revealed that Tommy had only recently moved into the neighbourhood, which meant the McBrides might not have joined a local congregation yet. The Reverend Gray was always on the lookout for new members. He fingered the briar in his lap. He would have loved another pipe, but had

19

already smoked his quota for the day. 'What's the boy's address? I'll send his parents a letter inviting them to morning service the Sunday after next.'

Star once more faced the flames. 'They live in Millbrae Crescent, but I don't know the number. I'll find out for you if you want.'

The Reverend's hand tightened over his briar. Millbrae Crescent! Only top-drawer and monied families lived there. A few new members from Millbrae Crescent would be a most welcome addition to his congregation. Most of the 'better' families preferred the bigger kirk over at Langside, which had several titles, including a Knight of the Thistle and an ex-Lord Provost, amongst its numbers.

'What does Mr McBride do?' he asked casually, thinking about future donations to the church fund.

Star shook her head. 'I've no idea. Tommy's never mentioned.'

'On second thoughts, rather than write I think it would be better, as you're already friendly with the lad, to call on them personally. And you can accompany me. Speak to this Tommy as soon as you can and ask him to ask his parents when it would be convenient for the pair of us to visit.'

'As you wish.'

The Reverend nodded his satisfaction, and hoped that Stanley Carrell over at Langside hadn't beaten him to it.

Star looked up at the McBrides' beautiful house. She guessed there were four or five bedrooms, which made it almost as big as the manse.

A glance at her watch told her it was one minute to eight; they were due at eight. Her father was a stickler for being punctual.

The Reverend was noting the thick velvet curtains hanging inside the window nearest to him. Those must

20

have cost a fair packet when they'd been bought before the war, he told himself.

'Pull the bell handle dear,' he instructed Star, and hoisted a smile on to his face.

Tommy was on his feet the moment the first clang reverberated through the house. He almost ran to the front door in his eagerness. He'd been excited about Star's coming since she'd broached the subject two days earlier.

In what they called the parlour Jim McBride glanced at his wife Jeannie and whispered for her not to be nervous. He rose from his chair and she did likewise.

As soon as she stepped into the hallway Star knew she liked this house, it had a warm and welcoming family feeling about it. As she walked behind Tommy and her father her eyes were darting all around, taking everything in.

There had been a lot of fresh painting done, which surprised her. Paint was still hard to come by even two years after the war. And the carpet underfoot was new, another surprise for the same reason.

'How do you do. It's kind of you to have myself and daughter into your home,' the Reverend said on entering the parlour, and extended his hand to Jim to be shaken.

The Reverend's practised smile wavered fractionally when he saw that instead of a right hand Jim had a hook.

Jim was well used to this situation. In a twisting motion he took the Reverend's outstretched hand with his left one, and shook heartily. 'Pleased to meet you, Reverend Gray.'

By the time the introductions had been completed Star had already decided she liked the McBrides. As she'd taken to their house, she took to them right away.

'A cup of tea?' asked Jeannie McBride.

'Or how about something stronger? Whisky, or a drop of Amontillado perhaps?' Jim added.

The Reverend beamed with pleasure. 'I haven't tasted Amontillado since 1942,' he declared. 'I'd be delighted to have a glass. It's always been my favourite.'

Jim produced a bottle of finest Amontillado from a well-stocked drinks cabinet and poured three schooners for the adults. For Star and Tommy he poured out fresh orange juice.

'Welcome to Battlefield!' said the Reverend to the McBrides, raising his glass in a toast. His expression was one of deepest appreciation as he tasted the contents of his glass.

'Perhaps Star would like to see over the house,' Jeannie suggested to Tommy.

The Reverend Gray blanched. His daughter's chosen name always embarrassed him. 'Silly name that, but she flatly refuses the good Christian one given her by her mother and me,' he said to Jeannie and Jim. He'd done everything in his power to get her to stop using such a ludicrous name, but in the end he'd had to admit defeat.

Jim McBride stared at Star across the rim of his schooner. She had all the signs of a real looker. Give her a couple of more years, he thought, and she'd be a cracker. It seemed she was also a determined young lady, a quality he admired. He could well understand why Tommy seemed so attracted to her.

The minister sipped his sherry and tried to gain his usual composure. It had been a shock for him to hear how the McBrides spoke. Star hadn't told him they'd come from Govanhill. Why, their accent was so common! Broad Glasgow. He certainly hadn't expected that, not in Millbrae Crescent. *Nouveaux riches*, he thought, and inwardly sneered.

Jim switched his attention back to the minister. A right sanctimonious fart was how he summed him up. He knew, however, that being accepted by a local church would make settling into the area all that much easier, and so was prepared to play his own game with Gray.

Jeannie gave the impression of being totally relaxed,

22

but in reality she was churning inside with anxiety. It had been against her wishes that they'd come to Millbrae Crescent in the first place, where she'd said they'd stick out like a sore thumb. But Jim had been insistent. He'd always fancied living with the toffs, and now that they could afford to they damn well would. Anyway, he'd argued, it was to Tommy's advantage that they do so, as it would give him the opportunity to meet some decent youngsters and make some good connections for the future. She didn't want him to turn out a lout like the other lads in Govanhill, did she?

Star was hesitating, unsure whether or not her father wanted her to remain by his side. When he still gave her no indication either way she said to Jeannie, 'Oh I'd adore to see round the house.'

There were five bedrooms, as it turned out. Star admired each one in turn. They were all newly decorated. Tommy's, where they ended up, was done in an exceptionally nice, tasteful wallpaper.

Star stared out Tommy's bedroom window at the falling snow. 'How did your father lose his hand?' she asked in a quiet voice.

He came up behind her. 'In the war. He was badly wounded at the Battle of Keren in Abyssinia. Besides having his hand blown clean off he also took some shrapnel in his right leg. You might not have noticed downstairs but he limps rather badly.'

Star thought of her cousin Haldane who'd gone to the war, and hadn't come back. She'd been very fond of Hal who'd been ten years older than she. Hal and two of his pals had gone into the army on the same day; none of them had survived.

The war had played such a large part in her life that as a child she'd come to believe it would go on for ever. She'd asked her father how Gentle Jesus could allow such awful things to happen, but her father's answer had been completely unsatisfactory.

Standing only a few feet behind Star, the smell of her

was driving Tommy wild. He tried to imagine what it would be like just to touch her hair.

'Why did you choose the name Star for yourself?' he asked, his voice husky.

She roused herself from her reverie, and gave a little smile. That was a question she didn't always answer. It all depended on who was doing the asking.

'When I decided I'd change my name I considered hundreds, but none of them were really right. Then one day I picked up a book of Familiar Quotations and there it was. Have you ever heard of *Elmer Gantry*?'

Tommy shook his head.

'It's a novel by an American writer, Sinclair Lewis. The quotation is from the character Elmer Gantry himself who says, *"What is love? It is the morning and the evening star."* I was so taken with those words that I named myself after them. And so Jessie became Star.'

The story intrigued Tommy. He'd never heard anything so wonderful, or beautiful. This is no ordinary girl, he told himself. This girl was very very special.

Meanwhile, in the parlour, the Reverend Gray was saying that it was time he and Star headed back home. Jeannie went and called up the stairs for Star and Tommy to come down.

'I'll look forward to seeing you on Sunday, then,' the minister said to Jim. It had already been agreed that the McBrides would be taking a section of a pew from now on. Jim had paid for this privilege with a cheque for a year in advance.

Jim had a sudden thought while they waited for Star and Tommy. Telling the Reverend he'd only be a moment or two, he hurried from the room. When he returned to the parlour he was carrying a bottle of Amontillado identical to the one from his drinks cabinet.

'Oh no I couldn't!' the Reverend protested, but only half heartedly, when Jim attempted to press the bottle on him.

24

'I insist. If for no other reason than as a token of gratitude for Star's kindness to Tommy,' Jim said.

'If you put it like that,' the minister replied, trying to appear reluctant, and accepted the bottle.

At the front door hands were again shaken, and hearty goodbyes made.

As soon as the Grays had gone Tommy rushed back upstairs to his room where he sat savouring the smell of Star that still lingered there.

'The morning and the evening star,' he said once to himself, and smiled.

Tommy lay wide awake in the darkness. He'd been in bed for ages but couldn't sleep for thinking of Star. How she fascinated him! He was drawn to her like iron to a magnet.

But, although he thoroughly enjoyed her company, he wasn't always totally at ease in it. She was so different to the lassies he'd been used to in Govanhill, so refined. She often made him feel downright uncouth. What could a boy like him offer a girl like Star? And yet there was that fascination, that magnetism.

He decided what he would do next. He would take her out someplace, a proper taking out, not just the Fives after the B.B.

He racked his brains. He could take her to a James Craig tearoom for a cream tea, or high tea even. Better the cream tea, he told himself. If there was one thing a lassie liked more than a gooey cake, it was two gooey cakes.

Then he had it. It was so obvious, it was amazing he hadn't thought of it before. It was far better than a cream tea. The school Christmas Dance – he would take her to that.

Excitement filled him at the prospect. Low lights, Star in his arms, the smell of her in his nostrils. He was a terrible dancer, it was true, but he'd make a special effort between now and then to get better.

He would ask his mother to work with him on his steps in the parlour. For Jeannie was a grand dancer, his Dad had always said so.

That decision made, he finally began to drift off. He dreamt he was Fred Astaire and Star was Ginger Rogers.

Star was worried about her Latin. Despite her best efforts, she was continuing to do extremely badly in it and dreaded to think what her end of term mark was going to be. It wasn't that she lacked intelligence. She excelled in other subjects. When it came to Latin, however, she found herself up against a stone wall of incomprehension.

She knew it wasn't the teacher's fault; no one could have been more patient than Mr Orr. But even he despaired when she constructed a sentence without a verb in it.

A smile turned her lips upwards when she thought about music. Now that was a different kettle of fish entirely. She was head and shoulders above most of her year when it came to that. Besides piano, she played violin and clarinet, and had even scored several compositions. Miss Hamill, the music teacher, said she was a natural. For her the music classes weren't work, they were sheer pleasure. The minutes of music class zipped past, while those of Latin dragged along on leaden boots.

'Star!'

She turned to see Tommy racing after her. She waved happily and waited for him to catch up.

It had started snowing again, and there was thick slush underfoot. When he arrived by her side his cheeks were red from a combination of the biting wind and his exertion.

'I missed you at the main gate,' he said, falling into step beside her.

'I left by the back one because I was coming from the Science Labs,' she explained.

A tram rattled by to stop at Battlefield Rest. It was a cream, green and orange coloured building, the Corporation's colours, where the crews changed over. They crossed behind the Rest and in front of the Victoria Infirmary.

They walked in silence. Finally he took a deep breath and said in a rush, 'I was wondering if you'd go to the Christmas Dance with me? I'd like very much to take you.'

She stopped and turned to him in surprise. The look on his face made her realize that their friendship meant something totally different to him than it did to her. How stupid she'd been! She should have realized before now what was happening.

Damn you for a fool, Jessie Gray! she thought. So upset that she called herself by her real name.

'I'm afraid I can't,' she replied lamely.

Tommy had never even considered the possibility of her turning him down. The scenario had been simple as far as he'd been concerned: he'd ask, she'd accept, and that would be that.

'Why not?'

She was going to hurt him again, she knew, but what could she do? 'I've already been asked by Alec Muir, the chap you met in the Fives that night,' she said softly.

'Oh!'

She went on, knowing she had to. Tommy had to be given the full facts, for his own good. 'You see, Alec and I have more or less been going out together for a while now.'

Tommy seized this slender thread of hope. 'What do you mean more or less?'

Star sighed inwardly, he wasn't making this any easier. 'All right, we've been going steady,' she snapped in reply, hating herself for snapping.

Tommy felt such an idiot. 'I hadn't heard round school. No one ever mentioned it.'

'I thought you knew. I mean, I just presumed you did, everyone does.'

'Seems I was the exception,' he answered, and tried to smile. The smile that came out as a grimace, and made Star want to sweep him into her arms and hug him tightly. He looked just like a wee boy. A wee boy who'd taken something precious out to play for the first time, and lost it.

Tommy fought to keep himself under control. Somehow, and it was an awful struggle, he managed to assume a nonchalant if unconvincing pose.

'Thank you for asking, though,' she said gently.

Emotion clogged his throat; the nonchalant pose disintegrated into drooping shoulders. 'See you then,' he mumbled, and walked hurriedly away, in quite the wrong direction for Millbrae Crescent.

Star stood watching his retreating back. She could kick herself for what had just happened. Why hadn't she seen he was getting sweet on her? She must have been blind.

She watched him till finally he disappeared from view, telling herself she'd lost a friend, and the Boys' Brigade their new recruit.

That Friday proved her right about the latter.

Jim McBride hummed as he drove. He always enjoyed being out in the Arrole Johnstone, which he'd bought only eighteen months before. During the last years of the war the car had been owned by an American Air Force mechanic stationed at Prestwick who'd converted it from an ordinary gear shift to automatic.

Automatics were still a rarity in Britain, and Jim had jumped at the opportunity of owning one when he'd heard about the Arrole Johnstone being for sale. Even with a hook he could still drive an ordinary gear shift, but for him automatic made life a great deal easier, and safer.

His humming ceased as he turned into the Candleriggs, a street he knew every stone and cobble of as his entire working life before the war had been spent in it.

Halfway down he drew the Arrole Johnstone into the kerb and stared across the street at the building on the other side. Murison's Carpet Factory, proclaimed the sign in faded letters – letters that had been shiny bright when he'd first seen them at the age of twelve.

He vividly remembered his start there; the terrible deafening noise, the huge looms that were awesome – at least to his inexperienced eyes – the weft and warp threads interlacing those looms that were being transformed into chenile carpet, the smell of linen and jute which had seemed such a stink to him at first. In time he'd got used to both the stink and the noise.

Then, years later, after Big Sandy Peggie and others had taught him his trade, came that glorious day when he'd been made a foreman. Oh that had been a day right enough! He'd been certain his heart would burst he'd been so proud.

Shortly following that Jeannie had come along, and the wee house in Boyd Street where Tommy had been born. Hard times, but good times, until that awful morning when war had been declared and he'd known he'd be going for a soldier.

When he'd left, old Murison had come down to the floor to say goodbye and wish him all the best. 'And rest assured your job will be waiting for you when you come back to us, McBride,' Murison had said. But it had been a different story after he'd been invalided out of the Army and returned, with his hook and limp, to confront the old man. It had been a different story then, all right!

There had been soft words of sympathy, and a large dram to go with them. Then the knife had been slid in. He couldn't resume his position of foreman, not when he was so badly disabled. And for the same reason operating a loom was quite out of the question.

He'd agreed about operating a loom, but argued that his disabilities wouldn't affect his work as a foreman. A foreman supervised, chivvied those under his control, saw there was no slacking and that all minor problems were resolved. How did his hook and limp affect him doing that?

But Murison, though apologetic, was adamant. That was the way of it, there were no exceptions.

So what position *was* open to him, he'd wanted to know.

Murison had poured more whisky, and considered that. The offer, when it finally came, was that of a nightwatchman's job, the wage a quarter of what he'd earned as a foreman.

He'd been outraged. How could he possibly keep a wife and kiddie on that sort of money, he'd demanded to know.

Murison's reply was brief but blunt. It was a case of take it or leave it.

He'd told Murison to stuff the nightwatchman's job up the arse, and gone stomping out past the now all-female workforce.

That night the real reason why Murison refused to have him back as a foreman dawned on him. It was because the foremen were now all forewomen, and women were only paid half what a man earned. He'd realized then how advantageous the war was proving for Joseph Murison, whose factory was now churning out various types of materials for the War Department. Full production, full order books, minimum wage outlay – Murison was coining it.

He hadn't been bitter after losing his hand, or learning he'd limp for the rest of his life, or even when it seemed certain that he'd lose his entire arm due to the continuing re-infection of his stump. But he'd been bitter then. Bitter, disgusted, and so angry at Murison he would happily have swung for the bastard if it hadn't been for Jeannie and Tommy who needed him.

Jim smiled wryly to himself, thinking it was an ill wind. For if Murison hadn't done the dirty on him he'd never have got tied in with Paddy Swords to become the wealthy man he was today, and getting steadily wealthier with every passing week.

If it hadn't been for Murison's greed he'd still have been a foreman and living in Boyd Street. Instead he now had his own set-up and lived in Millbrae Crescent amongst the nobs. In a way, he owed Murison, but, as the saying went, if Murison had been on fire he wouldn't have peed on the bastard.

He saluted the factory with his hook then headed off down the Candleriggs to the Trongate and the Docks beyond.

At Queen's Dock he made for the North Basin where the M. V. Swan was tied up. It had arrived earlier that day from Dublin. He nodded with satisfaction to see his lorry parked alongside the Customs and Excise shed. In the lorry were a driver and three others on his payroll. He brought the Arrole Johnstone to a halt beside the lorry, had a quick word with Matt, the driver, then went into the shed where he found Willie McAllister brewing up.

'A cup of java?' Willie asked.

'Aye, that would go down a treat.' He offered Willie one of his cigarettes. 'Ten crates this trip,' Jim continued, letting Willie know, as he always did, that he was aware of the exact number of crates in the consignment. It was a precautionary measure. He might trust Willie, but only to an extent. Mind you, it would have been downright stupid of the Customs official to doublecross him, kill off the goose that laid the golden eggs so to speak, but stranger things had happened before now.

Willie handed him a cup and saucer, then pointed to some forms lying on the desk.

Crossing to the forms Jim swiftly signed them, acknowledging receipt of the crates.

'Your bills of lading,' Willie said to Jim, and gave Jim ten further forms, these large and yellow. Each form stated that the crate whose stencilled number it carried contained specialist machine parts. Jim's business, situated in the Calton district, was ostensibly a repair shop. Which it was, and made a nice profit, too. But that was only a front for the way in which Jim really made his living.

Jim tucked the bills of lading into his inside jacket pocket, then took out his wallet. He counted off a number of five pound notes and gave these to Willie.

Willie recounted the notes in front of Jim; at the outset of their dealings together Jim had insisted on this, another precautionary measure. With the money recounted in front of him Willie could never come back at a later time to say the amount hadn't been correct.

'On the button as usual,' said Willie, and tucked the wad of fivers away.

'Next consignment is a week tomorrow. It's arriving on the S.S. *Hercules*, again from Dublin,' said Jim.

Willie digested the information, nodding. 'The S.S. *Hercules*, a week tomorrow. I'll make sure I'm the one on duty,' he replied.

Jim finished his coffee, accepted the release docket from Willie, then went out to the lorry to hand over the docket and tell the lads to secure the release of the crates and load them aboard.

Willie watched Jim through the shed window. He didn't know what was really in those crates, nor did he care. All that concerned him was the bung he got every time he passed a consignment through.

He grinned suddenly, remembering he was taking the new bint out that night. Her name was Sandra and she was a smasher! He'd buy her the best meal in Glasgow, then suggest the second house at the Alhambra. When the show was over it would be coffee and brandy in his West End flat.

It was the sort of night out he could only have afforded once in a while on his pay from the Customs and Excise. Thanks to Jim McBride he now did it all the time.

Star was in the school toilet with Lizzie Dunnachie, the pair of them sitting in cubicles next to one another.

Lizzie was in the middle of telling a filthy joke, and already had Star in stitches long before the punchline. Lizzie was the best filthy joke teller in the entire school, and had a seemingly endless supply of them. It was Lizzie's close secret where she got her jokes from.

The punchline was finally delivered, convulsing Star so much that she nearly fell off the w.c.

'Here listen, what's that?' asked Lizzie, as their laughter subsided.

Star caught her breath, listening. Then she heard it too, a commotion outside in the playground.

Just then Maev Whiteford, another 2A girl, came dashing into the cubicle on the other side of Star. 'Jesus!' she gasped, 'I thought I was going to get caught short there.'

'What's going on outside?' asked Star.

'That new boy . . . Tommy whatever his name is . . . he's having a fight with Korky Niven. It's a real humdinger, too, from what I saw as I dashed past.'

Tommy in a fight! And with Korky Niven! Korky was huge and a brute who enjoyed throwing his weight about. Star reached the toilet door with Lizzie right behind her. A crowd had gathered in the centre of the playground, heaving this way and that like a rugby scrum.

'Teacher,' muttered Lizzie, and gestured to where Mr Apsley, the P.T. teacher, was hurrying towards the crowd, black cape streaming out behind him.

Star and Lizzie reached the crowd at the same time as Mr Apsley, following in his wake as he carved a passage through the throng.

Star caught her breath when she saw Tommy. Blood was gushing from his nose, and the top buttons of his shirt had been ripped away. His tie had been jerked right round to the side of his neck. But though Korky was far larger than Tommy, the fight hadn't been one-sided. Korky's right eye was so swollen it was almost shut. There were also teeth marks on the cheek below the swollen eye.

The instant Korky saw Apsley he fell back from Tommy. 'Please sir, he started it! He attacked me with no provocation whatever, I swear that's the truth.'

'It's a lie,' hissed Tommy.

Mr Apsley stared hard at each lad in turn. He knew Korky to be a notorious bully, but that didn't necessarily mean he was the instigator of this. Tommy was more or less an unknown quantity to him, and did come from Govanhill, a right rough area.

'Why would he attack you without provocation?' Mr Apsley asked Korky at last.

Korky looked out innocently from his good eye. 'Please sir, I think he wanted to show everyone how tough he is, make a name for himself like. I was only defending myself, honestly.'

Mr Apsley wasn't yet convinced. 'Did anyone here see what happened?' he asked, addressing the crowd.

Korky had an inspiration then. 'Alec Muir saw and heard everything,' he said quickly staring directly at Alec.

Mr Apsley rounded on Alec, who was one of the school's most upright pupils. Mr Apsley knew Alec to be sound and reliable, a veritable paragon of virtue. If Alec confirmed Korky's account then that account was true.

Alec wanted to break eye contact with Korky, but couldn't. He was the rabbit mesmerized by the snake.

'Well, Alec?' demanded Mr Apsley.

'What Korky says is right enough sir,' Alec replied in a low voice.

Tommy couldn't believe that he'd just heard what he had. Why? Why was Alec lying? Wrongly, he concluded that it had to with Star. She must have told Alec about his asking her to the Christmas Dance, and this was Alec's revenge.

'Right then, it's the Head for you, my lad,' said Mr Apsley, and gestured to Tommy to start walking towards the Main Building, where the Head's study was located.

Korky congratulated himself on getting out of that one. He didn't envy in the least what was going to happen next to Tommy. He'd been up several times in the past before Commando McGee, and shuddered at the memory.

Alec saw Star, but didn't cross to her. Instead he backed off into the crowd at his rear and disappeared. He felt sick, and thoroughly ashamed of himself. He wanted to run and hide somewhere dark, just as he'd used to when wee and had done something wrong.

Star watched Tommy and Mr Apsley vanish into Main Building as around her the crowd began to disperse.

'Your friend Tommy will be for the high jump, that's a certainty,' Lizzie said to Star, for it was well known that Commando McGee couldn't abide fighting amongst his pupils and punished it severely.

Star looked round for Alec, wanting to talk with him, but he was gone. That's strange, she thought, for she knew he'd seen her. It was unlike him not to come over. He must have had something urgent to go off and attend to she told herself.

The bell rang, and those in the playground began to make their way into the four buildings that comprised the school. Star's next period was a study one, supervised by a Prefect. Impulsively, she decided not to attend. It was unlikely she wouldn't be missed, for the Prefects didn't take roll in study classes. Instead she'd wait for Tommy. After a session with McGee there was no telling what state he might be in. Maybe she could be of some help.

Star walked over to Main Building, the largest of the school's four buildings. On another impulse, she didn't go in but went round the side to stand directly beneath the Head's window. She wanted to hear what happened, and perhaps learn why Tommy had attacked Korky. It didn't really seem like the sort of thing Tommy would do.

The Commando was a small man with tremendously

35

broad and powerful shoulders. He'd been given the nickname Commando because he'd been one during the war. It was rumoured in the school that he'd killed half a dozen Germans, though not all at once, in hand to hand combat. He'd never been known to raise his voice, but when he was angry that voice took on a terrifying tone. That was the tone he was using now.

Tommy's guilt had been proven, so Commando McGee, to Star's disappointment, didn't bother going into the whys and wherefores. Rather he lectured Tommy about the behaviour he expected in his school, and that, as far as he was concerned, fighting was one of the two most heinous school crimes there were. Cheating was the other.

'Right then, it's twelve of the best. Six on the hands, six on the backside,' Commando McGee pronounced sentence.

Star gulped. Twelve! That was the maximum punishment allowed, and rarely administered. Tommy must be getting it because his attack on Korky had been unprovoked.

Star could imagine the Commando taking the black leather tawse from the cardboard box in which he kept it. The tawse was about eighteen inches long, three quarters of an inch thick, and sliced into fingers at the hitting end. She'd heard it said that the Commando periodically soaked his tawse in vinegar which supposedly made a blow from it more painful than it would otherwise have been, but she didn't believe that.

'Hold out your hands and cross them,' the Headmaster instructed.

She hoped Tommy knew not to partially draw away when the strap came down, for if it was only a partial hit then the Commando wouldn't allow it, even though a partial hit could sometimes be more painful than a full one. Or so she'd been told, she'd never had the strap herself.

She heard the whistle of the tawse through the air,

36

followed by the crack of it landing. She winced at the thought of what that must have felt like.

At the completion of the third stroke her clenched fist was grinding into her mouth, and she was shaking. Six times the tawse rose and fell with not a sound from Tommy.

'Now bend over the desk, boy,' ordered McGee.

Star knew the next stroke would be given a sideways motion, similar to the way a housewife beats a carpet hung over a low-slung washing line. Instead of the crack of leather on flesh there was the thud of leather striking material.

When it was finally over, Star's stomach was churning and she was still shaking. Turning away from the window, she stumbled back to the building's entranceway where she paused to collect herself. Then, straightening her shoulders, she went inside.

Minutes ticked by but Tommy didn't appear from the direction of the Head's study. Finally she had to come to the conclusion he must have left the building by some other way.

She'd missed him.

The tenement where Alec Muir lived with his mother and father was made of red sandstone that was visibly crumbling away. The windows staring out into Overdale Street had a mournful look about them, like eyes lost in memory, thinking of far better and more prosperous days. The stairs in the close Star walked up were concave from use.

Alec himself answered her agitated knock. He led her through to the sitting room, explaining that his mother was out doing some late shopping and his father was of course still at work.

Star always enjoyed being in the Muir house, there was a grace about it that attracted her. Once the contents would have been stunning, but now they were faded and, like the stairs in the close, well worn from use and the passage of time. Carpets, curtains, furniture, all mere shadows of their former glory, had been originally bought by Alec's great-grandfather when Queen Victoria was still on the throne. Today, however, she was too upset to take much comfort from it. 'I looked for Tommy coming out of school but didn't see him. I can't think what on earth possessed him to do what he did. Can you?' she immediately demanded. Her face was pale with concern.

Alec shifted uneasily from one foot to the other. He was still feeling wretched about the incident in the playground. He'd tried praying earlier, but for once that hadn't helped. 'No,' he mumbled so softly he was barely audible.

Star wondered what was wrong with Alec, he looked so hangdog. 'Are you all right?' she queried.

He nodded, wishing she hadn't come. Her presence was making him feel even worse.

'Well, what happened? Did Tommy just go up to Korky and belt him one? Was that how it was?'

Alec went over to the fireplace and leant on the mantelpiece. He was going to have to tell her; if he didn't then Tommy would when she saw him. He groaned inwardly, damn that Korky Niven! Damn Korky to all the terrible fires of hell.

'I've no idea,' he replied.

Star blinked. 'But you must have, you saw it all,' she said.

'I saw nothing. When I arrived on the scene the pair of them were already at it hammer and tongs.'

He was pulling her leg, he had to be. 'Of course you saw what happened, I heard you tell Mr Apsley you did. You said Tommy launched an unprovoked attack on Korky.' She didn't move her eyes from him.

He stared at the smooth marble of the mantelpiece. At that moment he couldn't have faced her if his life had depended on it. 'I verified Korky's story because I knew fine well what Korky would do to me if I didn't,' he said at last in a thick voice.

Star heard again the crack of leather on flesh, the dull thud of leather on material. Until this moment she'd always looked up to Alec Muir, thought of him as infallible, an inspiration to all around him. Now she was seeing him in quite a different light.

Alec went on. 'Korky would have made me pay for not backing him, he'd have given me an awful bashing. The truth is I can't stand physical pain, never have been able to, and Korky knows it. That's why, apart from the fact that the masters think a lot of me, he picked me out of that crowd.'

She was filled with distaste – and pity. Tommy hadn't made a single sound when being belted by Commando McGee, but she could now visualize Alec screaming the place down at the very sight of the tawse, long before he'd even been touched by it.

'Look at it this way, Tommy didn't suffer because of me, the Head would have given him the belt anyway for fighting. My backing Korky's lie only meant that Korky didn't get belted too, that's all,' said Alec desperately.

'That's not true, Alec. Because you said that Tommy's attack on Korky was unprovoked he got twelve of the belt. He would never have got that much otherwise. He's never been in trouble before. It's your fault he got so many.' She glared at him, breathless with rage.

Alex wilted. Twelve of the tawse! His own flesh crawled at the thought. 'I can't help being a physical coward, that's the way I was born and I can't change it. Please say you understand and forgive me. Please, Star?'

She was startled to hear him sob, her heart softening.

'What else could I do?' he whispered.

She wanted to retort scathingly that he could have stood up to Korky like a man, but she didn't. A coward, and weak, that was Alec Muir, and it was a revelation to her. But he was right. He couldn't have stood up to

39

Korky Niven. And she reminded herself, he did have his good qualities. He was gentle, considerate, and highly intelligent – and he was really very kind. Her distaste melted away. Hadn't she ever done things she'd been ashamed of? This only proved him human, with faults like everyone else, and not the saintlike figure he'd previously seemed.

Alec's body shook with sobs as the tears washed down his cheeks. He felt Star come closer to him till she was standing only inches from his back. He shrank fractionally away from her, but her hand came to lightly rest on his shoulder.

'It's all right, Alec,' she said quietly. 'I do understand.' She felt that she wanted to protect him, the way a mother might her child.

He whirled round and clasped her tightly to his breast, his heart soaring with relief.

They stood there for a while in silence. Star waiting for his weeping to run its course. When it finally did, she kissed him full on his wet mouth, not a passionate kiss, but a kiss that was warm and reassuring.

'I'll make a pot of tea, we could both use a cup,' she said.

As she went through to the kitchen she decided she'd go from here to Tommy's house in Millbrae Crescent, she had to talk to him after what Alec had told her.

Tommy wasn't home when Star called. Mrs McBride said she thought he might have gone down to Lovers' Lane, a path running alongside a section of the River Cart. It was the only part of the riverbank in Battlefield and Langside accessible to the public, and Mrs McBride added that it had become something of a haunt for Tommy of late.

Star had gone to the McBrides on her bicycle, so she now cycled down to the river, only a few minutes away, then slowly cycled along the path. There was only a crescent moon that night, and the secluded path was extremely dark and shielded by a screen of trees from the nearest houses. The opposite bank was on the edge of the Albert Park, a private park, so there was no illumination from there.

Star was nearly at the far end of the path, and thinking that if he had come this way she must have missed him for the second time that day, when suddenly her bike light picked out a solitary strolling figure.

'Tommy, is that you?' she called.

The figure stopped. 'Star?'

She dismounted by his side. 'Are you feeling sorry for yourself?' she asked, which wasn't at all what she'd meant to say.

Tommy stiffened. 'What can I do for you?' he asked coldly.

'I wanted to speak to you.'

'About what?'

'The fight.'

He started to walk away from her and she had to hurry to catch him up. 'What really happened between you and Korky?'

'You heard what your boyfriend said, I attacked him without provocation.'

In the darkness it was difficult to make out his face. 'I saw Alec after school, he admitted he lied because he was scared of what Korky would do to him if he didn't.'

Tommy laughed harshly. 'Feart was he? Well at least he admitted what he did, that's something.'

Suddenly Tommy was irritating her, making her cross. 'We can't all be tough and brave,' she said cuttingly.

Tommy stopped again, and she did also. 'You don't have to worry about Alec, I won't touch him for what he did, if that's what you're here for.'

It had never occurred to her that Tommy might want revenge. 'And what about Korky?' she asked to cover her confusion.

'By now everyone in school will know he made a fool of me by getting Alec to lie for him. Well, I can't have that. I *won't* have it. We'll have to settle it between us.'

'You mean another fight?'

'Yes, another fight.' Tommy's voice was the only sound in the darkness.

Apprehension gripped her. She must try to dissuade him. He'd been lucky once against Korky but it was unlikely he'd be lucky twice.

'You did all right against Korky today,' she said as coolly as she could. 'But that would soon have changed if the fight had been allowed to continue. Take my word for it, you've no chance against Korky Niven, he'll mollicate you.'

'Then mollicate me he will, because I'm going to fight him. It doesn't matter if he beats me, it's the principle of the thing that's important. I'll not be a laughing stock, no matter what it costs,' Tommy replied, thinking he was damned if he was going to let those toffee noses at school have a laugh at his expense.

Her irritation changed to something akin to admiration. What a spirit he has, she thought. He had more integrity than anyone else she could think of.

There was a soft plop in the middle of the river. Tommy turned towards the sound, thinking it must have been made by a fish. Rivers and fish were still new to him. After the dirty, narrow streets of Govanhill this spot along the river seemed like a paradise on earth.

'I wouldn't totally dismiss my chances against Korky,' he went on more calmly. 'He may be big lad, but he isn't a street fighter. I know that from today. But *I* am. I had to learn to be in order to survive in Boyd Street. And I can use it to survive here.'

He wasn't to be talked out of this thing, she could tell that much. His voice told her so. He wasn't at all like the shy, sensitive chap who'd asked her up to dance in Miss Parrot's assembly, this was quite another side of him. It was certainly her day for seeing the other side of folk, she

42

said to herself, thinking of Alec and what had been revealed to her in the house in Overdale Street.

'You still haven't told me what happened between you and Korky.'

'He called me a name.'

'It must have been something awful for you to get so het up about it.'

Tommy stared grimly out at the gently moving river. 'It was.'

Star sighed in exasperation. 'Well *tell* me for goodness sake!'

Thinking about the name made Tommy seethe inside, just as when Korky had called him it. He knew that part of the reason for his rage was because it was true, he was what Korky had said – and, desperately, he wished it weren't true.

He liked living in Millbrae Crescent. He liked the beautiful house and the posh neighbourhood. He liked having money and not living around people who beat each other up all the time. For the first time, he felt that he mattered, that he had the same chances as everybody else. Of course, he and his parents were a bit like square pegs in round holes, but given time they could adapt, change, be accepted. That was what he wanted; what he'd planned.

'Korky called me a scruff,' he said so softly she only just heard him.

His voice told her how much the name had hurt him. She could hear him breathing beside her in the dark, but she couldn't find the words to tell him that it didn't matter.

He suddenly pulled himself together. 'I'll see you,' he said in his normal voice. 'And don't worry about your boyfriend, he's safe from me.' Before she could reply, he strode off into the night and was quickly lost to view in the darkness.

Star wheeled her bicycle round. There had been no need for him to be so cold towards her. And there had

43

been contempt in his voice when he'd repeated that she needn't worry about Alec. Who did he think he was, talking to her like that?

Part of her wished she hadn't bothered to seek him out, part of her was pleased she had.

And another part was sick at the thought of what Korky Niven would do to him.

The word quickly spread through Queen's Park that Tommy McBride had challenged Korky Niven. The fight was to be held directly school let out that afternoon, and was to take place in what was known as the wild ground.

The wild ground was exactly that, it consisted of rough grass, clumps of heather, stunted bushes and a scattering of trees.

It started two streets away from the school, and went all the way over to the long grey dyke, a distance about the length of six hockey pitches. Beyond it was railway land and the railway line.

In length the wild land was a little over twice its breadth, with dykes on every side. Two of these dykes fronted on to major roads, the last on to a quiet residential street. The lie of the wild ground was such that once into it it was impossible to be seen from the outside. Which made it the perfect site for a fist fight and was why Korky had suggested it.

Star's final period of the afternoon was music. Normally she was blissfully happy during music, but today she was fidgety and on edge, one eye forever straying to her watch. When the bell rang she and almost everyone else would be going to the wild ground to watch the fight. She was dreading it.

If Star wasn't her usual self it didn't show in her playing. Miss Hamill beamed at Star as she played, until a Prefect arrived with a message and Miss Hamill had to leave the room.

If Miss Hamill had been beaming before she was called away, when she returned she was positively aglow. The class, restless to be gone, didn't notice.

At last the bell rang. Instantly instruments were downed and begun to be put away.

'Star and Janet,' said Miss Hamill above the noise. 'Stay behind, please, I want a word.'

Miss Hamill had Star and Janet Carnegie, 2A's other outstanding musician, stand by her desk till the rest of the class had hurried out. Then she smiled at them, unable to contain her excitement. 'Girls,' she said almost breathlessly, 'I've had a telephone call from an old and dear friend of mine who's on his way here right now. I'd like you to meet him. His name is Solomon Goldman. I'm sure you're aware that he is Conductor of the Glasgow Symphony Orchestra.'

Solomon Goldman! Star had seen the great man only three months ago when her father had taken her to the St. Andrew's Halls to hear Jose Iturbi who was on a British tour at the time. Goldman was a conductor of international repute, it was an undreamed-of honour to meet him.

Then she thought of Tommy, and her excitement vanished. Although she was dreading the fight, she wanted to be out there on the wild ground, cheering him on.

'How do you know Mr Goldman, Miss?' Janet Carnegie asked.

Star tried to listen to Miss Hamill's reply, but her mind was on the wild ground with Tommy. Very shortly he would be squaring up to Korky Niven.

The recent snow had vanished thanks to a sudden warm snap in the weather. The ground underfoot was dry and hard, perfect for fighting on. Tommy scanned the loose ring of people surrounding him and Korky, but failed to see who he was looking for. He glanced in the direction from which they'd all come, but there were no straggling figures, all those coming had arrived – and Star wasn't one of them.

With a shrug, he put his disappointment behind him and started to concentrate on the matter in hand. He wasn't exactly nervous, apprehensive more like, and wound up like a clockspring inside. He removed his jacket and handed it to someone near him, then watched Korky remove his and toss it casually to a crony.

Korky was about two and a half inches taller than Tommy and a good two stone heavier. His fists were thick and square, and Tommy knew from experience that they were veritable piledrivers once they swung into action.

He reminded himself that he mustn't let Korky get him in a stranglehold or bearhug. With his extra size it would quickly be all over if that happened.

'Let's be having you then, *scruff*!' Korky jeered and moved towards Tommy.

Tommy went forward to meet him.

'Perhaps I could hear you girls play,' Solomon Goldman was saying to Star and Janet.

Miss Hamill happily clapped her hands together, pretending that this was a delightful surprise when in reality it was what she'd been angling for ever since Solomon had arrived, as well he knew.

Hell's teeth! Star swore inwardly. Up until this moment she'd been hoping she'd still be able to make the fight. Korky was the sort to continue ladling into Tommy even though it was obvious Tommy was beaten. And Tommy was the sort to keep fighting as long as he was still conscious. She prayed that someone would step in and stop the fight before it was too late.

'A little Beethoven I think,' smiled Miss Hamill.

*   *   *

46

It was only Tommy's experience from the streets of Govanhill that had allowed him to survive this far, but he was taking a terrible pounding and knew he couldn't last much longer. He was aware only of the pain and of Korky goading him on.

The onlookers were silent. They'd started off cheering and shouting, but that had died away as the vicious fight progressed.

Repeating what had happened in their first bout, Korky had landed several vicious punches on Tommy's nose causing it to bleed profusely, the bright red stain covering his chin and spreading down his shirt. Tommy had also badly scraped the back of his left hand, so that his left fist looked as though it had been dyed crimson.

One of Korky's eyebrows had been cut and blood from there dribbled down his face. Although he didn't know it yet, he had a broken rib and two cracked ones.

Exhausted but still angry, the combatants closed again. Korky's fists flailed while Tommy shuffled heavily one way, then another. Tommy got in a swift jab to Korky's face, and received a glancing body blow in reply. He tried to shuffle in a circular motion, but his legs no longer obeyed the commands he sent them. Against his will, he stopped and sagged where he stood. This is it, he thought. Now I'm really for it.

Korky, realizing his opponent was done for, moved in for the kill.

During the war years the Army bivouacked often on the wild ground. Probably that was why the iron rod had come to be there. As Tommy's hand closed around it he thought it was a miracle.

He'd been sent sprawling by a mighty punch from Korky who was now kicking him in the side. If Star had been there she would have intervened now, or attempted to. Despite her fervent prayer in Miss Hamill's classroom, however, no one did any such thing. They were all too terrified of Korky Niven to risk getting in his way.

The rod was about a quarter of an inch thick, and approximately a yard long. Tommy swung it in a backhand arc. It hissed through the air.

More by luck than good judgement, the rod took Korky smack across the forehead, sending him pitching headlong to the ground beside Tommy. Painfully, Tommy struggled on to his side to stare at the still figure of his enemy.

'Fucking arseholes, he's killed Korky!' a male voice exclaimed.

Tommy gasped in breath after breath. Killed Korky? He kept staring at the apparently lifeless form.

'Jesus Christ!' Lizzie Dunnachie said, eyes popping.

Realizing he was still clutching the rusty rod, Tommy threw it from him. Bending, he caught hold of Korky and pulled him over so that he was lying face up. Korky's colour was waxen, except for the nasty red imprint across his forehead where the iron rod had caught him.

Stanley Munro, one of Korky's chinas, made a move towards him, but stopped when he saw the look on Tommy's face. '*Is* he dead McBride?' Stanley demanded in a shaky voice.

Tommy put his ear to Korky's nose. Relief flooded through him. Korky was still breathing. Then Korky groaned, rolled over, and was sick.

Tommy hauled himself unsteadily to his feet. Now that he knew Korky was all right there was no pity in him as he watched Korky continue to spew. He knew it was only luck that he hadn't been the one nearly killed. Korky deserved all he had got.

'He's all right, but he's going to have a bloody awful head on him for a while,' Tommy said to Stanley.

Tommy's chest felt tight and his legs were wobbly, but despite this he felt fine. Just fine. He was the victor, and that was sweet. Very sweet indeed.

He retrieved his jacket, had a last look at the still prostrate Korky, then staggered through the ring of people clapping him on the back and congratulating him, delighted that someone had finally beaten Korky Niven at his own game.

As he went, a pair of eyes filled with admiration followed his departure. The eyes belonged to one of the prettiest girls in the school. Her name was Eve Smith, and she was just deciding that Tommy McBride was for her.

When it came to the lads, Eve Smith always got whoever she set her cap at.

Always.

Margaret Muir, Alec's mother, was hunched in an armchair, watching her son get ready for the Christmas Dance. She had a cigarette in one hand and a glass of whisky in the other. She was indulging herself with a dram because it was the festive season. Normally, they couldn't afford to have drink in the house.

Her thoughts drifted to her husband Geoffrey, out at a Masonic meeting, and her lips twisted downwards into a thin, disapproving frown. It was Geoffrey she disapproved of, not the Masons. In fact, it had been at her instigation that he'd joined the Masons. She'd hoped they would help him in his career, as they'd supposedly helped so many others. But they hadn't. She was certain she knew why. As she had, the Masons must have come to recognize Geoffrey for what he was: third rate and a born loser. There was no point in helping someone who would only let you down.

She swallowed a mouthful of whisky, enjoying the harshness and pungency of its taste. She had always enjoyed things hurting her, as long as the hurt wasn't too great. With another man, this was something she might have introduced into their sex life. But Geoffrey was as boring in bed as he was out of it.

Her expression changed fractionally to one of contempt – contempt for her husband and for herself for being stupid enough to marry him in the first place.

Oh, he'd been handsome then. Devilishly so. She hadn't been the only one after Geoffrey. But she'd been the *lucky* one who'd caught him.

Her hero; Margaret thought scathingly. He'd dazzled her with the tales of the success he was going to be in the banking world. He was still only a lowly teller, he'd told her, but it wouldn't be long before that changed. He would be a branch manager before he was thirty; and after that, who knew! The sky was the limit. He might go into merchant banking, he might aim for a seat on the Board of the bank he was already with, and beyond that seats on the Boards of other banks.

Pipe dreams, pie in the sky, hopeless fantasies, that's all it had turned out to be. Alec had been five years old, and her figure long gone with the carrying and nursing of him, when it had at last come home to her that Geoffrey's big talk was just that, big talk and nothing else. Finally she'd understood that he would never amount to anything, that he would always be the lowly teller he'd been when they'd first met.

'Which tie, Mother?' Alec asked, holding out a choice of four.

She regarded the ties, then pointed to the grey with thin blue stripes as the one that was the best for his suit.

Her eyes narrowed as she watched her son finish dressing. He might be weak like his father, but, thank the Lord, he'd inherited her brains. She fully intended seeing they were put to good use. And although Alec wasn't nearly as handsome as Geoffrey had been, he was a good looking lad and he did have charm, when he wanted to use it.

All these were assets that she literally intended to cash in on. Alec was her last hope. It was her intention that he would rebuild the family fortune lost by his grandfather and restore them to their former glory.

The great idea had come to her a few years back. Ever since, she'd been busy scheming and making contacts, doing everything she could to further her plan. The

50

Muirs might be poor, but they still had standing in Scottish society.

She smiled to herself, thinking of the list of suitable girls she'd been steadily compiling. The parents of these girls had either become friendly with her or were about to.

Top of the list – because her family was the wealthiest – was Morag Hutchison. Second was Ishbel Doig, whose father was big in the grocery trade. Third was Juliet Abercrombie, whose family was in nuts and bolts. These three girls, like the rest on Margaret's list, had one thing in common; they would bring money and opportunity when they married. She was determined that Alec would eventually find his bride amongst them.

This religious nonsense Alec was going through was merely a phase which she would allow to run its course. If he didn't give up on it naturally, then she would see to it herself. Alec being a minister in the Church, with the miserable stipend they earned, didn't figure at all in her schemes.

'How's that?' Alec asked nervously, smoothing back his hair, a stray piece immediately popping up again.

Rising, Margaret crossed to her son and inspected him. 'You'll do,' she replied shortly.

'I'll be home about eleven, don't wait up.'

She brushed a bit of lint from his shoulder. 'Of course I will, I'll want to hear all about it.'

Alec pecked his mother on the cheek, so excited he could barely take the time to say goodbye. He was due to pick up Star in ten minutes, he'd timed it just right.

Margaret knew Alec was taking Star, and that he was fond of her. A puppy romance was how she saw it. Alec was only fifteen, just beginning to spread his wings. It would be a couple of years yet before she started introducing him to the girls on her list. In the meantime there was no harm in him going out with Star Gray.

No harm at all. If anything, it was good experience for him.

*   *   *

While Alec was getting dressed, Star was also getting ready for the school Christmas Dance.

She was delighted with her dress. It was a pre-war one of Alison's that Alison had remade for the occasion by cutting it down a little, and totally altering the sleeves, which hadn't suited Star at all, to mutton-chop. It was beige with a large bow on the left hip and tassly things round the collar and bust. The matching shoes were an old pair that had been newly soled and heeled before being dyed the same colour as the dress.

'You look a proper treat,' Alison said, admiring her daughter from a few feet away. 'That dress really suits you.'

Star looked at herself in the mirror. She was bubbling with excitement, it was going to be a marvellous night, she just knew it. Her hand strayed to her face – if only . . . 'Couldn't I wear just a smidgin of make-up, please?' she pleaded softly.

Alison sighed. Why was it young girls always thought make-up made them prettier. 'Even if I thought you needed it, which I most certainly don't, I couldn't allow you to put on any. Your father would go through the roof.'

Star sighed resignedly. Her father had a phobia about 'painted Jezebels', as he called them, and had even spoken on the subject from the pulpit. To him a painted woman was no better than a common prostitute. He was not a man to move with the times.

Alison was about to say that there was no make-up in the house anyway, then realized that if Star was asking to wear some there must be. Better not let your father catch you out my lass, she thought grimly, for if he did there would be Laldy to pay.

'And he'll want to see you and Alec before you leave. He's in his study writing Sunday's sermon.' Alison added, just in case it was in Star's mind to try and sneak some make-up on before going off.

Star peered into the mirror. 'A teensy weensy bit would

52

have been nice, though,' she said wistfully.

A few minutes later the doorbell rang. Alec had arrived.

A great deal of time and effort had gone into making the gym look as nice as possible for the Christmas Dance. There was a large tree at the rear with – a real novelty in 1947 – electric fairy lights on it in every colour of the rainbow. Paper chains had been strung from corner to corner and side to side across the gym. Some theatrical floodlights had been borrowed from the Citizens' Theatre and these provided the general illumination.

Star's eyes were everywhere, taking it all in – the music, the decorations, the smiling couples. She saw Lizzie Dunnachie arrive with James Ledingham, and a few seconds later Catherine with Bobby Douglas who was in his fifth year and coming up to take his Highers.

When Alec excused himself to go to the toilet, Star wandered over to where Lizzie and James Ledingham were standing to have a natter with them.

Lizzie was in brilliant form, her patter even better than usual, which was saying something. She told the filthest joke Star had ever heard, the joke made even funnier by James being so embarrassed at being told it by a girl. They where still giggling when Alec returned, looking serious. In a low voice, he told them that a group of lads in the toilet had a bottle of whisky and were passing it to one another. 'I think it's shocking,' he said in an outraged voice. 'I'm going to report them.'

'Don't be soft, that's the last thing you want to do,' Star said.

'But these boys are all in the first year, and drinking at that age is wrong,' argued Alec.

'Right or wrong it's none of your affair,' put in James. 'If that's how they want to enjoy themselves then leave them to it.'

God Squad! thought Lizzie, they could be a right pain in the bum at times.

Their argument was interrupted by a sudden comotion round the far entranceway. Star craned her neck to see what was going on. A couple seemed to be the centre of attention, though she couldn't make out who they were.

The band struck up a lively Military Two Step. Star was about to suggest she and Alec take the floor again, when suddenly the couple who'd been receiving all the attention emerged from the crowd surrounding them. Star's jaw fell open in amazement. Tommy McBride and Eve Smith! The pair of them were arm in arm, Eve staring adoringly up at Tommy as though he were a Hollywood god just stepped down off the Silver Screen.

'Well, well,' murmured Lizzie, having also caught sight of the couple. She glanced quickly at Star to see what Star's reaction was, for she knew that Tommy had asked Star to the dance.

Star was speechless with rage. Eve Smith, of all people! Why the girl was . . . *notorious*!

'I wonder when that happened?' mused Lizzie.

Tommy's left hand was still bandaged from his recent fight with Korky Niven, and his nose had a new, splayed look about it, but he looked better than she'd ever before seen him. He no longer looked shy or out of place; he radiated confidence and pride.

Star hadn't realized how much of a celebrity Tommy had become since beating Korky, but she did now. Every second or so someone called out to him, gave him a friendly wave, or punched him playfully on the shoulder. And Eve, the cow, was all over him, positively basking in the reflected glory.

Why was she so angry? Star asked herself the question, but couldn't answer it. Tommy McBride meant nothing to her. She'd tried to help him settle into school, and that was all. He was the one who'd been keen on her, for goodness sake!

'That suit he's wearing cost a couple of quid,' James commented. And it was true. Tommy's suit was the very best material, and beautifully tailored.

Star's gaze narrowed on Eve's face. Eve's lips were a crimson slash and her eyes were accentuated by a bold black line along the lids. Expertly applied shadow highlighted her cheeks. The overall effect – though it hurt Star to have to admit it – was quite ravishing.

Star's gaze dropped to Eve's dress, and her dismay turned to despair. Eve's dress was a simple black sheath that did for her figure what her make-up did for her face. In short, it was sensational.

Star's hand went to her own dress. Compared to Eve's, it was a rag. She realized now how over fussy it was; how dowdy and frumpish. And to think how chuffed she'd been with it at the beginning of the night! She bit back tears, and wished herself anyplace but where she was.

'She could be twenty-one or -two got up like that,' Lizzie said enviously.

All Star wanted was to go home, but it was far too early for that. If she left now it would only cause comment, perhaps even get back to Tommy, which was the last thing she wanted. And what could she give as an explanation?

Turning to Lizzie she said, a triumphant tone in her voice. 'Forget the rest. Look at her ankles, they're positively *fat!*'

Lizzie smiled to herself. If those were fat ankles then she was the Empress of China. 'Oh aye, they are that, regular treetrunks,' she agreed, aware of how jealous Star was. Now that, thought Lizzie, is very interesting, and amusing.

Time passed, but Tommy didn't once glance in Star's direction. He might at least have had the courtesy to say hello, she thought testily. At one point she considered going over and saying hello to him, but then she remembered how her dress compared to Eve's and decided against it.

Tommy was well aware of Star staring over at him from time to time, but he refrained from acknowledging those stares. After all, why should he bother about someone who didn't even care enough about him to come to the fight he'd had with Korky?

Eve squirmed in his arms. Jesus, she was sexy! Tons more so than Star, he bet himself; he was far better off with Eve. She was the lass for him.

'How did it go?' Alison eagerly demanded later, when Star got in.

'Oh, all right,' Star replied vaguely, then in the same vague tone said she was straight off to bed, she was dog tired.

Alison stared perplexedly at Star's back as she sauntered from the room. Now what on earth's got into her, she wondered? 'Young people!' she muttered to herself. You never knew where you were with them.

2

It was January, 1948, and Queen's Park Senior Secondary School had been back from the Christmas holiday for two weeks.

The other girls in 2A were getting dressed after P.T., and as usual the changing room was crowded and noisy. Star was tugging on her jersey when the door flew open and in streamed the girls of 3D who were about to get ready for indoor netball. The already close space became jam packed with girls either struggling to put clothes on or take them off.

By chance, Eve Smith and several of her pals ended up beside Star and Lizzie Dunnachie. Without so much as a look between them, Star and Lizzie immediately tuned in to what Eve was saying, and it was clear from the loudness of her voice that Eve didn't care who heard her.

'He's absolutely gorgeous. He's the best boyfriend I've ever had,' Eve practically purred as she undid her blouse.

Lizzie caught Star's eye. It had to be Tommy that Eve was talking about.

'What do you mean *had*?' Kirsty Cairncross teased.

A sudden hush fell round the vicinity, all eyes turned to Eve, all ears waited for the reply.

She raised an imperious eyebrow, looked down her nose at the owlish Kirsty, and said. 'You're old enough to know what the word "had" means.'

There was a faint chorus of gasps following this statement. To actually *admit* such a thing in public! It was unheard of, it was scandalous, it was the most exciting thing to ever happen in either 2A or 3D!

Eve grinned to herself, pleased with the reaction she'd got. She felt like a movie star surrounded by fans.

Star spoke before she'd realized it. 'You're disgusting,' she snapped, her face flushed.

Eve rounded on Star, fixing her with a hard look. 'Did you speak Miss Goody Two Shoes?' she asked in a voice of mock sweetness.

There were a few titters; Kirsty Cairncross laughed behind her hand.

'Yes,' said Star determinedly. 'I said you're disgusting, Eve Smith,' she repeated, matching the older girl's stare.

Eve already knew that there was a lot of truth in the cliché that the best defence is a good offence. 'I suppose you're just jealous because no real boy would be caught dead with you,' she said condescendingly.

Star went pale. She wasn't sure exactly what Eve was getting at, but she knew it wasn't going to be good.

'There's nothing wrong with Alec Muir,' she replied quietly, wondering why she had such a terrible urge to launch herself at Eve and claw her eyes out.

'There's nothing right with him, either,' snapped Eve. 'He's wet as they come. But I guess that's why you like him. You're such a perfect couple. He probably couldn't get it up even if he wanted to.'

Get what up Star wondered. Then it dawned on her what Eve meant.

'Not that I suppose you would know one way or the other being such a *nice* girl,' Eve was going on, making the word 'nice' sound like some dreadful disease. Then Eve delivered her final blow. 'I wouldn't be at all surprised if Alec Muir goes with you because he doesn't really like girls.'

Star went cold all over. Except for Lizzie, all the girls were laughing at her now. Eve's laugh was so harsh and strident it might have been a piece of broken glass being dragged along a stone wall.

Time to get out of here, thought Lizzie, and picking up the remainder of her and Star's clothes, she took Star by the shoulder and gently propelled her towards the door.

'Don't even deign to reply, it isn't worth it,' she said in a loud voice, giving Eve a sideways glance that warned, say anything smart to me and you'll get the edge of my tongue, and you know what that'll be like.

Eve got the message. Lizzie's tongue was renowned, and not even Eve wanted to get into a verbal duel with her.

Outside in the playground Star started to shake. 'What a bitch,' she said through her tears.

'Don't pay any attention to her,' said Lizzie. 'She just likes to hear herself talk.' Privately, though, she thought that Star had asked for that one. She should have had the sense to keep her mouth shut.

Star took a deep breath, then another, which stopped her shaking. She was angry, confused and bewildered. Goody Two Shoes, was that how people saw her? Surely not, she was nothing like that. She was bright and strong. She was going to be somebody.

'I'll say this for Eve Smith, she's got one hell of a brass neck. Imagine admitting she's no longer a virgin straight out like that. That takes some nerve.' Lizzie's voice was tinged with admiration.

Star frowned, unable to see what was admirable in what Eve had done.

'There's not another girl in Queen's Park Secondary would have made such an admission,' added Lizzie.

'There's not many could,' Star said.

Lizzie gave a knowing smile. 'There's a lot more goes on around here than I think you realize.'

Star was intrigued. 'What do you mean?'

'Just that. Most of the girls go in for no more than holding hands a goodnight kiss, but there is more than one has gone a lot further than that. Not that they'd publicly admit it, of course.'

'Yes, but . . . they don't actually go all the way, do they?' Star queried, her frown deepening.

'Of course they do. Particularly the ones who go steady. After a while it's more or less expected.'

Star was astonished. 'I never knew that.'

Lizzie gave her a funny look. 'So what about you and Alec, doesn't he ever try it on?'

'No,' she said slowly. 'No, he never has. Not once.'

Lizzie gave a long low whistle. 'He must be even more religious than I thought,' she laughed. 'I didn't think there were any boys like him left.'

They had time before the next class, so Lizzie suggested they go behind the bicycle shed so she could have a fly puff. Star, deep in thought, agreed absentmindedly. It wasn't until Lizzie had lit up that Star asked, somewhat coyly, her voice choked with embarrassment, 'Lizzie . . . have you . . . ?'

Lizzie cracked a grin. 'Just between you, me and the drainpipe here?'

'Cross my heart and hope to die.'

'Yes. It was Hamish McInstray, but it was more his idea than mine.'

Star stared at Lizzie as though she had just arrived from the moon. 'How often?'

Lizzie held up four fingers.

It was a complete revelation to Star. 'And you say lots of girls are . . . are doing it?'

The look on Star's face had made it hard for Lizzie not to giggle, but now realizing how serious Star seemed to be she got suddenly serious herself. 'Oh aye, but you have to take precautions, mind. You mustn't let them near you unless they're wearing an Ef-El, or you'll be in the club before you know where you are.' Ef-Els were French letters, or condoms.

'Why didn't you tell me all this before?' Star demanded.

Lizzie looked away, and blushed slightly. 'I don't really know why, you being my best china and all. I suppose it's because your old man's a minister. It didn't seem right talking about all that sort of thing to a minister's daughter. Not even you.'

'Just because my father's a minister doesn't make me different from the other girls,' Star snapped, surprised by the force of her feelings. It was as though there had been a conspiracy to make her the only girl in the entire world who didn't know what was going on. Was there something wrong with her? Was that why?

They walked in silence all the way to Latin class, where Star did even worse than usual. On being asked to decline Amaveram she could only get as far as Amaverat.

Mr Orr's comment about that was caustic in the extreme.

The Reverend Kenneth Gray was in the middle of his sermon, and going great guns. He always thoroughly enjoyed delivering sermons. There was a lot of the actor in him and he revelled in having an audience.

Star was sitting with her mother. To her left were Alec and Mr and Mrs Muir, and on her right, near the front, were the McBrides. Mrs McBride was wearing one of the most ostentatious hats she'd ever seen. Star pretended not to notice Tommy sitting between his parents.

Star fastened her attention on to Alec and tried to imagine what it would be like going to bed with him. She tried to imagine Alec getting carried away with passion, and couldn't. Somehow images of Alec getting carried away like that just wouldn't come. But then it was so

60

unlike Alec to get carried away about anything, except, possibly, religion.

She gnawed her lip. Could what Eve had implied be true? *Could* he be . . . queer? Of course he's not, she told herself. He's just reserved, that's all.

Her gaze accidentally shifted to Tommy. Suddenly, so clear it could have been happening right there in front of her eyes, she could picture him making love to Eve Smith. She had no trouble picturing Tommy carried away by passion. Her throat had gone dry, and a sensation had blossomed in her, a warm feeling that seemed to emanate from the very core of her being.

She tore her gaze away from Tommy and returned it to Alec. Why couldn't she imagine him making love to her when she could vividly imagine Tommy making love to Eve?

Was it just because of the type of person that Alec was, or was there more to it than that? Was it something to do with her? Not only had Alec never tried to touch her, *no* boy had. Lizzie said it was normal for them to, so what was wrong with Star?

Did boys merely like her to talk too, to be friendly with, but never to fancy? Was that it, that she didn't have any sex appeal? That she was so plain and prissy that she was unattractive?

There were such women, she knew. Women who were not particularly ugly, or different – just more or less ordinary, except that men never thought to go to bed with them.

Panic and self-doubt flared through Star. Was she herself like those women – a female who completely lacked sex appeal?

She was suddenly aware of Margaret Muir smiling at her, and she smiled back. She liked Mrs Muir. Now there was a woman with sex appeal. Even though she'd gone to fat, her sexiness was still there. Star was certain that a lot of men, given half the chance, would have fallen over themselves to get into bed with Mrs Muir.

Alec must take after his father, she decided. And yet Mr Muir had married Mrs Muir, so perhaps he wasn't as bland as he seemed. In which case, Star concluded miserably, the problem really did lie with her.

The Reverend Kenneth Gray wound up his sermon, thinking smugly to himself that it had gone well, as usual, and sat down. Immediately the congregation relaxed, some shifting on the hard wooden pews, others getting rid of the coughs they'd been holding back.

The organist gave them about ten seconds to get sorted out, then went into the opening bars of 'Onward Christian Soldiers', the next hymn on the board, and the Reverend's favourite.

Star got to her feet, still so preoccupied with her thoughts that she failed to grimace, as she would normally have done, when the organist inadvertently played a wrong note.

Jim McBride looked forward to his weekly drive through to Edinburgh, and the safety deposit box that lay at the end of it.

The box was registered in the name of Ronald McArthur, a pal of his who'd fallen in the war.

The reason he'd chosen Edinburgh was that he knew no one there. In Edinburgh he could be Ronald McArthur, and no one would ever know otherwise. Glasgow had been too dangerous for his purposes; it might be a large town in many ways, but it was awfully small in others.

Thinking of what lay inside his safety deposit box brought a smile to Jim's face, as it always did. Seventeen thousand and three hundred pounds, all in used notes, all his. Seventeen thousand and seven hundred and fifty pounds, he corrected himself, that's what it would be shortly, after he'd added the notes now nestling in his inside jacket pocket.

It would all have to end someday of course, that was

inevitable. But in the meantime he was making money hand over fist, and the sky above, no matter what the weather, was always blue.

As Jim McBride passed the Edinburgh City boundary marker, Jeannie McBride was alighting from a tram opposite her beloved Boyd Street where she and Jim had spent, as she saw it, so many happy years together.

Oh, but it was grand being back! She fair loved these visits, lived for them really, for Jeannie, unlike her husband and son, hadn't settled in Millbrae Crescent, nor would she ever.

There was Mrs O'Leary, the Irish wifie, leaning out of her window just as she'd been doing time out of mind, watching what was going on and hoping someone would stop for a chin wag; and there was Young's the wee newsagent shop which sold farthing ice lollies Granny Young made in the rear shop in that pre-war refrigerator old man Young had dug up from somewhere, and which had paid for itself a thousand times over with the number of lollies they sold.

Jeannie sighed. This was her place true enough, and it had broken her heart to have to leave. But Jim was right when he said Millbrae Crescent was a doorway through which Tommy could step into a whole new, and better, way of life.

She breathed in that well remembered smell, so different from Battlefield. Millbrae Crescent smelt quite antiseptic by comparison.

She spied Elsie Murtagh and hurried across the road, calling out to her as she went.

Elsie clasped her close. 'Look at you!' she exclaimed. 'You look wonderful! Life amongst the toffs must suit you.'

'Oh it's very nice, but not like it is amongst *real* folk,' Jeannie replied, trying not to sound as sad as she felt.

'I've heard the folks you're living beside now are so grand they don't ever have to go to the cludgie,' Elsie joked, her voice crackling with mirth.

'Oh they go all right,' laughed Jeannie. 'But they call it the toy-let, not the cludgie.' She pronounced 'toilet' in an exaggerated Kelvinside manner that had Elsie doubled over, slapping a heavy thigh with an equally heavy fist.

'Och, you always were a right one, so you were,' she grinned, straightening up and slipping her arm through Jeannie's.

Jeannie glanced fondly and longingly around. 'East west, home's best,' she said simply.

Elsie knew exactly what her friend meant. 'Toy-let,' Elsie answered, using the same exaggerated pronunciation Jeannie had.

Laughing fit to bust and holding one another up, they made their way down the street in the direction of Elsie's room and kitchen.

Sunday afternoons, prior to tea and evening service, and weather permitting, Star always went for a walk, to the Linn Park, a little over a mile from the manse.

This Sunday afternoon Lizzie Dunnachie was with her, for as Lizzie always said when she accompanied Star on these jaunts, what the hell else was there to do in Glasgow on a Sunday afternoon? Everything, but everything, was either closed or shut tight, even the childrens' swing parks, the swings themselves chained and padlocked.

In Glasgow on a Sunday there was one commandment, and one only: Thou Shalt Not.

Both girls were wearing the obligatory hat and carrying the equally obligatory umbrella. It was unthinkable for a decent lassie to go out without these badges of respectability. The only exception was the umbrella, which could be left home in high summer, but the sun really had to be cracking the sky before even that exception could be made.

They'd been through one extremely large section of the park, and were now leaving by the Snuffmill Bridge end, where a bridge crossed the River Cart as it roared and churned far below.

Deep in conversation, the girls were unaware of Tommy, walking up the road towards the bridge. He'd only just discovered the park, but already it had become his favourite place. The first time he'd come he'd stared in awe at the great cathedral of trees which seemed to stretch on and on forever. Now he came to the park at every opportunity. For him, it was a magic place.

Looking up suddenly, instinctively, Star noticed Tommy before Lizzie. She set her face into an impassive mask when she realized that he was coming over to them, a big smile on his face. Star was still not over the scene in the locker room. In fact, the more time passed the more horrible the whole thing seemed to her. She was sure that everyone was still laughing at her, and she wondered what Eve had told Tommy about the incident. She took his smile not as a friendly greeting, but as a sign that he, too, thought she was a silly fool.

'Well, hello,' he said when he finally came to a stop beside them.

Tommy was in a frivolous mood. When the girls did not immediately respond, he decided to have a wee dig at Star.

'I hear you and Eve had a bit of a run-in,' he said. 'Is it true she called you Goody Two Shoes?' He laughed.

Star coloured. So he did know. She could easily imagine what Eve had told him, prissy little Star Gray making a fool of herself in front of two classes, no wonder even her own boyfriend wasn't interested in her. 'I wouldn't call it a run-in exactly,' said Star softly.

Star's obvious discomfort spurred Tommy on to even more laughter. 'Eve can be quite a girl when she wants to be,' he grinned.

'Well, you'd be the expert on that,' snapped Star.

Something in her voice and the look in her eyes made the next joke die on his lips. 'And what's that supposed to mean?'

'You know what it means,' said Star, unable to control her voice or anything it said. She wished she were home, she wished she had never come for this walk, she wished she had never been born. She wished she would shut up and just go away. 'And by now the entire school probably knows as well.'

Tommy looked at Lizzie. 'What's she talking about?'

'I'm talking about the run-in, as you call it,' interrupted Star. 'Surely Eve didn't forget to mention the anouncement she made to 2A and 3D?' Having gone so far, Star's fears had been supplanted by contempt. She was so angry now, so angry and so disgusted, that she didn't give a fig what Tommy McBride or his cheap girlfriend thought of her.

Tommy stared at her coldly. 'What announcement would that be, then?'

'That you and Eve are sleeping together,' Lizzie said quickly, wanting only to get Star moving again.

Tommy felt as though someone had kicked him in the stomach. It would never have occurred to him to tell anyone about Eve, and he had assumed that the same went for her about him. 'She what?'

'She told everyone that you and she were having it off,' Lizzie said sweetly.

'That's a lie!' Tommy exploded. 'You're making it up!' He looked as though he was about to grab Star by the shoulders and shake her.

'It's the truth and you know it,' Star shouted back, shaking off Lizzie's hand which was trying to pull her away. 'Didn't she tell you what our fight was about? That it all started because I said she was disgusting when she started going into details?' The look of horror on his face made up for everything. Now she had the power, now she was the one in control. 'Don't tell me you're ashamed of her,' she laughed, taking an uncharacteristic pleasure in twisting the knife.

This time Tommy did grab Star by the shoulders, holding her so that she had to look him in the face. 'No,

Miss Goody Two Shoes, I'm not ashamed of her,' he said quietly.

'Well maybe you should be,' said Lizzie.

Tommy let go of Star and rounded on her. 'And just what do you mean by that?'

Lizzie gave him one of her sweetest smiles. 'Nothing much. Just that it takes all sorts.' Her tone made it clear just what sort she thought Eve was.

Tommy was as angry now as he had been when Korky called him a scruff. 'I'll not hear anything said against Eve,' he said to Lizzie but his eyes on Star. 'Not by you or anybody else. She's a first class bird and that's all there is to it.'

Lizzie, realizing that she'd gone far enough, took a step backwards and said nothing.

Star, however, was far beyond caution. 'First class,' she laughed. 'You call that first class?'

Tommy's fingers clenched and unclenched, but he made no more moves to grab Star. 'Yes, I do,' he said evenly.

'Well, all I can say is your standards can't be too high if you think that little tart is first class,' said Star. 'What I can't fathom is what you see in her.'

'You wouldn't understand,' said Tommy in a voice that was menacing because it was so controlled.

'Oh, I don't know. We're both females, after all.'

Tommy searched for the most cutting retort he could think of, and found it. 'Only she's a lot more so,' he announced in triumph.

As though he'd slapped her across the face, Star stared at him, speechless. All the nightmares of the past few days came back in full force, and she realized even more strongly that she was the outsider, she was the one who was the object of ridicule.

This time Lizzie physically stepped between them. 'Why don't you go and find a stone to crawl under,' she said to Tommy.

Tommy didn't move his eyes from Star. 'Because I'd

probably find you two there first,' he said, then strode past the two of them in the direction of the park. He didn't turn around to see the tears begin to stream down Star's face.

Star wiped at the tears with her sleeve. Her shoulders heaved, but she didn't make a sound. Everything in her life had been marvellous until the fateful day she met Tommy McBride in Miss Parrot's dancing assembly. Since then nothing had gone right, and everything that had always seemed so perfect now seemed wrong. And all through him, as well. Everything was his fault.

As soon as Tommy was out of sight, Lizzie put her arm around Star's shoulders, 'Don't pay any attention to him,' she soothed. 'His sort wouldn't know a first class girl if she came with a label.'

Star wiped the last tears from her face. 'I don't want to talk about it,' she said in a whisper. 'I just want to go home.'

Leaving Star and Lizzie far behind him, and feeling almost crazy with anger, Tommy hurried straight to Eve's house, in such a state that he barely noticed how he got there.

'Why, Tommy,' said Eve in happy surprise when she opened the door. If she noticed the expression on his face she pretended not to. 'I wasn't expecting to see you.'

He shook off the hand that reached out to touch him. 'I want to talk to you.'

'Well, then you'd better come in.' She called through to her mother that it was Tommy. 'We're going up to my room,' she added. He followed her up the stairs as he had done before, but this time with none of the touching and giggling of his previous visits to her room. 'Jill's gone out with some friends,' Eve explained, speaking of her sister who shared the room with her. 'So we won't be disturbed for hours.' She opened the door and he fairly shoved her through it. 'Hey! What's wrong with you?'

He shut the door behind him and leaned against it. 'Just what do you mean by telling everyone that we've been making love?'

Eve's eyes widened. So that was it. 'Making love, is it? Since when did you start calling it that?' she teased, her laughter sounding like tiny bells.

He leaned towards her, his eyes still hard with rage. 'I don't care what you call it. What I want to know is why you had to make a public announcement about it.'

'I didn't exactly make a public announcement,' she said, not moving an inch. 'I made a suggestion and let them come to their own conclusions. But even if I did, so what? Why are you so upset about it?'

'Because there are some things between people that you don't broadcast to all and bloody sundry. And as for going into details, that's the most offensive thing of all.'

Eve watched him with not the slightest trace of fear. He was lovely when he was angry. The power and violence in him made him all that more attractive. Just as he'd been the day he nearly killed Korky Niven, the day she realized that she wanted him for herself.

She laid a hand on his shoulder, bringing her body just that much closer to his. 'Who told you I went into details?' she asked gently.

'Star Gray. I met her and Lizzie Dunnachie up at the Snuffmill Bridge a little while ago.'

Eve slowly moved her hand along his shoulder till she was caressing his neck. 'All I said was you were the best boyfriend I've ever had. I hardly consider that going into details,' she whispered silkily.

The nearness of her made it difficult for him to concentrate on his anger. 'You wouldn't lie to me, Eve?'

'On my word of honour, that was all I said. She got so upset because I said I thought Alec was so wet I doubted he could get it up.'

Tommy couldn't help but laugh. That was just the sort of thing a Boyd Street lassie might have said. Perhaps it was that side of Eve that was so attractive to him. In some ways they were two of a kind. 'What else did you say?'

'That I wouldn't be at all surprised if her precious Alec didn't go with her because he wasn't really interested in girls.'

Tommy whistled under his breath. No wonder he'd received such a frosty reception from Star! If he'd known he wouldn't have teased her, but Eve had only told him they'd had a bit of a spat and hadn't elaborated.

'I don't like that girl,' Eve went on, her arms now around him. 'She's got such airs and graces. And as for that silly name she uses, how daft can you get? *Star*, indeed!

'She doesn't like you much either,' Tommy grinned.

Eve made a face. 'I don't want to talk about that pretentious little madam. She's as boring as that dreary Alec Muir she's so possessive about.'

'Are you possessive about me?' Tommy teased, his anger now completely gone.

Eve smiled with the realization that she'd won. Tommy's anger had evaporated. She'd wound him round her little finger, as she'd known she would. 'Yes,' she said simply, and drew him to her in a kiss.

'You're absolutely certain your mother won't come up?' he asked after a while.

'Absolutely.'

Star and Alec were on their way back from the Fives where they'd met up after her B.B. Maze Marching and his Scripture Union class.

Star had been brooding all week long, her mind filled with questions to which she desperately wanted answers.

They arrived outside the manse. 'Let's go round the side,' she whispered, and taking his hand led the way to where a wall returned, in the seclusion of which they'd be screened from all prying eyes.

Alec was intrigued. 'What's wrong?' he asked once

70

they were in the still darkness of the return. Her recent mood had made him think something had happened, and he assumed that she was going to confide to him.

She stood facing him. 'Kiss me, Alec,' she commanded.

'What?' That was the last thing he'd expected her to say.

'Kiss me! Or don't you want to?'

'Now?'

'Don't you want to?'

'Well . . . of course.'

'Then do it.'

This was most unlike Star. Giving a mental shrug, he pecked her on the cheek.

Her mouth set hard in disappointment, and secret fear. 'Is that the best you can do?'

'You mean you want a proper one?'

The secret fear began to grow inside her chest. 'Please.'

Clumsily and gauchely he took her in his arms and put his lips on hers.

It was not a passionate kiss. She might as well be kissing a dead mackerel, she thought. Or one that was almost dead.

And that was the way he always kissed. It had never bothered her before, but it did now.

'Now what's all this about?' he demanded as they pulled apart, asking his question lightly in an attempt to inject some humour into the situation.

Star scowled. She didn't see his tone as humorous at all, but as patronizing.

'Don't you find me attractive?' she asked at last in a faraway voice.

Alec gave a low laugh that only irritated her more. Did he think this was a joke?

'Of course I do. I wouldn't go out with you otherwise, would I?' He took her hand in his.

'Are you sure you're not confusing liking me as a person with finding me attractive?'

71

Her hand was cool and limp. 'Of course not. I think you're one of the most attractive girls I know.'

She relaxed slightly. 'Then why haven't you ever tried to touch me?' she asked, her voice sounding desperate in the quiet of the night.

What was she going on about? 'But I have touched you,' he said, frowning in bewilderment.

He was being dense, she thought. Or else evasive. She found his hand and placed it against her breast.

Alec jerked back his hand as though it had been burnt. 'What the . . .'

'I mean touching me, not just when we're dancing or you take my hand to cross the street. Really touching me.'

She waited for his hand to come back to her breast, to actually *feel* her breast, but the hand remained motionless at his side.

Alec was completely perplexed. He couldn't understand any of this. What *had* got into her? This wasn't the Star he knew.

'Well?'

'That's dirty,' he said simply, oddly embarrassed. 'I think more of you than that.'

It was the reply she would have expected – but was it the truth, the *whole* truth?

'But if we were married, man and wife, would you want to then?' she pushed.

'You know I would.'

'I do nothing of the sort. If I did I wouldn't have to ask,' she snapped back.

He coughed, glad of the darkness that was hiding his inflamed face from her. 'I would like nothing better than to touch you,' he said in a whisper.

'You're sure?'

'Of course I'm sure.'

She took hold of his hand a second time and returned it to her breast. 'Show me how it would be. I want you to, I want to know,' she urged him.

This was ridiculous! 'I can't. We're not married.'

'Try,' she said fiercely.

Tentatively, he uncurled his fingers, and almost immediately pulled his hand away again. 'You've no bra on!' he exclaimed in shock.

His tone was so outraged she almost wanted to laugh. 'So what?'

'I can't touch a bare breast, I'm going to be a minister one day.'

'But it's not bare, my woollie's over it.'

'You know what I mean.'

Her questions were still unanswered, she told herself. 'I don't believe you find me attractive at all,' she said at last in a small voice.

He ran his fingers through his hair. 'Yes I do.'

'You say so, but you don't act as if you do. Any normal boy wouldn't have reacted as you did. Any one else would have jumped at the chance. And I don't think there's anything dirty in that.'

'I explained. I'm going to be a minister one day. It wouldn't be right and proper. . .'

'Oh, nonsense. Are you sure you're not just using that as an excuse?'

He stared at the dark space from where her voice had come, wishing he could see her face, could read her expression. 'Excuse for what?' he asked hesitantly.

Star took a deep breath. If she wasn't so desperate she would never have gone so far. 'At school they're saying you don't really like girls,' she said quickly.

His mind reeled. Don't really like girls?

She went on. 'There's something wrong between you and me. There's something not normal about our relationship. I want to find out what, and why.'

He tried to speak, but no words came. Were they saying there was something wrong with him? 'Who says I'm not interested in girls?' he croaked at last.

'That doesn't matter. What does is the answer. Are you a homosexual?'

73

'Of course I'm not,' he answered quickly.

'Perhaps you don't know yourself yet. Perhaps you just think you're normal when actually you're not.'

Normal? Of course he was normal, he assured himself. Then doubt assailed him. Was he? Could she be right, could he only *think* he was? After all he'd never sat down and considered the possibility of his being abnormal; he'd always presumed he was just like other boys.

His doubt deepened into the beginnings of panic. Like Star, he also had to find out, he needed an answer.

'What am I going to do?' he asked eventually.

Star told him.

Tommy, home from school, let himself into the house in Millbrae Crescent and headed straight for the kitchen where he expected to find his mother waiting, ready with a little something to tide him over until tea together when Jim got home.

But Jeannie wasn't there, nor was she in any of the other downstairs rooms. There was an unsettling quiet about the house.

He eventually found her in her bedroom, slumped in a green Lloyd-Loom chair, tears streaming down her face.

'Mum?' he said quietly, shocked to see her like that.

She gave a startled exclamation at the sound of his voice. 'Oh, Tommy,' she said, wiping at the tears. 'I didn't hear you come in.'

'The door was open,' he said gently. 'I thought you heard me.'

Jeannie tried to smile, but the tears refused to stop. Her face was pale and drawn.

Tommy had never seen his mother cry before. The sight was quite unnerving. 'Can I get you something?' he asked. And she nodded, 'I'd like a glass of water, thank you.'

By the time she'd had a sip from the glass he brought

her she was once more in control of herself. 'I'm sorry about that,' she apologized. 'I didn't realize it was so late and that you were due back.'

He took the glass from her and laid it on the mantelpiece above the fire. 'What's upset you?' he asked gently.

She looked at her son through eyes still misty from tears. He wasn't a boy any more, she thought, he'd become a man. At some point during the past weeks or months a transformation had taken place, and this was the first she'd noticed it. She studied him carefully. There was a lot of Jim about him – in his expressions and in the way he held himself. As he was now he reminded her a lot of Jim when they first got married. And he was determined like Jim, with that same streak of wildness that Jim had still.

'It's your father, I worry about him,' she said flatly.

'Is there something wrong with his health?'

Jeannie shook her head.

'Then is it the business, is it starting to fall away?'

She wondered what he would say if he found out what his father really did? Probably ask to get involved, she thought, which made her grin inside in spite of herself. Aye, that would no doubt be his reaction right enough. She hoped and prayed he would never find out what Jim was up to, a young man starting afresh from the likes of Millbrae Crescent shouldn't have such knowledge about his dad.

Not that she was ashamed of what Jim was doing. Born and bred in Partick, she was well used to shady goings-on of all sorts. But in the new life Tommy was leading such things were not at all acceptable. She had even worried that in the years ahead Tommy might come to despise his father for what he was doing now.

By Jeannie's lights, Jim was only trying to earn a living for his family. With that hook and limp of his, he might well be idle, might never have got back on his feet after the war. She respected Jim's guts and endeavour. Not only was he earning a living, he was earning a damn fine one at that, and giving Tommy the chance in life that neither of them had ever had.

'It's not the business, that's going from strength to strength,' Jeannie assured him. This was partly true, and partly a lie. It was the business that worried her, though not because it was failing.

'So what is it then?'

She made her face smile. 'I suppose I'm worrying about nothing at all. Anyway, we women love a good greet once in a while, we feel the better for it.' Then changing the subject, she said, 'I went down to Boyd Street the other day and saw some of the old neighbours. Do you ever miss it?'

'Not me, that place is a hole. As far as I'm concerned, we're well away. If I never clapped eyes on Boyd Street again it wouldn't bother me one little bit,' he replied, matching her smile.

Already he'd adapted, she thought. There was none of her sense of being an outsider in him.

'Now I'm here I can't imagine living anywhere else,' he went on, thinking this was what she wanted to hear. 'It's so terrific just being able to go to the Linn Park. Did I tell you I saw an otter last time I was there?' his voice rising with excitement.

As they went downstairs to the kitchen Tommy raved on about the Linn Park, and what an absolutely magic place it was, and how he must take her and his father there soon so they could see for themselves.

Ever eager to please Tommy, Jeannie said perhaps they could all go the following Saturday or Sunday, even though the image he conjured up of endless trees and flowers made her shudder. Jeannie McBride was strictly an urban creature – the thought of being amongst that lot made her flesh creep.

Jim McBride was in the largest of the four small warehouses he rented. Two of them were near his own premises in the Calton district, the other two in Springburn. This particular one was one of the latter.

The latest consignment from Paddy Swords in Dublin had just been unloaded and was now stacked in front of him. It consisted of fourteen crates, all the same size.

Jim prised open the nearest crate with a jemmy, adroitly manipulating it with his left hand. Even so, sweat was beading on Jim's forehead when, with a final agonized creak of protest, the crate's lid was finally undone.

Inside the crate were thick white sacks, each with the marking 10 lbs stencilled in black on its front. Each sack had been screw tied at its neck with baling wire.

Jim selected a sack at random, undid the wire at its neck, then spilled a little of its contents into his hand. Bringing his hand to his mouth he licked the white substance on his palm. He gave an approving nod. Best quality sugar, always the best, never any grit or additives, that was Paddy for you.

He knew the sugar was refined in the south of Ireland from beet, but who did the refining, and where the refinery was, he had no idea, nor did he particularly want to know. As long as Paddy was able to keep shipping the beautiful stuff to him that was all that mattered.

Sugar might not be exactly worth its weight in gold, but it did command a hellishly high price when you sold it outside the points system – hoteliers, restaurateurs, and the like were his chief customers; less than twenty-five per cent went for ordinary domestic use. With ration books in force, and all foodstuffs coming under the points system, any food, especially one like sugar which had been in such short supply since the war, realized a tremendous mark-up when sold on the Black Market.

Nine times out of ten what Paddy shipped to him was sugar, the tenth time it was clothes, another thing which rationing had made expensive.

He re-did the sack and put it back with the others in the crate. There were fourteen crates in all. He made a few mental calculations, and figured the profit coming to him. It would take him less than forty-eight hours to shift the entire consignment, and he'd paid cash in hand, the *only* way he did business. Not a bad few days' work, not at all. He smiled as he thought about Paddy, or Paddy The Mad Irishman as he'd first been introduced to him.

His right stump had finally been on the mend and he'd been sent to a large house on the outskirts of St. Andrews for a period of convalescence. Fresh Air House the inmates called it, and that's exactly what it had been with the wind forever whipping in off the Bay and the cold North Sea beyond. The windows only closed at night. By God, he'd been in tip top shape when he'd finally left, or escaped as the immates termed it.

He and Paddy had become fast friends during those four months. They had quite a bit in common, of course. They were both working class lads from tough city neighbourhoods. And they had both lost their right hand.

He'd just told old man Murison where to put that insult of a nightwatchman's job, when Paddy had turned up out of the blue wearing a flashy suit and driving an even flashier car with a crate of whisky in its boot.

He remembered only too well his disbelieving look when he'd been shown that crate, an entire bloody crate when you really had to be in the know, *and* pay through the nose, to get a single bottle.

What a pish up that had been! The pair of them had ended up completely legless, with Paddy being sick into Jeannie's best vase. And during the bevy he'd told Paddy what had happened at Murison's, and how he hadn't been able to find a job since. With a hook and limp no one wanted to know.

The next day, Paddy had taken him aside and brought the subject up again. 'Us right handed hooks should stick together, and help one another out when we can,' Paddy had said, giving him a fly wink. And then Paddy had asked him how he'd feel about doing something strictly illegal, but extremely lucrative.

He'd listened carefully to Paddy's proposition, asked a few questions, and the deal had been struck. They shook hooks on it, an old gag of theirs from Fresh Air House.

Paddy would fund him initially to set up the Glasgow side of the operation, capital he would repay in time, and they would be partners, splitting everything straight down the middle after expenses had been deducted. From that day to this he'd never looked back. The money, as the saying went, just kept rolling in.

The sugar and clothes racket weren't the only ones Paddy had going, he knew Paddy had other fiddles in operation throughout the Irish south. But he never inquired about those, they were none of his business. All that concerned him were the sugar and clothes that arrived in Glasgow.

Locking the warehouse Jim got into the Arrole-Johnstone and set off for the town. He had customers to visit and orders to take.

Alec Muir was petrified. He had never been so scared in his entire life. He gripped his legs to stop his hands from shaking, certain they could be seen even through the cloth that covered his front.

Alec was having a haircut. The barber, Max Kyriacou, was also the owner of the shop.

Max employed two other men. One of them was also cutting hair, the other was sitting on the bench by the wall waiting for the next customer to walk in. Alec kept glancing at them nervously.

He had never patronized Max's before, and was only there now on the recommendation of a school chum who'd assured him that the Greek's was the best place to go for contraceptives as Max sold them to anyone, no matter what the person's age.

For the umpteenth time Alec glanced in the mirror facing him, seeking out the image of the Durex box that was in a prominent position beside the till.

79

'Lotion sir?'

Alec roused himself from his reverie. 'Yes, please,' he answered, his voice quivering at the edges.

A packet of three, that was the correct way to ask for them, Alec reminded himself. A packet of three, a packet of three, a packet of three, he repeated over and over. Lines from a doggerel he'd heard years previously flashed through his mind causing him to give a sort of hysterical snicker: 'It's only me with a packet of three, Barnacle Bill the sailor!'

Anything less like a Barnacle Bill than himself he couldn't imagine.

He watched Max's comb move through his hair. The haircut was going to be finished any moment now, then it would be the short walk to the till to pay his bill *and . . . and . . .* He groaned inwardly. Was he actually going to have the courage to ask for them? Was he really going to be able to speak those words?

He suddenly wanted desperately to go to the toilet, an almost uncontrollable urge to urinate having taken hold of him. He wanted to go to the toilet. He wanted to be outside. He wanted to be anywhere but standing in front of that till.

'How's that?' Max asked, brandishing a mirror behind Alec's head so he could see what the haircut was like at the back.

'Very nice,' Alec choked.

Max Kyriacou was enjoying this. He knew exactly why Alec had come to his shop – Alec's repeated glances at the Durex box in the mirror had long since given the real reason for Alec's visit away.

When the scared young lads came in for contraceptives it was a long-standing game of Max's to bet with himself as to whether or not the boy concerned would have the gumption to make the request when the time came. In this instance, his bet was that Alec would funk it at the last second and leave without the condoms.

Max replaced the mirror on its hook on the wall, then

whipped the cloth from around Alec's neck. He smiled benignly as he shook the cut hairs on to the floor.

Alec's legs were leaden as he swung them off the chair. He stood rigidly still as Max dusted down his shoulders.

The barber on the bench glanced up from the newspaper he was reading and his mouth thinned into a tight grin. He'd also seen Alec staring at the reflection of the Durex box in the mirror.

The barber placed his newspaper on the bench beside him, folded his arms, and leant back against the wall. Like Max, he loved these little dramas, they made a long day shorter.

He was going to wet himself, Alec thought. He couldn't help it, it was going to happen right there in the middle of the barber shop.

Max strode to the till and banged up the price of the haircut, the drawer of the till shooting open with a ting! 'That'll be one and six please,' he said.

Alec fumbled in a pocket, bringing out the ten shilling note he'd previously put there especially. Going to the till he silently gave the money to Max.

Knew you wouldn't son, Max thought, taking the note and making change. He counted the change into Alec's sweaty hand. 'Anything else, sir?' he asked. Behind Alec, the man on the bench's grin turned into a smirk.

Alec didn't reply.

'A bottle of lotion perhaps?' Max suggested, extending the agony.

'A thracket of pee please,' Alec said in a rush.

The other barber quickly covered his mouth to stop himself from laughing out loud.

Max was taken aback. 'Eh?'

There was a waterfall of noise in Alec's ears. 'A thracket of pee please,' he repeated, only then realizing the muddle he'd made of the words. He felt his face start to go red.

Max was disappointed that he'd lost his bet, and

decided to make Alec suffer a little more. 'Sorry, son. I'm not quite with you.'

Alec's face was now as bright as a beacon. Lifting a hand he pointed at the Durex box. 'Those,' he stuttered, his whole body shaking.

Max took pity then. Anyway, further torment would cease to be funny, merely cruel. 'Certainly, sir,' he replied, and lifting a packet from the box laid it in front of Alec.

Alec handed over half a crown, and willed himself to wait for his change. As he accepted the coins he picked up the Durex packet with his other hand.

'Come again, sir,' Max said.

Alec nodded, and walked stiffly to the door. Back on the street he maintained a walk till he was out of view of the barber shop window, then broke into a mad run.

As he raced along the filthy pavement, its gutter running with litter and refuse, he was quite delirious with excitement.

Leaping into the air he punched at the sky, 'Yippeee!' he shouted, to the astonishment of passers-by.

When he finally collected himself he realized he'd never before felt so marvellous in all his life. Then it dawned on him what it actually was he felt.

He felt a man, and oh but it was grand!

Star was standing in front of the bathroom mirror, applying some of the forbidden make-up. After the dab of rouge and the trace of red on her lips, she intended to smooth in just a whisk of powder with a fat pink puff.

The make-up had been taken from its hiding place in her bedroom the moment her parents had left for Reverend Carrell's annual whist drive over in Langside. Although the Grays always complained that the Carrells' whist drive didn't measure up to their own they always stayed on to the bitter end, probably, Star reasoned, because it gave them that much more to complain about. It would be hours before they returned.

Star put a dab of scent behind her ears, gave herself one last critical appraisal, then stepped out of the rest of her clothes and slipped into her dressing gown. She was ready.

She quietly made her way down the hallway and stopped outside her bedroom door for a moment. Taking a deep breath to compose herself – this was a momentous step, after all – she went inside.

Alec was already in the bed, looking rather scared, the covers drawn up almost to his chin.

'Are you sure we're doing the right thing?' he asked as she came to the side of the bed.

'Shhh,' she said, shrugging the dressing gown from her shoulders in what she hoped was a provocative manner. 'Don't say anything.'

But Alec was staring at her with an expression on his face she had never seen before. 'You're lovely,' he said in an awed whisper. 'You're the loveliest thing I've ever seen.'

Star felt a chill run through her that had nothing to do with the temperature of the room. 'Do you mean that? You're not just saying it?'

He reached out to touch the swell of her hip. The feel of her skin beneath his fingers was like nothing he had ever experienced before. It was like touching satin, he thought. Warm, vibrant satin.

Star slipped into the bed beside him, trembling. Her stomach muscles were jumping as if an electric current was running through her.

'You're more than lovely,' Alex whispered. 'You're beautiful. You're the most beautiful girl in Scotland.'

Star's voice came like a sigh. 'Really?'

'Really.'

'But am I *sexually* attractive?'

'Yes,' he breathed.

'Then kiss me, Alec,' she urged. 'Kiss me now.'

His lips reached for the sweetness of her lips, and his hands reached clumsily for her breasts. He could feel her nipples rise against his fingers and hear her breathing quicken. But his mind couldn't forget that God was watching him, watching him with disapproval. The instant he remembered God a war between his body and his conscience began. He caressed and kissed her longingly, but the erection which came so easily at times when it was least wanted refused to come now.

'What is it?' whispered Star, sensing the tenseness in him.

'Nothing,' pressing himself against her with renewed force.

'There's something wrong,' she persisted, suddenly knowing what it was. 'It's me, isn't it?' she asked, pushing him away. 'You just don't fancy me like this.'

His voice, when it came, sounded far away. 'No,' he mumbled. 'It has nothing to do with you.'

Tears filled her eyes. 'You don't have to lie,' she said, disentangling herself from his desperate embrace. 'It's all right.'

But when at last she could look into his face there were tears streaming from his eyes as well. 'Oh, Alec,' she cried, tenderly brushing the tears from his cheek.

'I'm sorry,' he whispered. 'Oh, Star, I'm so sorry.'

Star hugged him to her, gently stroking his hair, her own tears trickling down her face. Could it be that Alec simply wasn't attracted to her in a sexual way? And if so, was that because she lacked sex appeal, or because Alec would never be attracted to a woman? Star sighed. This fiasco certainly hadn't provided any answers.

Still crying, Alec laid his head against her breasts, his hands unthinkingly stroking her smooth, soft skin. Like two lost children in a storybook, they clung to each other until their fears were forgotten.

With surprise, Alec suddenly realized that his arousal had begun. 'Star,' he whispered, almost afraid to speak.

'Star.' He took her hand and placed it on himself, feeling the heat rise in his groin. 'Oh, Star . . .'

An eternity later, they pulled apart, their hands still touching. Alec felt like crowing. Any doubts he'd had about his own masculinity were gone for good. He was a man now. A real man.

Star stretched like a cat in the sun. All of her doubts were gone as well. She had aroused Alec to a pitch she wouldn't have believed possible – to the point where he was no longer reserved, methodical Alec but a man possessed by a wildness she had never before seen. She was a woman now, a desirable woman, a woman with oodles of sex appeal. As much as Eve Smith – as much as anyone.

Pulling herself to a sitting position, she let her gaze run down his body. Instantly, the look of satisfaction turned to one of horror. 'Alec!' she said in a strangled voice. 'Alec, where's the . . . the thing?'

Alec stared down at his naked penis, where the Durex should have been. 'Oh, Jesus!' he whispered.

'You did put it on, didn't you?'

'Of course I did,' he snapped. 'You saw me put it on.'

'Then where is it?' she wailed.

They tore the bed apart and shook out the blankets. But when they did find it it was in the worst possible place of all.

'It doesn't matter,' Alec said when at last his speech returned. 'Nothing's going to happen after just one time.'

'You're right,' said Star, trying not to panic. 'The odds against it must be a million to one.'

'A billion more like!'

'Maybe as much as a trillion.'

Alec laughed, but it was a nervous laugh that crackled at the edges.

Star felt the tears burning against her eyes again. She wanted him to take her in his arms and comfort her, to promise her that everything *was* going to be all right.

But Alec wasn't thinking of Star, he was thinking only of himself. A voice in his mind was telling him that he deserved this, that it was God's punishment for the awful sin he'd just committed. He should have known better. He should have been stronger. He shouldn't have let his doubts tempt him. He could hear God himself berating him for his weakness – and right behind God he could hear his mother.

'We have to beg for forgiveness,' he said suddenly, jumping out of the bed. 'We have to pray to God that nothing will come of what we've done.' Grabbing hold of Star's arm, he dragged her to the floor beside him. Joining his hands in supplication, he began, 'Our Father in Heaven . . .'

Halfway through Alec's fervent prayers, Star realized that she was still holding the useless condom in her hands.

Margaret Muir finished reading the solitary letter that had come in the morning post with an enigmatic sigh. The news it had brought had quite taken her breath away.

Cosmo Dunbarr was home from Kenya! And he'd brought his and Ginty's wee girl with him. Not so wee, she corrected herself with a smile; Virginia was the same age as her Alec.

Cosmo Dunbarr, the Earl of Clyde, was what Margaret Muir considered a darling, darling man. Ginty, her best friend since childhood, had married him in Glasgow Cathedral in what had been the wedding of the year. Cosmo had been Scotland's most eligible bachelor at the time, as well as possessor of one its greatest fortunes. As for the Dunbarrs, they were among Scotland's oldest families, far older than the Muirs, as well as among its canniest. Over the centuries they'd accrued enormous wealth, always managing to hold on to and increase it, no matter what the political or economic situation.

Margaret sighed. Poor Ginty, dead ten months now from the awful asthma that had plagued her since childhood. It was because of the asthma that Cosmo had bought the farm in Kenya, and why he'd taken his beloved Ginty there to live. But the Kenyan weather hadn't cured Ginty, it had merely extended her life. But the extension had run out, and Ginty had passed away one night in her sleep.

According to the letter, Cosmo hadn't been able to bear remaining in Kenya now that Ginty was dead. Her ghost had been everywhere, and so he'd decided to return to Scotland. He'd taken up residence again in the family town house. No. 56 Lindsay Drive, Kelvinside. It had already been arranged for Virginia to attend Laurel Bank School for girls, beginning next term.

Margaret nodded her approval of the Laurel Bank School. There were some preferred Craigholme, but in her estimation Laurel Bank was superior.

Alec suddenly appeared to her thoughts. She'd always wanted him to go to Hutcheson's, but the money hadn't been available. Instead Alec had had to go to Queen's Park Secondary, a local school of no particular merit, either academic or social. Another black mark against Geoffrey, one amongst many.

Margaret brought her mind back to Cosmo's letter. He'd gone on to say that he was looking forward to renewing his friendship with her and Geoffrey, and that he hoped they would call at Lindsay Drive in the very near future.

Margaret remembered Lindsay Drive with affection. She'd spent some marvellous evenings there when Ginty and Cosmo had first been married. Ginty had adored giving small, intimate dinner parties. Invitations to them had been much sought after, but Margaret had always had one.

From Lindsay Drive her thoughts went to Bonnydykes, Cosmo's family estate in Renfrewshire and seat of the Earls of Clyde since the 14th century. It was a magnificent estate, and the memory of it fired all of Margaret's old dreams.

Lindsay Drive, Bonnydykes – Ginty's life may have been a short one, but by God she'd prospered during it. And Margaret? What had she ended up with? A house in Overdale Street and a worthless husband, less than worthless, *useless*.

Strangely enough, Cosmo had always liked Geoffrey, though she'd never been able to understand why. It could only be some male thing she just didn't understand.

She decided to reply to Cosmo's letter immediately, suggesting that she and Geoffrey call this coming Saturday after lunch. Alec would go along too, of course, Cosmo would want to see how he'd grown up. Just as they'd want to see how. . . The thought hit Margaret like a bombshell. Lady Virginia Dunbarr, Cosmo and Ginty's daughter, would be Cosmo's heir now that Ginty was gone, heiress to one of the largest fortunes in Scotland, perhaps even the largest. And then there was the title itself which would go to Virginia's eldest son. Suddenly, Margaret could see it all as though God had written it on the wall for her.

To Hell with Morag what's her name, Ishbel Doig, Juliet Abercrombie and that upstart crew! It was Virginia Alec should woo and wed. It would be a match beyond her wildest dreams!

She was so excited she began pacing around the room. Was it possible? Was it really possible? She answered the question herself: Why not?

For the next half hour she walked up and down, thinking, planning, scheming. Finally, she wrote her reply to Cosmo's letter.

Margaret was shocked to see Cosmo after all these years. She still remembered him as the young and dashing man who'd had all the girls swooning over his charms. How he'd aged! His once handsome face was worn and lined, his hair had thinned to such an extent that the scalp shone through, and his fine physique had gone to fat. She could barely keep the shock out of her face.

'Margaret!' he cried, holding out his arms. She rushed into them, hugging him with all the old affection. Geoffrey stood behind her, smiling.

While all this was going on, Alec studied Virginia. His mother had been talking non-stop about her since *the* letter had arrived. She was attractive enough, he thought, although it was somewhat startling to see a girl so brown she could almost have passed as an Indian, if it hadn't been for that straw-blonde hair and those washed-out blue eyes, that was. She had a good figure, too, he noticed, and coloured a little. He hadn't been the same since his episode in bed with Star. Losing his virginity had opened up areas within himself that he would never before have guessed existed. And all the prayers in the world wouldn't change that.

Virginia, virginity, he thought, and smiled inwardly. He wondered if she still was?

'You've both got fat,' Geoffrey laughed as they finally pulled apart.

'Beauty is in the eye of the beholder,' said Cosmo unsmilingly. 'And as far as I'm concerned Margaret is still as beautiful as she ever was.'

Margaret simply scowled at her husband.

'And this is Virginia,' Cosmo went on, gesturing towards his daughter.

She was Ginty to a T, Margaret thought, except that the girl was clearly bursting with health. 'Lady Virginia,' Margaret smiled, slightly wary now, for the lass had a mind of her own, that was evident in the haughty way she was staring back at her.

Virginia extended a hand. 'I've heard so much about you, Mrs Muir,' she said politely.

Margaret took her hand and shook it. 'I was hoping it might be Margaret. That's what it always was to your mother whose dear and devoted friend I was,' she replied.

Virginia immediately softened under this combined entreaty and overture. 'Then Margaret it shall be. But you must call me Virginia, as my mother would have wanted.'

That was that hurdle out the way Margaret told herself with relief. Things weren't going to be too difficult after all. She introduced Geoffrey and Alec. Then they all followed Cosmo into what was called the Chinese Room for drinks.

As Virginia entered the Chinese Room beside Alec she was thinking again how she hated Scotland. It had turned out to be even worse than she'd expected. She hadn't been warm since arriving; even when every fireplace in the house was ablaze she was still freezing. Every night she dreamt about Kenya, and woke next morning wishing she were back there under the blue sky, with that soft, gentle wind that was like velvet on the skin.

Alec had been primed by Margaret to concentrate on Virginia, whether he liked her or not, and this he did, like the obedient son that he was. The last thing he wanted was to encounter his mother's wrath.

'The house is in a dreadful state I'm afraid,' apologized Cosmo. 'After lying empty for so long, it's going to take some time to get it back to what it was.'

Margaret gazed about her critically. If the Chinese Room was anything to go by, he was right. Years of neglect had taken their toll. Suddenly it reminded her of their own house in Overdale Street, and she shuddered inwardly. But then an inspiration hit her. A way of getting Virginia under her influence. 'Why don't I help by organizing a total revamp for you?' she asked. 'Virginia and I – if she'd like that is – could do it together before she starts school. It would be a good way of introducing her to Glasgow. We'd have to visit all the big shops.'

'Would you do that?' Cosmo was obviously delighted.

'It would be my pleasure. What do you say, Virginia?'

Virginia thought for a moment, then nodded assent. Things couldn't get worse.

'Excellent!' Margaret declared, and took a sip of her whisky.

'How big is your farm in Kenya?' Alec asked Cosmo, genuinely interested, but also tired already of talking to Virginia.

'A hundred and twenty-five thousand acres,' Cosmo replied proudly.

Margaret's eyes glittered. She'd forgotten just how vast the farm was. And that was only one of Cosmo's many assets.

'Who's looking after it now you've left?' asked Geoffrey, also interested.

'I've appointed a manager, a Welshman called Roberts. He'll be running cattle on half of it, and growing tobacco on the other half. We employ local men, a friendly bunch from a tribe called the Kikuyu.'

Margaret's gaze flickered over to where Alec and Virginia were sitting silently and slightly apart. Alec had done all the talking between them so far. Virginia's replies, at least those she'd overheard, were restricted to monosyllables.

She brought her attention back to Cosmo. He was repeating how marvellous it was to see her and Geoffrey again, after such a long time. 'It's only too bad Ginty couldn't be here to share this,' he concluded, but at the mention of his dead wife's name his face darkened in sorrow, and his eyes took on a faraway look. Margaret knew it was Ginty he was seeing.

After a while Margaret suggested that Alec might take Virginia for a walk. It was such a lovely day, the sort of day young people should be out and about, not sitting in musty drawing rooms listening to their elders talk about times gone by which must be boring for them.

Alec took up his cue. 'It'll be nice down by the Kelvin,' he agreed. 'There's a lovely walk along the banks.'

Virginia sighed. Better to be bored in the fresh air, than in this mouldering old house.

Shortly after they had gone, Margaret said to Cosmo, 'It must seem like the end of the world to you with Ginty passing away, but just because her life is over doesn't mean yours is. It's not impossible, although it might seem so at the moment, that you'll meet someone else, and get married again. After all, we may all be getting on but none of us are exactly beyond it yet.'

Cosmo shook his head. 'I'll never marry again Margaret, of that I'm absolutely certain. I'm strictly a one woman man, and Ginty was the woman.'

Margaret's expression was serious and sympathetic, but she was jubilant to hear him say that. It meant the title was safe with Virginia. Grandmother to an Earl. The thought almost made her forget not to smile.

Later, when they'd returned to Overdale Street, she drew Alec aside. 'How did you get on with the lassie?' she demanded abruptly.

Alec had no idea of what his mother was up to. He thought she wanted him to get on with Virginia because Virginia was the daughter of an old friend. 'Well enough. She wasn't very friendly to begin with. Until I asked about Kenya that is, then she wouldn't stop talking. She misses the place like mad.'

'And you liked her?' Margaret pressed.

'Oh aye, she's extremely nice.'

Good, Margaret thought. Very good indeed. 'And do you think she liked you?'

Alec couldn't understand his mother's extreme interest, but it didn't occur to him to question it. 'I'd say she did, particularly after I showed interest in Kenya.'

Margaret had another brainwave. 'There's a picture about Africa on in town next week, why don't you take her to see it? You could go Friday night.'

'But Friday night is my Scripture Union class,' objected Alec.

Margaret shooed his objection away. 'To miss it once

in a blue moon won't hurt. Anyway, you can regard it as putting into practice what you've been learning about being a Christian.'

A film about Africa, he'd rather enjoy that he thought. 'What's it called?' he asked.

But Margaret was no longer thinking about him. She was wondering how to get him with Virginia on Saturday as well.

'Are you all right?' Ding A Ling asked Star concernedly. She'd just finished playing for the Maze Marching, and if he'd thought she hadn't looked too clever on arriving in the hall, she now looked positively dreadful.

'I suspect I've got a cold or the flu coming on,' Star replied in a tremulous voice.

'If I was you I'd get right up to bed, and I'd take some hot lemon if your mother's got any.'

Star rose from the piano and gently lowered its lid. She'd banged out a dozen tunes for the marching, and couldn't remember playing a single one of them. 'I'll away then,' she said distractedly, and slowly made her way from the hall.

Once into the corridor she forgot all about the officers' cups and saucers that she normally washed, dried and put away, and broke into a run, scalding tears streaming down her face.

She burst into the toilet at the far end of the corridor, slamming the door closed behind her and locking it. Collapsing on to the w.c., she held her head in her hands and wailed her fear and grief. Her period was a whole week overdue, and it had never been even one day late.

She just knew it wasn't going to come now, she just knew!

3

Spring was in the air, Star could smell it. Soon the buds would be appearing on the trees and the first flowers in the gardens.

Star and Alec were in Lovers' Lane at her request. She'd told him at school that afternoon that she desperately needed to have a word with him. She'd suggested Lovers' Lane because it was quiet there, a good place to say what she had come to say.

'I'm pregnant,' she stated bluntly.

Alec could only stare at her. With the passing of time he'd almost forgotten about the possible consequences of the condom coming off. Almost, but not quite. Every so often the worry had re-emerged at the back of his mind, but he'd pushed it aside. For some reason neither of them had talked about it, preferring to leave it there like a bad smell they both hoped would suddenly disappear. Only it hadn't disappeared and the secret nightmare had now become a horrible reality.

'Are you sure?' he asked at last, if only because he had to say something.

'I've missed three periods, and I've never missed one before,' she said in a choked whisper. 'I consider that pretty conclusive. Wouldn't you?'

His head had gone light; the inside of his mouth was dry as dust. He wanted to take her hand but he couldn't move. 'Have you told anyone else?'

She shook her head. 'No. You had to be the first.'

He would never be a minister now, he thought. That balloon had just gone bang. Never be a minister! Just for one lapse! It was a catastrophe!

'Well?' said Star, worried at his silence. 'Say something!'

'I'll stand by you,' he replied quickly. 'I'll do the Christian thing.'

'Don't do me any favours!' she snapped back.

He stared at her, his feelings a combination of affection and dislike. If it weren't for her, none of this would ever have happened. This was God's vengeance, he told himself. He really was being paid back for his moment of weakness.

'I'm sorry,' he said more gently. 'I didn't mean that to sound so bald. What I meant was we'll get married. I know we're awful young, but it isn't exactly unheard of for couples to get married at our age. A bit unusual in Battlefield perhaps, but there we are. People will talk of course, there'll be lots of that, but that can't be helped.' Once he'd started he could barely keep the words from tumbling out, he was so terrified.

A surge of relief went through Star. She hadn't really doubted what his reaction would be, but the worry had been there. At least the baby would have a father and the father's name. 'The sooner we get everything settled the better,' she said trying to sound brave.

He picked up a chukkie and threw it into the water. If only she'd been two months gone instead of three. They might have been able to explain the baby's early arrival as its being premature. Three months no one would believe.

'I wish you'd told me before this,' he said.

'I kept hoping I was wrong, that it would come next time round.'

The local gossips were going to have a field day, he thought bitterly. His mother would go daft!'

'It was bad luck as we only did it the once,' Star said miserably.

Bad luck! That was the understatement of the year, he thought.

'We'd better tell our parents right away,' she said. She wanted it over with as quickly as possible.

'I wonder if your Dad will lose his job over this?' Alec

mused, knowing this could be a distinct possibility. After all, a minister with a fallen daughter wasn't exactly the pillar of moral rectitude a *Scottish* minister should be.

Star paled. She'd been so concerned about herself she'd failed to consider that. If her father lost Battlefield Central he'd never ever get another kirk. A horrifying scenario, and her fault entirely.

Alec took her cold hand in his. 'We'll go to Overdale Street first because that's closest to here.' As ye sow, so shall ye reap, he thought, and wanted to be sick.

As they trudged in the direction of Overdale Street Star felt incredibly small, frightened, and vulnerable. She reminded herself it could have been worse. Alec might have left her in the lurch.

'What!' Margaret screeched, her features contorted with fury.

Geoffrey Muir stared at his son in total astonishment. What Alec had just announced was the last thing he'd ever expected to hear the boy say. It seemed there was more to Alec than he'd ever given him credit for.

Margaret, however, was so beside herself Alec thought she must either have a heart attack or a seizure.

'Get her a dram,' Geoffrey instructed.

Alec hurried to obey, pouring her a large one. The bottle of whisky was one of twelve, a crate which Cosmo Dunbarr had sent over as a small token of appreciation for what Margaret was doing at Lindsay Drive. With that crate had been another of best claret.

Margaret's gaze bored into Alec, but what she was seeing was a large black hole down which all her dreams and aspirations for him, and herself, were disappearing. Pregnant! Marriage! The words sizzled in her brain as if they were burning there in letters of fire.

She took the dram from Alec and tossed half of it down, paused for breath, then drained the glass. 'Give me another,' she ordered returning the glass to Alec. The stupid wee bugger, she thought, watching Alec's retreating back. What on earth had come over him? There was only one answer, of course, Star bloody Gray, that was who. It had to be Star who seduced Alec, she couldn't even begin to imagine it happening the other way round, not with Alec. Well, one thing was certain, she told herself, she wasn't going to let Alec marry Star, not when Lady Virginia Dunbarr, and all the Dunbarr money, was in the offing.

Alec handed his mother the second dram, noting her eyes had taken on that calculating, scheming look he knew so well. Margaret was at her most dangerous when she wore that look.

Geoffrey Muir thought of Star again, and suppressed a smile. If he were Alec's age he wouldn't mind a go with her himself. But then his attention went back to Margaret. God but she was in a right mood this time. She was going to make his life even more of a hell from now on. And as for Star . . . he could only pity the lass. He knew roughly what was bound to happen next. He wasn't privy to Margaret's plans for Alec, but he was aware there were plans, and that they were hardly likely to include Star Gray, fine lassie that she was.

In a flash of insight it suddenly dawned on Geoffrey that it was Virginia Dunbarr whom Margaret had in mind for Alec. That was why she had been pushing the two of them together ever since Virginia had come to live in Lindsay Drive. Why hadn't he seen it before? If that was the case then Star was really on a hiding to nothing. His pity for Star deepened.

'And you said Star is outside on the landing waiting to meet us?' Margaret asked at last.

Alec nodded. 'That was my idea. I thought it best I break the news alone. Will I get her in now?'

Geoffrey lurched to his feet and made for the whisky bottle. If Alec thought he'd defused the situation by breaking the news to his mother alone he was wrong, as the lad would shortly discover.

Star gave a tight smile when Alec opened the front door. 'You're to come on through,' he said.

She stood aside while he closed the door behind them. He squeezed her arm, a gesture of encouragement, then led the way to where Margaret and Geoffrey were waiting. 'We're here,' he announced quite unnecessarily when he and Star were in the room.

Margaret fixed Star with an unblinking look, but didn't speak. Nor did Geoffrey; at that point he wouldn't have dared.

The pungent smell of whisky in the room made Star want to sneeze, or perhaps it was only her nerves. She had imagined what Alec's parents might say, but Margaret's first words hit her like a brick.

'How do we know it's Alec's baby?' she asked abruptly, going immediately on the offensive.

Star blinked, completely thrown. 'Who else's could it be?' she whispered in embarrassment.

'That's for you to know, I'm sure. But it's something I can always find out.'

Star had turned pale. 'But . . . but Alec is the only boy I . . . everybody knows we've been going together . . . I . . .' her words trailed off as she stared into Mrs Muir's cold, hard eyes.

Margaret twisted her face into a disbelieving sneer. 'There have been more lads trapped with that lie than you've had hot dinners,' she hissed.

'But there is no one else,' Star repeated frantically.

Margaret drew herself up to her full height. 'Let me tell you this, girl. You may be a minister's daughter, but as far as I'm concerned you're nothing more than a common trollop.'

Star recoiled, feeling as though she'd been physically assaulted.

'Mother!' Alec exclaimed, shocked.

'Quiet,' Margaret commanded.

Star glanced over at Alec, willing him to continue in her defence. Surely he wouldn't allow his mother to accuse her of such things, such lies! He knew the truth, as surely as she did.

'There'll be no wedding, at least not with my boy,' she continued. 'You'd better understand that, and accept it here and now.'

'But he *is* the father!' Star wailed.

Geoffrey stared down into his glass. This was bloody, and getting bloodier, just as he'd known it would be.

Margaret took a step towards her. 'If you put it about that he is then I'll stand up in your own father's congregation and cry you whore in front of everyone,' she threatened.

Star staggered backwards. 'You wouldn't!' she whispered, her eyes wide in disbelief.

'Oh, but she would,' said Geoffrey quietly.

'I'll do more than that,' Margaret raged. 'With Holy Bible in hand, I'll swear Alec has never slept with you and that you're only saying he has in order to trap him into marriage and give your bastard a name.'

Star turned to Alec, who was transfixed by his mother's glare. 'Alec?' she pleaded.

But Alec was no match for Margaret. He could no more go against his mother's wishes, or orders, than he could have sprouted wings, jumped out of the window and flown away.

'Alec?' Star pleaded again.

He turned to her. 'I'm sorry,' he mumbled and dropped his eyes to the carpet.

Game, set and match, thought Geoffrey, disgusted at what had just taken place. Disgusted he might be, but it never crossed his mind to interfere. He and Alec were alike in that respect.

'Now get out of our house, and never set foot in it again, you little *slut*,' Margaret ordered.

Before Star had felt small, frightened and vulnerable. Now she felt completely and utterly alone as well.

She turned to go, then stopped in front of Alec. 'I

realized you were weak, but now I see I was wrong. You're worse than that, you're pathetic.'

Margaret was at the window watching when Star came out into the street below. 'That settles her hash. And good riddance,' Margaret said.

Geoffrey rose from his chair and poured himself another drink. Maybe if he got drunk enough he could forget what had just happened.

He could be a minister after all, Alec told himself, so elated it made him want to jump for joy. Later, in the privacy of his bedroom, he got down on his knees and thanked God for relenting towards him. Then he added a prayer for Star.

Lizzie Dunnachie was stunned by what Star had just told her. The pair of them had come direct from school to the Fives.

'Pregnant!' Lizzie breathed.

Star nodded.

'And it was only the once?'

Star nodded again, her face showing just how wretched she felt.

Lizzie gave a low whistle. 'So what are you going to do now?'

Star waited while their coffees were placed in front of them, then replied, 'Tell my folks, I suppose. What else can I do?'

Lizzie lit a cigarette and drew on it pensively. Trust it to happen to Star, she thought, and her only having done it the once. There was no justice right enough.

'Why don't you . . . you know, lose it?' Lizzie asked slowly, aware that her heart had suddenly started going thump thump thump.

Star stared at her friend in shock. 'But that's murder,' she replied in a whisper.

Lizzie knew that if it had been she who'd had the misfortune to fall pregnant she wouldn't have hung back.

'If you go ahead and have it you'll never get married. Glasgow boys won't touch unmarried mothers, at least not for marriage. You'll ruin your whole life.'

It was true enough. Unmarried mothers became outcasts in this town. Oh, she'd get plenty of proposals all right, but not for a ring and wedding lines. And there was her father and his job to think about as well. If she lost the baby he need never know and his job saved.

Star could feel herself relenting. It was a solution, if a horrible one.

'Look at it like this, it can't be murder in the true sense when the wean hasn't been born, when it hasn't been out in the world yet,' Lizzie argued.

'That's just playing with words,' Star countered. 'The baby becomes alive at conception. Killing it now is as much murder as if I was to pull out a gun right here and blow your head off.'

'Well I don't agree,' Lizzie answered, wanting to remain unconvinced in case there ever came a time when she had a similar decision to make. 'All I can say is, it's either it or you. And the choice is yours.'

Star looked at Lizzie's cigarette, and for once wished she smoked. She could have done with something to hold on to right then. 'Even if I did decide to have an abortion, how would I go about it? I mean, I don't know anyone.'

Lizzie didn't know anyone either, but she did have information on the subject. 'You don't need to know anyone, you can do it yourself.'

Star didn't like the sound of that at all. 'How?' she asked cautiously, the chill running through her body.

'A piping hot bath and a bottle of gin. You sit in the bath, as hot as you can bear it, and drink the gin. You then lie back and let Mother Nature take her course.

A hot bath and gin! That didn't seem too awful. The chill subsided. 'Are you sure that works?'

'I've heard it on good authority. But don't ask me whose, that's my secret.'

101

A bath and a drink and all her troubles would be over, Star thought. She could go back to being the Star she'd been before all this had happened. No more worries about a baby, not getting married, her father's job, the family being turned out into the street, the shame, the humiliation, the . . .

'How would I get a bottle of gin?' she said.

'If you can raise the necessary to buy one then leave it to me,' Lizzie replied obviously relieved.

It was *murder*, Star thought, but she was coming to realize that in life there are things worse than that.

'I'll give you the money tomorrow morning at school,' she told Lizzie.

Star smuggled the gin into the bathroom inside her briefcase. She'd sought out her parents before going to the bathroom, explaining the briefcase by saying she intended doing some homework reading while enjoying a good long wallow. After her bath, she'd said, she'd go straight up to bed and have an early night.

Outside the door of the room where she'd just left her parents talking, she'd paused to take a breath. With that breath she'd begun to shake.

She was still shaking as she turned off the taps and tested the water in the bath. Any hotter and she'd scald herself, she thought. Sitting on the w.c., she took her briefcase on to her lap and opened it, then she opened the bottle of gin.

She screwed her face up at the gin's perfumed smell. It was going to be absolutely ghastly to get down, but get it down she would. She had to.

Her instructions from Lizzie were to get into the bath before starting on the gin, so rising again she shrugged herself out of her dressing gown, then removed the flannelette nightdress she was wearing beneath. She stared down at her belly, thinking of what was inside there. A shudder ran through her.

She fought back the tears, if they came she'd never go through with this, she knew that.

The bath was so hot it took her all of ten minutes to get into it and fully sit down. On finally accomplishing that, she reached for the gin bottle and the toothbrush cup she'd placed beside it. She filled the cup half full, raised it to her lips, forced herself not to think what she was doing, and drank. She managed to drink off the entire contents of the cup in one go.

Normally she liked hot baths, but this one was torture. She might have been in a cannibal pot being boiled alive.

She poured more gin. It wasn't too bad once you got the taste of it, she thought, and drank that lot back, this time taking two goes.

Alec was a rat, a weak, snivelling, mummy's boy rat. She was far better off without him, he'd have been a diabolical husband, she could see that now.

'Alec you're a rat,' she said aloud, and sipped more gin.

She felt a stirring deep within her. It happened again, but this time the pain was so intense that it made her squirm.

The pain passed away. 'Bye Bye Baby,' she sang softly to the tune of 'Bye Bye Blackbird', and giggled. She was getting drunk, she realized, and thoroughly pleasant it was proving too.

She swallowed more gin, focused her wavery gaze on the bottle, and saw she'd already consumed more than half. She was doing damn well for a beginner, she thought, and giggled again.

The bath was beginning to cool a little so she let out some of the water and poured in a fresh stream of hot. The painful sensation returned with a vengeance, knotting her stomach and causing her to groan. Eventually the pain subsided, and as it did she found herself again wanting to burst into tears. 'Mustn't, mustn't, mustn't . . .' she repeated over and over.

She drank yet more gin.

It was well over an hour later that Alison Gray

knocked on the bathroom door. 'Are you all right, Star? You've been in there a gey long while.'

Star had used the entire tank of hot water and was sitting in a bath that had gone stone cold. She was nursing a head that was threatening to blow itself apart from the inside.

'I said are you all right, Star?' Alison repeated, knocking the bathroom door a second time.

'I'm all right,' Star replied miserably. 'Nothing's happened mother, nothing at all.'

It was the period of the day between evening and night which the Scots call the gloaming, a soft ethereal twilight that makes the world seem like a fairlyland.

Finding himself at a loose end, Tommy McBride had decided to go down to Lovers' Lane. He would have preferred a walk to the Linn Park, but it was too late for that.

Spring had arrived in the last week, wakening the earth from its winter slumber. The birds overhead were crying from the joy of it, and here and there crocuses had appeared to brighten the landscape with their yellows, blues and purples.

Tommy stopped beside a goosegog bush, visualizing it heavy with fat, succulent berries. He smiled at the picture, and promised himself he'd come back in the summer and pick a big bagful.

He was about to move off again when he caught sight of Star about a hundred yards ahead of him. She was standing on the side of the bank staring pensively into the slow-moving water.

He wondered where she'd appeared from, she certainly hadn't been there when he'd stopped at the bush. She shouldn't stand so close to the edge, he thought, the bank could crumble or give way. He'd heard it was notorious round here for that.

He stood watching her. God, but she was lovely. Eve

Smith wasn't a patch on her, he'd known that all along. Eve was great fun, and a laugh, but Star, well she was special – at least to him she was. Alec Muir was a lucky so and so, that was certain. He was still staring at her when, to his complete astonishment and horror, Star stepped off the bank into the water and began wading out into the murky brown depths.

For the space of a few moments he stood paralysed, as though rooted to the spot, but then the spell was lifted and he sprang into action.

The river bed squelched under Star's feet and the freezing water lapped its way up her thighs, but she was aware of none of it. She was thinking about her father. Time and again she'd tried to tell him of her predicament, but each time the words had died in her throat. Every time she looked at him her guilt overwhelmed her. Every word she spoke to her father brought home her betrayal again. There was no doubt in her mind that they would all be better off if she was dead.

Tommy had shouted several times, but she'd been oblivious to his cries. Seeing her tense to dive, he threw himself across the last few feet, managing to grab hold of her the second before she jumped.

'Let me go!' Star screamed, twisting in his grasp. 'Let me go!'

She struggled like a demon, hitting and scratching as though she meant to kill him too.

In the end he knew there was only one way to stop her insane behaviour. He punched her hard on the jaw. Then he half dragged, half propelled her to the bank, pushing her roughly up on to dry land, swinging himself up beside her. Gently, he brushed the wet tangle of hair from her face, then glanced round to see if there was anyone else in the Lane. He and Star were quite alone.

'You should have let me die,' she whispered at last. 'You shouldn't have bothered.'

'Shhh,' he said, taking her hand in his. 'We'll talk later. But first we've got to get you out of those wet things.' He got to his feet, pulling her up as well. 'We're going to my house.'

Star made no objections. His punch had knocked all the fight out of her.

Taking one of her arms in his, he supported her as they walked, at the same time making sure that she couldn't get back to the river.

As they made their way to his house, Tommy talked to her in a soft, easy voice. He told her about something funny that had happened in one of his classes earlier that week, and he told her how nervous his mother had been that first time Star and her father had come to tea. 'You'd have thought he was visiting royalty or something the way she carried on.' Star listened in silence as he rambled on, comforted more by the sound of his voice than the words he was speaking. She relaxed against him, suddenly not afraid any more. And then she realized, as they walked down his street and he described with great glee each neighbour behind each curtain, that she no longer felt alone.

Once inside his house, he took her to the room she and her father had been in on that day that seemed so long ago. He sat her down in the most comfortable chair. 'My parents won't be back for at least another hour,' he said as he poured them each a whisky. 'That gives us some time to dry your clothes and have a little talk. But first you've got to drink this,' and he thrust the glass into her hand.

'Oh, I couldn't drink this,' protested Star, trying to hand it back.

'Drink it,' he insisted. 'It'll do you good. At the very least it'll warm you up a bit.'

It was only when she brought the glass to her lips that she realized she was shivering. Obediently, she sipped at the liquid, instantly feeling its warmth flow through her.

'Better?' he asked with a grin.

Star nodded. 'Much better.' Before, she had thought that the difference between Alec and Tommy was that

Alec was serious and well-bred and Tommy was at heart wild and a ruffian. Now she was beginning to understand that that wasn't the difference at all. She wasn't sure how Alec would have behaved if he were in Tommy's place right now, but she was certain how Tommy would have behaved had he been in Alec's.

'The next thing,' said Tommy, putting his glass down on the table, 'is to get you into something dry. You can put on my mother's dressing gown and we can lay out your clothes by the hearth. I'll show you where you can change.'

Star put her glass down on the table beside his, and prepared to follow him out of the room.

'And then you can tell me what all that nonsense down at the river was about.'

'I see,' said Jim thoughtfully when Star had finished recounting her story. He and Jeannie had returned to find Tommy and Star waiting for them. Tommy had said Star needed his help, then told them about Star's attempt to commit suicide. Star, calm by then, had gone on to explain what had happened.

Jim was both shocked and horrified by her tale. Shocked to think how desperate she had been; horrified at the Muirs' – particularly Mrs Muir's – behaviour. He glanced across at Jeannie. Her face told him she felt all the emotion he himself was feeling.

'So what do you want me to do?' he asked quietly.

Tommy glanced at Star and took a deep breath. 'Arrange a proper abortion for her,' he said quickly.

Star looked down at the floor.

Jim turned to Jeannie, who gave an almost imperceptible nod.

'I don't know anyone you see,' said Star in a strained whisper. 'And I don't have any money, even if I did. The bath and gin were my only hope.'

A lump came into Tommy's throat. He wanted to

sweep Star into his arms and hug her tight. Instead, he looked at his father questioningly.

Jim took a deep breath. He didn't know anything about abortions or abortionists, but he'd find out. One thing was certain, it wasn't going to be some dirty old wifie with a knitting needle. It would be a proper doctor, in proper surroundings, no matter what the cost. 'It'll have to be done quickly, I suppose. Leave all the arrangements and details to me,' he said, sounding more confident than he felt. 'We'll have everything sorted out in no time.'

Jeannie rose as though on cue. 'I'll put the kettle on. I don't know about anybody else, but I could certainly use a cup of tea,' she said briskly. But then, just as she was about to pass Star, she suddenly stopped and embraced Star fiercely. 'No' to fash yourself any more lassie,' she said warmly. 'You'll be all right now, my Jim'll see to that.'

Star had been examined by the gynaecologist, and now she and Jim sat in a reception room, waiting quietly but impatiently for the results of the doctor's tests.

'We'll get a time set for this week,' Jim said reassuringly, 'It'll be all over and done with before you know where you are.'

Star smiled her gratitude. She had never met anyone as kind before in her entire life. With the McBrides on her side she no longer felt either guilt or fear.

Some time later the gynaecologist came into the room, looking extremely pleased with himself. 'I've got some good news for you,' he said, laying a hand kindly on Star's shoulder. 'You won't be needing that operation after all.'

Star regarded him blankly. 'What's that?' asked Jim.

'I was more or less certain after the examination, but I did a few tests just to be certain. The young lady is not pregnant, and never has been.'

Star stared at him in disbelief. 'But what about the three periods I've missed?'

'Going on what you've told me, it would seem that what's happened is a combination of guilty conscience and worry. Deep down you were convinced you'd become pregnant, so your body did its best to oblige you, though you weren't. It happens more often than you'd think.'

'But I feel pregnant!' Star exclaimed.

'I'm sure you do,' said the doctor gently. 'But it's all in the mind, I assure you.'

'Thank God,' breathed Jim.

Star put a hand to her forehead, suddenly lightheaded. Not pregnant! All that fear and despair – and all for nothing.

But then she saw the look of relief and affection in Jim's eyes. At least she had discovered who her friends were.

Outside the house Star stared up at the sky, feeling as though she'd been reborn.

'That's that, then,' Jim said with a sigh.

'That's that,' she echoed.

That Saturday, to celebrate the fact Star wasn't pregnant, Jim took her, Tommy and Jeannie to the Grand Hotel in Charing Cross for lunch.

The Grand Hotel, though now well past its prime, was one of the most impressive buildings in Glasgow. Inside, the once plush opulence had faded, but the ghosts of its grandeur remained.

Star was dazzled by her surroundings. Her eyes darted everywhere, taking everything in. This was the first time she'd been in a restaurant, and she was fascinated by all that was going on around her.

'Has Tommy told you that if he can get a good enough pass and land a place he's going to go on to university after school,' Jeannie said proudly to Star.

Star gave an exclamation of delight. 'But that's wonderful. What will you read?' she asked, turning to Tommy.

'I thought I might have a bash at botany. I've become really interested in it since moving to Millbrae Crescent.'

'Imagine, a son a mine at university!' Jeannie exclaimed, excitedly raising her voice so that it was overheard by those at the adjoining tables.

'Ma!' Tommy hissed in embarrassment. That sort of thing might go down all right in Boyd Street, but not in the Grand Hotel.

'And what about you Star?' asked Jim. 'Have you any plans in that direction?'

'I wish I had, but I'm afraid my father's stipend doesn't run to higher education. But if I could go on , it wouldn't be to university but to a music college. I'd give my eye teeth to go there.'

'She's a fantastic musician,' Tommy said enthusiastically.

Jim remembered Tommy mentioning something about this in the past. 'What do you play?' he asked Star.

'You mean what *doesn't* she play!' Tommy laughed.

'Clarinet, piano and violin,' Star answered.

'I'm fond of the piano myself. Though I suppose the sort of music I like wouldn't be to your taste,' Jeannie said.

'Puccini or Jolson, it depends on the mood I'm in,' Star replied truthfully.

Jeannie wondered who the hell Puccini was? She must remember to ask Jim when they got home.

'You'd choose a career in music if you could, then?' Jim persisted.

'Oh yes! If it was ever possible.'

'What about a bursary?' Jim asked.

'There are two available for music every year, but neither has ever yet gone to a girl. I'll try for them of course when the time comes, but I'm not holding out much hope. I think the powers that be consider it would

110

be a waste of money to give one to someone who might pack in her career to become a housewife and mother.'

'Well, I can understand that point of view, even if I don't wholly agree with it,' Jim said.

Suddenly Star noticed that Tommy was staring over her left shoulder with a peculiar expression on his face. She turned in her chair to see what he was looking at. There was Alec Muir staring at her.

'See what the cat has just dragged in,' Tommy said in a hard voice.

Star transferred her attention to the girl at Alec's side. She was whispering in Alec's ear in such a way as to make it clear that she and Alec were good and close friends.

Well, thought Star, it hasn't taken him long to find someone else. One thing was certain, whoever she was her parents weren't short of a bob or two, the clothes she was wearing were foreign, and clearly expensive.

Margaret had asked Cosmo Dunbarr to meet her and Virginia that morning to give final approval on a number of fabrics they'd selected and which were being held for them. As Cosmo was joining them, it had seemed natural for Alec to do likewise – or so Margaret had thought.

Cosmo had been so delighted with the choice of fabrics (as he was delighted with everything Margaret and Virginia were doing for the house in Lindsay Drive) that he had suggested they all go on to the Grand Hotel for luncheon.

Margaret, chattering nineteen to the dozen, glanced round the restaurant to see if there was anyone there worth being seen by. Her chattering ceased abruptly when she spotted Star.

'Something wrong?' Cosmo inquired solicitously.

Margaret forced a smile back on to her face, and caught her breath. 'It's nothing,' she replied lightly. 'Now, what was I talking about?'

When it came time to leave, Star realized they were going to have to pass close to the table where Alec and his party were sitting. Should she acknowledge them, she wondered, or ignore them? She decided that rather than let them bring her down to their level she would stop and say hello. Anything else seemed somehow petty.

Virginia was telling Alec another story about Kenya when he realized that someone had halted just out of his line of vision. Looking up he found Star looking at him. Immediately, he felt the colour rise in his face.

Star opened her mouth to speak, but before she could get out even one word, Margaret snapped in a threatening tone, 'Please move on, Miss Gray. My son doesn't speak to tarts.'

Star froze in embarrassment. Alec turned scarlet, looking from Star to his mother in horror.

Anger was raging in Tommy, standing behind Star. If Margaret had been a man, he would have punched her on the nose. As it was, he strode over to her and glared down into her scowl.

'You're a truly horrible woman,' he said. And then he picked up her almost full soup bowl and poured the contents into her lap.

Margaret screeched and leapt to her feet. Tommy took hold of Star by the arm and forced her towards the door. All around them customers were staring in either shock, amazement, or ill-concealed amusement.

Jim McBride managed to keep a straight face until they were outside the hotel. Then he nearly doubled over with laughter. 'That's the funniest thing I've seen in years,' he gasped.

Jeannie also began laughing, seeing again the expression on Margaret Muir's face as the hot soup landed in her lap.

Tommy's anger fizzled out, and he too started laughing. 'I wouldn't have dared do that if I'd stopped to think about it. And in such a swanky place too!'

Star, still stunned by Margaret's quite gratuitous insult, and Tommy's reaction, slowly began to smile. 'Did you see her face?' she asked. 'Even after it happened

I don't think she believed it.' The smile melted into a laugh.

The four of them continued laughing all the way to the car.

Star had just told her parents that she had broken irrevocably with Alec Muir. The Reverend Gray was furious.

'I had such high hopes for you two,' the minister fumed.

'You mean for your daughter marrying into the Muirs,' Star corrected.

'Don't be cheeky, Jessie!' Alison snapped. 'Your father only wants what's best for you.'

'Then he should be happy now.'

'I just don't understand how you came to fall out so badly,' he went on. 'You were such close friends.'

'Perhaps this is only a storm in a teacup and you and Alec . . .'

'No, mother, it's definitely finished between us for good.'

'I'm sure the day will come when you'll rue this decision, and your impulsiveness,' the Reverend said heavily. 'You won't find another lad like that very easily.'

'I certainly hope I never find another like him,' said Star. 'Once is enough.'

'You thought highly enough of him until now,' suggested Alison nervously.

'Aye, up until now,' Star echoed. 'Up until now.'

Willie McAllister was congratulating himself as he led Maggie Pettigrew up the stairs to his flat in Athole Gardens. He'd lumbered Maggie from a party he'd been to in Kelvinbridge.

Going into the kitchen for water for his drink, he'd struck up a conversation with the pretty red-haired lassie he'd found there, and after a few minutes offered her a dram from the bottle he was carrying in his jacket pocket.

Maggie had readily accepted, and gone on to match him drink for drink. He'd liked her sense of humour and the relaxed, easy-going manner she had about her. Not only that, but told him she was a Civil Servant. 'Snap!' he'd laughed. 'So am I. I'm a Customs and Excise official.'

Willie opened the front door to his flat and switched on the hall lights. 'Ta ra!' he cried, and made a flamboyant gesture indicating that Maggie should enter.

Maggie laughed as she went past him. She was high on more than alcohol. She couldn't believe her luck, meeting someone like Willie. He was a smasher, right enough, and it had been a long time since she'd met a man who attracted her in that special way. Willie had clicked with her right off.

Inside the lounge door he kissed her before switching on the lights. She responded eagerly.

'You promised me a dram?' she whispered when the kiss was over, trying to regain her composure.

Willie kissed her again, pulling away from her slowly. 'I'm promising you a lot more than that,' he said softly, 'but if the lady wants a drink then a drink she shall have.'

He crossed the room and threw open the drinks cabinet. 'Glenfiddich, Glenmorangie, Glenlivet, or how about a nice Armagnac, Salignac or vodka or gin even?'

Maggie blinked in astonishment. 'You're well stocked,' she replied slowly.

'You name your poison and Uncle Willie has it,' he boasted.

'My God,' she said. 'You've even got tequila. I thought it was impossible to get.'

He gave her a fly wink. 'Nothing is impossible for those in the know, and with the wherewithal,' he smiled.

While he went into the kitchen for salt and lemon, Maggie gazed round the lounge, taking in the deep pile carpet, expensive furniture, magnificent bakelite wire-

114

less set, and the dozen or so other items, including the lead crystal glass she was holding, that spelled out plenty of money. He must have private means, she thought, this set-up is well outside the pocket of an ordinary Customs and Excise official.

Rich as well as a smasher! She'd fallen on her feet here, she told herself.

Maggie felt ill as she stared at the dark green door through which she knew she was going to have to walk to say her piece on the other side.

She offered up a silent prayer that she might be wrong, but deep down she was certain she was right. God damn you, Willie McAllister, she raged inwardly. And God damn her job and the rotten suspicious mind she'd had to develop to go with it.

She'd been seeing Willie a month now, and during that time had established that there were no private means. And yet, on each occasion they'd gone somewhere he'd spent a small fortune. So where was the money coming from?

She sighed with frustration. She'd fallen hard for the charming Willie, and would have seen him as husband material if not for her fears.

She focused again on the dark green door, wondering for the thousandth time if she was doing the right thing. But it had to be done, she reminded herself, there was nothing else she could do.

Oh hell, best get this over with, she told herself, and, rising, crossed to the dark green door.

'Enter!' called out a male voice.

As Maggie came into his office Inspector Tom Beaton looked up from the report he'd been reading and smiled.

'I wonder if I could have a word sir?' W. P. C. Pettigrew asked her boss.

★   ★   ★

Jim McBride noted that Willie McAllister's hand was trembling when Willie gave him the release docket for the twelve crates that had arrived that morning on the M.V. *Kathleen*.

'What's wrong with you, then?' Jim asked, staring at the trembling hand.

Willie followed Jim's gaze, saw what had prompted the remark, and hurriedly stuffed the hand into his trousers' pocket. 'Too much of the cratur last night, I suppose,' he mumbled.

Jim had had the shakes quite a few times in the past. 'How's your head?' he grinned.

'Terrible,' lied Willie.

'I'd watch it if I were you. The booze can soon get hold of you if you're not careful,' Jim said in a fatherly tone.

'Aye, I'll do that.'

'I'll see you next Tuesday then when the *Orion* gets in,' Jim said.

'I'll arrange my shifts accordingly,' Willie replied, wishing this was all over. Judas goat, that's what they'd made him, and it wasn't a nice feeling at all. But the rock solid guarantee of a good word being spoken to the beak on his behalf was not to be turned down, not when it could mean a couple of years off his sentence.

A minute later Jim was outside the shed handing Matt, his driver, the release docket. Matt and the other two men that had come in the lorry went off to collect the twelve crates and load them up.

The eighth crate was being hefted over the lorry's tailgate when, out of the corner of his eye, Jim caught the unmistakable blue flash of a police uniform.

There were three bobbies, with truncheons drawn, advancing on the lorry.

Jim knew then what had been wrong with Willie. It had nothing to do with the shakes, it was because the bastard had fingered him and known this was about to happen.

Behind the now barred shed door Willie sat staring

vacantly into space. Filled with self-pity, he silently began to weep.

Jim glanced over at the main entrance to the North Basin, and saw two police Rileys parked there blocking the entranceway. Another Riley appeared behind the three policemen advancing on foot. Jim looked over at Matt and the other two lads, who were as yet unaware of the police closing in on them.

Jim's mind was racing furiously; he had a contingency plan all worked out for just such an eventuality. He would pick the money up from the Edinburgh safety deposit box, get himself over to Ulster, then sneak across the border where Paddy Swords would pick him up. He would simply disappear in the Republic after that. Paddy would fix him up with a new identity.

Of course, this meant leaving Jeannie and Tommy behind for the time being, but that couldn't be helped. Paddy would ensure they knew he was all right, and that money got through to them on a regular basis. Sometime later, when this had blown over, Jeannie and Tommy would join him in the Republic. From there they would go to another country, Canada, perhaps, or Australia.

But first of all he had to escape this police trap, and he knew exactly how he was going to manage that.

He dived into the Arrole-Johnstone, switched on the engine, and peeled away in a burn of tyres. The Riley behind the policemen immediately set off in pursuit.

Matt looked up in surprise when the Arrole-Johnstone went screaming off down the dockside, then he saw the three policemen who were on foot charging down on the lorry. He gave a yell of warning to his two mates, and all three of them scattered in different directions.

Each policeman chose a man and followed him. More policemen on foot emerged from behind the two parked Rileys.

Jim had noticed some time before that the wall of wooden planks that divided the North Basin from the rest of Queen's dock was extremely old and rotten, the

117

wood so soft and spongy in parts that it fell away to the touch. He now headed the Arrole-Johnstone directly at this wall with the intention of smashing his way through.

He hit the wall with a muted bang, and, as he'd known would happen, the Arrole-Johnstone ploughed through the wood with no bother. What he wasn't prepared for, however, was the ancient rusty capstan that had been cut from the dockside and dumped on the far side of the wall where it was waiting to be taken away for scrap. The Arrole-Johnstone hit the capstan a glancing blow, which sent it slewing sideways.

Jim cursed his luck as he fought to regain control of the car. Of all spots in the wall he'd had to pick that one!

Jim pulled the steering wheel in the opposite direction to the way the car was travelling, then, at what he judged the appropriate moment, stamped hard on the accelerator. The Arrole-Johnstone came out of the skid as Jim had intended, but two things happened which he hadn't intended. The steering was gone and the accelerator was jammed to the floor. Jim's concentration turned to horror when he realized the car was headed for the dry dock filled with water.

Hastily, he fumbled at the door, proposing to open it and throw himself out, but just as the door began to open the Arrole-Johnstone left the dockside and sailed out over the dry dock.

'Shit!' exclaimed one of the officers in the pursuing Riley.

The Arrole-Johnstone hit the water in a downward angle, sinking immediately.

For Jim the world had suddenly turned into a watery nightmare. He managed to keep the car door open by wedging his hook in it. The moment it came to rest on the dry dock bottom he put his shoulder against the door and his feet against the edge of the front passenger seat. He pushed with every ounce of strength he could muster.

Despite the depth pressure, the door gave way, allowing Jim to wiggle out of the car. He kicked for the surface, but was barely moving upwards. He kicked harder, and harder still. Far ahead of him he could see the shimmering light that was the surface. But despite his frantic efforts he wasn't making any progress. And then came the awful realization of what was holding him back. His hook! His bloody solid steel hook. He clawed at the harness straps, normally so easy to undo, but immensely difficult now. He got one strap loose, and was working on the second, when suddenly the water got darker and darker.

With a sudden, terrifying rush the darkness closed in on Jim McBride.

Tommy stared in disbelief at the two large policemen who'd come into their house. His father dead. Drowned while trying to evade capture?

The policemen were both Highlanders, and each was trying to give the impression of sympathy – and finding it hard to do. It was obvious that they considered men like Jim McBride to be scum.

Black marketeer! The words rang inside Tommy's head. That's what these two were accusing his dad of being, a black marketeer!

'It's a fucking lie!' Tommy burst out suddenly.

'I'm afraid not, son . . .' Constable Donaldson began in his soft Highland lilt.

Tommy knotted his hands into fists. He didn't care if they were police, they weren't going to say such a dreadful thing about his father. 'You'll take it back and apologize to my ma,' he threatened.

Donaldson and McTaggart exchanged glances. It was clear the boy hadn't known what was going on.

'I'm afraid it is the truth,' McTaggart said gently. 'We wouldn't have said it if we didn't have the proof.'

But Tommy was beyond reason. He flew at McTaggart, and succeeded in getting in several solid blows to

119

the huge Highlander before McTaggart pinioned his arms by his side.

'You'll take back your filthy lies!' Tommy screamed.

Donaldson looked at Jeannie. 'Missus?' he appealed.

'We don't want to book the lad after what's happened, but we will if he forces us to,' McTaggart added.

'Come here, Tommy,' Jeannie said, nodding to the policemen to let him go.

Tommy went to his mother's side. She clasped his hand in hers. 'You mustn't go to jail, you're the head of the family now,' she said in a voice that was choked with tears.

Tommy personally escorted the policemen to the front door – not to be polite, but to make sure they'd actually gone. When he returned to Jeannie he found her slumped against the mantelpiece, clutching an old picture of Jim.

'It was a lie, wasn't it, Mum?' Tommy asked.

Jeannie shook her head. She took a deep breath, then went over to the drinks cabinet. If ever she needed a hard drink it was now. Jim gone! Gone just like that! That was going to take some time to sink in, a long time.

Tommy's gaze never left his mother. 'I don't understand,' he said softly.

'Let's sit down and I'll tell you all about it,' Jeannie replied taking a large sip of her drink.

Jim's death was reported on page two of the next day's *Glasgow Herald*. It was there over breakfast, that the Reverend Kenneth Gray learned the truth. He read the article through once to himself, then aloud for Alison's and Star's benefit.

'A black marketeer!' he breathed, eyes gleaming. 'I always suspected there was something fishy about McBride. Well now we know.'

Poor Tommy, thought Star. And his mother, what a hell she must be living through right now.

The Reverend Gray had a sudden uneasy thought.

Would Jim having been a member of his congregation reflect on him? 'I shall denounce McBride from the pulpit,' he declared.

Star stared at him aghast. 'Isn't that a bit strong?'

'I'm sure your father knows what's right and proper for him to do,' Alison said immediately.

'But what about Tommy and his mother?' asked Star. 'You will go and see them?'

'I shall do no such thing. The man was a criminal. I'll have nothing further to do with those he's left behind.'

'You can't just abandon them,' cried Star. 'You're a minister!'

'Your father's quite right,' Alison stated primly. 'There are some people beyond Christian charity.'

'I thought it said in the Bible that we should forgive, so that we'll be forgiven,' countered Star.

'Don't try and be clever with me young lady!' her father thundered back.

Star didn't flinch, she'd heard that bullying tone too often before. 'If you won't go over there, then I will,' she said, rising from the table.

'You'll do nothing of the sort. And what's more, I absolutely forbid you to speak to young McBride ever again. Is that clear?'

'You can't be serious!' Star gasped.

'Oh, but I am. I won't have a daugher of mine associating with that sort of trash.'

She stared at her father's hard, unyielding face. Tommy McBride was worth ten of him. As for Tommy, he'd need a friend now, and she'd stand by him just as he'd stood by her. She wouldn't let him down.

She wouldn't go to Millbrae Crescent just yet, though. In the circumstances, it might be embarrassing to Mrs McBride. She'd wait until Tommy came back to school. When he did return to Queenie she'd be there waiting.

'I'd better get along or I'll be late for my first period,' she said.

'Mind what I told you now,' the Reverend growled.

'I won't forget.' Of course she wouldn't forget, it was just that she had no intention of complying with his orders, that was all.

'Say that again!' Tommy exclaimed.

'The money your Dad had is lost to us,' Jeannie repeated.

'*All* of it?'

'With the exception of twenty-two pounds I retrieved from the Calton office a couple of hours ago.'

'But how?' Tommy demanded. Twenty-two pounds certainly wasn't going to get them very far.

Jeannie ran a hand through her dull limp hair. It was three days now since Jim had died, three days of shock and grief. Then late that morning, when Tommy was out at the undertaker's, she'd suddenly remembered about Jim's 'special arrangements' as he'd called them.

She'd gone straightaway over to the Calton repair shop in the hope there might be a sizeable amount of cash in the safe, but there wasn't. Twenty-two pounds was all there had been.

'When your father started in the business he realized he couldn't bank the large sums he was making without starting people asking questions. So he hired a safety deposit box, and kept the money in that,' Jeannie now explained.

'Where is this safety deposit box, then?'

Jeannie gave a grim smile, shaking her head. 'I don't know. Your father never volunteered that information, and I never inquired. It is in a bank, but I couldn't tell you which bank far less which branch. All I do know is that the box was hired under a phoney name.'

'What name was that?'

'I've no idea. He never mentioned that either.' Jeannie took her teacup and held it in her hands to try and warm them. She'd been so cold since Jim died, she'd come to half-believe she'd never be naturally warm again. 'Even if I knew the name, bank and branch I still wouldn't be able to get into the box. To do that I'd have to produce a death certificate in the phoney name, plus identification proving I was his next of kin. All impossible, of course. That money is lost to us forever, we just have to accept that.'

But Tommy couldn't give up. 'What about the bank account Dad had for the repair shop, surely there's something in that?'

'Jim always managed to keep his legitimate business account in overdraft, so in point of fact *we* owe *them*.'

'There's always the house, you've forgotten about that,' Tommy said, brightening.

'The house was bought on a mortgage, again because of the tax people. When we default on the mortgage at the beginning of the month, as we'll have to, then the house goes by the board.'

'How about Life Assurance?'

This time Jeannie merely shook her head.

Twenty-two pounds! Despair filled Tommy. That wasn't even enough to cover the funeral.

'What about furniture, carpets and all that sort of thing? Surely they belong to us and we can sell them to raise cash?'

Jeannie had forgotten all about the household contents. 'Oh, aye,' she said in a dazed way. 'There's that.'

Tommy let out a sigh of relief. At least that was something. What was important now was getting his mother out of here and to a new life as soon as possible. It was only then, he knew, that she stood a chance of surviving her enormous grief. The prospect of the future was still bleak, but not as totally bleak as it had been a few minutes ago. They'd still lose the house, but hopefully they'd have enough money to keep the pair of them until he got a job, although a job at what he didn't know.

'I'll telephone the Crown Showrooms and arrange for them to pick everything up directly after the funeral,' he said. The Crown Showrooms specialized in auctioning off household and office contents.

'I don't want you to think less of your da for what he did. Remember, he did it for us, you and me.'

Tommy forced a smile on to his face and took her hands in his. 'I know,' he said warmly. 'I know.'

Star walked down the hill that was Millbrae Crescent. It was the Monday of the second week since Jim McBride's death, and still Tommy hadn't returned to school. Worried, she'd decided to go to him and not wait for his reappearance after all.

The moment the McBride house came into view she knew there was something different about it. She was almost at the door when it dawned on her that there were no curtains showing in the windows any more. Every last curtain at the front of the house had been removed.

She knocked and waited. Even the sound of her knock seemed strangely hollow.

She pulled the bell handle, and its reverberating clang sounded hollow as well, as if it were being rung inside a drum.

She knocked and pulled the bell handle again, and still there was no reply. Lifting up the letterbox she gazed into the hall. Where was the hall carpet? And where was . . . Standing up, she peered into the nearest window. The room was empty, every stick of furniture gone. A look in the window on the other side showed only walls and floorboards.

She squatted and had another look through the letterbox. There could be no doubt about it, the entire house was empty.

Why hadn't Tommy contacted her to say they were going? Because he'd been so ashamed of what Jim had been doing that he hadn't wanted to face her? Or because he'd heard what her father had said about Jim in church and had assumed that her father's view was hers? And where would Tommy and Mrs McBride have gone? With Jim's story splashed all over the Glasgow newspapers, it seemed likely that they'd left the city for good.

All at once she realized that she was never going to see Tommy McBride again. He'd gone out of her life forever.

Suddenly she felt like the house, completely empty inside. With tears washing her face, she made her way back up the hill.

PART TWO

Jessie
1955–58

4

Lizzie Dunnachie lit a cigarette and sank back into the train seat. 'Whew,' she gasped. 'I almost didn't make it that time.' She'd been late as usual, galloping down the station steps to catch the 8.20 by the skin of her teeth. Unknown to her a male passenger from Burnside further up the line regularly made book on her.

'You'll be late for your own funeral so you will,' Jessie laughed.

It was October, 1955, and both girls were now twenty-two. Being off to work, they were both soberly dressed in the manner approved by business. Lizzie wore a grey costume, Jessie a dark brown skirt with matching cardy, and both sported the beehive hairdo that was all the fashion.

'So where's it to be the night?' Lizzie asked. It was Friday and Friday night was the first of the two traditional nights for going out.

'Whitecraigs, I suppose,' Jessie answered without any enthusiasm. Whitecraigs was the name of the posh tennis club on the outskirts of the city which held a dance every Friday night during the winter in support of the club. It had the reputation of being frequented by a 'better class' of person.

Lizzie wrinkled her nose. 'I'm getting right fed up with there. We're getting older and older, and the male talent is getting younger and younger. When they get me up nowadays I feel like their big sister instead of a potential lumber.'

Jessie laughed. It was true enough, though. The lads there were getting on the young side for them.

'How about the Plaza then?' Jessie suggested. The Plaza was a swanky dancehall down at Eglinton Toll.

Lizzie pulled a face. It's just the opposite there. When they come out with their patter you expect it to be about their exploits in the First World War, if not the one against the Zulus.'

'So much for the Plaza,' Jessie replied. At the rate they were going they would end up staying in.

Jean Semple, a member of the Croftfoot contingent, leant forward from the other end of the carriage. 'I couldn't help but overhear you,' she said quietly. 'Can I make a suggestion?'

'Fire away,' said Lizzie.

'Do you like Rockabilly?'

'Rocky who?' Lizzie asked. Jessie laughed. She knew all about Rockabilly, having listened to a number of records in the shop where she worked. She'd never heard it live though.

Jean rolled her eyes heavenwards. 'You two aren't just old, you're bloody decrepit,' she teased. Jean was seventeen, just.

'Many a good tune played on an old violin I'll have you know. And anyway, less of your cheek, Miss. Have a wee bit of respect for your elders,' Lizzie snapped back with exaggerated dignity.

'I went to a new dancehall a fortnight ago called The Black Raven,' Jean went on. 'Well, it's not actually new, it's the Trocadero tarted up somewhat and its name changed. But I had a smashing time there. The music was this really fab Rockabilly, and the male talent enough to make you drool.'

Lizzie was immediately interested. Droolable talent! That sounded just the ticket.

'What sort of crowd go?' asked Jessie.

'Mixed. Some students from the Uni, people who work in town offices, a few workies; all ages and all sorts like.'

Lizzie snapped her fingers. 'I think we should give it a try. What do you say, Jessie?' she asked eagerly.

Jessie wasn't so sure. It didn't really sound like her sort

of place. She enjoyed Rockabilly enough, but the people she associated it with were definitely not her sort. 'Well . . .'

'Come on, nothing ventured nothing gained,' Lizzie urged.

'Oh, all right. The Black Raven it is then,' Jessie decided, unable to resist the pleading look in Lizzie's eyes.

It was a decision that was to change her entire life.

Jessie saw him elbow his way through the crowd and instinctively knew who it was he was making for. Oh, God, she thought. She'd noticed him on the dance floor a while back, pawing and mauling the lassie he was with, the girl clearly too terrified to protest.

He was a rough looking Teddy Boy in a maroon drape jacket, black brothel creepers and a headful of grease. Jessie cringed at the thought of him holding her in his arms. A quick glance around confirmed that she was hemmed in. It was impossible for her to slip away before he reached her. She would refuse him, she told herself; there was no way she was going to let him get her on to the floor.

He stopped right in front of her, looking as though he thought he was doing her a favour. It's amazing how arrogant ugly men can be, she thought.

'Are you dancing?' he said, and, without waiting for a reply, reached out and grabbed her by the arm.

'Not this one, thank you,' she answered hastily, forcing a pleasant smile on to her face. She should have stayed home.

He blinked. 'You what?'

'Not this one, I don't feel like it.'

His grip tightened, making her wince. 'Are you refusing me?'

Jessie desperately wished for Lizzie. Lizzie might have been able to deal with him, but Lizzie was at the far end of the floor with a chap she'd danced the last three numbers with.

'To be honest, I'm not feeling very well, I was just about to go to the Ladies',' she said trying to look ill.

'You're a liar,' he scowled. 'You're refusing me, and no bird does that.'

Jessie'd heard how dangerous Teds could be and couldn't stop the fear that was beginning to grow. She drew herself up to her full height nonetheless and tried not to appear frightened. She was aware that a ring of silence had descended in her immediate vicinity. 'I don't want to dance,' she repeated.

His grip tightened even more and he tugged her towards him. 'I said. . .'

'She said she didn't want to gēt up, so why don't you just piss off, toerag,' said a male voice quietly.

The man who'd spoken was another Ted, dressed completely in black. There was an authority about him that even she recognized. Her eyes moved from one to the other, and it was obvious that the first Ted felt it too. He let go of her wrist and took a step forward, but there was a new look of wariness in his face. 'And just what do you think you're doing on my patch?' he hissed.

The second Ted reached out and brushed an imaginary piece of lint from the other man's collar. 'Just visiting. Why? Don't tell me you have some objections.'

Jessie had been about to simply fade away into the crowd and get out of here as fast as she could, but the sound of the Ted's voice made her stop and look at him again. That voice, she thought, trying to recognize the face beneath the waterfall hairdo. That voice . . .

The first Ted's eyes flicked this way and that, checking on his friends.

'There are six of yours here,' the other Ted said with a thin smile. 'I've already counted.'

Ken Young, the first Ted, stared into the insolent eyes of his adversary. Ken was good at pushing women around; he was even good at pushing his own boys

132

around, but he was not good at pushing around men who were stronger and smarter than he was. It was too early yet for most of his boys to be here, and even he could understand that that wasn't by chance.

'To save you asking,' the second Ted went on, 'I'm here mob handed. I've got twenty-three of my boys with me, and they're all looking right at you.'

Ken was carrying a bicycle chain, but as much as he would have dearly loved to use it he knew that any move like that on his part would be suicidal. He glanced quickly around, but there wasn't even one of his men in sight. 'Don't think I'll forget this effrontery,' Ken said with as much menace as he could muster. 'Don't think I will. Another day and you won't catch me by surprise.'

Jessie was suddenly aware of the number of Teds who'd quietly materialized around the black-clothed figure during this exchange. They were as ferocious looking as the press always claimed, despite the bright colours of their drapes. Only her rescuer was dressed in black. She turned her attention to him again. There was something so familiar about him, something in the way he stood, something in the expression of his eyes.

The second Ted laughed. 'You were always a great one for the scintillating repartee, Young. Another day I'll catch you by a lot more than surprise.' He jerked his thumb. 'Get lost, or I may forget my manners.'

Ken gave him one more belligerent look, then did as he was told, disappearing into the crowd.

'I do want to thank you,' began Jessie to the black back. 'I mean, thank you, if it hadn't been for you . . .'

And then he turned, grinning like a school boy – like the school boy she used to know. 'Hello, Star,' he said. 'Don't you recognize me any more?'

For a moment she couldn't react at all – couldn't move, couldn't speak, couldn't even think. Tommy. Tommy McBride. She wanted to fling her arms around him, to make sure that after all these years it was really he and not a dream. Instead, she heard herself saying, 'It's just plain Jessie now.'

A Ted in a bright yellow drape leaned towards Tommy. 'Do we stay or go?'

'We go,' decided Tommy instantly. 'We've had our laugh coming here, let's leave it at that.'

Jessie could see Lizzie pushing her way through the crowd towards them.

'What do you say?' asked Tommy. 'Do you fancy a drink, just plain Jessie?'

She hesitated for a moment, thinking of what her father would say if he ever saw her out with a Ted, or what any of her friends would say for that matter, but then she looked into Tommy's eyes and saw the nervousness there, like the first time he had asked her to dance in Miss Parrot's class. 'I'd love a drink,' she said. Then added, unexpectedly, 'I never thought I'd see you again.'

At that moment Lizzie broke through the crowd. 'Are you all right?' she demanded. She hadn't been able to see much from where she'd been standing, but she had been told that the trouble was over a girl, and she'd assumed the worst. She was more than willing to take on a roomful of Teds in defence of her pal.

'I'm fine,' laughed Jessie. 'Look who came to my rescue.'

It was a rare thing for Lizzie Dunnachie to be at a loss for words. Like Jessie, however, she couldn't believe her own eyes. 'My God,' she said at last. 'It's Tommy McBride! What are you doing here?'

Tommy winked. 'I've come to take two old school friends out for a drink.'

Once outside, Tommy linked an arm through one of Jessie's and one of Lizzie's. 'It's just like old times,' he grinned as they made their way down the street, flanked on either side by his boys in drapes and beetle crushers. As they walked along, people quickly stepped out of their way.

134

When they got to the pub, Tommy whispered something to one of his boys, and the next thing Jessie knew Lizzie was being shown to a table well away from where Tommy was inviting her to sit. She could see Lizzie turn to her and wink.

Tommy placed their order with another of his Teds, and sat down across from her. The eyes were the same, the eyes and his smile, but everything else was hard and new. She might have passed him on the street a hundred times and never known it was him.

'Well,' he said, staring at her as though she might suddenly vanish, 'it's been a long long time.'

'No one knew where you'd gone,' she said, looking back at this stranger who seemed like someone from another world. 'I went to your house to tell you how sorry I was about . . . about your father . . .'

He played with the ashtray in the centre of the table. 'It was all a bit of a rush,' he said, lowering his eyes. 'I just wanted to get Mum out of there as fast as I could.' He stared at the table top for a few seconds, then shook himself from his reverie. 'Why Jessie?' he asked suddenly. 'I thought you hated that name.'

She smiled wrily and shrugged. 'I suppose I just outgrew Star. I thought it made me sound special, you know. But now I guess I'm old enough to live with reality.'

He looked up as a Ted approached with their drinks. 'I guess that's something we've all had to learn to do,' he said softly.

She moved her eyes everywhere – from the floor to the table to the people around them – but not to him. 'I thought that, after all that there was in the papers, and your father so well off . . .' She stared at a point just beyond his shoulder. 'I thought that you would have left Glasgow for good.'

He laughed, but it was far from a happy sound. 'Dad had money, all right. But none of it came to us. He had it so safely stashed away that we didn't know where it was.

So we moved back to Boyd Street, and I finally managed to get a job.

At last her eyes rested on him. There was a look in them that he couldn't quite recognize. 'So that's where you've been all this while.'

'Aye,' he nodded. 'Right back where we started from.'

'And what's your job?'

He shrugged, looking young again, almost like the boy she remembered. 'It's not much. I'm a packer in a china shop. The one underneath Highlandman's bridge.' He smiled bitterly. 'It's not a great achievement, but it's the best I've been able to do.'

Her heart went out to him. He'd been such a promising student – so full of dreams, so full of spirit. 'I always imagined you were a botanist somewhere,' she said softly. It had never occurred to her that he hadn't gone to university, as he'd planned; that he hadn't made those dreams come true.

His eyes took on a far-away look. How it hurt him even now to remember that dream, those plans he'd felt so sure about. In only a few years he had moved a lifetime away from them. 'And what about you?' he asked, bringing himself back to the present abruptly. 'What's happened to you?'

Not a damn thing, she wanted to say. Time had passed, but she had nothing to show for it other than the days marked off on the calendar – the days, the weeks, the months, and then the years. She'd drifted along as though her life hadn't begun, as though it were still about to happen, kidding herself that something would happen to change the boredom and blandness of her life.

'I applied and auditioned for those two bursaries at the Music College, but I got nowhere. Now I work in a music shop. It's not exactly the same as being a professional musician, but it seems to be the closest I'll ever get.'

'And are you happy?'

She looked straight into his eyes. 'Are you?'

But instead of replying, he said, 'Seven years . . . in some ways it's a life time, but in others it's just like yesterday.'

'Yes,' she agreed softly. In some ways it was just like yesterday, a yesterday she'd never forgotten, whose dreams and promises haunted her still.

'You never got married, then?' he asked, taking her ringless hand in his.

She shook her head. 'And you?'

'Not me,' he said airily. 'I'm too busy enjoying myself.'

'You mean playing the field?' she teased, wondering at the pang of jealousy that stabbed through her.

'That and being a Ted,' he answered slowly.

She took in his appearance again, what a transformation from the Tommy she'd known at Queenie! There was something frightening about him now, but something fascinating, too. 'Why did you become a Ted?' she asked.

His mouth twisted into a crooked grin. 'There's excitement in being a Ted,' he said with real enthusiasm. 'A packer's life, even a head packer's life, is never more than dull. There were mornings, before I became a Ted, when I'd wake up wanting to scream at the thought of the day stretching ahead, Becoming a Ted changed all that. It makes me somebody.' He took a deep breath, then went on. 'I was the first in Boyd Street. Then a few others became Teds, and that's how the Boyd Street Boys came into existence.'

She understood what he meant about boredom, about one day just melting into the greyness of the next. 'And the others elected you leader?'

He shrugged. 'There was no election, it just fell out that way.'

Jessie took a sip of her shandy. 'What about fights, do you get into many of those?'

Tommy gave her a sideways look. 'They happen now and then. When challenged you have to hold your own, you can't be a Ted otherwise. But I wouldn't believe everything you read in the papers.'

'And do you. . .' searching for the right word. 'Do you enjoy them?'

'And how!' he grinned. Something in his tone sent a cold shiver down her spine.

Tommy patted his pockets, took out a cigarette packet, and opened the packet to find it empty. He made a sign to one of the Teds at an adjoining table who immediately jumped to his feet and came over to offer Tommy one of his fags.

Power, Jessie thought. That was what Tommy had now. And he had all the charisma of a born leader as well. Another pang of jealousy lanced through her as she realized how attractive he must be to the lassies he now moved amongst. Suddenly, she felt confused. 'Lizzie is a shorthand typist with the Gas Board,' she said in a different voice nodding in Lizzie's direction.

'Good for her, but it's you I want to hear about.'

She smiled shyly. 'There's not much to tell.'

'What about the Fives, do you still go there?'

'Not a lot, a younger set have taken over nowadays. If I do go to a cafe it tends to be the one up at the top of Battlefield Road, the one facing the school dinner hall.'

He grinned. 'I remember. The dinner hall in the church basement?'

'That's it,' she nodded.

'And what about the Boys' Brigade? Still playing piano for them?'

'No, I gave up doing that years ago.'

'Aye, of course you're not still playing for them. Tonight's a Friday, you'd have been there if you had.'

An uneasy silence fell between them. She stared into her glass as though it might tell her something to say. One minute he was Tommy McBride, the friend she'd missed for so long, and the next he was a tough, aggressive young man, leader of the Boyd Street Teds.

'And boyfriends, I suppose you've had quite a few of

138

those since the old days?' Tommy leaned back in his chair, affecting an uneasy, unconcerned manner.

'Oh aye, stacks and stacks,' she replied quickly, and gave a nervous, self-conscious, laugh. There had been boyfriends to be sure, but not that many and none who'd mattered. 'What about you? You must have a girlfriend or two.'

Tommy shook his head. 'They come and go, you know what I mean.'

Was he sleeping with them? Had to be, she told herself, Teds didn't go in for holding hands and a chaste good-night kiss as her boyfriends had.

'What is it? What's funny?' he demanded.

She'd been imagining him kissing a girl good night. 'Nothing.'

'There has to be something!'

'Just a memory, that's all.'

He glared at her. 'About me?'

'No, not about you. You're not the centre of the universe, you know.'

He dragged on his cigarette.

Touchy, she thought. That was interesting. Perhaps he wasn't quite as hard as he liked to make out.

She swallowed more of her shandy. Lizzie seemed to be doing all right with Jack. The pair of them were engrossed in conversation.

'It really is smashing seeing you again,' she said on a sudden impulse, and just as suddenly reached out and squeezed his hand.

'It's good to see you, too.'

She could hear in his voice that he meant that, and it pleased her. It pleased her a great deal.

They reminisced some more, and then, catching sight of the time, she announced that it was high time for her and Lizzie to be making tracks.

She and Tommy led the way out into the street, Lizzie and Jack right behind them. The other Teds fanned out around the two couples.

As they walked, Tommy said quietly to Jessie, 'Funny how things happen. If I hadn't decided to go to the Black Raven tonight to have a laugh at Ken Young's expense, and if you hadn't picked this particular night to go for the first time, we'd never have met up. If you'd come in later, even, I'd have gone.'

'It must be fate,' she laughed trying to sound more light-hearted than she felt.

'Now that we've met up again we mustn't lose touch,' he went on.

She nodded. 'No, we mustn't.'

They walked a little way in silence, not so much as looking at one another. They turned a corner and Jessie and Lizzie's tramstop came into view. Seeing the stop, Tommy slowed his pace fractionally, and the others followed suit.

'There's our tram now!' shouted Lizzie, pointing.

'Och, let it go, there'll be another along in a minute,' Tommy said quickly.

Jack, who'd been about to make a sprint for it with Lizzie, came down off his toes, and, taking hold of her elbow, resumed walking slowly, forcing her to do the same.

'No hurry is there?' Tommy asked Jessie with a sideways glance.

She continued to look down at her feet. 'A few minutes longer won't make any difference.'

The tram clattered by as they came up to the tramstop. Tommy drew Jessie a little way aside. 'It really is good to see you again,' he said awkwardly.

'You've already said that, and so have I,' she reminded him.

He flicked back a slickened lock of hair. 'I was wondering . . . uh . . .'

She waited, guessing what was coming next, but not knowing what her answer was going to be.

'Me and the lads have a dancehall we go to. It's in Govanhill. It's a bit rough, mind you, but interesting, oh aye, very much that. I was wondering um . . . if you had nothing planned for next Friday, what about me taking you there to see the sights?' He paused, then added. 'You might enjoy it.'

She pretended to be interested in something across the road.

He shifted from one foot to the other. 'It was only a thought. You probably have something else planned.'

She made her decision, not at all sure it was the right one. 'Where shall we meet?'

He froze for a second, then swiftly regained his composure. 'How about Battlefield Rest?'

That was too close to home; she didn't want to be seen by anyone who might report back to her father and mother that she'd been in the company of a Ted. 'Outside Pearson's, the big ironmonger's in Victoria Road,' she suggested.

'That's fine,' he replied, nearly laughing with relief. 'That's perfect.' A second tram came clanking along. He shook her by the hand, a strangely formal gesture for a young man of his appearance. 'Till next Friday night then.'

'I'm looking forward to it,' she replied. She hesitated for a moment, then disentangled her hand and stepped aboard the tram.

'Let's go upstairs so I can have a fag,' Lizzie said, and headed up the metal stairs.

They sat in the back seat. Jessie watched Tommy till at last he was lost to view, just as he, illuminated by the harsh white street light, stood watching her.

Jessie was in a quandary about what to wear. All her dresses and outfits were of the sort acceptable at Whitecraigs or the like, but they weren't suitable for a Govanhill dancehall full of Teds.

She heard her father moving about downstairs. Her parents believed she was going out with Lizzie that evening. She could easily imagine their reaction if they knew the truth – that she was going out with Tommy McBride, the criminal's son, and that Tommy was a Teddy Boy now and was taking her jigging in Govanhill.

Her father would have had a canary, she thought, and smiled. As for Alison, hysterics at the very least.

She suddenly remembered the day Jim McBride had taken them all to the Grand Hotel and how Alec had been there with his mother and the girl he eventually married.

The marriage had made all the newspapers, even the London *Times*. Lady Virginia Dunbarr, daughter of the Earl of Clyde, weds Alexander Henry Muir in a ceremony in Glasgow Cathedral. Not all that long after the wedding Alec and his wife had gone to Kenya where he was now managing the Family's huge farm. That had also been in the paper.

Jessie wondered what had become of Alec's ambition to be a minister. Lady Virginia must have changed his mind about that. It was a pity in a way. Alec would have made a good minister. As for his being a farm manager, she couldn't imagine how he was making out at that.

She brought her mind back to the present. What ever was she going to wear?

He was waiting for her outside Pearson's. She was early, which meant he'd been even earlier.

Lord! she thought, momentarily seeing him as a Ted and not as Tommy. His sideboards were thick and bushy, his D.A. brushed to perfection.

This time he was wearing a black waistcoat below his black drape, with a watchchain dangling between the waistcoat's two pockets. He had five rings on his left hand, each gaudier than the next.

'Hello,' he said when she came up beside him.

142

Going up on to her tiptoes she brushed her lips against a point just below the left hand corner of his mouth. 'Hello,' she replied, surprising even herself.

The Cameo dancehall had a crumbling facade that was extensively covered with graffiti, a lot of it about the Boyd Street Boys.

Tommy led Jessie through to the foyer where she left her coat with the attendant. She noticed him giving her green and white polka-dot dress the once over out the corner of his eye, but he didn't comment.

Inside the hall itself a band called The Bad Angels was playing a loud rock song. Jessie was startled to see that a Ted was doing a handstand on the piano, while others were standing nonchalantly on top of the side booths and tables watching the action taking place on the floor. She gasped when she noticed that one of the dancing Teds was naked from the waist down. She looked quickly back to Tommy when the dancing Ted whirled round to expose his front.

'You were right about there being some sights here,' she grinned weakly.

Tommy laughed. 'And it's still fairly quiet yet,' he said ominously, and laughed again at the horrified expression on her face.

Despite her shock, it didn't take long for Jessie to become fascinated by the dancing. She'd never seen anything like it in the clubs she frequented. The music had something raw and almost primitive about it, and the dancing couples had about as much to do with the lessons learned in Miss Parrot's class as lovemaking has to do with business etiquette. The blatant sexuality of the dancing nearly took her breath away.

By Jessie's reckoning, there were somewhere between 80 and 100 Teds present. A good half that number, Tommy informed her, were not Boyd Street Boys but 'friendlies' from round about.

And then there were the girlfriends, equally exotic in appearance though not quite as calculatedly menacing.

Ted after Ted gave Tommy a sign that expressed not merely acknowledgement, but fealty as well. She suddenly felt as though she were visiting a strange and ancient tribe.

Affecting enormous dignity, Tommy took Jessie round introducing her. Everyone he spoke to seemed enormously pleased at the attention of the head man himself.

The reaction to Jessie was not quite so positive. It was clear they weren't at all sure what to make of her. They'd all heard about how he'd taken her away from Ken Young in the Black Raven, and the whisper was already around that she was an old friend, someone from his past.

Despite Tommy's efforts to make her feel at ease, Jessie couldn't feel comfortable. She stood out like a sore thumb amongst this lot. So great was the difference between her clothes and her behaviour and theirs that she might have been someone dumped down in the midst of a group of beings from another planet. All eyes were on her, sizing her up. She wanted to go home, but didn't want to leave Tommy. He seemed oblivious to either her discomfort or the looks she was getting, especially from the other girls.

'Well, I don't think the bitch is anything special!' a female voice suddenly boomed out behind her.

Jessie turned to find herself facing a striking blonde, standing with her hands on her hips. There was no doubt in Jessie's mind who this was.

'Lena!' Tommy warned.

'He's screwing me you know, so don't get any ideas,' Lena spat the words at Jessie.

Tommy gave an exclamation of anger, and made to go for Lena, but Jessie grabbed his arm. 'For heavens sake, you can't go around fighting everyone,' she hissed.

Lena tossed her pony tail. 'I want to know what's what,' she said staring defiantly into Tommy's eyes.

'I do as I please. Nobody owns me, and that includes you,' Tommy said in a quiet, measured voice.

Lena coloured with anger. 'You're no' coming here with another bird and making me a laughing stock.'

'The only person making you a laughing stock is yourself.'

Lena glared at him, then sauntered over to Jessie. She fastened her gaze on Jessie's feet and worked her way up inch by inch, until finally she was looking Jessie straight in the eye. 'Like I said,' she declared, 'nothing special at all.'

Jessie was so sure that Tommy wouldn't let anything happen to her that she wasn't even slightly afraid.

Suddenly, Lena's palm cracked against Jessie's cheek.

Without thinking, Jessie threw a punch at Lena which took Lena right on the end of the nose and threw her backwards.

Jessie couldn't believe what she'd done. Nor, from the amazement on their faces, could anyone else, least of all Tommy.

Lena scrambled back to her feet, puzzlement and a grudging respect in her eyes. 'You couldn't do that a second time,' she challenged.

Jessie gave the blonde a sheepish smile. 'To be honest, I didn't know I could do it a first.'

As quickly as it had sprung up, the situation was defused. 'Och tae hell with it, I wanted a change as well,' Lena said, almost friendly. She turned to Tommy and gave him a long kiss. 'That's for good-bye,' she winked.

'Would you like to dance or sit down?' Tommy asked Jessie when they were finally alone again.

'Sit down, before I fall down.'

He guided her to a side booth whose inhabitants vacated it when Tommy made it known he wanted to use it.

He stared across at her in open admiration. 'That was really something,' he said with his lop-sided grin.

Jessie frowned. 'You should have warned me you had someone here.'

145

'I told you in the pub last week, there's nobody important in my life.'

'Lena seemed to think she was.'

'She was wrong, and she should have known better.'

Jessie glanced down at the hand she'd hit Lena with, still unable to believe she'd actually done such a thing. Two of her knuckles were grazed. What would her parents say if they found out she was in a place like this, brawling?

'She's very attractive,' she said at last, not taking her eyes from her hand.

'Who?'

'Your friend, Lena.'

'Oh, she's that all right. I do have taste you know.'

Jessie sucked the grazes, all at once feeling what a mistake this date was. 'I hope you don't regret having asked me here tonight.'

'Why should I regret it?'

'Me being so . . . so normal compared to your friends.'

'You're not so normal,' he laughed. 'Not with that right. Anyway, if I have a regret it's for what happened with Lena there. I'm sorry.'

'She's fond of you, I could see that.'

He shrugged.

'I wish . . .' she stopped herself from saying that she wished he wasn't a Teddy Boy, that he was normal, like she was, that he was more like he used to be.

'Wish what?' he prompted.

'Nothing.'

'Is all this. . .' making a gesture that encompassed the entire dancehall, 'is all this hateful to you?'

'No, no . . . I don't hate it – I just feel out of place. I really love the music, though.'

'There are nights I come here after a day's work completely washed out,' said Tommy thoughtfully, 'and then I meet these people, and hear that beat, and I feel life's worth living again.'

'I don't suppose you mind the way they all treat you either,' she teased.

'I'd be a liar if I denied it. During the day amongst the cups and saucers, the teapots and chanties I'm no one at all. But here I count.'

Jessie smothered a laugh. 'You don't sell chanties there do you? I thought they went out with Queen Victoria.' A chantie was a chamberpot.

'I'll have you know there's still a big demand for them. Why, would you like one? I can get you a nice bone china one with roses on the outside.'

'No thank you,' she laughed.

'That's what comes from living in a manse with inside cludgies, you don't know what real life's all about,' he said, not quite joking. 'If you stayed in a tenement you'd find a chantie very preferable, having woken in the early hours say, to going down ice cold stone stairs to a middle landing lavvy.'

She glanced down at the table. 'I take your point.'

'Fifteen minutes by tram from Queen's Park and Battlefield to Boyd Street, fifteen minutes that'll take you back half a century, from one world to another.' He took a deep breath. 'Here's me getting all intense and maudlin and it's the last thing I want to do. How about a dance? Do you think you could brave the floor?'

She stood up. 'I just hope your dancing's improved, that's all. You used to murder my feet in Miss Parrot's class.'

'Oh I think I've improved a wee bit since then.'

And he had. In fact, he wasn't just a good dancer now. He was terrific.

'I'll see you home,' Tommy said as they walked to the tramstop.

'You'd better not,' she said slowly, not wanting to hurt his feelings. 'For the same reason I didn't want you to meet me at Battlefield Rest. You know as well as anyone what my father's like.'

147

He nodded. 'I think I can remember.'

They halted at the tramstop, the only ones there. 'I enjoyed myself tonight, thank you,' she said softly, suddenly feeling awkward and shy.

Silence fell between them.

Jessie glanced at her watch. 'Shouldn't be long before a tram comes along.'

'No, they're pretty frequent,' making a show of looking up the road.

Suddenly Tommy laughed, startling Jessie. 'I'll never forget Lena's expression as she got up off the deck after you'd hit her. It was priceless!'

'One night out with a Teddy Boy and already I'm thumping folk,' she replied, and then regretted her words when she saw the expression on his face. 'I'm sorry, Tommy,' she whispered, 'I didn't mean it like that.'

'Well, as I said before, we do live in two different worlds, don't we?'

'Yes, I guess we do.'

He lit a cigarette, striking the match, viciously almost, against the box. 'What's that expression? East is East and West is West and never the twain shall meet?'

'Kipling,' she mumbled.

'Whoever, I suppose they're right. We're not kids any more, are we?'

She studied him in the glow of his cigarette. There was still something in him that reminded her of the Tommy of old.

'I don't suppose there's any point in asking you out again, you'd only refuse.'

Did she want to see him again? She looked into his eyes. She was being mad, she thought, he was a Teddy Boy! But he wasn't only a Teddy Boy, he was Tommy – the same Tommy who'd once saved her life, the Tommy for whom she'd had a deep affection. *Still* had a deep affection for, she corrected herself.

'How about next Friday, same time same place?' she suggested.

He stared at her hard, then nodded. 'That's fine by me.'

'I'll look forward to it then.'

'Me too.'

When the tram came he kissed her quickly on the lips. It was a somewhat gauche kiss, which pleased her. She'd have bet a week's wages he'd never kissed Lena like that.

The tenements in Boyd Street were made of red sandstone rather than the usual grey. The street itself was long and lowering. Despite the time of year, wifeys were hanging out the windows, chatting to one another and watching the passing scene. A host of ragged children played on the pavements and in the gutters.

They came to Tommy's close and started up the stairs. It was early Saturday evening, and Tommy and Jessie had been going out together for a month now. She was on her way to have tea with him and Jeannie. It was the first time she'd been to his house in Boyd Street and the first time she'd met Jeannie since Millbrae Crescent.

Tonight Jessie was wearing a black knee-length skirt, a lilac blouse and black tinted nylons. It was hardly full Teddy Girl gear, but enough to help her blend in more easily with the Cameo crowd. She and Tommy were off to the Cameo after their tea.

The McBrides' room and kitchen was three stairs up and on the left of the landing. He let them in with a large iron key that was almost medieval in appearance. They found Jeannie dozing in a chair by the fire. An appetizing smell filled the tiny home.

Jeannie woke with a start when Tommy banged the door closed. 'Oh, there you are,' she said, quickly getting to her feet. 'I was just resting my eyes for a minute.'

'Do you always snore when you're resting your eyes?' Tommy teased.

She was about to protest, but then she saw the grin on his face. 'Ach, you,' she said fondly. And then she turned her attention to Jessie. 'Just look at you,' she said, taking

149

every inch of Jessie in. 'What a handsome young woman you've turned out to be.'

Jessie found herself unexpectedly overwhelmed with emotion. The years dissolved away, and she was back in Millbrae Crescent with Jeannie's warm voice telling her that everything was going to be all right. 'It's so good to see you again, Mrs McBride,' she choked out at last. 'It really is . . . I . . . I . . .'

Tommy looked from one to the other. Both women were close to tears. 'Do I smell something burning?' he asked in mock horror, winking at Jessie.

'My stew!' cried Jeannie, rushing to the cooker. She was peering frantically into the pots on the stove when Tommy's laughter stopped her. 'All right, my joker,' she said, laughing herself, 'just for that you can help me get the table laid.'

'Oh, no,' interrupted Jessie. 'Let me.'

While she helped Jeannie get things ready she took in the McBride's new surroundings as surreptitiously as she could. It was a far cry from Millbrae Crescent, that was for sure. It was small and cramped and decorated not out of taste and money but out of necessity. If the house in Millbrae Crescent symbolized limitless opportunities and comfort, then the rooms on Boyd Street symbolized a lifetime of struggle and hardship. And yet, as she watched Jeannie bustling around the tiny room it came to Jessie that Jeannie McBride was far happier here than she had been in Millbrae Crescent. The nervousness and unease were gone, she was home at last. But Tommy wasn't. Although he'd never said a word to her, it was obvious from the way he'd strode down the street with her – obvious from the way he dressed and from the anger that was always there in him, just below the surface – that he resented being back, resented the stigma and the squalor.

They had a homey tea of stew and boiled potatoes and homemade scones. Jeannie made a few polite inquiries about Battlefield, but it was clear to Jessie that she wasn't

150

at all interested, and had blocked out Battlefield and its memories as best she could. Then, when Tommy got up to rake the fire, she suddenly asked, 'And how are you getting on with Tommy's crowd? They're a bit different to what you're used to, I'd guess.'

'More than a bit!' Jessie laughed.

Tommy came back to the table. 'There's nothing wrong with them,' he said, frowning. 'They're good sorts, all of them.'

'I wasn't criticizing,' Jessie said softly.

'You better not,' said Tommy with a wink to his mother, 'or they'll be after you with chains.'

Jessie ignored him and went on to Jeannie. 'Let's just say that as long as I'm with Tommy they're prepared to put up with me.'

'Aye,' said Jeannie. 'I know what you mean.' Although she would never say anything to Tommy, she didn't approve of his winching Jessie. If living in Millbrae Crescent had taught her anything, it was that people should stay where they belonged. No good came, in her mind, in putting yourself above your place. As much as she liked Jessie, she couldn't see that anything would come of her and Tommy other than more pain and grief.

'And she puts up with *them*,' Tommy chipped in.

She leaned across the table and gave him a playful punch. 'It's you I put up with,' she laughed.

As soon as the table was cleared and the dishes done, Jeannie went off to visit a friend whose husband was working the late shift. 'She's expecting her fifth,' Jeannie explained, 'and she doesn't like to be alone all night.'

Jessie sat down in the chair by the fire.

'I'm just going to get washed and changed before we go out,' Tommy said, pointing at the sink. 'I'm afraid Boyd Street doesn't run to private baths.'

He boiled a kettle, poured the contents into the basin of the sink, and took off his shirt.

Jessie, who'd been chatting to him while he made his preparations, caught her breath. His body was marked

151

by four ugly scars, three cutting across his chest, and another along his left shoulder blade. Besides the old wounds, his upper arms were decorated with tattoos; a large spider on the left and crossed hatchets dripping blood on the right. It was the scars that made her shudder. She watched him as he washed, unable to take her eyes from his mutilated torso. At last, as he began to dry himself, she asked gently, 'How did you get those, then?'

'These here,' he said, pointing to his chest, 'were from a little argument with a fellow with a knife. The other one wasn't as civilized, that one was done with a broken bottle.'

Her eyes stayed on the jagged marks. 'It must have been very painful . . .'

He laughed at her concern. 'It hurt them a lot more than it hurt me,' he joked.

But instead of joining in his laughter, she got up and came slowly towards him. Very gently, she touched the scar on his shoulder blade. The hardness of it made her shiver. Slowly, almost delicately, she ran her finger along its length. 'Poor you,' she whispered, her breath warm against his skin. 'Poor you . . .'

Suddenly, she was in his arms, their lips meeting in a kiss that left them alone in the universe, their bodies pressed against one another in a yearning embrace. A passion she had never known before burned through her like a fever. All she knew at that moment was that she wanted his lips on hers, wanted his hands on her body – wanted him.

And then, just as suddenly, he gave a muffled exclamation and pulled himself away.

She stared at him in amazement. 'Tommy . . .'

He picked up the towel he'd dropped and ran it over his face. He was still breathing heavily. 'I'm sorry,' he mumbled from under cover of the towel. 'I . . . I forgot that you're not like the others.'

'What do you mean I'm not like the others? That I'm not as attractive to you? That I'm . . .'

He threw the towel onto the counter and laid a finger on her lips. 'I mean you're special, that's what I mean.'

'But I'm a woman, too,' she whispered, her voice close to breaking. 'I . . . I've never been with anyone since Alec. But you . . . with you . . .'

'I don't care about where you've been, Jessie,' he said, his fingers now tenderly stroking her cheek. 'But I do care about where you're going. You've always been special to me, you know. Always. I'm too close to having my dreams come true to want to rush things now.'

She held his hand still with her own. There was a glint of tears in her eyes. 'You're kind of special yourself, Tommy McBride,' she said.

It was New Year's Eve and the Cameo was in full swing. The band, new to the Cameo, was called the Rocking Quiffs. Their singer wore a drape with gold thread interwoven through it, and a Mohawk haircut, the entire head shaved except for a central strip of hair.

Jessie was sitting in one of the side booths with Tommy, watching the band, and thinking about the conversation she'd had half an hour before with the sax player during the break. She'd been surprised to learn how much money there was in rock bands. She'd never realized that a band could be more than a hobby, it could be a living as well.

Her thoughts were interrupted by a commotion at the main door. Excited and angry voices could be heard above the din of the band.

Tommy came to his feet as Jack, the same Jack who'd been at The Black Raven with Tommy when he'd rescued Jessie, was hustled towards him. Instantly his expression became grim. Jack's face was bright with blood, and his right ear partially torn from the side of his head.

'He's been whipped with a bike chain,' said one of the Teds who was holding Jack up.

'And had a couple of bad strokes from a razor,' added the other.

The band stopped playing. Tommy helped the others lay Jack down on the seat of the booth.

'He was dumped outside from a car, just like you see in those Yankee gangster movies,' a Ted called Vince said.

'A Zephyr. I saw it speeding off, but not who was inside,' Vince's girlfriend added.

Tommy leaned over his stricken friend. 'Jack! Jack! Can you hear me?' Jack moaned. 'Ken Young said I was to give you his regards,' he mumbled, and then he passed out.

Jessie guessed that the facial injuries weren't the only ones Jack had received. He'd probably been given a kicking as well. 'We need to get him to a hospital, and fast,' she said.

Tommy looked hesitant. 'Now, Tommy,' she urged. 'Right now.'

One of the Teds said he had a motor outside; he'd be glad to take Jack. Immediately, Jack was gently lifted and carried back out the way he'd just come.

Jessie could see from Tommy's expression what he intended to do.

'Tommy,' she said, grabbing hold of his arm. 'Listen to me before you do anything foolish.'

Tommy was white with fury. He barely felt her hand gripping him, all he could think of was revenge. His plan was to get Boyd Street Boys, and as many 'friendlies' who would come with them, and go straight to The Black Raven to have it out with Ken Young and his lads.

'Can't you see this is a set-up?' she asked, making him look at her. 'Strike back now and you'll be doing exactly as Young wants.'

Tommy blinked. 'What do you mean?'

'Go charging over to The Black Raven now and they'll be waiting for you. You'll be walking right into their trap.

Tommy forced himself to cool down, to think clearly

154

and rationally. She was right, of course. Doing over Jack and then dumping him outside the Cameo was a come on. It had to be.

Ken Young would have a host of Teds over at The Black Raven waiting the arrival of the Boyd Street Boys. Young wouldn't make a move like this unless ke knew he had them outnumbered. Well, he wasn't going to let Young call the tune. *He* would do that. When the Boyd Street Boys exacted revenge for what had been done to Jack it would be at a time and place of his own choosing.

He put his arm around her fondly. 'You can stop looking so worried,' he chided. 'You win. It would be suicide to do anything tonight. But Ken Young's going to be bloody sorry for what he did this Hogmanay.' His eyes were far away. 'Bloody sorry.'

That night Jessie lay in bed, staring at the ceiling. But it wasn't the shadowy ceiling she was seeing, it was a vivid picture of the forthcoming fight between the Boyd Street Boys and Ken Young's Teds. And there in the thick of it was her Tommy, the enemy swarming all around, each one of them trying to do his worst to Tommy. She shuddered to think what the bloody outcome might be.

If only she could stop the fight taking place. There had to be a way, some ruse or argument she could come up with.

Dawn found her still wide awake and wracking her brains.

Jessie and Tommy were in the Seaforth Bar, around the corner from the Cameo. They were having a quiet drink at her suggestion.

'I really don't understand why you feel you have to fight Young,' Jessie said, changing the conversation.

Tommy stared at her in astonishment. What was she havering on about now? 'Because of what has been done to Jack,' he replied, his tone condescending at having to explain the obvious.

Jessie ran a finger round the rim of her glass. 'All Ken Young was doing was retaliating for what you did to him that night in The Black Raven. You were there for a laugh at his expense, and he repaid it by having Jack beaten. So why don't you just leave it at that. As it stands at the moment, the pair of you are quits.'

'And what about Jack?'

'Getting more of your boys cut up isn't going to change what happened to Jack.'

'No, but cutting up Young and his lads would.'

She laid a hand on top of his. 'You had your laugh, then Young had his. So now you're even. Leave it like that, don't escalate matters,' she begged.

'Young would have escalated matters by having us go to The Black Raven after Jack was done over,' Tommy persisted.

'But you didn't go, so nothing happened.'

There were times when Jessie infuriated him, and this was one of them. He gave a long sigh of frustration. Arguing with her was like arguing with a brick wall. 'You just don't understand,' he said, and took a swig of his beer.

She waited patiently till he'd put his glass back on the table. 'The trouble with you is you can't bear not to come out on top. A draw isn't good enough for you, you have to be a winner,' she said angrily.

Tommy glared at her. Her analysis was absolutely correct, but he certainly wasn't going to give her the satisfaction of admitting it. 'I can't call it quits, the others wouldn't allow it. One of us has been hurt, so we've got to hit back. It's as simple as that.'

'Since when do you take orders from them?' She knew she'd got through to him when she saw him colour. It might have been a beneath the belt blow, but it had worked. When he didn't reply she went on. 'Sometimes the hardest thing of all to do is nothing, Sweet Fanny

156

Adams. You've told me often enough how fond you are of the Boyd Street Boys, right?'

Tommy nodded slowly.

'You fight Ken Young and his Teds and how many of the Boys are going to end up in hospital? Broken arms, legs, mangled faces, gouged out eyes, maybe even some of them dead.'

'We're Teds, and Teds fight, it's part of the creed.'

'You may think it's manly to do that, but I don't. It would be far more manly not to force this fight, to have the strength and guts to say enough is enough, let's call a halt while it's all square.'

'I've told you, I can't call this fight off.' he replied stubbornly.

'So you're nothing more than a figurehead who takes orders from his own men.'

'I'm nothing of the sort!'

'Then if you're the leader, damn well lead. Save your friends from what's in store for them if they go up against Young.'

'I'm not a coward.'

Jessie leaned towards him urgently. 'Only a brave man will do what he thinks is right over what he knows is popular.'

Tommy stared at her. Could he convince the Boys to leave the situation as it was and not seek revenge for Jack? It was a hell of a challenge but the more he thought about it the more sense it made.

'You were aye God Squad Jessie,' he said after a while. Their laughter echoed through the bar.

It was early Friday evening and the Reverend Kenneth Gray was writing the first draft of his sermon for that Sunday. The theme was 'Man's Inhumanity to Man.'

Jessie was sitting over from him sipping a cup of coffee. When she finished that she intended going up to her room to get dressed. She was meeting Tommy in just over an hour and a half. She was thinking about the new, bright pink lipstick she'd bought that lunchtime, and hoping Tommy liked it.

The Reverend paused in what he was doing to glance across at Jessie. She'd been different of late, a lot happier, and he wondered why. As he sat gazing at her a possible explanation came to him.

'Is it the dancing again tonight?' he asked.

'Yes, Dad,' she smiled.

'Seeing someone special, are you?'

She immediately became wary, what on earth had prompted him to ask that? Had she been seen with Tommy? Had something been said?

'Why should I be seeing anyone special?' she replied as casually as she could.

So he was right! The minister gave himself a mental pat on the back for his powers of deduction. He then explained how he'd arrived at that conclusion. It was a relief to know he was talking in the general, and not the particular. Her secret was still safe.

She faked a blush, then put on a coy look, giving the impression she was embarrassed to discuss the subject.

'Did you meet him at Whitecraigs?' her father continued.

'Yes,' she lied, mumbling into her cup.

The Reverend Gray nodded his satisfaction. If the lad went to Whitecraigs he must come from a good family, Jessie would be all right there. 'Perhaps you'd like to bring him to the house one day so your mother and I could be introduced?' he suggested.

She'd better get out of here before this went any further, Jessie thought. With a quick guilp she finished her coffee, and rose from her chair. 'I'll do that when I think he's ready for the third degree. If he's ever ready for the third degree,' she answered, making a joke of it.

After Jessie had left the room the minister wondered what the lad's name was, he'd forgotten to ask.

★   ★   ★

Ken Young was sitting in the Bluebird cafe moodily stirring his espresso. What was wrong with that bastard McBride? What did he have to do to get a reaction? When the Jack Gowrie business hadn't provoked McBride he'd engineered more proddings, but none of them had worked either.

He licked his spoon, and thought of how much he hated Tommy McBride. Partly it was a chemistry. He just had to be in McBride's presence to experience the almost overwhelming urge to banjo the bastard. But over and above that he hated McBride because Tommy was the only other serious contender for the position he saw as justly his, King of the Glasgow Teds.

He wanted McBride destroyed, and the Boyd Street Boys along with him, for he knew they would never give allegiance to any other than one of their own.

Ken Young's scowl deepened, as he recalled the time in The Black Raven when McBride had not only called him a toerag and told him to piss off, but stolen away the bitch who'd been refusing to dance with him, and whom he'd just been about to sort out.

To add insult to injury, McBride had not only stolen the bird away but had taken up winching her. From what he'd heard the two of them were now thick as could be.

Slowly, a smile spread across Ken Young's face. Now there was a thought, a right humdinger of one!

Jessie was re-stocking the sheet music when her boss came over. 'There's a personal telephone call for you in my office,' Mr Elvin said frostily. The receiving of personal calls wasn't forbidden, but it wasn't exactly encouraged either. The unspoken rule was that any calls had to be extremely important.

'Is it my mother or father?' Jessie asked anxiously, thinking that something might have happened at home.

'Neither. It's a *young* girl,' Mr Elvin replied crisply.

Puzzled, Jessie thanked him, and hurried to his office at

the rear of the shop. Could it be Lizzie Dunnachie? Lizzie's voice was hardly that of a young girl. Wondering, she picked up the receiver.

It wasn't Lizzie, but a lassie she didn't know who said she worked alongside Tommy. 'He can't come to the telephone himself, so he's asked me to ring instead. He says it's urgent he speaks with you before you go home the night, and he's given me an address where he wants to meet you directly after your work.'

The arrangement had been for Jessie to meet Tommy later on, to go dancing at the Cameo. Something must have come up and he was going to cancel their date, Jessie thought. She smiled, it was just like Tommy to want to tell her in person rather than have it done by someone else over the telephone.

'What's the address?' She jotted it down on a pad, and then jotted down the directions as well. It wasn't a street she knew.

She thanked the lassie and hung up, then seeing that Mr Elvin was busy with a customer, she made a hasty call to Battlefield to say she'd be late back and not to wait tea for her.

Jessie frowned. Linton Street was deserted, the tenements on either side were derelict. No smoke came from any of the chimneys, and many of the windows were boarded up. It was a condemned street waiting to be pulled down, she realized with a sudden rush of fear. Had she got it wrong? Was there more to this than Tommy merely cancelling their date? Was he in some sort of trouble? It was certainly a peculiar place for a rendezvous.

She hurried through the drizzling rain, her shoes resounding on the worn cobbles. She found the close number she was seeking half way down the street on the right hand side. The more she wandered in this deserted place, the more apprehensive she became. There was no name plate on the peeling brown door. The bell pull was long gone, either stolen for scrap or vandalized. She knocked and waited, convinced now that Tommy was in some sort of trouble.

She heard the tread of footsteps, then the door swung open.

'Surprise, surprise!' smiled Ken Young.

Jessie froze in shock. Only when Ken Young moved did she, but it was too late, and she was too slow. He grabbed her before she'd even got off the landing. She screamed as his strong arms encircled her, pinioning her own to her sides. With the struggling, still screaming, Jessie locked tightly in his grasp, Ken congratulated himself. His plan had worked a fair treat, and it was so simple. But then all the best plans were.

'You might as well stop screaming, there's no one to hear you. Except me that is,' he crooned sadistically. Lifting her up, he carried her into the damp and musty smelling house.

Jessie was propelled into the first bedroom they came to. He threw her right across the room to bang against the opposite wall. She fell to the floor and before she could pick herself up again heard the click of a padlock outside the door which had been slammed shut behind her. Seconds later the main house door also slammed shut. An eerie silence descended through the house. She knew it was useless, but tried the bedroom door anyway. The padlock she'd heard clicking closed held it fast.

The solitary window was partially boarded, but moonlight and street light streamed in through the unboarded part. A quick check showed that, four flights up and with a straight drop to the street below, there was no escape in that direction. Terrified, she looked around her. The bedroom was a ruin, the floor littered with old newspapers, rusty tins and other rubbish. Someone had defecated in a corner and covered the mess with a sheet of newspaper. The stink was nauseating. The only furniture was an ancient iron bed that had a couple of tattered blankets over its stained and ripped mattress.

161

After a while, Jessie sat on the bed, which was preferable to sitting on the floor, not allowing herself to imagine what would happen next.

Hours later, she heard laughing voices out on the landing. One of them she recognized as Ken Young's. She listened to the sound of the main door opening, then the scrape of a key in the padlock securing the bedroom door.

They'd been at the bevy, she could smell it the moment they entered the bedroom. Besides Ken Young there were four others, all Teds, all drunk, all loud, all menacing. Young held aloft a lighted storm lantern, casting weird dancing shadows around the room. 'And how are you hen?' he leered.

Jessie didn't answer. Fear was making her heart pound so loudly she was sure they could hear it.

'You're right Ken, she's not bad at all,' crowed one of the Teds.

Ken Young laughed without a trace of humour. 'I'm going to really enjoy this, so I am. Get her lads!'

The other four Teds swooped on Jessie and threw her backwards on to the bed, holding her down. She knew then, without a shadow of a doubt, what they intended next.

Ken Young sauntered over, ripping her clothes until she was completely exposed.

'Now that's what I call lovely,' he crooned, roughly handling her breasts. 'Don't you boys agree?'

This wasn't happening, it was a nightmare from which she was going to awake at any second. 'You're nothing but a pack of animals,' she screamed.

Young's hand lashed out to crack across her cheek, knocking her head sideways. Her head was knocked the other way when he hit her again.

'Watch this lads, I'll show you how an expert does it,' he boasted to the others. 'And then you can all have a turn.'

*   *   *

Lena McGurk was about to go into the Cameo when a Zephyr came screeching to a halt at the pavement. A door flew open, a bundle came rolling out, then the car was away again, peeling off down the road and out of sight.

There was a dull ache between Jessie's legs, and she felt as if every last ounce of energy had been drained from her body. Dimly, she became aware of Lena staring down at her, then Lena was kneeling by her side and talking, but she couldn't quite understand the words.

The girl from the cash desk came hurrying across, 'Go get Tommy, and hurry!' Lena ordered, taking off her cardigan and throwing it over Jessie's half-naked body.

Tommy was lounging against a pillar, watching the dancers, when the girl from the cash desk appeared by his side. One look at her face told him something was wrong.

He'd waited half an hour for Jessie at the tramstop where they'd arranged to meet. When she hadn't shown, he'd assumed she'd had to cancel and not been able to tell him, or else, for some reason or other, was going to be late, in which case she'd make her own way to the Cameo. Although nothing like that had ever happened before, it hadn't worried him. It had just never crossed his mind that something might have happened to her.

Tommy came thundering out into the street with a posse of Boyd Street Boys behind him. He stopped abruptly when he saw Jessie lying there, her head in Lena's lap.

He didn't have to ask her what had happened.

'It was Ken Young,' Lena said. 'I saw him clear as I'm seeing you. They dumped her from the same motor they dumped Jack from.'

'Have they hurt her?' Tommy demanded kneeling beside her.

Lena didn't say what she suspected. 'She's not been marked,' she assured him. 'And there are no bones broken.'

163

Tommy gently scooped Jessie into his arms and carried her to the foyer. The manager told him to take Jessie into his office where there was a fire and bottle.

By this time most of those inside had come crowding out into the foyer which was jam packed as a result. Tommy shouted to be let through, and followed the manager to his office.

Tommy heeled the office door closed behind him, then laid Jessie on the chaise longue that was drawn up beside the blazing fire. He muttered his thanks when the manager handed him a large glass of whisky for Jessie. 'I'll leave you two alone,' said the manager softly, and immediately left the room.

Tommy stroked Jessie's forehead. She was hot and feverish. He lifted her head and put the glass to her lips, but she moaned that she didn't want any. Well, he certainly did.

She was reviving quickly, thanks to the heat of the room and Tommy's presence.

'So what happened?' Tommy asked quietly at last.

She didn't want to tell him, knew she shouldn't, but the sheer horror of what she'd been through overcame her and the words came spilling out.

When Jessie was finally finished, she started to shake. Tommy, tears streaming down his face, clasped her to him and held her there.

'You mustn't retaliate, it's another set-up,' she sobbed.

'Aye, I know that,' he replied in a whisper.

He couldn't bear to think of what had been done to Jessie. There were no words to express the depth of his outrage. One thing he knew for certain, he was going to do his damnedest to make Ken Young pay for the violation of his Jessie, his Star. He held her tightly until she fell into an exhausted sleep.

Tommy covered her with a travelling rug that had been over the back of a chair and poured himself another large dram.

There was a sink in the corner where he washed his

face. When he'd towelled that dry he took another dram, after which he kissed Jessie on the cheek.

Then he went looking for Ken Young.

They came out of the night to descend on The Black Raven, forty-nine Boyd Street Boys and 'friendlies' with Tommy at their head, all carrying weapons.

There was music playing inside The Black Raven, but the music was muted, almost hushed. Outside the dancehall's front entranceway stood a lone figure, that of a wee boy of maybe ten or twelve.

'Which one of youse is Tommy McBride? I have a message for him' the wee boy's voice quavered.

Tommy stepped forward to stand towering over the small child. 'I'm McBride, what's the message?'

The boy licked his lips. 'I'm no part o' any of this, mister. Kenny gave me half a sheet to deliver the message, and that's why I'm doing it. I'm not involved.'

Tommy nodded that he understood.

'Not here, Kenny says it's too public. He says he'll be waiting for you and yours at Linton Street. Do you know where that is?'

Linton Street! Where Jessie had told him they'd taken her. 'I know,' Tommy replied evenly.

'That's it, then,' and the wee boy scurried away.

Linton Street, it was a fitting venue for what was going to happen, Tommy thought.

'Let's go,' he ordered, and he and the other forty-eight disappeared back into the night.

Jessie came awake with a start. She'd been dreaming she was in that awful bedroom again with Ken Young and the four others, only this time it *had been* a nightmare.

'Tommy?' she called out blearily.

'Tommy's gone, I'm to look after you,' said a voice close by.

Jessie struggled onto an elbow to discover Lena sitting on a chair by the chaise longue. 'Gone where?' she demanded, a new fear chasing the last traces of sleep.

Lena evaded the question. 'Tommy told me to take you home by taxi when you were fit enough to travel,' she answered instead.

'How long was I asleep?'

'An hour, maybe a little longer.'

'Has he gone alone or with the Boys?' Jessie asked. Lena's evasiveness had told her what she wanted to know.

Lena could see that Jessie had guessed what the situation was. There was no point in lying further. 'All of them.'

Jessie knew then what she had to do.

'You can call that taxi now,' she said, getting to her feet.

Ken Young stood directly in front of the house where he and his boys had raped Jessie. Every so often he grinned at the memory.

Young already knew that this time he'd been successful and that Tommy was on his way. Word had been phoned through from The Black Raven. Not long now and McBride and the Boyd Street Boys would be destroyed, leaving him uncontested King of the Glasgow Teds. He might even have a coronation, he thought. A coronation at The Black Raven! Aye, he liked that idea, King of the Glasgow Teds.

'They're coming!' a voice warned urgently

Ken Young reached for the bayonet he had tucked into the waistband of his drainies.

The night editor of the *Scottish Daily Record* was reading through copy about a small blaze in a bonded warehouse just off St Enoch Square when he was handed a note. A glance at the note, from a regular and thoroughly reliable outside source, caused him to raise an eyebrow in interest.

In two straight lines running down from his own desk were those of the reporters. Spying John Cameron staring off into space, he shouted to Cameron that he had an assignment for him.

A few minutes later John Cameron and photographer Fraser Tulloch hurriedly left the *Scottish Daily Record* building for Linton Street.

Tommy and his contingent stopped when they came in sight of the army of Teds waiting for them. They were well outnumbered, but they'd known they'd be.

'Just remember, unless I go down Ken Young is mine,' Tommy said in a loud, clear voice. He gazed down Linton Street. To actually see the place where Jessie had been raped further fuelled his already awesome anger.

Somewhere in the far distance a police siren sounded, its harsh wail rupturing the stillness of the night.

Tommy moved forward, and his people with him. As they neared Ken Young additional enemy Teds swarmed out of the closes nearest Young to swell Young's numbers even more.

'I'm claiming you!' Tommy yelled at Ken Young.

And with that battle was joined.

Jessie moved in her seat nervously as the taxi sped through Glasgow. Getting into the taxi, she'd told Lena that she'd left her purse behind in the manager's office, and Lena had immediately volunteered to return and get it for her. The moment Lena had vanished, Jessie had passed the driver five bob and told him to leave right away, and that their destination was now Linton Street, not Battlefield Central Church. It was Lena who'd found out where the big fight was to take place, although Jessie didn't know how.

167

As the taxi turned into Linton Street the driver swore and stamped on the brake, bringing the cab to a screeching halt. There were Teds fighting everywhere. 'This is as far as I go,' growled the man. 'And I'm not waiting.'

Jessie jumped from the taxi, handed the driver a pound note, and told him not to bother about change. He did an incredibly fast, reverse three-point turn, then roared off back the way he'd come.

Jessie recognized one of the Boyd Street Boys, Sammy McGlinchie, lying in an ever widening pool of blood that was coming from a knife wound in his side.

Another Ted, an enemy, was hunched against a lamppost clutching his face that had been cut in ribbons, keening in agony.

But where was Tommy? That was all that interested Jessie as she dodged between the countless individual fights that were going on, too obsessed with finding him to be afraid.

Razors flashed, bicycle chains swished, lead pipes filled with cement thudded, and occasionally a bottle shattered. Some fought in silence, others howled and shrieked, and one of the combatants, his nose spread flat across his face, was actually laughing.

She raced on, interested in only one thing. And then there was Tommy, back to a tenement wall, Ken Young prostrate at his feet, fighting off three who were attacking him simultaneously. Tommy had a small hatchet in his right hand while his left was encased in bloody knucklers.

It happened quickly, one second Tommy was still upright, the next he'd lost his footing and gone down with a jarring thump.

No thought went into Jessie's reaction, no conscious decision. She saw her man in desperate trouble, and leapt to his defence. As she ran, she bent and snatched up a half brick that had already been used in the fight. Tommy was still fending off his opponents, though flat on his back. She took a deep breath and hit the nearest Ted on the head

168

with the brick. To her surprise, he crumpled, senseless, to the ground.

The smaller of Tommy's remaining attackers whirled on Jessie, his flick knife raised in a stabbing position. Jessie's long nails desperately swept the length of his face, making trails of blood from forehead to chin. The Ted made a lunge with his knife, but she neatly side-stepped the descending blade.

A length of chain whistled towards Tommy's neck. He managed to catch it around the handle of his hatchet, and wrench it from the last Ted's grasp. A solid kick took the Ted full in the crotch.

Jessie's Ted, blood obscuring his vision, blundered after her, his knife hand lancing out again and again at the ever moving shadow he knew to be her.

Tommy despatched his Ted with a side blow of the hatchet, then he turned on Jessie's assailant, punching viciously at him with his knucklers. The boy pitched headlong to the pavement.

Jessie flew into Tommy's arms.

'It's all over. Drop your weapons, son,' a voice commanded.

Tommy looked up to find he and Jessie were surrounded by police, all with truncheons drawn.

Tommy gazed round him. There were Black Marias at either end of Linton Street, while the street itself was overrun with bobbies.

Tommy released his hatchet and knucklers which fell to the ground beside the stricken Ken Young who was still unconscious, badly wounded from the hatcheting Tommy had given him.

He brought his attention back to Jessie, who was clinging to him as though she would never let him go.

'I love you,' he whispered.

'And I love you.'

He held her close. She laid her head on a shoulder, closed her eyes, and thanked God that she'd been in time, that he was safe. She was filled with so much joy and love that she felt she might burst with it. Nothing mattered. Not the police, not her parents, nothing mattered but them.

She looked up into his face, and he kissed her with all the passion in his heart.

A flashbulb popped. It was Fraser Tulloch taking their picture.

'You and I forever,' Tommy whispered when the kiss was over.

'Forever,' she agreed. Arm in arm, Jessie and Tommy were led to the nearest Black Maria. Ragged cheer after cheer from the Boyd Street Boys, still standing followed their progress.

'Who are they?' John Cameron asked one of the Boys.

'That's Tommy McBride, our leader and undisputed King of the Glasgow Teds.'

'King of the Glasgow Teds!' John Cameron breathed, already visualizing the words in print.

Jessie was sharing a cell with a prostitute and a middle-aged, middle-class woman held for shoplifting who kept saying over and over that it was all a horrible mistake.

The night had been long and bitterly cold. Jessie had done her best to sleep on the palliasse she'd been given, but thoughts of all that had happened had kept her restless.

There was a rattle of keys at the door, and a policeman appeared, bringing their dinner.

'About effing time, too!' snarled the prostitute, grabbing the first tray.

Jessie was not due up before the beak until the afternoon, but she knew that Tommy and the others had been scheduled for the morning session.

'Any idea what Tommy McBride got?' she asked the policeman anxiously.

'Two years,' he said shortly.

My God, Jessie thought. Two years was an eternity.

'You're famous now, quite the celebrity,' the police-man said suddenly, and handed her a folded copy of the *Scottish Daily Record* along with her tray.

Jessie laid the tray on the floor, then shook open the paper. The page 1 headline and the picture beneath it made her gasp.

The King and Queen of the Glasgow Teds screamed the headline in thick black type. Beneath it was a picture of her and Tommy kissing, Tommy's clenched and bloody fist draped around her neck. The accompanying story was a hair raising account of the fight that had occurred in Linton Street. Thankfully, no one had been killed, although apparently in several instances it had been a near thing. Ken Young, described as the leader of the North Glasgow Teds, a name John Cameron had invented, was reported to have multiple wounds and severe concussion.

Queen of the Glasgow Teds! Good Lord! She dreaded to think what her mother and father were going to say. The family didn't take the *Record*, but sure as eggs were eggs some 'friend' in the congregation would bring it to their attention.

The minister and his wife were on their knees praying when Jessie arrived home. As she entered the room, both glanced up to give her an accusatory stare.

After hearing Jessie's full story, it had been abundantly clear to the beak, an astute, wise, and widely experienced man, that she wasn't the wild Teddy Girl the *Scottish Daily Record* had made her out to be. In sentencing her he'd taken into consideration the circumstances which had both caused and brought her to the fight, as well as the fact that she came from a good family and had never been in trouble before.

However, regardless of the whys and wherefores, she had actually taken part in what the newspapers were describing as The Battle of Linton Street, and had been observed hitting an opponent with a brick. He therefore sentenced her to six months, sentence suspended.

She'd been overwhelmed with relief. Now, seeing her parents, she knew that her relief had been false.

The Reverend Gray got to his feet.

'Pack what you wish to take, then leave this house for all time,' he said, looking at her as though he didn't know her.

Jessie turned to her mother.

'How could you?' Alison whispered. 'After all we've done for you?'

'Tommy McBride of all people, a criminal just like his father,' he continued bitterly. 'You're no daughter of mine. You belong with the scum.'

In her mind's eye, Jessie saw a piece of string and scissors. The scissors opened and closed, and what had been one piece of string was now two. That was her relationship with her parents. Up until then she'd been part of the family, one with them. Now she was separate, for ever.

'I think you should know that I love Tommy,' Jessie said in a still voice. 'And he loves me.'

'How can you love someone who's no more than a common thug?' Alison asked scornfully. 'Don't you realize that your father could lose his job over this?'

What small people they really were, Jessie thought. When she was young, she'd seen her parents as giants, while in reality they were pygmies.

'There was a time I would have bent over backwards to save Dad's job, but not now. I know it's a strange thing to say after all the years he's been one, but I can't help wondering if he didn't make a mistake in becoming a minister.' And with that, she went upstairs to pack.

5

Jessie glanced at her wristwatch; it was only three minutes more to eleven a.m. Tommy was due to be released on the hour. He'd served eighteen months, with six months off for good behaviour.

Barlinne Prison was an evil place, you could smell it like some invisible, poisonous cloud.

She'd come alone, leaving Jeannie behind to cook the dinner. She'd been staying with her at Boyd Street since the day her parents threw her out. Jeannie had taken her in, given her Tommy's inset bed in the kitchen, and made her welcome. The pair of them had grown close over the long months of waiting.

Tommy was the last of the Boyd Street Boys to leave prison, but not the last of those who'd taken part in what was now widely known as The Battle of Linton Street, for there were still a handful of Ken Young's followers inside, those with previous records.

Ken Young himself had got out a few months back, a lot of the stuffing knocked out of him after his defeat by Tommy. Within a week of leaving the Bar-L, as Barlinne was often cried, he'd departed the city for London. Rumour had it he was running with a group of Willesden Teds.

Jessie frowned as she looked across to where half a dozen cars were parked. The Press had come in force to cover Tommy's release.

The small green door inset in the larger green one swung open, and Tommy McBride stepped out into the August sunshine.

He had a grey pallor, and was thin to the point of skin and bones. She hadn't noticed either of these things during the many times she'd visited him.

She walked hesitantly towards him, suddenly shy, although she couldn't think why that should be. Tommy was shy also, she could read it in his face, and that made everything all right somehow.

'Hello,' he said in a low voice.

Her answer was to move into his arms for the kiss she'd been dreaming of for so long.

He laid a hand against one of her cheeks, and momentarily closed his eyes. 'You don't know how good it is to be able to touch you again,' he whispered.

'Oh, but I do. You just wait and see.'

He smiled at her, a smile so warm and deep she felt she could have fallen in it and drowned.

His eyes flickered over her shoulder to take in the cars, and the reporters and photographers waiting expectantly by them.

'The Press have come to interview the newly released King of the Glasgow Teds, are you up to it?' she asked following his gaze.

'Do I have a choice?'

'I doubt it. They all appear the type that'd hound you till they got what they wanted.'

'Then let's get it over with. Then we can go home.'

Jessie waved to the pressmen, and they hurried over.

As soon as the photographers were close enough the flashbulbs began to pop.

The Boyd Street Boys had planned a welcome home party at the Cameo that night. They dressed in style for the party. Jessie, having decided to play the part she'd been given, had a brand new outfit she'd bought for the occasion. Tommy was wearing his best black drape, a gaucho string tie, and a thick black belt with a silver death's head buckle. Jessie a black pencil skirt, body hugging deep purple sweater, purple stilettoes and black mesh stockings.

She'd parted her hair down the middle, and combed it

to fall straight on either side. The other girls at the Cameo would have high, back-combed bouffants, but she preferred to be different. If she was a queen, she'd show it.

The Boyd Street Boys were standing in facing twin lines, with a corridor down the centre. The moment Tommy and Jessie appeared everyone began shouting, whistling, cheering and clapping.

Tommy and Jessie slowly made their way between the rows of Teds. Everyone wanted to shake their hands. After that, Jack Gowrie made a speech welcoming Tommy home. Tommy said a few words of thanks. Then the band struck up, and Tommy and Jessie led off the dancing.

It was about an hour later that the first strange Teds, from Balornock, appeared to offer fealty on their group's behalf. As the night wore on, though, more and more strange Teds arrived to pay fealty.

Perhaps they really were the King and Queen of the Glasgow Teds, she thought to herself.

The chimes of midnight found everyone well into the spirit of things. One of the band, guttered out of his skull, staggered off the rostrum to go and call for Ralph.

Tommy watched the sax player go, and had an idea. He turned to Jessie suddenly. 'I'll tell you what, if you'll play that saxophone up there I'll sing.'

Jessie stared at him in astonishment, wondering if he'd had even more than she'd thought. 'I didn't know you could sing.'

'I'm sure there are lots of things about me you don't know,' he answered, giving her a wink.

Jessie waited for the punchline, but none came. He really was serious. She glanced over at the saxophone; knowing how to play the clarinet meant she could also play that, but it had been so long since she'd had an instrument in her hands. She was bound to be rusty. The last thing she wanted was to make a fool of herself in front of all these folk.

'Are you scared?' Tommy whispered mischievously.

'I'm nothing of the sort,'

Tommy lurched to his feet and drew her to hers. 'Can you manage Rock Around The Clock?'

'Can you?'

His reply was to take her to the rostrum, jump onto it, and pull her up after him.

After a word with the band, Tommy faced the floor and gestured for silence. 'I've been saving my voice for the past year or so for an occasion like this,' he announced. 'And Jessie's going to be kind enough to drown out my mistakes with the sax.' The dancehall was filled with a veritable Hampden Roar of approval.

A wave of pleasure surged through her to be holding an instrument again. She didn't know why she'd given up playing since going to live in Boyd Street, she'd just never felt the urge. She did now though, the hunger to play suddenly revitalized within her.

A tapping of the feet, one, two, three, and they were away. Immediately, she felt herself take control, every cell of her body knowing exactly what to do.

The big surprise for her was Tommy's singing voice. Not only was it not bad it was better than good. It had character and sexuality, a rasping greyness that was Glasgow personified.

But, apart from his voice, what impressed Jessie was the way Tommy was handling himself, reaching out for the audience through his personality to grab them and make them listen. He was not only charismatic, he was a natural performer. What a transformation from the shy lad she'd first met at Queen's Park Senior Secondary, she thought with an inward grin.

The number finished to tumultuous applause, which only died down when Tommy started singing again, this time Johnnie 'Cry Guy' Ray's, 'Such A Night'. Jessie and the band went with him.

When it was finished Tommy moved over to Jessie who'd been standing a little apart from him: his eyes were glowing, as were hers.

'That was fab!' she said, and, realizing he hadn't heard because of the battering waves of applause that were reverberating round the dancehall, put her mouth to his ear and repeated herself.

He nodded, then put his mouth to her ear. 'I was going to ask you later on tonight, but why not here! Will you marry me?'

She was sure she hadn't heard him right. 'What?' she screamed.

'Will you marry me?' he shouted back.

In a million years she'd never have imagined a proposal like this. 'Yes,' she yelled. 'Yes, I will.'

Her acceptance was drowned by the noise, but that didn't matter to him, he could see what her answer had been.

Tommy faced the audience, held up his hands and kept them there till he finally had a semblance of quiet. 'I have an announcement to make,' he stated.

Jessie unhooked the sax and placed it in its case, then laid the lanyard alongside it. What a day it had been. Tommy out of prison, the party, and now his proposal! She felt lightheaded with joy.

'I first met Jessie here years ago,' Tommy was saying. 'And I think I knew even then that I wanted to marry her. Well tonight I've proposed, and she's accepted. We'll be getting wed just as soon as I can make the necessary arrangements.'

The cheering and applause was the loudest yet. Unable to help herself, Jessie burst into tears. It was hardly the thing for the Queen of the Glasgow Teds to do, but she didn't care about that. At last she knew that she'd been right to follow her heart. A new chapter in her life was beginning. A better chapter than any that had gone before.

Jeannie was already in bed, fast asleep. In the kitchen, where Jessie had been sleeping in Tommy's inset bed, some spare sheets and blankets had been put out. Jeannie had tactfully avoided any mention of new sleeping arrangements now that Tommy was back, and Jessie had seen no reason to bring them up either.

'I'll stick the kettle on,' Jessie said, suddenly feeling shy and awkward.

Tommy stood staring at the sheets and blankets, then nodded. 'Aye, that would be best. I'll make a bed up in Mum's room for myself,' he said.

'There's no need for that,' she said softly, her back to him so he couldn't see her face.

'We'll be married soon enough. After waiting for so long what's a wee while longer?'

She laid out the cups and saucers. 'Will you stop havering, Tommy? Do you love me or don't you?'

He blinked. 'Of course I do. I've told you!'

'And I love you, and we're to be married. We're already living in the same house together. It would be downright silly not to share the same bed.' She paused in what she was doing, her hands shaking. 'All right?' she whispered.

He came up behind her, his arms around her. 'All right.'

Jessie was on the tram coming home from work. Following The Battle of Linton Street, and her picture appearing in the paper, she'd been sacked from the music shop, Mr Elvin telling her sniffily that he had no place for the likes of her in his establishment.

It was Jeannie who'd come to the rescue. The job in the laundry was no great shakes, but it kept the wolf from the door, for which Jessie was grateful. She tended the counter with a woman called Jane Lamont.

As the tram rattled along Jessie was worrying about Tommy who'd been going to drop by his old place of employment that afternoon to find out if they'd take him back. He hadn't said anything, but she knew he hadn't been holding out any great hope, and in truth neither had she – not after the new pictures that had appeared in the newspapers the previous week, showing Tommy's release from Barlinne.

The trouble was that jobs were hard to come by, times weren't good in Glasgow, and hadn't been since the war. In some areas every street corner you passed had a gathering of lounging, unemployed men on it, just passing away the day.

Thank goodness she and Jeannie were grafting, even with Tommy to feed they could aye get by on what the pair of them brought in, but it would be far from a life of luxury, that was sure.

She'd bought a copy of that night's *Evening Citizen* and was glancing through it. An item on page 2 now caught her attention: 'Lady Virginia Muir, formerly Lady Virginia Dunbarr, and daughter of the Earl of Clyde, her husband, Mr A Muir, and young son Cosmo Muir, were murdered by the Mau Mau at their farm in Kenya. . .' Jessie read it through twice unable to believe her eyes. There were no real details, only that Alec, his wife and son had been the sole Europeans on their farm when the attack had occurred. They'd been buried on the farm where they'd died.

What a terrible thing to happen. She left the paper open on her lap. It was funny how life turned out so differently to what you'd imagined it would be. Everything had seemed so clear cut when she'd been young. Alec would be a minister; she, she'd hoped, his wife. Instead he'd married a titled lady and become an African farm manager, while she'd become Queen of the Glasgow Teds, living in a slum.

Who could have foreseen his death so many miles from home – or her new life a world away from her past?

Closing her eyes she offered up a prayer for the soul of Alec Muir.

★   ★   ★

She found Tommy sitting at home staring moodily into the empty grate. It was obvious what the outcome of his excursion into town had been.

'No luck, eh?' she said, giving him a sympathetic smile.

Tommy roused himself from his reverie. 'I thought the bastarding boss was going to shit himself when I strolled in through his door. He went green with fright.'

Jessie filled the kettle and put it on the stove. She always made the tea as Jeannie came in after her. Jeannie always washed and put away the dishes.

'You'd think I was Genghis Khan and Attila the Hun rolled into one,' Tommy muttered.

'That's probably how he now sees you,' Jessie said gently. This was just what she'd feared. She gave Tommy a sideways look. 'If he was so scared of you couldn't you have done a wee bit of not-so-subtle persuasion? Like cleaning you nails with a flickie as you requested employment for a second time?'

Tommy laughed. It was rich to hear Jessie suggesting such a thing. But then he knew she wasn't advocating he use violence, just hint that the possibility could be there; make his reputation work for him rather than against him.

'To be honest, I considered doing something like that, but what if it backfired and he called the police as soon as I'd left him? It wasn't worth the risk.'

'Aye,' she said. 'I know. Everything's harder now.'

'It's not that big a problem. I'll soon find a job elsewhere,' he said in a confident tone, but she could hear that it lacked conviction.

'Do you want to postpone the wedding until you get work?' she asked quietly.

In answer, he grabbed her to him, and sat her on his knee. 'Don't think you're getting out of marrying me as easily as that. A week on Saturday and it's down to Martha Street where it'll be ring and paper. It'll take The

Big Yin Himself to stop us getting spliced, I promise you.'

Later that night, they decided to treat themselves to a night out. They went into a pub for a couple of drinks and there decided to head for a club in the Broomielaw where they'd gone together several times before Tommy had been sent to Barlinne.

The Omar Khayyam – a pretentious name for a club Jessie had always thought – was a place where the arty set hung out. It served drinks and simple meals, and the babble of talk was usually about philosophy, literature or the theatre rather than music or sports.

At least that was how the Omar Khayyam had been the last time they'd been there, but in the intervening eighteen months all that had changed.

To begin with, the club had a new management who had gutted the premises from top to bottom. The mouldering Arabian décor had been replaced by Hessian wallpaper, a great deal of plastic, and spotlights that hung from the ceiling in clusters, making Jessie think that many-eyed monsters were peering down at her. The only thing about the club that remained the same was the name.

As soon as they went inside Tommy and Jessie were hailed by several Teds who neither Tommy or Jessie knew, but who recognized them instantly. Drinks were conjured up and pressed on Tommy and Jessie, and when those drinks were finished more appeared.

The music before had been modern jazz, which Jessie had a taste for, but that had also changed, as they now found out.

A nattily attired chap bounded onto the stage area, and a hush fell amongst the clientele who were as different from the previous clientele as the music was going to turn out to be.

'Ladies and gentlemen, I'd like you to put your hands

together for one of Glasgow's sons who's made a big success in the South. Down there he's taken them by storm with what can only be termed his own individual way of doing things. I am, of course, referring to the one, the only *Lonnie Donegan!*'

'Who's Lonnie Donegan? Never heard of him,' Tommy whispered to Jessie, who shrugged; she'd never heard of Donegan either.

Lonnie Donegan turned out to be a flat-faced young man with a shock of hair that gave the appearance of standing up from his head as though in fright. Donegan cracked jokes as his band formed up behind him. They can't be serious, Jessie thought, for they didn't have instruments – at least not the conventional sort.

There was a tea chest with a broom handle sticking up from it, and a gut string running from the top of the handle to the chest itself. It wasn't until they started playing that Jessie realized this was a primitive bass. Besides the tea chest there was an empty suitcase, a partially galvanized washboard, a seven-gallon Jug and a kazoo.

'What is this?' Jessie whispered to one of the Teds who'd been buying her and Tommy drinks.

'It's called Skiffle.'

Jessie recalled then that she'd read something about Skiffle being popular in the Twenties and a name, The Mound City Blowers, popped into her mind, but this would be the first time she'd either heard or seen it.

'Rock Island Line,' Lonnie Donegan announced.

It worked surprisingly well, Jessie thought as the number got under way and Donegan certainly had star quality that stood out a mile.

'Is he a real musician?' she asked the Ted who'd told her what it was they were hearing.

'I think he played with Ken Colyer for a while, banjo or something like that.'

That impressed Jessie. Ken Colyer was well respected, as was Chris Barber who also played with him.

'I like this,' Tommy said to Jessie, who agreed with him. She liked it too.

They got smashing weather for the wedding, but September often produced sunny days for Glasgow.

When they arrived at Martha Street in a hired car Jessie gasped to see the crowds, mostly Teds from all over the city, but there were a contingent of the press and spectators come to see the King and Queen of the Glasgow Teds at their wedding.

The Boyd Street Boys had gone on ahead of Tommy and Jessie, and now formed twin lines – just as they'd done in the Cameo on the night of the party – from the car to the door of the Register Office. As Tommy helped Jessie from the car the photographers went daft. So many flashbulbs popped it was like silent machine gun fire.

The reporters tried to get to speak to them in person, but were held back by the Boyd Street Boys who linked arms as if they were policemen.

There were policemen present as well, but they'd wisely restricted their presence to the fringes where it was their intention to stay unless trouble broke out. Which, thanks to the festive mood, it didn't.

Tommy, because it was expected of him, had insisted on wearing a drape for the occasion. Jessie had therefore decided that if she had to dress in Ted gear she'd do so spectacularly. She wore a cream-coloured pencil skirt with matching mesh stockings and four-inch stilettos. Her top was a man's cream-coloured shirt, with brass links at the cuffs, and old-fashioned brass bands on her upper arms. Round her neck she sported a cream-coloured tie done in a Windsor Knot. She'd combed her hair in the fashion now identified with her, hanging straight and parted in the middle. She had black shadow on her eyelids, and on her left cheek she'd painted a white butterfly which she'd outlined in black.

183

Tommy, in contrast to her cream, was dressed entirely in black, for once without rings or any other metal adornment.

Glasgow had never seen the like before.

When the ceremony was over they emerged to a cloud of confetti and cheers from the Teds. Then it was back into the car, a repeat of the silent machine gun fire, and off home to Govanhill and the Cathcart Road T.A. Hall where the reception was being held.

Invites to the reception had been restricted to immediate family – Jessie had sent an invitation to her parents but hadn't even received a reply – the Boyd Street Boys, the Boyd Street neighbours, and some 'friendlies' and other pals from the Cameo. All in all, 260-odd people crowded into the hall.

There was a large cardboard box at the end of the bar and into that went cash donations to help cover the cost of the reception.

At ten o'clock after a marvellous party, Tommy and Jessie decided to be off. Not that they were going on honeymoon, there was no question of that. They were headed back to Boyd Street where they'd be alone for the night as Jeannie had arranged to stay with a friend.

They left the hall surreptitiously, Jessie via a trip to the toilet, Tommy out a side exit. The reason they went in this fashion was because they didn't trust the Boys not to have some sort of surprise cooked up, and as they later found out, such a surprise had indeed been scheduled. So they escaped that.

Once home, Jessie kicked off her shoes and sank into a chair. Tommy produced a bottle of whisky that he'd lifted from the reception, but she didn't want to know about any more alcohol, it was tea for her. Tommy poured himself a stiff dram, and said he'd make the tea.

'Are you sure you know how to?' she teased. It was rare he turned a hand to anything round the house that came under the umbrella of 'women's work'.

'Go and raffle your doughnut,' he said indignantly. 'I can make a pot of tea with the best of them, as you will soon find out.'

While he was making the tea he said suddenly, 'It would have been nice to go doon the water for a couple of days, Largs or Dunoon maybe.'

'It doesn't matter to me,' she said, her eyes on him. 'I'm happy just being with you.'

He smiled, but he continued to feel guilty.

'We'll do it later, after you've got that job,' she suggested.

'Aye, and we'll make it a fortnight, not a couple of measly days,' he said with false enthusiasm.

She got up and put her arms around him. 'It was a grand wedding Tommy, I couldn't have asked for better.'

'Oh? And how does it feel to be Mrs Thomas McBride?'

'Lovely.'

'What happens if I never get another job?' he asked quietly, voicing the fear that had been growing daily within him since being released from jail.

'We'll cope somehow. We've got each other, and in the end that's all that really matters,' she answered softly, running a hand through his hair, and thinking how much she felt for this man who'd come to be so dear to her.

She was naked, held in a spreadeagled position by the four grinning Teds, and an equally naked Ken Young was leering down at her. 'First me, then the others, each in turn,' he crooned. She tried to scream, but for some reason no sound would come. She twisted her head this way and that, seeing the five faces watching her expand and contract, expand and contract, over and over. If only she could escape, if only she could jump up and run away from this terrible place, if only Ken Young and the other four would disappear, if only . . . 'And when we're finished we'll go back to the beginning and all do it again,' Ken Young laughed. She couldn't make a sound, no matter how hard she tried. No! she screamed in her brain. No! No! NO!

Jessie came awake with a start to find she was drenched in sweat and shaking. She hugged herself to calm herself down.

There were variations of the nightmare. In some of them Young and the others got as far as actually raping her. In others it was just the threat, over and over again.

She wiped the wet from her forehead using the sleeve of her nightdress. The nightmares weren't occurring as often as they once had, but she was certain that she'd never be entirely free of them, that they'd be with her for the rest of her life.

It would be a good hour before she'd get back to sleep, it always was. She lay in the darkness and thought about Tommy snoring by her side.

It was three months now since he'd got out of Barlinne, and he still didn't have a job, not even the sniff of one. He hadn't spoken since their wedding night about his fear that he never would find another job, but she knew the fear was still there, she'd seen it in his eyes when he wasn't aware she was watching him.

If only she could do something to help, but what? If she'd known an employer she could have approached on his behalf she'd happily have done so. But she didn't know any employers.

She was being as supportive and encouraging as she could, but it didn't seem enough. She wanted to do more; felt she should be doing more.

If only he hadn't been King of the Glasgow Teds, if only he hadn't received that publicity for The Battle of Linton Street and the huge amount of coverage that had accompanied their wedding. If only. . .

When she finally dropped off again she dreamt again. In this one Tommy was a successful botanist, who

186

looked like everyone else, and he and she lived in a nice part of town.

That was a lovely dream.

It was Jessie's twenty-third birthday, and they were celebrating at the Cameo. Tommy was in great form, as he'd been all day. He'd been out in the morning after breakfast, returning with a bunch of flowers. She'd thanked him for them, then asked where he'd got them. His reply, delivered with a cheeky grin, had been, ask no questions, get no lies. She'd known from that he hadn't paid for them, and suspected he might have pinched them out of a greenhouse somewhere.

Tommy had a fair old skinful in him, though he wasn't drunk, just extremely happy. They'd been to the Seaforth Bar before coming in, and as was always the case there at the weekend they hadn't paid for anything, others being only too eager to buy for them.

Tommy excused himself and went over to talk to Jack Gowrie who, after a few seconds, glanced in her direction. Something was planned, she thought, that look of Jack's gave the game away.

Tommy left Jack and crossed to Sammy McGlinchie who was soon nodding vigorously at whatever Tommy was saying. So Sammy was in on it too. She hoped it was nothing that was going to embarrass her.

Tommy and Sammy disappeared into the crowd, and when she glanced back to where Jack had been it was to find that he also had done a vanishing act.

Minutes passed without either of that threesome reappearing, then the band completed their session and left the rostrum for a break, taking their instruments with them.

The lights suddenly went out, plunging the dancehall into darkness. A girl screamed, another was heard to say loudly, 'Keep your hands to yourself you dirty bastard!'

'What's going on?' a female voice demanded.

187

'Bugger if I know hen,' a male voice replied.

A single green light snapped on to reveal Tommy standing on the rostrum. Jessie could make out that there were others on the rostrum with him.

'As most of you know, it's my wife Jessie's birthday today, and to give her a bit of a giggle, because I know she likes one, me and a couple of the lads have organized the following. Jessie darling, this is for, and dedicated to you. A brand new band, folks! The Boyd Street Skifflers!'

The green light snapped off, and the normal lighting came back on. Tommy, Jake, Sammy and Jake 'The Rake' Stewart could now all be seen, and with them was the same weird assortment of instruments that Tommy and Jessie had watched Lonnie Donegan and his band play at the Omar Khayyam.

Jessie sniggered and put her hand to her mouth. Jack was on the tea chest and broom handle, Sammy the washboard, and Jake 'The Rake' the seven-gallon jug and kazoo. Tommy was the singer.

'Rock Island Line,' Tommy announced, and gave Jessie a broad wink.

There had been several times during the past couple of weeks when Tommy had gone off mysteriously in the evening, not telling her where he was going as he usually did. Now she knew that he'd been practising for this.

It might have been meant as a joke, but that wasn't at all how they sounded. They were extremely good, especially Tommy.

And that was when the great idea came to her. She sat there, forgetting everything around her, wondering why she hadn't thought of this before.

She said nothing to Tommy until they were home and getting ready for bed. The kitchen was lovely and warm as Jeannie had had a fire going all night.

Jessie sat curled in a chair, a shawl round her shoulders,

188

a cup of Ovaltine in her hand. Tommy was just getting into his pyjamas.

'I've had a thought,' she said as casually as she could.

'Oh, aye?'

'Tell me one thing, though, do you trust my musical judgement?'

He stopped and stared at her. What a funny thing to ask. 'You know I do. What are you leading up to?'

She took a deep breath. 'Just that I think you're a smashing singer. Not only that, but you put yourself across well and you know how to handle an audience.'

'Well, thanks very much,' he grinned, chuffed with himself. Such a compliment from Jessie was a compliment indeed.

But Jessie hadn't finished yet. 'The others who got up with you, can any of them play real instruments?'

'Sammy knows a few tunes on the mouth organ, but that's about it. Why?'

'So why did you choose them?'

'I put it to Jack and he roped in the two others. There weren't any special reasons. Does it matter?'

She shook her head. 'No. It's just that you all worked so well as a group.' She was watching him closely. 'In fact you were so good that I think you should try and make a go of it together.'

He stopped tying the cord of his pyjama trousers and looked at her sharply. What was she havering on about now? 'A go at what?'

Jessie was nearly jumping with excitement. 'A go as a skiffle band.'

'You mean do it properly. For real?'

'You're looking for a job, why not this? I'd bet anything your band would be popular.'

He sat facing her, dazed by her suggestion. 'Why should our band be popular?' he asked slowly.

She gave a wry smile, sometimes he was so naive. 'Because of you. You're the King of the Glasgow Teds, wherever you play the Teds in the area will flock to hear you. And then the 'straights' will come to get a charge out of being in the same hall as an outlaw like yourself.' Her eyes were sparkling.

But Tommy didn't look delighted. He had a vision of all those 'straights' coming to gawp at him, and it made his flesh creep. 'That's what they did to Sitting Bull,' he said slowly.

'Sitting Bull?'

'They put him on show, made him no more than a circus clown. Is that what you want for me?'

'Of course not.'

'I'd be a laughing stock.'

'You'd be nothing of the sort. Once they've heard you no one will be laughing. I promise I know I'm right.'

Tommy didn't like the idea at all. It was one thing to get up at the Cameo, those were his friends and mates, but to get up in front of a lot of strangers was something else. Aye, and it frightened him, too. He'd rather fight a Ken Young any time.

'The whole notion's preposterous,' he said shortly, ready to dismiss it completely.

Jessie was beginning to lose her temper. Why did he have to be so obstinate? Here was the perfect solution to their problems, and all he could do was turn up his nose at it.

'Give me one reason, one *good* reason, why you shouldn't have a go?'

'I just have. It would be demeaning.'

'It seems to me to be far more demeaning to be jobless and living off your mother and me. Do you want to go on accepting handouts for the rest of your life?'

He went white as a sheet. How could she say such a thing? How could she be so cruel?

'I won't turn myself into a circus clown for you or for anyone else,' he replied.

'But you wouldn't be. You've got real talent.'

'No.' He turned away from her.

'Tommy. . .'

'I said no, and I mean no! Having a giggle like we did the night is one thing, what you're proposing quite another. And that's the end of it.'

'Silly bugger,' she muttered into her cup.

He whirled on her. 'What did you say?'

'I said you were a silly bugger!' she repeated loudly.

His gaze went to the wall. 'Sssh! You'll wake up Ma.'

'Good, then she can tell you you're a silly bugger as well!'

He stalked stiffly to the bed and got in, turning on to his side so that his back was to her.

She stayed in the chair till long after the fire was out and was so cold that she had to make a move.

She knew he was only pretending to be asleep.

What an end to her birthday! But that was unimportant. The real disappointment was his reaction to her idea. He so *badly* needed a job. As time passed he was getting more and more moody and ill-tempered.

Well she wouldn't give up her idea of the band, it was too good an idea.

'Jessie?'

Closing her eyes she pretended *she* was asleep.

Jessie was doing a bit of darning while listening to the Light Programme on the wireless, Jeannie was at a friend's and Tommy was out having a couple of pints with some of the Boyd Street Boys.

The socks she was darning were well past it, but she wouldn't be throwing them away, money was too tight for that. Despite the state they were in they'd just have to last a while longer.

She glanced up in surprise when she heard the outside door click open, she wasn't expecting Tommy back for at least another hour.

She leapt to her feet, the darning tumbling to the floor, the moment she saw him. There was blood all down the side of his face and his drape was ripped.

191

She rushed to his side. 'What happened to you?'

'Fight.' He collapsed into the nearest chair with a heavy sigh.

'Are you hurt?' she asked, kneeling beside him, her brow furrowed with concern.

'Just a bit. He nicked my cheek with his razor and he hit me on the shoulder with a hammer. That's fair giving me gyp. But I'm all right.'

The blood on his face had dried. As far as she could tell he was right, it was only a small nick about half an inch in length. She tried not to think what Tommy's face might have been like had that razor really connected.

She switched off the wireless, filled the kettle and put it on the stove. She wanted hot water to wash the blood away.

Returning to Tommy, she helped him out of his drape, then, being as gentle as she could, took his shirt off. 'Oh my God,' she whispered. His left shoulder was black and blue and swollen.

'I don't think anything's broken,' he said, flexing his fingers.

She had a feel of the shoulder. 'It's amazing, but it seems to be intact.' But it was a right sore shoulder all the same. She'd put a hot compress on it, that would help.

'How did the fight come about?' she asked, hunting in the press for the flannel for the compress.

'We were having a quiet drink in the Albion Arms when in comes this young Ted who announces he's been searching for me to challenge me for my title.'

'Had you seen him before?'

Tommy shook his head. 'Never clapped eyes on him till he walked into the Albion. He was from Garthamlock, pretty far out on the north side.'

Jessie's hands were shaking as she poured some of the hot water into a bowl, then put the kettle back on the gas. She'd clean up his face first, then tend his shoulder.

Tommy went on. 'So he and I went round the rear of the pub and got stuck into it. I'll say this for him, he was a bonny fighter, if he'd been a wee bit bigger or stronger he might well have had me.'

'Was he badly injured?' Jessie asked, gently daubing at his face.

'Jack rang 999 and told them to send an ambulance, so he'll be in hospital now.'

She knelt beside him, her hand on his. 'What future is there for you in all this love?' she asked softly.

'I didn't exactly *apply* to be King of the Glasgow Teds,' he snapped back.

She continued, 'Tommy, listen to me. You're on an eventual hiding if you go on as you are. You've been made King, but there will always be someone after your crown. Fight will follow fight will follow fight until one day you lose. You'll be the one coughing up blood or with a face razored to mincemeat. I can't bear the thought of that happening to you Tommy.' Warm tears sprang to her eyes.

'What can I do?' he asked in an agonized whisper.

'You know what I think you can do. You have two things going for you: your voice and the fact you *are* King of the Glasgow Teds.'

Tommy gnawed his lip. The skiffle band idea, they were back to that. It still frightened him to think of getting up in front of strangers, but it frightened him even more to think of being maimed or mutilated in some alley fight.

'You need an escape door from all this Tommy. The skiffle band could be that door. Will you at least give it a try, *please*?' she pleaded.

He stared at her lovingly, wondering what marvellous thing he'd done to be rewarded with his Jessie. 'You're wrong about me only having two things going for me, I have three, and the third, by far the best of all, is you.'

Her heart swelled with relief. She'd won him round, he was going to do it.

*   *   *

His singing was terrible, completely off key. The Tommy McBride Skiffle Band, due to open at the Yoker Palais the night after next, was in Jeannie's kitchen rehearsing their numbers, with Jessie supervising as Musical Director.

Jessie glanced at Jack who raised his eyes to heaven. If Tommy sang like this at Yoker it would be a disaster.

Finally she couldn't stand any more of it, and gestured them quiet. 'If I was outside listening in I'd think you were a chicken having its neck wrung,' she said to Tommy.

Tommy scowled at her, and stuck his hands deep into his pockets. 'I always said this was a bloody daft idea.'

'There's nothing daft about it!'

'Maybe Tommy's right,' Jake muttered.

Jessie ran a hand through her hair. There was no point in continuing with the rehearsal, she decided. The more it went on the worse Tommy became.

She told them that was it for the evening, and no, there wouldn't be another rehearsal the following evening, they were as ready as they were ever going to be.

Jack, Sammy and Jake took the cue and got ready to leave. Jessie saw them to the front door. 'Don't worry,' she whispered, 'I'll sort Tommy out. He'll be at his best at Yoker, you have my word on that.'

When she returned to the kitchen she found Tommy staring morosely out the window down into the back court. His hunched stance warned her that if she said the wrong thing he'd go off like a Guy Fawkes banger, and try to get out of the Yoker date.

'Can I get you anything?' she asked sweetly.

'I could murder a drink,' he muttered, knowing there was fat chance of that. Money was so tight it was some time since there had been booze in the house.

But he was wrong. Jessie had a large bottle of strong cider planked, and this she now got out.

He turned in surprise at the sound of the familiar chink, cider wasn't exactly a favourite of his, but it was a lot better than nothing.

'Now what's bothering you?' she asked, handing him a bubbling glass, half the contents of which he immediately downed in one swallow.

'Nothing.'

'It's obvious something is, so why not tell me?'

He shrugged and drank more cider.

Patience, she told herself, it would come, all she had to do was stand there and wait.

He finished the glass, and helped himself to more. 'Call it stage fright, nerves, or what you will, I suppose it's that,' he said suddenly, the words tumbling out in a rush.

Of course, she should have realized. He was terrified of what lay in front of him.

'I'm just worried sick that I'll make an idiot of myself,' he went on.

'You won't do that if you sing as you can, I promise you Tommy.'

'Just the thought of going out there makes me all tight inside, and if I feel that way now God know what I'll be like come the actual event.'

'A minute or two after you've started you'll be wondering why you were so worried,' she said reassuringly. 'It's just nerves.'

'Maybe so, but those first couple of minutes are going to be hell. What if my voice seizes on me like it did tonight? They'll laugh me off the stage, especially the 'straights' and I couldn't abide that.'

She topped his cider up yet again. If nerves did cause his voice to play up then they did have a problem. His singing career would be over before it had even begun.

'Don't forget that all the Boyd Street Boys and their lassies, will be there to give you support. It won't be all strangers, your friends will be there as well.'

Tommy began to relax a little. Jessie talked and talked, relaxing him even more. Their pals would be there when the doors opened, she assured him, she'd make sure word got round. She continued talking, but wasn't entirely satisfied with the result. What he still needed was an extra confidence booster to take him through those crucial opening minutes.

It was later when they were having a bite of supper that the answer came to her. She smiled at the memory of how the trick had worked on her and her class.

'Do you remember Mr Harrison at Queen's Park School?' she asked Tommy suddenly.

'Of course, he was a geography teacher.'

She went on to explain what she had in mind, and when she'd finished speaking Tommy was smiling, the first real smile she'd seen in days.

'How many do you think?' Tommy asked Jessie. They were in the wings of the Yoker Palais prior to the band going on stage. The Yoker Palais had a real stage that was at least three times the size of the rostrum at the Cameo.

Jessie peeked round the side of the heavy velvet curtain to see that it was already blue with fug in the hall which was nearly three-quarters full. That in itself was something – it was another hour till the pubs closed, the traditional time for most folk to come to the dancing.

It was gratifying to know such a large number had turned up, and so early, for the Yoker Palais had been doing rotten business of late. Tommy, as she'd predicted, was definitely a draw.

'Five, six hundred maybe,' she said to Tommy who, but it might have been the light, appeared to pale fractionally.

She squeezed his arm. 'You've nothing to fear, honest. Your voice was in cracking form when you sang for me this afternoon. Do Harrison's trick and you'll have them in the palm of your hand right from the off. It always worked for Harrison with a new class, so there's no reason why it shouldn't work for you.'

McLean, the manager, appeared. 'All set?'

Jessie glanced at Tommy, then Jack, Sammy and Jake. Jake gave her a cheery thumbs up sign.

'All set,' she confirmed.

'Good luck,' McLean smiled, and walked on stage to do an intro.

The band wouldn't be taking their instruments on with them, those were already behind the heavy velvet curtains. With the instruments was another little item that Jessie herself had put there, an empty biscuit tin. Harrison had always used a wastepaper basket, but she'd thought a tin box more appropriate to the occasion.

She was desperately nervous for Tommy, and trying not to show it. Everything depended on his confidence in those opening minutes.

'The Tommy McBride Skiffle Band!' McLean announced, completing his intro, and led the applause.

The curtains parted and Jack, Sammy and Jake 'The Rake' strolled on.

A buzz of expectation filled the air as the threesome took up their instruments, a buzz that became a questioning mutter. Where was the big man himself? Where was McBride?

Jessie let the tension stretch and stretch. 'Now!' she finally whispered.

Tommy made for the microphone, strolling as the other three had done. Just before the mike he encountered the tin box which was so placed that it looked as though it had been left there accidentally. He stopped to glower down at the box, as if furious that something was in his way. The audience stilled, wondering what was going to happen next.

With a snarl of pretended rage, Tommy lashed out with his right foot to send the tin box to the other side of the stage where it made a fearful clatter as it landed. He whirled on the watchers, his expression one that dared anyone to speak up against what he'd just done.

The moment was electric – and pure theatre.

'Aah!' gasped an ecstatic girl near the front, the only sound heard throughout the hall.

Tommy's nervousness subsided. He had them right where he wanted them. He was the boss in complete control. His reputation and Mr Harrison's little trick, had ensured that.

He completed his journey to the mike, stared out over the hall then slowly allowed his face to soften into a smile. 'Rock Island Line,' he said.

In the wings Jessie breathed a sigh of relief. Tommy would be all right now. And what a lovely piece of acting, he'd fooled even her, and she'd known what was going to happen.

She mentally thanked Mr Harrison, who'd used the trick to establish his authority with each new class. In the door he'd come, glower at the wastepaper basket in his path, and bang would go the basket, spilling its contents everywhere, and the class would be instantly awed into subjugation. None of the previous classes ever told the new class what to expect, or that Mr Harrison was in reality the sweetest man imaginable.

By the end of the opening set Jessie knew the Tommy McBride Skiffle Band was a great success. When those who'd gone to the pub prior to coming on to the dance-hall finally arrived they found the Hall Full signs out front, which hadn't happened at the Yoker Palais in years. Inside it was packed to bursting.

Jessie judged that about sixty per cent of those in the hall were Teds and their girls, the rest 'straights'. Both groups were quite clearly enjoying the music.

In the middle of the final set the manager appeared beside Jessie and asked her to follow him into the passageway outside.

'The lads have done well, I'm pleased. Do they have a booking for next weekend?' he asked.

'Not so far, but after tonight we shouldn't have any trouble in lining one up,' she said confidently, knowing what was coming next.

'How about them appearing here again then?' he proposed.

'Fine,' she said after a moment's consideration. 'But the fee goes up by half.'

McLean gave a small laugh. This girl was a born dealer, he'd realized that right from the beginning. 'Let's say an extra tenner because I think you're the prettiest lassie here tonight.'

Jessie ignored the flattery, he wouldn't get round her that way. 'It's half as much again or we go elsewhere,' she stated firmly.

'Maybe it's only a flash in the pan, maybe by next week the novelty will have worn off,' he challenged.

'If you thought that you wouldn't be standing here discussing them now.' she said shrewdly.

She had him there, and he could see she knew she did. 'All right, it's a deal. Half as much again it is. But with one provision.'

She became wary. 'And what's that?'

'You never forget it was me gave them their start,' he said.

Three weeks later, on a cold Wednesday night in February of 1958, Tommy was waiting at the tramstop for Jessie when she arrived back from work.

Her face lit up with pleasure when she saw him. His coming to meet her was a treat. 'Well, this is a surprise,' she laughed, hugging him.

'I've got something to show you,' he said mysteriously.

Right away her curiosity was aroused. 'What?' she demanded, hooking her arm in his.

'Wait and see.'

He led her along then turned into Allison Street, which ran parallel to Boyd Street.

'No hints even?'

'No hints even,' he laughed, delighting in her excitement and impatience.

Allison Street was older than Boyd Street and looked

it. It was also a far longer street, and wider, with shops dotted along its length.

The close he headed for was next to a newsagent's. Tommy took her to the second landing where he produced a yale key. With a flourish, he opened the door on a room and kitchen, similar to Jeannie's. It was empty now, but had been well cared for. She couldn't imagine why Tommy had brought her here.

'What do you think?' he asked eagerly.

'About what?'

'This.' His hand gestured around the room.

The penny dropped, and so did her spirits. 'You mean for us?'

He nodded. 'I heard on the grapevine that it was going, so I went straight to Meikle the factor and said we'd take it.'

Jessie gazed again round the room that overlooked Allison Street, but didn't reply. The wallpaper was hideous and the room itself seemed to speak of nothing but defeat.

'You don't seem pleased.'

She forced a smile on to her face. 'I am, yes. Of course I am.'

'It's a place of our own, Jessie.'

'Oh aye, another Buckingham Palace.'

'There's no need to be like that. I thought all that mattered was that we were together.'

'I'm sorry, it's just that it's so . . . so unexpected.'

He looked at her to say more.

After a pause she went on. 'I just thought we'd stay with Jeannie a while longer. Then, when we did move, we'd move right out of Govanhill altogether. I had dreams of us buying a house beside the Linn Park.'

His eyes gleamed. 'Do you really think that one day we could do that?'

'Why not? A year from now our lives could be entirely transformed.'

A house beside the Linn Park! 'I'll see Meikle again tomorrow and tell him we've changed our minds,' he said.

'No you don't. You were right to grab this house, we do need our own place. Just as long as we both know it's only temporary.'

'You really have set your sights high for me, haven't you?'

'I love you.'

'Well,' he laughed, 'There's going to be one big advantage of being in our own house, we won't have to wait till Ma goes to bed at night.'

'Is that the real reason you're so keen to take this place?'

'Can you think of a better?'

The Tommy McBride Skiffle Band was playing Logan's Dancehall in the London Road, and, as was usual wherever they appeared, the hall was mobbed with an appreciative audience.

Jessie was out front, mingling with the crowd. She liked to do that at least once a night to hear some of the comments made about Tommy and the band. One such comment now caused her to turn and stare at the speaker, for the truth of what he'd said was so blindingly obvious that she couldn't think why she hadn't seen it herself.

'Aye, you're right, Shughie, they should be doing their own songs,' a second Ted agreed with the first.

Their *own* songs, of course! So far, all their numbers were hits by, or closely identified with, already popular artists like Lonnie Donegan, the Vipers, Chas McDevitt and Nancy Whiskey, Johnny Duncan and the Bluegrass Boys etc.

If Tommy and the band ever hoped to join that group they could only do so playing original material. Therefore original material was the next step on the ladder. The problem was: who was going to write it?

'But where do we get original material?' Tommy asked. He was sitting in front of a roaring fire with a dram.

'London, I suppose. That's where the songwriters seem to be,' Jessie suggested.

Tommy sipped his drink, enjoying the heat of the fire washing over him. 'London!' London seemed a universe away.

Jessie was well away with her new idea. 'I could go next week and do the rounds.'

He didn't like the thought of her going to London on her own. On the other hand, he could hardly accompany her, the band was booked for four nights during the coming week and five the week after.

'What do you say?'

'I agree we should have our own material,' he said slowly. 'But I'm not so sure about you and London.'

She could read his mind. It amused her that he thought she might not be able to take care of herself. Men! Their egos made them forget how resourceful, capable women were.

Tommy's brow knotted in thought. He finished his dram and poured himself another from the bottle by his chair. Finally, he said, 'What you're proposing is to go to London and take pot luck at what you can find. Right? But it seems to me that it would be far better if instead of taking pot luck we had a number written specifically for the band.'

'You mean get a songwriter to come here from London, meet you, and then write his song?'

He shook his head. 'We could do it that way. But aren't there any Scottish songwriters around? If we're going to do new material, then it should be about us and the way we are. I don't want some Englishman telling me what my life is like.'

Jessie looked doubtful. 'I've never heard of any,' she said dismally.

The next thing Tommy said took her completely by surprise. 'What about you? Didn't you write music at one time? There certainly isn't anyone who understands me better than you.'

202

Jessie stared at him in astonishment. 'I have composed a bit, but that was years ago at school, and the sort of thing I composed was nothing like what you need.'

But Tommy wasn't to be put off. This time he was the one with the idea. 'Music is second nature to you, you know that. And you understand skiffle as well as anyone. So why don't you just see what you can come up with? We've nothing to lose, after all, except perhaps a wee bit of time.'

Write a skiffle number! Could she do it? But it had been so long . . .

'You told me to have a go as a singer, and that worked. So why shouldn't you have a go as a songwriter? You've certainly got more musical ability than I do.'

'What you're asking isn't as easy as you make it sound,' she answered, although it was clear from her expression that her resistance was weakening.

'Nothing worthwhile is every easy, you know that.'

'It's not just the music itself, there are also the lyrics, I've never tried my hand at those.'

'Well now's your chance,' he replied firmly.

She'd got herself into a proper pickle this time. How had her original idea come round to this?

'Perhaps a Glasgow theme, the local punters would certainly love that,' Tommy went on.

Jessie chewed on a strand of hair and thought about Glasgow. The docks, the shipbuilding, the heavy industry, the slums, the fierce pride of every Glaswegian. There was enough material, that was for sure.

'Well,' she said slowly, 'I could start working on something tomorrow night. But I'm not convinced I can pull it off.'

But she did. When her first number, 'King Of The Glasgow Teds', was introduced the following week it was the hit of the evening.

6

Jessie glanced at the clock on the mantelpiece, saw it was nearly 3 a.m., and groaned. She was going to be out on her feet at work tomorrow, but she wanted this new number finished so Tommy and the band would have a fair crack at rehearsing it before introducing it Friday night at the Locarno.

This would be the fourth number she'd written, and all of them had been extremely well received. The more new material the band had the better. The plan was that they'd eventually perform nothing but their own stuff, but that amount of songs was going to take a while for her to produce. She didn't want to churn out just any old rubbish.

Tommy was asleep in bed. They had spent the evening talking again about getting a disc cut, but that was proving a lot harder than they'd anticipated.

They'd had a demo made, reproduced, and sent off to quite a few London record companies, but so far they hadn't had a bite. It was becoming more and more apparent that talent and determination alone wasn't enough to get on, you needed contacts and that was one thing they didn't have.

But they'd come, she was sure of it. The thing to do was keep on building Tommy and the band as much as possible, eventually somebody would have to take notice.

If only they could get some wireless time, or on the newly popular television, either would be great.

The tune she'd been working on started buzzing again in her head, and her pencil flew. When she finally crawled in beside Tommy it was past four o'clock.

She was up again at seven.

*　　*　　*

The Locarno was crammed to capacity. There were Hall Full signs out front, as there had been every night Tommy and the band had played.

Jessie was in the dressing room while Tommy and the band were out on stage; from where she was sitting she could hear them performing her latest number. They'd done it twice already that night, and it had gone down a bomb each time. It was exhilarating to know that people could get so much enjoyment out of something she'd written.

She fell to thinking about the walk round inside the hall that she'd just had – or tried to have. Why, there must have been two and a half to three thousand people there, possibly even more. So how much did that mean the Locarno was taking in for the night?

She took out a pen and some paper, and made a calculation. The figure produced caused her to purse her lips in a silent whistle.

She compared that figure with what Tommy and the band were being paid, and the comparison was hardly a good one.

She decided this needed further thinking on.

Mr Bojangles wasn't only the largest dancehall in Glasgow, but the largest in all Scotland.

Ross Wylie was the manager. He was a wee, rat-faced man who twitched a great deal and smoked incessantly. 'The fee you ask is out of the question Mrs McBride,' he was saying. 'It's far far too high.'

Jessie smiled at him from across his desk. 'I admit it's a higher fee than anyone else in Scotland has been paid, but Tommy McBride will fill your hall for you, Mr Wylie, I can guarantee that.'

Wylie gave a thin, condescending smile. 'Tommy might have filled the Locarno, but Mr Bojangles is another matter entirely. We're double the Locarno's size.'

'I'm well aware of the size of your dancehall, Mr Wylie. But the sum I asked is what we want to play Mr Bojangles,' she answered, putting the very minimum of expression into her voice.

'Impossible, Mrs McBride,' Wylie said emphatically. 'Absolutely impossible.'

Jessie, keeping her face impassive, stared at Wylie. She knew he was keen for Tommy and the band to play Mr Bojangles, because they were rapidly becoming the hottest musical property in Scotland. The odds were in her favour.

The silence between Jessie and Wylie stretched on and on. She continued to watch him impassively, giving nothing away.

Finally it was he who broke the silence. 'If I do agree the fee you're asking, and Tommy fails to fill Mr Bojangles, then Mr Bojangles could be out of pocket. And that would be bad business,' he said reasonably.

That was a lie, Jessie thought, and a rather clumsy one at that. Mr Bojangles didn't have to be filled for the dancehall to make a profit on the deal, he must think her stupid if he imagined she'd swallow that.

'You're the one who came to us,' she said evenly.

'I'm a businessman, Mrs McBride,' he blustered. 'Not a patron of the arts.'

She counted twenty inside her head. 'Then I propose a deal whereby Mr Bojangles can't possibly lose.'

Wylie was immediately interested. 'And what sort of deal would that be?' he demanded.

'Put us on a percentage of the gross. That way you can't possibly lose on your fee.'

A percentage of the gross? He'd never heard of that being done in Scotland before. He knew some of the big stars, and particularly the Americans, arranged such deals in London, but London was London, and Glasgow Glasgow. 'It's novel,' he conceded.

'And fair. To Mr Bojangles as bookers, and to Tommy and the band as performers.'

He took his time about lighting a cigar while he thought about her proposition. 'What kind of percentage did you have in mind?' he asked at last.

She contained herself till she was out of the dancehall, and round the corner. There she let out a loud whoop of delight that startled several passers-by. A percentage of the gross was what she'd wanted all along, not the high fee she'd originally asked for. And what's more, she'd got a full percent and a half more than what she's had in mind when she'd walked into his office.

Now that the precedent had been set she fully intended that every contract from there on in would be on similar lines, and written down as a safeguard.

Ross Wylie might think himself a clever businessman, but she didn't consider him very clever, not very clever at all.

As was always the case on a Sunday, Glasgow was dead. It was a beautiful June day with the sun pouring down, making the area appear even more bleak, Jessie thought, as she stared out the room window into Allison Street.

Suddenly, she wanted away from there, if only temporarily. Maybe they could catch a red bus for the coast. They could go to Largs, or Dunoon, or Seamill. The day was just right for a bus run, and they both could certainly use a breath of fresh air after the amount of time they'd been spending in dancehalls of late.

And then she knew where she and Tommy would go. Not down the coast, but someplace far closer to home, and long neglected by them. A magic place.

She went into the kitchen where Tommy was sitting reading the *Sunday Post*. He never missed The Broons or Oor Wullie. 'Get your jacket,' she told him. 'We're going out.'

He demanded to know where, but she tapped her nose. 'Don't you mind where. You'll enjoy it, I promise.'

So as to keep him in suspense as long as possible, she

took him a way that was different to the one he'd used when he'd lived in Millbrae Crescent.

They got off the bus at Swanson's Garage in the Carmunnock Road, just below the blight of houses that was Castlemilk and crossed over into Simshill, a newly built private estate. Emerging from the far end of Simshill Jessie led Tommy to a hedged path that eventually dipped down to the golf course, the bottom end of which was adjacent to the southern boundaries of Linn Park.

Tommy stared out over the park, a crooked smile on his lips and the gleam of happy memories in his eyes.

'It's been an awful long time,' he said, a catch in his voice.

Hand in hand, they entered the park, stopping a few hundred yards further on to watch raucous rooks dart about a clump of horse chestnut trees, then moving into the small fir forest that went up one side of the brae, and down the other towards where the river twisted.

A young lad and his lass, out for a walk same as themselves, gawped at them as they passed one another, and it suddenly dawned on Jessie that she and Tommy, dressed in Ted gear, must look incongruous in these surroundings.

'Mind I bumped into you and Lizzie Dunnachie here once?' Tommy asked, laughing at the memory. Jessie remembered it well. She could visualize herself as she'd been then – the clothes she'd worn, the hat and umbrella, the hair-do. What a contrast to the way she was now!

'Whatever became of Lizzie?' Tommy went on.

'I've never seen or heard of her since I left the manse. I suppose I should have let her know where I'd gone, but I felt that she was part of my life as it had been, and Boyd Street was what it was now. I suppose I thought that if I tried to continue the friendship it would have gradually ended. It seemed better to stop it cleanly so that the good times we'd had didn't get lost in other things.'

There was sadness in her voice that cut right through him. He'd known it had been difficult for her to go and

208

live in Boyd Street, but until that moment he hadn't realized just what it had really meant to her.

He looked around. They were in Old Castle Road with the Snuffmill Bridge over on their left, the derelict castle up behind them. 'Let's look at these houses, then,' he urged. 'Just for fun. If ever I do make big money this is where we'll live. It's my favourite street in all Glasgow.'

There weren't very many houses in that part of the road. Those there were, sat amidst large walled gardens. Most had been built early in the previous century, but one or two were from the century before that.

One in particular caught Tommy's eye. It was made of grey granite and somewhat smaller than the rest. He and Jessie went to the wrought iron gate in order to get a better view. It was an imposing building with a regal look about it. A plate on the left hand pillar into which one of the gates was fixed bore the name GREENDAYS. Jessie's gaze moved across the garden. There were a lot of fruit trees, mainly apple and pear, and a row of gooseberry bushes at one side. It would be a marvellous garden in summer.

'This house is the pick of the bunch for me,' said Tommy. 'I'm not sure why, but it's special.'

Jessie giggled. 'I can't help thinking about our house in Allison Street, and you say you'd love to live in one of these houses here. Talk about going from the sublime to the ridiculous!'

Tommy joined in her laughter. 'Some day, though, perhaps. Some day,' he fantasized as they continued on their way.

Jessie had been waiting for the appropriate moment to spring her second surprise of that Sunday, and decided now was it. 'How would you feel about going on television?' she asked casually, knowing full well what his answer was going to be.

There was something in her tone told him this was more than an idle rhetorical question. 'What do you know that I don't?'

'The BBC programme New Talent is coming to Glasgow in August. They want the nine best new acts in Scotland for the show,' she explained excitedly.

New Talent! Why that went out at peak viewing time and was tremendously popular. 'If we could win that we'd be bound to get a recording contract with a major disc company,' he said, already making plans.

Jessie gave him a hug. 'That's how I see it, too.'

'You're not telling me we've already been accepted for the programme?'

'It's not quite as easy as that, I'm afraid. There's a small matter of an audition first. An I warn you now, when I spoke to the producer's office there had already been over a hundred applications, and the applications don't close for another three weeks.'

'Does that mean there's the possibility we may not even get auditioned?'

'You will if I have anything to do with it,' she answered with determination.

Jessie was at the piano Tommy had bought her the week before. A dozen of the Boys had bought it up the stairs, and what a to-do that had been. It had ended up with the outside door and the door to the room having to be taken off their hinges before they could get it where she wanted.

She had been worried that the folks up and down the close might complain about her playing late at night, which was when she usually worked on new songs, but they'd all said they weren't bothered in the least when she played. The truth was they were all very fond of her and Tommy, especially Tommy who was something of a celebrity in the neighbourhood.

Jessie frowned as she stared at what she'd scored. She had the music all right, but as always it was the lyrics that were giving her trouble.

A wee while later Tommy returned from playing

snooker to find her gazing glumly into space. 'What's wrong, love?' he asked with concern.

'I just can't write lyrics,' she said crossly.

'Let's hear the tune first,' he said, leaning on the piano.

She played the tune through. 'That's great,' he declared when she was finished. The tune had zest and style, and guts. He liked it and was certain the audiences would too. 'Now play it again, and this time sing the lyrics you have,' he instructed.

When she'd finished he was looking thoughtful. He could see what she meant by having trouble. The lyrics were nowhere near the standard of the music.

'Well?' she asked him.

It had never entered his mind to get involved in this side of things, but it was obvious Jessie needed help, and he was there, and her husband. It was up to him to give her what help he could.

'You want honesty?' he asked.

'Of course. Just don't be too honest.'

'It seems to me your trouble is that you're unclear about what you're trying to say. What you've written is vague and fuzzy. Soft, if you like. But it should be as sharp and hard as a diamond. Every word has to count. Now, what precisely *are* you trying to say?'

He was right of course. That was still unclear to her. She'd been hoping it would crystalize as she went along, but it hadn't.

With Tommy taking the lead they soon hammered out a story line, which they now had to transform into actual lyrics themselves. 'You're going to have to scrap what you've already done and start over.'

He brought a chair over to sit beside her at the piano. 'You play, we'll both suggest what we think should be put down, and as we agree I'll write it for you,' he said, taking up her pencil.

They started off suggesting equally, but it was very quickly evident to Jessie that Tommy was far better at the words than she. Before long she was merely playing

211

while he spoke aloud, bouncing lines off her, she nodding, and he scribbling them over the previous lyrics.

It took them half an hour, and then they were done. Jessie played the tune through, and Tommy sang the lyrics. They were a perfect match.

'I sort of got carried away there,' Tommy said, realizing he'd taken command.

'Don't apologize, those lyrics are streets ahead of what I had. In fact, they're better than anything I've written,' she added ruefully.

'Do you really think so?'

'I most certainly do. You have a talent for writing lyrics, Tommy, that's plain as the nose on your face. From now on in, you're going to write all of them for us. I'll score the music, but you'll write the lyrics.'

He went over his lyrics again, they *were* good. Well how about that!

Jessie was puzzled. Tommy's talent wasn't at all raw as she would have expected, but appeared to have been worked at. But how could that be? Unless he'd been writing lyrics without telling her. 'Have you been writing songs on the side without telling me?' she teased.

'Not a one. It never occurred to me.'

'How about poetry, have you been penning some of that on the fly?'

He blushed, delighting her. Tommy McBride, King of the Glasgow Teds, blushing like a lassie! That was one for the book.

'Not for years now, but I did used to jot down the odd piece when I was at Queen's Park,' he admitted shyly.

'You've never said.'

He shrugged. 'There was no reason to. Anyway, only Crossmyloofs and English public school boys talk about poetry.'

'Do you still have any of it?'

He shook his head.

She was fascinated, who would have imagined

212

Tommy writing poetry! Although sensitive, he hadn't seemed quite the type. 'What was it about?' she pursued.

He blushed again and glanced away. 'A lot of it was about Lovers' Lane, the river, the Linn Park, that sort of thing,' he mumbled.

'What sort of thing?' she prompted.

'Animals, trees, fish and the like.'

He was holding something back, she could tell. 'And?'

'There were also some about you. Quite a lot in fact,' he replied reluctantly.

'Oh, Tommy! And you never said a word.' She was thrilled – Tommy writing poetry about her!

'You're not to laugh now,' he said.

'I wouldn't dream of laughing. I just wish I'd known before now how good you are with words, you'd have saved me an a lot of sweat and worry.'

'But most of your lyrics were smashing!' he protested.

'They were acceptable, and the people liked them, but they weren't in the same class as yours, believe me.'

Tommy was chuffed to hell to hear that. He'd never thought he had any talent.

'Listen, there's another tune been rattling around inside my head this past week, but I haven't actually put it on paper yet. If I do, will you have a go at doing the lyrics for it?'

'I don't see why not,' he answered, excited at the prospect.

It took her ten minutes to write down the tune. It took him twenty to produce the lyrics which were even better than the first set.

'This could be quite a partnership,' Jessie said, and to celebrate took her new found lyricist off to bed.

The BBC was situated in Queen Margaret Drive, the squat grey pile overlooking the River Kelvin.

The audition was for three o'clock, Jessie and Tommy McBride Skiffle Band arrived by taxi at quarter to, because she was terrified of arriving late and being told they'd missed their chance to audition.

The receptionist, a middle-aged woman dressed in twin-set and fake pearls, goggled when they presented themselves before her. She'd never seen the like in those hallowed premises. The poor woman recoiled when Jake 'The Rake' flicked his brylcreamed quiff and leered at her in a suggestive manner. Just for a laugh he almost pro-positioned her, but refrained from doing so knowing Jessie would murder him if he did.

Jessie intervened and told the receptionist who they were, and what their business was. Reluctantly, as if she feared they'd contaminate the upholstery, she asked them to take a seat.

Jack put down the tea chest he'd humped from the taxi. It was a brand new chest he'd bought specially for the audition; it had Made In India stencilled on every side.

Sammy, who played the washboard, not to be out-done by Jack's new tea chest, had purchased five new bright shiny thimbles for his strumming hand.

The receptionist rang an internal number, then called across that someone would be coming for them. Jessie thanked her. The woman was clearly surprised to be thanked. Good manners from Teds were the last thing she'd expected.

For the umpteenth time since it had arrived, Jessie re-read the letter stating the time and place of the audi-tion. It was signed by a Mrs Baxter, personal secretary to Alan Hood the producer.

Jessie was amazed that they were apparently the only ones there for an audition; she'd been prepared for thousands all waiting their turn. And then she looked up and saw a face that struck a familiar chord in her mem-ory. The woman was about the same age as herself, maybe a little older, wearing a blue suit and matching blouse that positively screamed money.

'Hello Tommy, hello Star,' the woman said, coming to stand in front of them.

It was Tommy who recognized her. 'Eve Smith!' he exclaimed.

'Eve Baxter, now. I'm married to a staff cameraman,' Eve smiled in reply.

Tommy kissed her on the cheek, saying how grand it was to see her again. Then Eve kissed Jessie.

Tommy *was* pleased to see Eve again. He had many fond memories of her. He could hardly credit her popping out of thin air like this, and after so long!

'I don't call myself Star anymore, I went back to Jessie,' Jessie explained coldly, still bewildered by this sudden turn of events.

Eve nodded, thinking to herself that Jessie was as good looking as ever – but those outlandish clothes! They didn't do anything for her at all. Eve thought with satisfaction of the suit she had on. She'd selected it for this meeting after great deliberation, wanting to look her absolute best. Alan had personally chosen it for her in London's Bond Street, and when he'd paid for it there had only been pennies change out of fifty pounds.

'So you're Mr Hood's personal secretary,' Jessie said.

'That's right. And I must admit this is no surprise to me, I knew it was you two when you applied for the audition. I've seen your pictures in the papers.' Turning to Tommy she said, 'Barlinne wasn't it?'

'Yes,' Tommy acknowledged. It didn't faze him to have his imprisonment referred to. It was something he'd long since learned to live with.

'Must have been terrible for you,' Eve said, relishing the shiver that ran across her belly. There had always been a wild, explosive, quality about Tommy McBride, Eve thought. It was a quality that excited her. Tommy was also the only man to ever ditch her. She'd never forgotten that, or forgiven it.

'I wondered why there was no one else here for the audition. Are we getting special treatment because of you?' Jessie asked in a whisper.

Eve gave Jessie a conspiratorial wink. 'What sort of a

person would I be if I couldn't help a couple of old school pals?' she whispered back.

Tommy introduced Eve to the lads. Then Eve said she would take them to the rehearsal room where they'd be auditioning. Alan Hood was already there waiting for them.

As they headed for the rehearsal room, with Tommy chatting to Eve, Jessie thought about how much Eve had mellowed since Queenie Park. This sophisticated, well made-up and exquisitely dressed young lady was completely unlike the tarty Eve Smith of those days.

But then she herself was also totally different to what she'd been then. Eve could hardly accuse her of being Goody Two Shoes now, you could hardly label the Queen of the Glasgow Teds as that!

Long forgotten memories came flooding back to Jessie. She recalled the barney she'd had with Eve in the changing room that time. How shocked and scandalized she'd been. She remembered saying Eve was disgusting, and Eve retaliating by calling her Goody Two Shoes.

Who would have thought the notorious school hussy would end up a svelte BBC television producer's secretary? Or the minister's daughter Queen of the Glasgow Teds?

Eve told Jessie she was living out in Bearsden, one of the poshest areas in Glasgow, she and her husband Norman had a bungalow there. She didn't ask Jessie where Jessie and Tommy were staying, she knew from the application for an audition that they were living in Govanhill. Down amongst the peasants was how she'd phrased it in her mind.

Eve recalled to herself the occasion she'd seen Tommy and Star's picture in the *Scottish Daily Record* after The Battle of Linton Street. What a mouth gaping shock it had been to realize that her old lover was now King of the Glasgow Teds – and that Miss Butter-Wouldn't-Melt-in-Her-Mouth-Goody-Two-Shoes was his queen.

Eve brought her thoughts back to the present as they

arrived at the rehearsal room where Alan Hood was waiting. Dear Alan, she'd had him under her thumb since shortly after becoming his secretary, a job she'd schemed and connived to get because it was one of the best positions for a woman in Queen Margaret Drive.

Alan was a non-descript man with red hair and very pale freckles, of medium height and medium weight. He lurched to his feet the moment Eve came through the door. As hands were shaken and introductions made he said how pleased he was to meet them all, and that he was looking forward to their audition.

Jessie didn't fail to notice how Eve controlled the situation. It was Eve who told the band to set up, and who suggested the most appropriate place in the room for them to do so. It was also Eve who organized coffee and jollied Hood – a bit of a cheek Jessie thought – into lining up the chairs for those who'd be watching.

Tommy had thought he might be nervous but wasn't. Hell, it was only Eve he'd be singing to, and as for Hood, the producer was about as frightening as a bowl of cold porridge.

Jessie learned from Eve that they were the only people auditioning that day. Eve had accorded them extra special treatment indeed, for which Jessie was uneasily grateful.

Eve was dying to hear Tommy sing. Word on the grapevine, for she'd made inquiries, had it he was good. How strange it was to think of him as a singer, so unlike the image of the Tommy McBride she'd carried in her mind all these years. Mind you, until seeing that picture in the *Scottish Daily Record*, that image hadn't been of him as a Teddy Boy either.

Tommy and Jessie had already decided he and the band would perform the two numbers he and she had collaborated on together. In Jessie's opinion those two numbers were by far the best in their repertoire of original material.

'Ready when you are,' Alan Hood smiled, and, hunching his shoulders, sank in on himself, a body posture he felt made him appear not only important but also extremely knowledgeable.

Jessie crossed two fingers for luck, and offered up a silent prayer. This was so important to Tommy.

Tommy tapped out the beat on the wooden floor, and they were off. Jack twanged the homemade bass, Sammy rattled on the washboard, Jake blew the seven-gallon jug, and Tommy sang.

What a hunk he'd turned out to be, Eve thought, her eyes glued on Tommy. He'd been fanciable as a school-boy, but he was certainly not a boy any more. As for his singing – that definitely did things to her as well.

Alan Hood was greatly relieved to discover Tommy and the band had talent. It would have been a sod if they didn't and Eve insisted he put them in the show. He would have argued with her, of course, but the outcome would have been inevitable. Eve always got what she wanted.

Tommy's eyes met Jessie's, and she gave him a nod of encouragement, a nod that confirmed he was doing well, and to keep it up.

The band performed both numbers, then it was over. Jack and Sammy were grinning, for they were sure it had been a success. Jake 'The Rake' also looked highly pleased with himself, as if he'd just pulled the most beautiful doll in Glasgow. Tommy tried to hide how chuffed he felt.

Eve applauded loudly. Alan Hood not quite so loudly, but enthusiastically. Jessie didn't know whether it was right for her to applaud or not, and decided she might as well.

'So what do you say, Alan?' Eve demanded, knowing full well what he would say, for he always said the same thing to applicants.

'You'll be hearing from me in due course, but I want you to know I was most impressed, *most*,' Alan Hood said to Jessie, Tommy and the band.

Jessie glanced at Tommy. That sounded to her like it was in the bag. She could see he thought so, too.

Getting ready for bed that night Jessie put on the most seductive of her nightdresses and dabbed scent behind her ears and in the cleavage of her breasts.

Already under the covers, Tommy was still full of the audition, and didn't think he'd be able to sleep for ages yet. Because of this he'd brought a cowboy novel to bed with him to read.

Jessie had been thinking about Eve Smith, or Eve Baxter as she was now, ever since leaving the BBC. Eve had been so sophisticated and successful looking. And she'd been wearing the sort of clothes Jessie would have loved to wear, rather than the eccentric ones she did. Next to Eve, Jessie felt like a child. But to be truthful, it wasn't merely the clothes. Tommy was a one-time lover of hers. He must have noticed how attractive Eve was now. Must have noticed and wondered.

Tommy closed his eyes and pictured himself on television, losing himself in a fantastic dream. He suddenly realized that Jessie was talking. 'What did you say?'

'I thought the new Eve was quite a dish, didn't you?' she repeated.

He had indeed thought the new Eve quite a dish, a right cracker, but he had no intention of saying so to Jessie. There was a jealous streak in her, and her expression, which she thought was guarded, told him that streak was now very much to the fore.

'She was all right,' he shrugged, and pretended to begin reading his novel.

'I was wondering if you still fancied her? Couldn't say I'd blame you if you did,' Jessie went on.

'Eve could never hold a candle to you as far as I was concerned, you know that,' he replied without looking up from his book.

'Still?'

'Still.'

Jessie sighed. It was good to hear that, at least it relieved a little of her anxiety.

'So you *didn't* fancy her then, even though she was so much dishier than she used to be?' Jessie persisted.

Tommy gave an inward groan. Women! How they could go on when they got a bee in their bonnet about something.

'Not even a flicker of interest,' he lied convincingly.

'Jake fancied her.'

'Jake fancies anything that wears a skirt, as you know. Anyway, I don't see what you're driving at. Eve's clearly settled down now, in love with her husband, and living in happiness in posh Bearsden.'

Jessie snuggled up close to him. Using two fingers she walked her left hand over his thigh, and then down into the slit of his pyjama trousers where she took hold of him.

'How about it?'

'What if I don't feel like it?' he asked coolly, pretending indifference.

She gave a small, but sharp tug. 'If you don't I'll pull the bloody thing off,' she threatened.

'A very convincing argument,' he answered hastily.

Jessie put extra effort into her lovemaking. Just to be on the safe side.

Mid-morning the following Monday, as Tommy was brewing himself a pot of tea, there was a knock on the outside door. Opening the door he found a strange young man standing on the landing.

'Mr McBride?' the young man asked.

'Yes.'

'I'm a photographer from Auntie,' the young man said.

Tommy was baffled, what sort of gag was this: 'Auntie who?'

'Sorry, the BBC.'

Tommy shook his head, he'd never heard the expression before. Then excitement gripped him. A photographer from the BBC! It could only be something to do with the audition, the result of which he hadn't yet been notified.

'I've been sent by Mr Hood's office to do some photographs of you,' the young man explained, brandishing a camera.

Tommy immediately asked if that meant the band had been accepted for the show, but the photographer had no idea, he hadn't been given any information, only told to take a number of photographs.

Tommy ushered the young man through to the kitchen where he offered him a cup of tea, which the photographer refused.

'What about the other lads in the band, don't you want them too?' Tommy asked.

'Nope, only you.' The photographer produced a light meter. Squinting at it he asked casually, 'All alone?'

'Aye, the wife's at work.' Tommy decided he'd put on his best black drape for the photo session, the one he'd been married in.

The photographer muttered in exasperation, and said it was no use, there just wasn't enough light in the house. Would Tommy mind going out to a location? He had a car parked nearby.

Tommy answered that he wouldn't mind in the least, and told the photographer to wait while he got changed.

The photographer said he thought Tommy was fine as he was, there was no necessity to put on other clothes. Tommy considered insisting, but decided against it. He would have preferred the photos to have been of him in that particular drape, but there was no point in arguing.

The car, a Bentley, was parked around the corner. Its rear window blinds were drawn. As Tommy slid into the front passenger seat he realized there was another person in the back of the car. Turning round he found himself staring at Eve.

221

'The chap never said you were here,' Tommy said in surprise.

She smiled enigmatically. 'Drive on,' she instructed the photographer.

There was something fishy going on, Tommy suddenly thought. They didn't want the other lads in the band, only him. And now Eve had put in an appearance. 'What's your game?' he demanded bluntly.

'I wanted a chat, that's all. Knowing Star was at work I would have come up and knocked on your door myself, but you know what neighbours are like, always seeing what they shouldn't, and jumping to wrong conclusions. That's why I had Pete here do the knocking for me.'

'So there aren't to be any photos?'

'Sorry for the subterfuge. No photos, just a chat,' Eve said.

Tommy stared at Eve, not trusting her one iota. He remembered only too well the Eve of old. 'What kind of chat?'

'Relax, I just wanted to find out more about you and how you've been. Your plans for the future. Just a friendly interest in someone I used to be very fond of, okay?'

They drove to the Queen's Park, and swung into a side street, eventually coming to a halt adjacent to the bandstand.

Eve said they'd get out there, and waited for Tommy to open the door for her. When she was on the pavement beside him she hooked her arm in one of his.

'I thought we'd come to the bandstand,' she smiled. 'Not only is it the ideal place for a quiet chat, but you can see the school from there.'

At the bandstand Tommy looked in the direction of the school to see the spire of north building jutting into the sky about half a mile away.

'Imagine our paths crossing again after all this while,' she said softly. 'And you so transformed – King of the Teds and a singer.'

Something about her was making him uncomfortable. 'I haven't heard the outcome of the audition yet,' he said.

'You will,' she replied, lighting a cigarette.

They crossed to a wooden bench and sat down. Birds were singing and a warm breeze was gently blowing; it was a beautiful day.

'Tell me about being King of the Teds,' Eve coaxed.

Tommy didn't think there was any harm in that, so he recounted what it had been like for him since he'd been given the title.

Eve wanted to know all about the Battle of Linton Street, so he described what had happened, including the details of his fight with Ken Young. She listened with bated breath.

She asked about the reasons for the battle, causing Tommy to tense, wondering if she'd heard anything about what had happened to Jessie. That was something he never spoke of except to Jessie, and very occasionally to one of the Boys who'd been there. It was strictly private.

'There was a long standing grudge between me and Ken Young, that's all. One day it came to a head.'

Eve was satisfied with his explanation.

It gave Eve a thrill to have Tommy describe his exploits as King of the Glasgow Teds to her. She thought of Norman, her dull husband, and shuddered inwardly at how deadly boring he was. Any thrills Norman had once given her had long since vanished. 'And how did you become a singer?' she asked, coming out of her thoughts.

'It was Jessie's idea. She told me my voice was good enough for me to have a career in music.'

'I agree with her, it is.'

Tommy gazed off into the distance, but it wasn't the park he saw, it was his cell in Barlinne. If there was a hell hole on Earth it was that prison. 'When I came out of prison I discovered no one would employ me, so I was stuck without a job. Singing started me working again.'

223

'And you enjoy it?'

'Oh, aye. I was nervous at first, but soon got over that. Now I believe I can really go places, given the breaks that is.'

'You're ambitious then?' she prompted, watching him nervously.

'I am that. Jessie says I have it in me to go to the top, and that's where I'm going to do my damnedest to get.'

Eve smiled, he *was* ambitious, just as she'd hoped. Ambition made him vulnerable. 'So getting on the show really is important to you,' she said slowly.

'Winning it is even more important,' he replied with a grin.

She dropped what remained of her cigarette on to the grass and ground it underfoot. 'I can help you, you know,' she said simply. 'And not only with the show, but at the highest levels of the industry.'

He tried to hide his keen interest, but it shone through. 'How?'

Eve opened her handbag, took out a private card, and handed it to him.

'Come to lunch tomorrow at twelve. I'll show you then the power I have.'

He glanced down at the card, it was a Bearsden address. 'Shouldn't you be working then?' he asked quietly.

'I have an arrangement with Alan, and part of that arrangement is that I can have time off whenever I want. Within reason of course.' She got to her feet. 'And anyway,' she smiled, 'it is working.'

'And is the swish Bentley that brought us here also part of the arrangement?' Tommy asked.

Eve's eyes gleamed. 'Alan's a rich man in his own right.'

Tommy didn't have to ask Eve what her side of this arrangement was. He could guess.

*   *   *

Tommy had never been in Bearsden before. Walking down the street where Eve lived he decided he didn't like it. There was a sanctimonious air about the place which reminded him of Jessie's father, whom Jessie had never seen from the day she'd been chucked out to this.

The bungalow was painted beige with a red tiled roof. What originally had been a small garden out front had been concreted over. Sacrilege that, Tommy thought as he pressed the buzzer, wincing when a brassy scale of bells rang out.

Eve was wearing a light summer frock, no stockings and open-toed sandals. Her only make-up was scarlet lipstick. She looked a knockout. 'Right on time,' she laughed. 'Just like always.'

She took him through to the lounge where she poured him a generous whisky and herself a gin and tonic.

'Won't your husband mind you entertaining a man when he's not about?' Tommy asked, nervous now that he was actually here.

'I do as I please, Norman never complains,' she answered coolly.

Tommy glanced round, thinking there might be a photograph of Norman, but there wasn't. 'And what about neighbours, don't yours gossip?'

Her reply was to give him one of her enigmatic smiles, and sip her drink. He wasn't at all sure what to make of that.

'Did you tell Star you were coming here?' Eve asked.

Tommy shook his head. 'And she told you, it's Jessie nowadays.'

Still smiling, Eve crossed to an open bureau and lifted two sheets of paper from the desk. These she gave to Tommy. They were letters, both addressed to him, but as yet undated. He read them through.

One said the Tommy McBride Skiffle Band had been awarded a place on New Talent, the other was a polite rejection, saying the Tommy McBride Skiffle Band had failed to be selected.

'I decide which of those two letters gets sent to you. Not only that, if you do appear I can ensure you win,' Eve said.

'Hood?'

'As producer Alan names the winner. If I tell him to name you, then that's what he'll do.'

Tommy thought of the New Talent show. Winning it could make the Tommy McBride Skiffle Band a national name. It would be an enormous break for them.

'You mentioned the highest levels of the industry the other day?'

'I'll give you an example. You've heard of M.M.T. Records?'

Tommy nodded, M.M.T. was a top recording company, ranking alongside Decca in size and the number of first class artists they had signed to their label.

Eve gestured to a bright yellow telephone in the corner. 'I want you to do this yourself so that you know I'm not conning you in any way. Pick up that phone, ask for M.M.T.'s London number, then have the operator put you through. When they answer the party you want is Miss Grierson, the managing director's secretary, say you're ringing on my behalf. When Sally Grierson comes on the line you can then hand the phone over to me,' she instructed.

Tommy did as he was bid, handing the phone over once he'd been connected to the pleasant sounding Sally Grierson.

The ensuring conversation was about a big name star who would shortly be appearing on a BBC Glasgow Light Entertainment programme. Eve hung up, sat again, and stared at Tommy, that enigmatic smile on her lips.

'Sally Grierson is only one example of the contacts in high places that I have, there are dozens more. Being Alan's secretary I deal with these people every day. As a matter of course, and business, we do each other favours from time to time. It helps make life easier all round.' Eve

226

paused, then said slowly, and with emphasis. 'If I asked Sally to put in a good word for you at M.M.T. she would. It's a virtual certainty that a recording contract would follow.'

Tommy's heart jumped. A contract with M.M.T. would be an open sesame to the charts and playing the number one London venues.

'If for some reason it didn't, I guarantee I'd get you one with another top outfit,' she continued.

Now for the punchline, Tommy thought with dread. He was pretty sure he knew what it was going to be. 'What do I have to do for all this?' he asked.

'Agree to start sleeping with me again, and I'll do all the things I've just said. And more,' she promised. 'Lot's more.'

He stared at her, his eyes hard. 'Why?'

She treated him to one of her enigmatic smiles. 'Because I want you. It's as simple as that. I usually get what I set my heart on, and for now it's set on you.'

'What about Hood and hubby?'

She shrugged. 'Neither need know. And if they did it wouldn't matter, they're both broadminded.'

He found the whole thing disgusting. It told him a great deal about Alan Hood and Norman Baxter, that was for sure.

Eve played her ace. 'I might also mention the other side of the coin. I can pull strings on your behalf,' she purred. 'Or *against* you.'

He went cold all over, his mouth suddenly dry.

'Doing the dirty on you would be even easier than building you up. A dropped hint here, a little lie there, and soon . . . Well, you might continue to be booked by the Glasgow dancehalls, but you'd certainly never get any further than that. TV and radio would be closed to you, London wouldn't want to know. Tommy McBride, thug and ex-jailbird, and his skiffle band, would have a reputation that stank a mile high,' she said sweetly.

227

Oh you bitch, you rotten bitch, he thought. She'd certainly grown up.

Eve rose and smoothed down the front of her frock. 'Don't give me an answer now. Ring me at the Beeb, or here if you like, when you've decided,' she said, picking up the two letters from where she'd laid them and putting them back in the bureau. She turned to him with a smile. 'How about lunch? I'm ravenous.'

It was *coq au vin*, followed by raspberry fool.

It had taken Jessie thirty-five minutes to write down the music for their latest number. She'd finished that several hours ago, and Tommy had been struggling with the lyrics ever since.

She glanced over at the piano where Tommy was staring morosely off into space. It suddenly dawned on her that he looked pale and drawn, as if he was worried about something or ill. She hoped he wasn't coming down with something, for they had yet another booking for Mr Bojangles, opening the following night. They'd been lucky with health so far, none of the band having gone down with anything that had stopped them appearing.

Tommy was thinking about Eve's proposition, and feeling wretched as a result. She had him by the short and curlies, there was no getting away from it. He wondered if it would be any good reporting her to the BBC, but doubted it. Hood would back her up, and in the end if would boil down to his word against hers. He certainly didn't doubt that she'd stick the knife in him if he didn't comply, she'd stick the knife in and twist it, and smile that bloody enigmatic smile of hers as she was doing it.

With Eve against him it would take God alone knew how long to escape Govanhill, and being King of the Glasgow Teds, while every passing day increased the chances of his being involved in a barney he'd be carried out of feet first.

And then there was the fact that though he loved Jessie, if he agreed to becoming Eve's lover then the world was his on a plate. He'd win the New Talent show, there would be a contract with M.M.T., and from then on the sky was the limit – money, a smart car, all the luxuries you could think of. But most important of all, the escape from Govanhill that Jessie so craved, and his own escape from being King of the Glasgow Teds and his past. And if Jessie didn't find out, what was the harm?

'Are you all right?' Jessie asked, placing a hand on his shoulder.

He jerked away in surprise. 'I've got rather a headache I'm afraid,' he lied.

'Then you should pack this in for tonight, you're obviously struggling with these lyrics because you're not feeling all that hot.'

Abandoning piano and the few lyrics he'd managed, he crossed over to his favourite chair and slumped into it. 'Yes please,' he said when Jessie asked him if he'd like a cup of coffee.

As Jessie waited for the kettle to boil she saw that he'd closed his eyes and was rubbing his forehead. His headache must be worse than he was letting on, she thought.

Next morning he waited till the back of ten, he'd got the impression these people didn't go in for early starts, then walked along Allison Street to the nearest public phone box. From there he rang Eve at the BBC.

'Okay, I agree, but on one condition,' he said shortly.

Elation and self-satisfaction filled Eve. That, and a fluttering of sexual arousal. It wouldn't be long now before she had that gorgeous hunk in her bed. 'Which is?'

'On no account must Jessie find out.'

'She won't find out from me, you have my promise on that,' Eve replied.

229

They made arrangements for him to call at the Bearsden bungalow the following afternoon.

Eve answered the door in a clinging pale yellow silk dressing gown, a cloud of heady perfume hanging around her. Tommy slipped inside. She laughed at his furtiveness.

The truth was she didn't care what the neighbours thought about the various comings and goings at the bungalow. They'd long since stopped talking to her anyway.

She led the way to her bedroom where the curtains had already been drawn and a table lamp switched on. The bed's covers had been pulled back. On top of the vanity were two crystal glasses, a crystal decanter of whisky, and a plate of salmon sandwiches.

Eve stood with her back to Tommy, and undid her dressing gown, which fell in a whisper of silk to the thick fitted carpet. She was naked underneath. Going to the vanity, Eve picked up a sandwich and delicately bit into it. 'Help yourself,' she said to Tommy.

And gave him one of her enigmatic smiles.

Jessie slotted her key into the door lock, having just arrived home from work. It had been a tiring day with her never off her feet, and she still had the evening meal to make, with Mr Bojangles after that. She wondered about sending Tommy out for chicken and chips, which would at least give her time to have really good wash down at the sink.

Tommy was in the kitchen with a huge grin plastered all over his face.

'You look like you lost a tanner and found a pound,' she said.

He pulled a sheet of paper out from his inside jacket pocket and waved it at her. 'It's the New Talent show for us!' he exclaimed.

Jessie squealed with joy, throwing her arms around him. She kissed him on the cheek, the mouth, and the mouth again. Snatching the letter from him she hurriedly read it through.

'Have you told the others yet?' she asked excitedly.

'I wanted you to be the first to know. I'll tell them tonight at Bojangles.'

Her tiredness had vanished. She was now light as air, and full of energy. She felt as though she was going to laugh and cry at once. 'I can't tell you how pleased I am . . . I . . . oh, Tommy!'

She was so lovely, he thought, his beautiful darling Jessie. That look on her face made him feel that he'd done the right thing. Everything would be all right from now on. He wanted to take her to bed there and then, but he'd been with Eve nearly all afternoon and doubted that he could.

'Soon everyone's going to know who you are. Now we've been accepted for the show we've got to win it,' Jessie declared with determination.

Tommy took her in his arms. 'I've got a feeling about that,' he said.

Jessie was gathering their dirty laundry into a pile, as she did every week, to take it to work with her where it was done for nothing, one of the few perks of the job.

Her nose suddenly twitched at an unfamiliar smell. It was a nice smell, and one she couldn't place. She tried several of Tommy's shirts before she found the one it was coming from. It was a beautiful perfume, undoubtedly expensive, and quite different to the blue bottle she wore. Probably French, she thought, it smelled French.

Now how had Tommy got such perfume on his shirt? He didn't have another woman did he? Jessie laughed aloud at the idea, no it must have come from a fan, some lassie who'd rubbed herself up against him.

Another woman indeed, let him dare!

She thrust the shirt back into the pile and promptly forgot about it.

Jessie gnawed a nail, she'd already broken two others, and for the umpteenth time glanced at the wall clock. Twenty minutes till the show started and she wanted to be sick.

They'd been at Queen Margaret Drive since early that morning, the rehearsals culminating in a run-through that had finished an hour previously. The next run would be the real thing.

Jessie was in the dressing room allocated to Tommy and the band. Tommy and Jake 'The Rake' were chatting about snooker, while Jack and Sammy were off for their turn at make-up. She was expecting Jack and Sammy back at any moment.

Tommy was extremely relaxed, as if appearing on the box was a regular occurrence with him. Which meant there was one less thing to worry about. The more relaxed he was the better his singing would be.

She continued gnawing her nail and thought about the other acts. They were a mixed variety bag consisting of a juggler, a bicycle trio, a ventriloquist, a magician, three stand up comics, and a female singer. As far as she was concerned the singer was the main competition. The girl wasn't only exceptionally attractive, but she had a real belter of a voice, the sort of voice that could soothe you to sleep one moment and shatter glass the next.

'Come in!' Tommy called out in a reply to a rap on the door.

It was Eve, accompanied by a man about ten years older than herself. Snake hipped, dressed in casual clothes, he had a moustache and beard, and wore tinted glasses. The hair on his head was thin and balding. The eyes behind the glasses were small and sharp, reminding Jessie of a ferret. He had a thick gold chain around his neck, and a fankle of smaller gold chains dangling from the larger. He had three gold bracelets on his left wrist, a broad banded gold watch and another gold chain on his right.

He's queer Jessie thought.

'I'd like you all to meet my husband, Norman,' Eve said with a big smile.

Tommy was momentarily thrown, but swiftly recovered himself. 'Come away in, would you care for a hauf Norman?' he asked, indicating the bottle of whisky he personally had provided for after their performance and in case of visitors.

Norman replied he wouldn't, not just then anyway. He shook Jessie's hand, said he was delighted to meet her, then did the same with Tommy and Jake.

'I just wanted to wish you good luck,' Eve told Tommy.

Jack and Sammy arrived back from make-up, and were introduced to Norman by Jessie, who'd decided she didn't care at all for Eve's husband, he gave her the willies.

Norman made small talk by asking Tommy what the order of their appearance was in the show, and Tommy answered they were going on fifth. Eve said the fifth and sixth spots were generally considered to be the best.

The tannoy crackled into life, and the Production Assistant announced that there was now only fifteen minutes to go. He requested the acts to remain in their various dressing rooms, until they were called.

'Well, I'm going to take Norman out to his seat,' cooed Eve. 'Are you coming, Jessie? Your seat's next to Norman's so you'll be among friends.'

Jessie would much rather have sat beside total strangers than Norman Baxter.

'I'll be along in a minute.' She wanted to stay with Tommy for as long as she could.

Eve gave Tommy a big kiss on the mouth, wishing him good luck again. Jessie felt something stir at the back of her mind. She didn't know why, but that kiss annoyed

233

her. There seemed to be more to it than just good luck. She could, after all, have kissed him on the cheek. But then, Eve had always been a liberty taker.

When Eve and Norman were gone Jessie gave Tommy the once over to make sure he was as he should be and all in order, and then did the same for the lads. She insisted Jack do up his top shirt button, even though, he argued, he never usually did. That wasn't the point, she told him, he was going to appear before millions of people, and just because he was a Ted it didn't mean he had to look sloppy.

There was another rap on the door, and Alan Hood popped his head round. 'A quick all the best, I'm sure you'll do fine,' Alan smiled.

Tommy gave Hood the thumbs up, neither betraying to the other by even the smallest sign that it had already been decided that the Tommy McBride Skiffle Band was going to win.

At last she could find no more excuses for hanging around. She took one of Tommy's hands in her's and squeezed it warmly. 'Bring the house down,' she whispered.

'You can rely on it,' he whispered back.

She gave the lads a cuddle each, then fled the room for the corridor outside where she had to pause for nearly a full minute in order to collect herself.

Arriving in the studio she immediately caught sight of Norman Baxter who waved to her, then pointed at the empty seat beside him. She made her way across.

The stage consisted of a number of rostra surrounded on three sides by steeply banking seats. Jessie estimated there were about two hundred and fifty people in the studio which was already stiflingly hot.

When she was seated Norman gestured up into the gloom of the studio ceiling and there, on the side opposite, high above the hanging spots and floods, she could make out a pale green glow. He told her that was the director's box where Eve and Alan Hood were.

'How do you feel?' Norman asked, his eyes glinting behind his glasses.

Jessie gave him a weak, and very strained, smile. She wished he wouldn't keep talking, she would have preferred to suffer in silence.

Norman fumbled in a pocket to produce something which he slipped into her hand. 'Swallow that, it'll soon calm you down,' he said quietly.

It was a flat pink pill he'd placed in her palm. He was offering her drugs, she thought in a combination of disgust and alarm. 'No thanks,' she said quickly, trying not to sound contemptuous, or ungracious and returned the pill to him.

With a shrug he put it back into his pocket. 'I take them all the time myself,' he said. 'They're great when you need relaxing.

There was only a couple of minutes left now. Jessie squirmed in her seat, restless with anxiety for Tommy. She wondered if he was still as relaxed as he'd been when she'd left him. Oh, please, God, she prayed, don't let him lose his voice.

Then the P.A. was on the stage, welcoming the audience to the show, and cracking a few jokes to warm them up. He told them that at the end of the performances the V.T.R., the tape on which the show was being recorded, would be stopped and slips of paper passed amongst them. After they'd voted the slips would be taken away and counted, and when this had been done the V.T.R. would be restarted, and a decision announced, first, second and third, in the usual reverse order.

The lights shining on the audience dimmed, and died. 'Let's hear a large hand for our opening act, The Great McGregor, Magician Extraordinaire!' called the P.A.

The Great McGregor bounded onstage and right off produced a haggis from his ear. The audience, loving that, gave him a round of applause, and the show was off to a fine start.

Next up was one of the comics who'd clearly modelled

himself on Lex McLean who'd long been an enormous favourite with Glaswegians. By the end of his patter the feeling amongst the audience was that Lex wasn't in for any sleepless nights worrying about this particular competition.

The third act was the singer, a blonde girl in her early twenties, who had a magnificent figure as well as a magnificent voice. Somebody gave a wolf whistle before she began, another voice was heard to exclaim 'Wow!' The girl gave a charming smile, she was obviously used to that sort of attention.

When the singer was finished Jessie knew that Tommy and the band could be in trouble. She had been even better than the run-through, and she'd been damned good then.

The next act was the bicycle trio, which turned out to be comedic, although it wasn't supposed to be. The trio consisted of a father, mother and daughter, the father so nervous he repeatedly fell off his unicycle, at one point directly in front of the daughter who promptly ran over him.

Then it was the Tommy McBride Skiffle Band, who came to their instruments led by a scowling Tommy. The scowl and aggression were part of his act.

Jessie's heart was in her mouth. Without realizing it she'd taken hold of Norman Baxter's arm, clutching it so hard he'd have black and blue marks for a week.

She could hardly bear to look, and to begin with kept her gaze fastened to the rim of the seat in front.

The band's first number was the last she and Tommy had collaborated on, and their best to date. It was a raunchy, heavy beat number about a hard drinking dockie, out for a night on the town to drown his sorrows about his lost love who'd run off with his closest pal.

He reached out, took that audience by the scruff of the neck, and completely won them over. He'd had charisma before; now he knew how to use it.

The second number was poignant and bittersweet, and

Tommy sang it to perfection. The last note faded away, to be greeted with silence, a silence filled with emotion and pleasure. One person clapped and another, then they all were. Tears were rolling down Jessie's cheeks as she banged her hands together. That had been even better than she'd hoped. Tommy had surpassed even her expectations.

Norman Baxter leaned towards her. 'I'm very impressed,' he whispered. 'I think they have a good chance of winning.'

But Jessie didn't underestimate the threat of the blonde singer and her breasts. A lot of men in the audience would be voting for those breasts, it was the sort of thing men did.

The acts following seemed to fly by, then the P.A. was back on the stage saying the V.T.R. had been stopped, and voting would now take place.

The paper Jessie was given had the names of the nine acts on it, with a box against each name. Jessie's hand was shaking as she made her mark using Norman Baxter's pen. Throughout the audience pens and pencils were being passed back and forth.

The slips were collected, put into a cardboard container, and then the container given to the P.A. who disappeared off with it.

'How long do you think this'll take?' Jessie asked Norman. She was fidgeting with impatience.

'Not long. Eve will have it well organized, you can be sure of that.'

In the dressing room Tommy was pouring large whiskies, and congratulating himself on having done well. He didn't think he'd ever sung better, but then there had been no pressure whatever on him, as there had been on the other acts – he'd *known* he was going to win.

'Come on!' Jessie muttered, and glanced yet again at her watch.

In the director's box Alan Hood was finishing knotting his tie. He'd changed into a lounge suit, for he'd be going

237

onstage, in front of the camera, to declare the winner and runners up. The P.A. would run that last part of the show from the box.

Eve and Alan had personally, and in private, counted the votes and were surprised at the results.

Alan Hood made his way to the stage, where his appearance was greeted with applause. He held up his hands, gesturing for the clapping to stop. Hood made a brief speech about Scotland, the show, and the acts who'd performed that evening. Then he said, 'In third place, with forty-eight votes, The Great McGregor, Magician Extraordinaire!'

On hearing that he'd come third, the Great McGregor gave a whoop, and came bounding on stage to shake Hood's hand. When Hood had finally extricated his hand he found, to his own amusement as well as the audience's that he was holding a ring of black pudding.

So far so good, Jessie was thinking, bouncing in her seat.

'And in second place Roy Byrne!' Hood announced. Byrne was of the stand-up comics.

Despite the heat Jessie went chill all over. She'd thought first place was between Tommy and the female singer, in which case one of them should have come second. But they hadn't, Roy Byrne had! So either Tommy or the female singer wasn't placed at all, and she could hardly believe it was the singer, not with those sodding great tits!

Oh, Tommy, Jessie wailed inside. His big chance had ended in disaster.

'And in first place, with a hundred and three votes, the winner is . . .' Hood paused, drawing the moment out. 'The Tommy McBride Skiffle Band!'

They'd won! They'd won after all! Jessie leapt up and down with excitement and joy.

Tommy and the lads came onstage to shake Hood's hand, and give the audience 'thank you' gestures. Jake 'The Rake', so overcome by it all, was blowing kisses to every woman he could see.

238

Hood spoke into the camera, winding up the show. The P.A.'s voice boomed out from hidden loudspeakers saying that the show was over, and that the audience could now go.

Jessie left Norman Baxter, wriggling her way out to the aisle, and running down and over to where a beaming Tommy was being congratulated by The Great McGregor, Roy Byrne and Alan Hood.

She threw herself into his arms, and hugged him tightly. 'We did it! We did it!' she cried. 'You were wonderful!'

Tommy extracted Jessie and himself from the general confusion, and they returned to the dressing room where they toasted their success in whisky. Tommy confessed that he was also dumbfounded that the singer hadn't done better. Then he shut up about that, thinking the finagling of the votes he believed had taken place might well have accounted for the lassie's poor showing. The truth of the matter was, though, that it had done nothing of the sort. Eve and Hood had been just as surprised on counting the votes to discover the lassie had done so badly. As it had turned out, Tommy and the band had won fair and square, knocking the other acts for six. Eve hadn't had to do any finagling, something she never did tell Tommy. The figures Alan Hood had read had been exactly as cast.

Jack, Sammy and Jake arrived back in the dressing room, all three of them cock-a-hoop, and with another bottle of whisky which they gleefully declared they'd 'liberated'. Sammy, who'd been swallowing from the bottle as though it was lemonade, was already well on the way to getting paralytic, or 'deid mockit' as he would have put it.

Alan Hood appeared with a tall thin woman whom he introduced as his wife, Vanessa. 'I always take the winning act out for a meal after the show,' he said. 'You boys fancy a meal?'

During the drive to the restaurant Jessie snuggled up to

Tommy, she felt closer to him than she'd ever been, and so gloriously happy she must surely burst from it.

Tommy was still in bed the next morning, Jessie having long since gone to work, when there was a knock on the outside door. He'd been awake for a while now, but continued to lie there waiting for his muzzy head to clear. He'd drunk a lot the night before, as had everyone else. It had been a great celebration.

Getting out of bed he staggered through to answer the knock, to discover Eve standing on the landing. 'I've got news,' she said, and marched past him on into the kitchen. There she looked around in interest, though it was obvious from her expression that she didn't think much of what she saw.

'You're not on the phone, and there wasn't time to write, so I came in person,' she explained briefly.

'So I see,' he drawled, wondering what this was all about.

'I had a buzz about an hour ago from Sally Grierson at M.M.T. Daniel Silver watched you last night, and was most impressed.'

Tommy's ears pricked up. Daniel Silver was the boss of M.M.T., and, according to an article he'd read recently in *Melody Maker*, one of the most powerful people in the recording business. He was wide awake now. 'That's terrific!'

'It's more than that. He wants you and the others to fly down to London, at his expense, this afternoon to discuss your future.'

Tommy let out a yell, and punched the air. This was it, the big breakthrough. This was escape from Govanhill, and his past, and being King of the Glasgow Teds. This was the beginning of his dream coming true.

'My only worry was you might have a performance scheduled for tonight,' Eve said briskly. 'If so you'll have to cancel it.'

Tommy shook his head. 'We've nothing on, we're in the clear.'

'I've already booked you on the three o'clock plane. Sally Grierson will be meeting you at Heathrow.'

Tommy was fizzling inside, his hangover gone. He felt like he was walking on air.

'Do I deliver the goods or don't I?' Eve asked, standing right in front of him.

'You deliver,' he agreed.

'Then how about a little kiss of gratitude?'

He took her in his arms. 'Thanks,' he whispered. 'Thank you very much.'

Eve shivered. God but he was a hunk. The sense of danger he exhuded was an aphrodisiac that never failed to turn her on.

Their lips met, hers greedily on his.

Jessie sat down and clutched her head. Luckily they'd been quiet at work. She doubted she could have coped otherwise.

'Still bad?' Jane Lamont asked sympathetically.

'Worse if anything. It's a real blinder. I should have known better than mix grain and grape,' Jessie moaned.

Jane laughed. 'Always a mistake that.'

'It was a tremendous night mind, but I'm certainly paying for it now.'

Jane thought of the several favours Jessie had done her in the past. Here was her chance to repay at least one of them. 'Listen, I can see us being dead for the rest of the day, so why don't you hoof it? Way back to your kip and sleep. I'll manage here,' She suggested.

Jessie glanced up at her. 'Would you mind?'

'I wouldn't have mentioned it if I did. As you never take time off it seems to me you've earned the right of a skive. And to be truthful, you're not really very much help the way you are.'

Jessie gave a weak smile. 'I'd be eternally grateful.'

'On your bike, then. And don't worry, I'll see everything's all right here.'

Jessie left the shop a few minutes later, hoping Tommy was still in bed so she could cuddle up next to him.

Tommy was still in bed. He lay flat on his back with Eve astride him. He was paying the price for the news she'd brought. Not that it was all that difficult a price to pay, he'd have been lying if he said he didn't enjoy having sex with Eve.

He opened his eyes, and there she was staring down at him, smiling that damned enigmatic smile of hers. He gave a gasp of pleasure as she made a movement that was quite sensational. Then she did it again.

The fresh air had helped a bit, Jessie thought as she climbed the stair leading to the house. When she got in she'd have a nice cup of tea, and then get down underneath the quilt. A couple of aspirins, a few hours sleep, and hopefully she'd be right as rain again.

The first thing she noticed on going through the front door was that the lights in the bedroom were blazing, and then that the bedroom curtains were drawn. How odd, she thought. What was Tommy up to?

She snicked the front door shut behind her, then went into the bedroom. She came up short, blinking in disbelief at the sight confronting her. A naked Eve was on all fours, an equally naked Tommy crouched over her.

Tommy and Eve froze the moment Jessie entered the room. Tommy stared at Jessie in horror.

Whether it was a nervous reaction to the situation, or a manifestation of the nasty streak that ran all through Eve, was hard even for Eve to tell, but she started to laugh. It was a high, raucous laugh – and to Jessie's ears a triumphant and mocking one – that gutted Jessie where she stood. She gave a strangulated cry that was more animal than human.

Tommy, recovering his wits, threw Eve to one side, and tried to get to his feet. As he was doing that, Jessie spun round and fled.

'For God's sake, Jessie, stop!' he screamed, following her out of the house and down the stairs. At the close front, because of his nakedness, he was forced to stop. He watched in despair as Jessie ran up the street.

She ran and ran, not caring where to as long as it was away from the obscenity she'd just witnessed. She could still hear Eve's laugher, ringing in her head.

She found herself at a stop where a tram was picking up passengers, a tram that would take her back to work.

She jumped aboard.

During her return journey to the laundry, a strange intermingling took place in Jessie's mind. What she'd seen in her bedroom became mixed up with the rape she'd suffered in Linton Street.

Revulsion at what Tommy and Eve had been doing was as deep and profound as the revulsion she'd experienced then. She wanted to cry, to die, to be a million miles away. She stared out the tram window, but didn't see the passing scenery. Instead she saw herself spreadeagled, held fast, while Ken Young ravaged her, thrusting his flesh into hers just as Tommy had been thrusting into Eve. Then the picture changed, and now Tommy was one of the rapists, leering at her as he waited his turn.

He'd told her he loved her, he'd sworn it. The liar! THE LIAR!! If he loved her how could he do this to her? And in their bed; in their bed where they'd made love so many times. She heard Eve's laughter again, and cringed inside. She knew that laughter would haunt her for the rest of her life.

Suddenly, everything fell into place. She recalled the

expensive perfume she'd discovered clinging to his shirt, which she'd assumed had rubbed off from a fan. Fan indeed! It had come from Eve, she knew that as surely as she knew she had a nose on her face and five fingers on each hand. And that kiss in the dressing room last night . . .

'In the name of the Wee Man!' Jane Lamont exclaimed when Jessie stumbled into the laundry. Jessie's eyes were wild, her hair awry.

Jessie fled past the solitary customer, staring at her in amazement, and into the back shop where she flopped onto a wooden chair.

When the customer was finally gone Jane ran through to where Jessie sat slumped in the chair.

In a voice breaking with emotion, Jessie told her what had happened. Even though Jessie only hinted at the details, Jane was shaken. To think Jessie had walked in on the likes of that! No wonder the lass looked the way she did.

'I'll stick the kettle on, you need a coffee,' Jane said briskly, immediately suiting her actions to her words.

'In our bed, his and mine,' Jessie repeated. 'That was the worst thing of all.'

'Just forget about them for now.' Jane advised. 'You're getting yourself all worked up and it't not worth it.'

But Jessie couldn't stop torturing herself. 'I've been asking myself how often they've been there together. How often has he had her in our bed in the afternoon, then me at night, on the same sheets?'

Again, the scene she'd walked in on re-played itself in her mind, betraying everything her love for Tommy had stood for. 'I can never go back there, Jane. I'm leaving him.'

'Oh lass, be careful, don't do anything silly.'

Jessie shook her head. 'No I'm leaving him, my mind's made up.'

'I think you're making a bad mistake. If I was you, I'd fight for him.'

Jessie's eyes filled with tears. 'Why bother to fight for someone who can do that to me? He doesn't love me, he *can't* do. If he wants to replace me with Eve then let him, I'll make it easy for the pair of them by clearing off.'

'But where will you go? How will you manage?'

Jessie wiped away tears, but didn't reply. She was going to have to quit Glasgow altogether, that was something else she'd decided on the tram. She couldn't stay here, where everything would remind her of all she'd loved and lost.

In their own bed with another woman! He couldn't possibly love her to do that. No, she wasn't making a mistake, she was doing the right thing – the only thing.

Coming to her feet, she went to look amongst the parcels of laundry to search out her and Tommy's clean laundry, which she knew was there. When she found their parcel she opened it and separated hers from his. She regarded his pile thoughtfully for a couple of seconds, then picking it up heaved it into the garbage bin. There were three of his favourite shirts amongst that lot, which gave her some satisfaction.

She took a brown paper bag from the stock and put her laundry into it. It didn't amount to much, but it was better than nothing – at least she wouldn't be starting out with only the clothes she stood up in. As for money, she had cash in her purse that had been intended for several outstanding bills. She also had most of her previous week's pay left. Most importantly though, she had her Post Office book, which contained a fair amount as she'd been a regular saver since Tommy had started earning. Money, at least, wasn't a problem, at least not in the short term.

Taking a deep breath she turned to Jane whose face was drawn in doubt and concern. 'Don't worry, I'll be all right. Really, Jane. I know what I'm doing.'

'And what about your job here?'

'Apologize for me. Tell them I would have worked out

my notice had it been possible, but it's not. Make up any excuse you want.'

Jane broke down then, for she was terribly fond of Jessie. 'I'll miss you so I will,' she wept.

'And I'll miss you, too.'

They hugged one another, each squeezing the other tight. 'I love him more than life itself, and I believed he loved me,' Jessie whispered. 'That's why I never want to see, or be with him ever again.'

Disentangling herself, Jessie picked up the brown paper bag and left the shop. She turned once to wave to Jane standing in the window, then disappeared round a corner.

PART THREE

Mrs McBride
1959–62

7

Jessie gave the glass she was drying a final wipe, and stacked it with the other pint pots. A glance at the clock above the bar told her it was just gone half past eleven, they were done early for a Saturday night. At times it could be midnight, or later, before the last glass was put away.

'See to the staff drinks will you, darling!' Julian called out to his wife Pixie from the corner where he was sitting cashing up.

Julian was thirty-three, and had been to Eton. Jessie considered his aristocratic background a strange one for a pub landlord, but that was London for you.

Pixie, who Jessie thought a real sweetie, wasn't quite so upper crust, but good enough for Julian's family not to complain when he married her. At least that was what Pixie said, and Pixie wasn't the kind to lie about that sort of thing. In fact there was hardly anything Jessie could imagine Pixie telling a lie about, she was that type of person.

Besides Jessie there was another barmaid working that night in The Lonsdale Arms, a Cockney girl called Yvonne, who originally came from Hackney, but now lived in a flat across the road.

'I'll have a pint of bitter,' Jessie called. She'd developed a taste for beer since coming to work in the pub, and as far as her figure was concerned it was beginning to show. She'd put on more than a bit of weight since leaving Glasgow eight months ago. If she'd been interested in men it might have bothered her, but she wasn't, so it didn't. Men had become strictly past tense in her book. Since Tommy she hadn't wanted to know.

She lit a gasper, another bad habit she'd acquired. She'd

vaguely hoped that smoking might help her weight, but it didn't seem to make any perceptible difference.

The Lonsdale Arms was located in the St Mary Ward of the Borough of Islington. When Jessie arrived at Euston last September she booked into a cheap hotel in that neighbourhood, then the next morning started looking for digs. She hadn't fancied the Euston area, or the adjacent King's Cross one, so she'd hopped on a bus, getting off again in the next borough, which was Islington.

After several hours' fruitless viewing of rooms, all so bad she wouldn't have let a pig stay in any of them, she'd decided to give her feet a rest, and have a bit of a sit down. She'd headed for a cafe she'd passed earlier, but before coming to it had chanced upon The Lonsdale Arms and the sign in its window. Live-in Barmaid Wanted, the sign had said, which had set her thinking.

Inside, she'd ordered a drink and had a good look round. The pub hadn't been modernized with formica and chrome like many, but retained its original Victorian décor with highly polished wood and brass everywhere.

Julian had been behind the bar, talking loudly in that toffy voice of his (he always talked loudly she was soon to learn) and she'd thought he was a character.

She'd decided she liked The Lonsdale Arms. It had a good feel about it. You could just tell that the landlord and his wife were nice, and that the customers were nice, too.

She'd gone up and inquired about the job. 'Have you ever worked in a pub before?' Julian asked, taking her in without seeming to. Jessie didn't know how desperate she looked.

'Well, no,' she'd admitted. 'But I'm a quick learner, and I do need a job.'

Without blinking Julian had called Pixie out from the back where she was cooking, introduced them, mentioned what the job paid, and told Pixie to show Jessie the room that would be hers before Jessie made a decision.

Jessie had adored the bedroom. It had pretty floral wall-paper, a table covered by an old fashioned velvet cloth that had tassles on it, and there was even a continental quilt on the bed, something she'd read about but never seen. There was also a green painted hard backed chair, the same colour green as the cloth on the table. 'Oh, this is lovely,' she'd said enthusiastically, relaxing for the first time since she'd left Glasgow. 'Well, that's it, then,' Pixie had smiled, and they'd shaken hands on it, and Pixie had said to take that day to move in and get herself comfy, she could start work the next morning.

So she'd begun work at The Lonsdale Arms, and had been there ever since. She considered herself to have fallen on her feet. The job itself, the friendly chat and banter and camaraderie was exactly what she needed after the trauma of walking out on Tommy, and the enormous gap that had left in her life.

'How did we do tonight?' Pixie asked Julian, knowing without having to be told that business was down on the previous Saturday, which itself had been down on the Saturday before that.

Julian scrunched up his nose. 'Could be worse, I suppose, but I must admit this falling away of trade is getting me worried. And the brewery isn't happy about it either, not that they've said anything, yet, but I get this feeling every time I talk to them on the phone.'

'That big pub on Islington Green is packing them in,' Jessie said. 'I heard one of the customers talking about it the other night.

'It's because it's got that location. Being at the junction of two main roads is a lot different to being in an out of the way street like us,' Julian said sadly.

Yvonne sipped her gin, and looked thoughtful. 'You know what you want is a gimmick, something that will make this pub different, and have the customers wanting to come here rather than go elsewhere,' she said slowly.

Julian glanced at her with interest. Yvonne somehow gave the impression of being thick, but was anything but. When she made a suggestion it was always a good idea to pay heed.

'What sort of gimmick?' Julian asked.

'How about Morris Dancers?' chipped in Pixie.

'With their wee hankies and their jingly jangly bells?' laughed Jessie. 'Where would you put them all? And who would they attract?'

Yvonne sniggered into her hand.

'Then you come up with something!' Pixie retorted a little miffed that her idea had been received with such scorn.

Jessie racked her brain. What sort of gimmick would get folk into a pub? And the folk round here in particular, who were partly third and fourth generation working class Islingtonians, and partly the new young professional people who were moving in because it was relatively cheap, and they could affort to buy whole houses and do them up.

Darts were popular, of course, but lots of the pubs had that, many even ran their own tournaments. So darts were hardly a novelty.

'Live music,' Jessie said abruptly, remembering that in Glasgow you couldn't fail with live music, provided it was good. So why not here?

'Live music,' Julian mused, now there was a thought. There wasn't a pub in the district, as far as he knew, that had live music. The odds were high it would be a draw, especially with so many young people around.

'What sort of live music, jazz?' he asked Jessie.

Jessie made a face. 'Personally, I'd go for a modern group who would attract the young set, they're the ones with money nowadays. And they're the ones with few real venues.'

Julian turned to his wife. 'What do you say Pixie?'

'I think it's a smashing idea. It would liven things up no end.'

'Yvonne?'

'Should be fun, and I'm always in favour of that.'

Julian snapped a thumb and forefinger. 'Live music and a modern group it is, then. Jessie, take a gold star and go to the top of the class!'

Jessie laughed, top of the class indeed!

'This calls for another round on me,' Julian said, and got up to do the honours.

'I don't suppose you know any modern groups?' he asked Jessie, when he came back with the drinks.

Jessie gave a wry smile. 'Not in London,' she said softly.

'Then I'll place an ad in the *Gazette* and see what that produces,' Julian said. 'There must be lots of groups around dying for a place to play.'

They sat around for some time, making plans, then Jessie went up to her bedroom to get ready for bed.

Talking about live music and groups had brought on another bout of depression. She'd been suffering from recurring bouts since coming south. Jessie blamed beer for her weight problem, but that wasn't the whole answer. Her loneliness and unending unhappiness were also to blame. Part of her had simply given up.

When she was in her nightie, she went over to the old wind up gramophone she'd found in the pub basement which Julian had allowed her to bring up to her room to use. She'd bought a stack of 78s down Camden Passage, an antique market not all that far away, and she now selected one of these and put it on the machine.

Lavender blue dilly dilly,
lavender green.
When I am King, dilly dilly,
you'll be my Queen. . .

'When I am King, dilly dilly, you'll be my Queen,' she echoed, and started to cry, ending up sitting on the bed, rocking herself back and forth, while the tears cascaded down her face.

The band was called The Light, and Jessie thought them not bad at all. This was their first appearance in The Lonsdale Arms, and it was on a trial basis only.

The vocalist, and guitar player, was a tall, slim, flaxen haired young man; there was a young negro man on the drums, and a very intense looking fellow on the piano. They were a trio.

Julian sidled up to Jessie while the fair young man was in the middle of Buddy Holly's hit 'Peggy Sue'. 'What's your opinion of them?' he asked for once not talking at the top of his voice.

'I like. And you?'

He nodded. 'So do the customers I've chatted to. When they take their next break, give them a drink on me, okay?'

After 'Peggy Sue' the band played 'Love Is Strange', an Everly Brothers' hit, followed by 'Crying in the Rain', another Everly hit.

When they'd finished that the drummer gave a small roll, and the guitarist, apparently the band's spokesman and leader, announced they were taking a break.

Jessie caught the guitarist's eye and crooked a finger. He stood his guitar in a corner and came over.

'Julian says you're all to have one on the house, what'll it be?' she smiled.

'Three pints would be lovely,' he replied with a grin. 'I'm Phil by the way,' he added as she pulled the pints.

'I'm Jessie.'

'Pleased to meet you, Jessie.'

When she placed the final pint in front of him he leaned in towards her. 'Do me a favour and stick in a good word for us with the guv'nor,' he whispered.

Well, this one certainly wasn't shy in coming forward, she thought. But it was enterprising, and she liked enterprising folk.

'I already have,' she winked.

He stared at her for a second, and knew she was telling the truth. 'Do you have a favourite song?' he asked.

Her mind went back. 'Do you know "Rock Island Line"?' she asked softly.

It was the first number in their next set, and all the time

Phil was singing there was a dull ache in her stomach, a lump in her throat, and a blur before her eyes. Phil might be singing, but it was Tommy's voice she was hearing.

The evening was a success for The Light. Julian bought them another drink when they'd completed their final set, and asked if they'd play the following Saturday and Sunday, which Phil hastily agreed to.

Just like old times, Jessie thought.

Phil gave her a wave when the band left the pub, and she waved back.

This was the fourth weekend that The Light had appeared at The Lonsdale Arms, and they were proving popular, as Julian had been hoping.

His takings were up, a fact the brewery had seen fit to mention on several occasions. There had even been a hint of a bonus for Julian if the trend continued.

Earlier Phil had whispered to Jessie that the band had a surprise in store for that evening, and that surprise would be their closing number.

Jessie and Yvonne had been working flat out since nine, they were so busy Julian was having to do his own pot collecting, but he didn't mind that in the least. Pixie was upstairs with her two children, the youngest of which, Sally, was ill with the mumps.

Julian plonked some more glasses on the bar, then gazed around. This was the busiest yet, with many new faces to be seen.

'And now the last number of the evening, a little concoction of our own,' Phil announced, ' "Why Fucking Not!" We hope you like it.'

Jessie nearly dropped the sweet sherry she'd just poured. Had she heard right? A glance at Julian's astounded face told her she had. A number of customers were gaping at the band.

It was the most astonishing song Jessie had ever heard, thundered out to a crashing beat it centred round the

255

repetition of the line 'Why fucking not!' while Phil leapt up and down on the spot as if he was having a fit.

Jessie knew audiences, and she could feel this one respond with enthusiasm. The enthusiasm snowballed as the number gathered more and more momentum, until Phil was literally shrieking into the stand mike in a deranged manner.

When the number was finally over the customers gave the band a huge hand, some whistling and shouting, others pounding their feet in approval and appreciation.

In the ensuing babble of conversation that broke out nearly everyone was talking about the last number. Even the few who'd found it outrageous couldn't stop talking about it.

Phil, flushed and dripping with sweat sauntered over to Julian. 'I didn't tell you about that because I thought you'd forbid us to do it. But now you've heard it and seen the reaction, can we do it as a closer every night we play here?' he asked.

Phil was right, if he'd been asked beforehand he would have said no. But now Julian readily gave his consent. The song had gone down a bomb, and, despite its refrain it was strangely inoffensive.

'We think it's going to be a crowd puller,' Phil explained excitedly.

'Just as long as it doesn't pull the police as well,' Julian joked.

Jessie looked up from the sink where she was washing glasses to find Phil on the other side of the bar. 'Do you ever get a night off?' he asked casually.

He was going to ask her out, she'd known for several weeks that he would. She had already decided what her answer would be, and that was no.

'Every Monday,' she answered immediately.

'How about me taking you to the pictures next Monday, then?'

'I'd love to,' she said, and then realized with shock that she'd accepted when she'd fully intended refusing. Now what on earth had prompted her to do that? She wasn't interested in men any more, and yet it was as though the words had had a will of their own, not uttered as a result of a message from her brain.

'Seven o'clock then, I'll be in the bar here waiting,' Phil said, and, giving her a brief smile, returned to where Oscar and Len, the other two band members, were packing up.

Oh why fucking not! Jessie told herself, and shrugged.

They went to the Odeon in Upper Street where the picture was a real oldie doing the rounds for the umpteenth time, *Nanook of the North*, the story of an eskimo.

During the entire performance Phil sat enthralled, completely caught up. Jessie glanced at him occasionally, but his eyes never wavered from the silver screen. She might just as well have been there on her own, she thought.

When the picture was over they went out into the hot and sultry June night. Jessie didn't like this sort of weather at all, it was far too close and sticky for her taste, quite different to Glasgow where even when the temperature was high there was a freshness off the sea.

'I adore everything about eskimos and the north pole, I just find them fascinating.' Phil said, his eyes glowing with enthusiasm.

'So I noticed,' Jessie replied drily, but her sarcasm passed him by.

'The eskimo name for themselves is *Innuit*. It means The People,' he told her.

'You're not part eskimo yourself by any chance?' she said, and laughed, anyone less eskimo looking she couldn't imagine.

'No,' he said. 'I'm hundred per cent Jewish.'

She was flabbergasted. 'But you're so blond? I'd never have dreamt . . .' She trailed off, wondering if she was being rude.

'We don't all have huge hooters and need to shave twice a day,' he laughed. 'Some of us are fair and baby-faced and beautiful like me.'

'What's your last name, then?' she asked.

'Jacobs.'

Well that was Jewish enough, she thought. Phil Jacobs, it had a pleasant ring to it.

They walked towards Islington Green. 'It's early still, we could have a drink, or how about coming in for coffee? I live only over the road,' Phil said.

She was curious enough to want to know more about him, but didn't really want to go into a pub, six nights a week in one was sufficient. 'I'll have the coffee,' she answered.

They turned into St. Peter's Street, which ran down the side of the Camden Passage Antique Market where she'd bought her 78s, a long road of Georgian houses that were gradually being taken over and done up by the new people moving into the area.

He had a ground floor flat, a small reception doubling as bedroom, and an adjoining kitchen of the same size. He told her his bathroom was at the end of the entrance-way passage, where he had exclusive use of the bath, but had to share the w.c. with the nasty old biddy upstairs.

He closed the front curtains, having already switched on the lights, and went through to the kitchen where he started filling the kettle.

Jessie took the opportunity to look around. The walls and ceiling were painted white and on the floor was a fitted chocolate brown carpet that had seen better, and chocolatier days.

There were racks of bookshelves on either side of the chimney, each crammed to overflowing with books, mainly paperbacks. The original fireplace had been taken out and a gas one installed. The furniture consisted of a green moquette armchair, a pouffe, a single bed and a radiogram.

Switching her interest to the kitchen she saw there was

a pine table and two pine chairs there. The black and white squared vinyl floor didn't appear to have been acquainted with a brush or mop in ages, though the rest of the flat seemed clean and tidy enough.

'It's a nice place you've got here,' she said.

'Thank you. It's big drawback is the woman upstairs. I'm convinced she's quite mad. Would you believe she keeps a bucket upstairs which she pees in, and brings the bucket down once a week to pour its contents down the w.c.?'

Jessie screwed up her face in a combination of distaste and laughter. 'But why does she do that? Does she have trouble getting up and down the stairs?'

'Not her, she's as nimble as a mountain goat. I've no idea why, she just does, that's all. And I'll tell you this, it doesn't half pong after. She's no sooner back in her own flat than I'm out in the loo with Domestos.'

Jessie laughed at the picture of him chucking Domestos down the pan with one hand and holding his nose with the other.

He told her some more stories about Mrs Perkins which had her in stiches. She hadn't laughed like this for months.

'I've been wanting to ask, why do you call the band The Light?' she asked after a while.

'The light referred to isn't electric, but inner,' he answered seriously.

'Oh!' she exclaimed, taken aback by this new pretentiousness.

She judged Phil to be about twenty-four in which case he was a couple of years younger than herself. 'What do you do beside the band?' she asked, accepting a mug of coffee from him.

'Nothing, the band's it. I used to have a proper job, as the expression goes, but I gave it up once we got the band together. You see, I have every intention that the band will succeed.'

She was impressed; not only enterprising, but a man of

positive action and determination as well. 'And what was your so called proper job?'

'A stockbroker, as my father is, and his father before him. We're a family of stockbrokers.'

'It sounds as though your family is well off?'

He gave a thin smile. 'Stinking rich. We've got a house you could easily get lost in.'

'So what do your parents think about you breaking with family tradition?'

Phil laughed, and ran a hand in comb-like fashion through his shoulder length hair. 'Father gave me his blessing, but my mother! She had hysterics when I told her what I intended doing. She's round here at least once a week trying to make me change my mind and go back to the firm. She swears I've broken her heart.'

'Mothers tend to worry,' Jessie smiled.

'You can say that again.' Phil laughed. 'But she could let me be myself.'

'At least you've got a good solid profession to fall back on should you fail to make it in the music world,' she said.

'I'll make it, Jessie. Nothing, and no one, is going to stop me.'

She raised her mug in salute. 'Here's to your musical career then,' she toasted.

He acknowledged her toast by raising his own mug, then they both drank.

'I have some Bacardi if you prefer?' he suggested.

She was enjoying herself more than she'd thought possible. 'Sure,' she smiled. He poured them fairly large ones, topping the glasses up with coke, and they abandoned the coffee.

'How did you meet Oscar and Len?' Jessie asked once they were settled again.

'I heard about Oscar through a mutual friend, and Oscar knew Len,' he explained. 'It was as simple as that. Of course,' he continued, 'actually getting gigs isn't quite that simple. The Lonsdale Arms was our first.'

'What do you do the nights you're not playing The

Lonsdale Arms?' Phil told her they were managing two sometimes three, dates during that time, mainly private functions which they were getting through word of mouth.

'And "Why Fucking Not!" was that a joint effort?'

He grinned wryly, 'No, it was my baby, really. I wanted something completely different, something that would grab attention, make people sit up and take notice. "Why Fucking Not!" was what I came up with.'

'It's certainly different, I'll grant you that,' she laughed taking another drink of her rum.

'Now tell me about you,' Phil prompted.

The last thing Jessie wanted was to talk about her life up until then, so she gave Phil a much edited version. She told him she'd been married, that the marriage had failed, and that because of that failure she'd come to London to start afresh. She added that her parents were in Glasgow, but she wasn't in contact with them as they'd fallen out years ago.

Phil poured them each more Bacardi, and they talked about the current music scene, a subject he knew inside out. More Bacardi was poured, and more after that, then Jessie, feeling somewhat high by now, and unusually relaxed, excused herself to go to the loo.

When she returned Phil was waiting in ambush. She'd no sooner closed the door behind her than he'd taken her in his arms and was pressing an eager mouth against hers, a hand groping for her breast.

She pushed him away angrily. 'What do you think you're doing?' she demanded coldly.

He looked at her in confusion. 'I'm sorry, I got the impression you liked me. We were getting on so well together.'

'I do like you, but that doesn't give you the right to attack me.'

His face coloured. 'It wasn't meant as an attack. It wasn't meant that way at all.'

She took a deep breath, and told herself she was being

261

stupid, she should have seen how things were going, what had she expected? But she'd been enjoying herself so much that she forgot to pay attention.

'I'd like to go home now. You don't have to worry about walking me back, I'll be quite all right on my own,' she said softly.

Phil looked miserable. 'I've offended you,' he muttered.

She indicated what remained of her drink. 'Thank you for the Bacardi, I've really enjoyed tonight.'

He tried to insist on escorting her home, but she was even more insistent that he didn't. Finally she escaped out into the night, turning at the end of St. Peter's Street to find he was standing outside his flat staring after her. When he raised a hand in salute she waved in return.

She berated herself all the way home. She'd handled that extremely badly and felt guilty about being so cold and angry with him. It was just that he'd caught her so unawares, she told herself. For a while there she'd felt so much like her old self that she hadn't expected a pass.

Stupid stupid stupid, she told herself.

When she got back to the pub she went straight up to her room, and there got ready for bed. She looked at her naked body in disgust. She'd got so fat! She ran her hands over her thighs and hips.

How could Phil fancy someone so fat she wondered? And yet fancy her he did, even though she wasn't as pretty as she'd been less than a year ago – even though her own husband had found her so unattractive that he had wanted someone else.

Well, she thought as she climbed into bed. Phil didn't matter now, not after the way she'd behaved.

Much to Jessie's surprise, Phil asked her out the following Monday night, and to her further surprise she accepted. They went to the Upper Street Odeon again where, this time, there was a Cary Grant film on that was much more to her taste than *Nanook of the North*.

On coming out they went to a cafe for coffee, chatting over several cups before he took her back to The Lonsdale Arms.

Instead of trying to kiss her goodnight he shook her by the hand and said he'd found the evening a pleasure. She wasn't at all sure whether he was being polite and formal, or taking the Michael.

In the middle of the week he popped into the pub to say he'd like to see her that Monday, but he desperately wanted to watch a show that was on television, he'd just rented one he explained, and how would she feel about coming round to St. Peter's Street and watching it with him? 'I'll even throw in a home-cooked meal,' he grinned.

He was a perseverer, she had to give him that. 'That sounds great, Phil,' she found herself saying. 'I'd love to.' Then she moved off to serve a customer. When she returned to where he'd been he was gone.

Saturday and Sunday nights the pub was jammed to bursting. Everyone came to hear The Light, and this fantastic new number, 'Why Fucking Not!'

As Julian remarked to Jessie, The Lonsdale Arms was rapidly becoming the 'in' place in Islington. And not just Islington, either. Why, a couple he'd spoken to earlier had come all the way from Chelsea just to hear 'Why Fucking Not!'

On the Monday morning Jessie had the luxury of a long lie, after which, as it was a glorious day, she went for a walk down to a nearby leg of the Regents Canal where she watched the gaily coloured narrow boats chug past. She was feeling better than she had in a long time and then a boat which had thistles and bluebells on it went by, making her think of Glasgow and how much she missed it. Not Boyd Street and Allison Street and her being Queen of the Glasgow Teds, but the very essence of Glasgow itself that ran through its streets and its people alike.

She thought of Tommy, the Linn Park, the Boyd

Street Boys, they were all gone forever. She doubted she would ever return there, she could never go back to the source of her pain.

She thought about her parents and wondered; they could be dead for all she knew. And Lizzle Dunnachie, dear chain-smoking Lizzie, what had become of her? She thought of Battlefield, the Fives Cafe, and seducing Alec Muir because she'd been worried about not being sexually attractive.

And Eve Smith, now Eve Baxter, she mustn't forget Eve, and the image of Eve that was forever burned into her memory, or Eve's laugh, triumphant and mocking. A laugh that would haunt her till her dying day.

Putting a hand to her forehead, Jessie discovered it was cold with sweat. Going back to the pub she tried to sleep some more, but couldn't. Every time she closed her eyes she saw Eve and Tommy.

Tommy and Eve. . . .

Phil had cooked spaghetti bolognaise, and complimented it with the traditional bottle of chianti. They ate in the kitchen. The spaghetti was surprisingly good. 'I'm so impressed,' she laughed 'that I'll wash if you dry.'

When the bottle of chianti was finished, he produced a second, saying it was what posh folk called 'the other half'. With a full glass in her hand Jessie settled down in the green moquette chair while he turned on his new hired telly. When he had the channel he wanted he sat on the pouffe.

The show was called Espresso Coffee, and, as Phil explained to Jessie, was a forum for rock bands, both the well-known and the not-so-well-known. Jessie sat back in her chair, thinking to herself that she was going to enjoy this.

The first band were the Bepops, a coloured group who sang exceptionally well. Phil told her they'd just returned from a tour of West Germany.

'The next band this evening is the Tommy McBride Skiffle Band!' the compere announced, and a curtain flew away to reveal Tommy, Jack, Sammy and Jake 'The Rake'.

Jessie went very still, her heart thumping nineteen to the dozen, as she stared at Tommy. The band was already into their first number.

Phil glanced in her direction, about to say something, but frowned instead. 'Are you all right?' he asked concernedly. She looked as if she'd had a bad turn. When he got no reply he repeated his question with even more concern.

Jessie's mouth had gone so dry she had to consciously make an effort to speak.

'That's my husband,' she whispered, pointing to the box.

Phil brought his attention back to the set, as Jessie's surname was McBride she could only be talking about the vocalist.

He took in the black drape, black drainies, brothel creepers, gaucho tie, flamboyant white shirt and well greased quiff. 'Is your husband a real Ted?' he asked.

Jessie nodded. 'As real as they come. He's King of the Glasgow Teds.'

Phil pursed his lips in amazement, here was a revelation indeed. His barmaid, the shy and reserved Jessie, married to a King of the Teds. Who would have imagined such a thing?

Tommy hadn't changed since she'd seen him last, he was exactly as she remembered. She almost felt as though she could reach out and touch him, as though she could reach into the past and nothing would have changed.

'Tommy and I collaborated on the number he's singing,' she said just to hear herself say something.

Phil was further amazed. 'You write music?' he exclaimed.

'Only for Tommy and the band. I wrote some by myself, but the best were those where I scored the music

265

and Tommy added the lyrics. He has a feel for lyrics,' she said softly, her lips trembling.

The show wasn't from Scotland, but transmitted from Lime Grove, which meant Tommy was in London. Was Eve with him, she wondered? A jagged pang of jealousy shot through her so real that she almost cried out.

No doubt Eve was waiting for him in his dressing room even now, the pair of them intending to paint the town red once the show was over. She could see the two of them together, hear them laughing.

It suddenly hit Jessie that she was wasting what remained of her life because of Tommy McBride. If she went on as she had been she would be mourning him forever, afraid to ever trust another man, afraid to ever love again. And would Tommy McBride care if she spent the rest of her life lonely and unwanted? Would Tommy McBride care that she wasted her life, an old maid with a fondness for beer? Tommy McBride was obviously on top of the world, and Eve undoubtedly on top of it with him.

'Did you know this second number is in the Top Ten?' Phil asked eagerly.

It was another number she and Tommy had collaborated on. If it was in the top ten then she was due royalties from it, an amount which might even be substantial. Well, she might be due those royalties, but didn't want them. She didn't want anything from that past association. Her pub job paid what she needed, she had enough, she'd get by.

'The Top Ten? That's interesting,' she said drily.

When the show was over, they polished off what remained of the chianti. 'Did it upset you seeing your husband again?' Phil asked gently.

'Not in the least,' Jessie lied. 'He means nothing to me now, nothing at all.'

He watched her closely. 'You don't look like someone who'd be married to a Teddy Boy,' he said at last.

Jessie gave a soft smile, what clothes she'd brought

266

with her from Glasgow had long since been consigned to the dustbin, and the replacements she'd bought were all 'straight'. She'd even had her hair cut in a different style, now it was neatly cut and layered, the epitome of respectability.

'The last thing *you* look is Jewish.' She teased. 'And yet you are. Appearances can be deceiving.'

Rising, she crossed to the window and closed the curtains. 'Do you still want to sleep with me?' she asked, keeping her back to him.

Another surprise! She was just full of them tonight, he thought.

He came to her and placed his hands on her hips, taking a firm but sensual hold of them. 'Yes,' he stated simply.

Jessie trembled, the last male hands other than Tommy's to touch her that way had been those in Linton Street, hands of hated memory.

'Doesn't it bother you that I'm fat?' she asked quietly.

'You're not fat, just well covered,' Phil whispered. 'I think you're lovely.'

She places her hands on his. 'Have you any more of that chianti?' she asked, still without turning round.

'I can go out and get another bottle.'

When he returned with the wine he found her in his bed, waiting.

Tommy was sitting in the bar at the BBC Lime Grove studios with the rest of the band and some others who'd latched on to them. He knew he and the band had gone down well on Espresso Coffee, everybody had said so.

Jake 'The Rake', flanked by two make-up girls whom he was holding by their waists, delivered the tag line of a funny story he was telling, and the company burst into laughter.

Tommy's laughter died in his throat when he caught sight of a lassie who'd just come into the bar. Her face was in profile to him, and the likeness was uncanny. It might have been Jessie standing there.

267

Sadness overwhelmed him. In his heart was nothing but a terrible, aching loneliness. He thought back to that awful day when Jessie had discovered him with Eve, shuddering at the memory. He would have given everything he had to make that day never have happened.

For what might have been the millionth time he wondered how she was, and how she was doing. If only she hadn't bolted as she had, but stayed and let him try to explain. If only she had just talked to him. If only. . . The lassie he was staring at turned round so that she was now full face to him, and with that the spell was broken. Face on, she didn't look at all like Jessie.

'You all right, china?' asked Jack.

Tommy brought himself out of his reverie and smiled. 'Never better,' he lied.

Jake 'The Rake' launched into another story that was even funnier than the first.

Tommy pretended to listen, but really he was thinking, remembering.

Jessie lay smoking a cigarette while Phil snored gently beside her. It was impossibly cramped in his single bed, but she'd put up with it while she smoked, then she'd get dressed and return to the pub.

Being made love to by Phil hadn't been anything like being made love to by Tommy. The trouble was that when she'd been with Tommy their lovemaking had been exactly that, the making of love. At least it had been on her part for she'd been in love with him. With Phil it had been no more than sex, and the difference between the two was enormous.

She might not love Phil but she did like him – she liked him a great deal. If he wanted to continue seeing her she'd be agreeable, just as she'd be agreeable to their continuing to go to bed together.

It might have been sex rather than the true making of love, but it hadn't been that bad, and it might get better if she worked at it. At least her period of mourning was over and she'd found someone new, she was grateful for that.

Outside a bird sang, heralding the rising of the dawn.

She was about to slip from the bed when Phil, who'd been lying quietly awake for some time, pulled himself on top of her, and she discovered dawn wasn't the only thing that had risen.

The band was half an hour late, and as they'd never been late before Julian was fretting, glancing anxiously every other minute at the clock above the bar. Early in the evening as it was, the pub was already doing brisk business, many of those present there to hear The Light sing their notorious song later on.

Julian had had to increase his staff for the nights when The Light were appearing, those nights he now had three extra girls, besides himself, Jessie and Yvonne, working the bar.

Through one of the leaded windows Jessie saw Oscar's purple van draw up, and called out to Julian that the band had arrived. The van was used to transport their equipment, including Len's piano.

Phil came striding into the pub, glanced round as if looking for someone, then went to Julian who, much relieved, greeted him warmly.

'Sorry we're late, but Oscar and I had to take Len home again. He woke up with a dose of flu this morning which has got worse as the day's gone on. He thought he might make it despite that, but he flaked out on the way here. It's impossible for him to play tonight,' Phil explained.

'But you and Oscar can still manage something?' Julian asked, anxious once more.

Phil turned to Jessie who'd joined Julian during his explanation of what had happened. 'Of all nights to go ill Len couldn't have picked a worse one. I had a letter from Mick Marco of Vestal Records yesterday saying he intended dropping by this evening, I've been trying to get him here ever since we started, and now the bastard's picked this bloody night to come.' Phil said in despair, running a hand through his hair.

'How important is he?' asked Jessie.

'To us *important*,' Oscar said.

Phil looked like he might cry. 'Shit,' he swore.

'I don't think we should play as a twosome, we'd be completely out of balance and Marco might get the wrong impression of us,' Oscar said to Phil.

'That's what's been bothering me too. But if we let him down tonight there's no telling when he'll come back again, maybe never.'

Jessie felt for them, it was a case of the devil and the deep blue sea. 'Can I make a suggestion?' she asked hestitantly.

Phil waved his hand. 'Go ahead.'

'If Julian says it's all right, I'll play piano for you. That way Marco can hear you as a threesome, and you can explain to him after that I'm only a stand-in.'

'I didn't know you played piano,' frowned Phil.

'Well I do.'

'But can you play our numbers?' Oscar demanded.

'There's nothing you've ever played here that I can't play. And I've heard you so often now I know your style inside out.'

'If he likes us with Jessie then that might encourage him to come back soon and hear us with Len,' Oscar said to Phil.

'I won't let you down, I promise.' Jessie smiled.

She was the magician who kept pulling rabbits out of the top hat, Phil thought. 'Does she have your permission to become a member of The Light for this evening?' he asked Julian.

'Certainly,' Julian replied, calming himself by thinking he'd get Pixie down from upstairs as a replacement for Jessie behind the bar.

'Then let's give it a whirl,' Phil said, and with a word

to Oscar he and Oscar started back for the van to begin unloading their gear.

Jessie was suddenly nervous. Had she made a bloomer by volunteering herself? It had been a long time since she'd played after all. And there would be no sheet music, she'd have to play by ear.

Of course she could do it, she told herself, her ear was excellent, and as for the actual playing itself, playing a piano was like riding a bike, once you knew how, you knew for life. She might be a little rusty to begin with, but that would soon wear off as she got into the swing of it.

Jessie continued serving until Phil and Oscar were set up, then she went over and sat at Len's piano, a smallish instrument that had been reduced to a working skeleton to make it easier to be carted from place to place.

Butterflies fluttered in her stomach when she placed her hands on the keyboard, then Phil was blowing into the stand mike and telling the crowd that Len wouldn't be appearing that night because of illness, but that Jessie McBride, the barmaid they all knew and loved, would be tinkling the ivories in his place. 'How about a show of appreciation for Jessie, please?' he called.

Oscar gave Jessie a drum roll as she acknowledged the applause. Phil said what the first set would be, and the order it would be played in.

'Ready?' he asked her.

'As I'll ever be,' she replied, a smile wavering on her face.

And so, off they went.

Within minutes her nervousness had completely disappeared, and she was thoroughly enjoying herself, and surprising herself by playing as well as she'd ever done despite the time it had been since she'd last sat at a piano.

They played Presley numbers – 'Hound Dog', 'Blue Suede Shoes', and 'Heartbreak Hotel' – following these with Tommy Steele's 1956 smash, 'Rock with the Cave Man'. The audience shouted for more.

At the end of the fourth set, and relishing a pint sent over by Julian, Jessie said to Phil, 'Any sign of Marco yet?'

'He came in about ten minutes ago.' Phil replied softly out the side of this mouth, and went on to describe where Marco was standing and what he looked like.

Over the rim of her glass Jessie's eyes casually sought out Marco. He was a short, barrel-chested man of about forty, dressed in a very expensive Italian-cut suit. He was talking animatedly to a stunning woman half his age whose clothes suggested both money and class.

Announcing the fifth set, Phil explained again about Jessie standing in for the ill Len, this for Marco's benefit, and again Jessie was given an enthusiastic and appreciative round of applause.

Finally last orders were called, and it was time for the number everyone was waiting for. The conversation and general pub noise died down in anticipation.

Phil excelled himself, leaping about like a crazy man, while the crowd, as always, went wild. It never ceased to amaze Jessie how the public, and repeated, utterance of 'that word' could provoke such a reaction, but it did. Perhaps a psychologist could have explained it, but she certainly couldn't.

When it was over the crowd continued to cheer, shout, stamp their feet, and more or less act as if demonically possessed. 'Again! Again!' they cried to no avail, Julian was most strict about that, it was difficult enough getting them out at the end, and he knew the local police kept a watchful eye on his premises.

Mick Marco and his companions made their way over. 'Absolutely terrif!' Marco enthused.

'How about recording it then?' Phil put in quickly.

Marco gave a wry smile and shook his head. 'You know that's impossible, but I wish I could. If I could I would.'

Phil, who'd met Marco previously, introduced Oscar and Jessie, and Marco responded by introducing the girl with him whose name was Caroline.

When Caroline spoke Jessie realized she was very upper crust indeed, the sort whose daddy has a 'seat' in the country, and whose ancestors came over with Duke William.

Caroline had a beautiful figure and a face to match. Jessie, overweight and self-conscious as she was, felt dreadful beside her. There had been a time when she'd have held her own, she thought, but no more.

Marco listened sympathetically to Phil's account of Len's flu, then Marco said he thought Jessie had been an admirable stand-in, he'd been impressed with all of them.

'I'll tell you what, why don't I come back again next Saturday to hear the band as it should be?' Marco suggested.

Phil's face lit up. That was precisly what he'd been hoping for. Oscar was beaming fit to bust.

'That would be fab.' Phil grinned.

'It's a date, then,' Marco confirmed.

When a few minutes later the pub had finally been cleared, and the doors shut, Marco asked Julian if he could buy everyone a drink, to which Julian agreed.

After a while Marco and Caroline left, Marco repeating that they'd be back the following Saturday.

When Marco and Caroline had gone Phil told Jessie what a grand job she'd done for the band that night, she'd been marvellous, a sentiment Oscar seconded.

Oscar went to the loo, and Phil to the telephone at the far end of the pub to ring Len and tell him the good news.

Jessie lit a cigarette and took another swallow of beer. She was shattered, but high with elation. She'd enjoyed the evening tremendously, the more so because it had been so unexpected.

Stubbing out her cigarette, she began playing a tune that had been running through her mind lately. Going back, altering and re-phrasing as she'd used to do on her piano in Allison Street.

The tune had a haunting quality about it that appealed to her, it was a love-song, she decided, a sad love-song.

273

'I like that, what is it?' Phil asked coming up beside her.

She glanced up, unaware until he'd spoken that he'd returned. 'It doesn't have a name yet. It hasn't even been scored properly.'

'You mean it's one of yours?'

She nodded, and played it from the top as far as she'd worked out.

Phil took a stool and sat beside her. 'Can I ask you a favour?' he smiled.

'Ask away.'

'Will you write it for me? I've been looking for original material for some time, but so far I haven't come up with anything. I've tried Tin Pan Alley, but the decent songs there get snapped up by the established singers and bands with a name, not to mention their managers and agents.'

Jessie broke into 'Bony Moronie' while she thought about Phil's request. Why not? she asked herself, there was no reason why she shouldn't help him, and he was right, he did need original material. Playing other people's numbers was okay to start out with, but if a singer and band were to progress they couldn't go on that way.

'Okay, I'll write it for you,' she said simply.

Phil leaned over and kissed her on the tip of the nose. 'You're smashing,' he whispered.

It was the happiest she'd been since finding Tommy and Eve.

It was good to get back to writing music, she hadn't realized how much she'd missed it. As usual the music itself had been easy; as usual the lyrics were difficult.

She picked up her pencil, and laid it down again. She picked it up once more, chewed its end, and this time threw it down. She hummed the tune through, willing images into her mind, but nothing came.

She lit a cigarette and topped up her glass of whisky from the half bottle she'd bought in the off licence a block away.

A love-song, she reminded herself, that's what this is, a sad, haunting, love-song. Picking up the pencil she hastily scribbled 'Totti'.

Totti, what on earth did that mean?

She smiled as the answer came to her. Totti was the name of the girl the man in the song had lost. It would have to be a man losing a girl as Phil would be singing the song.

Losing someone, when had she decided that was the subject? She didn't know, what she did know was that it was right. The lyrics would be about her losing Tommy, only the sexes would be reversed. It would be a man losing a woman instead of the other way around, but the emotions and sense of loss would be the same.

She wrote:

> I miss my baby,
> I miss her, oh,
> why, oh why,
> do I still love her so?

And the chorus:
> She found another,
> and I found them.
> Together!

> I miss my baby,
> each and every night.
> I cry sad tears
> when I turn off the light.

> She found another,
> and I found them.
> Together!

When they were finished Jessie knew them to be the best lyrics she'd ever written – perhaps because they came straight from the soul.

She drank more whisky, then changed the single word

Totti to 'Missing Totti'. That would be the title of the song.

Switching out the light, she began to cry, just as she'd done so often at night when she'd been thinking about Tommy.

Just as she'd written.

'And now folks, we'd like to perform a brand new number especially written for the band, called 'Missing Totti'. It's by our very own Jessie McBride. A big hand for Jessie, please!' Phil said into the stand mike, gesturing to where Jessie was pulling a pint behind the bar. Oscar and Len led the applause.

Jessie blushed, feeling her face go quite red with embarrassment. She gave a half-hearted wave in response to the clapping, and slopped a wave of beer on to the floor as a result.

The evening had been going well so far. Phil was in fine voice and the band in good form. Because The Light was appearing the pub was packed and had been since before nine. Marco and Caroline, as promised, were present, and had wormed their way into one of the better viewing positions.

Marco was now staring at the still blushing Jessie in surprise, a song-writing barmaid! Whatever next? Then he remembered how she'd been on the piano the previous Saturday, and thought that maybe it wasn't so strange after all.

'I miss my Totti, nearly drives me bad. I always loved that girl, never treated her bad. . .' sang Phil.

The audience quietened, even those who'd been clamouring for drinks at the bar. Faces began to register the emotions of the song. Suddenly almost everyone in the pub looked sad.

The penultimate notes were on the piano, the last one of all a twang on the guitar, a twang that reverberated softly, then faded away to nothingness.

There were a few seconds of total silence, then the applause exploded. There could be no doubting that 'Missing Totti' had gone down a bomb. Phil waited till the applause finally began to ebb, then broke into the next number, 'Stand By Me'.

Jessie glanced across at Mick Marco who gave her the thumbs up sign, then she was back to pulling pints as it became pandemonium at the bar again.

By quarter past eleven the last customers had gone, ejected by Julian, and Phil, Marco, Caroline, Oscar and Len were sitting around a table while Jessie put a fresh tray of drinks, compliments of Marco, in front of them.

'Do you mind if I have Jessie join us here?' Marco called over to Julian, who replied that was all right by him. So Jessie sat beside Phil while the other girls got on with the washing and drying of the glasses.

'I'll come right to the point,' Marco said. 'I'd like to record The Light doing 'Missing Totti'.

'Hot damn!' Len muttered, and slapped Oscar on the back.

Phil wanted to give a loud whoop of delight, but refrained from doing so, thinking Marco would consider it juvenile.

'But, do you have another new number for the flip side?' Marco went on.

Phil glanced at Jessie.

'When do you want to tape?' she asked Marco.

He consulted a pocket diary. 'How about the week after next?'

'The Light will have a second new number by then, I promise you.'

Marco nodded slowly. There was more to this girl than met the eye. Her reply hadn't been boastful, but confident – the confidence of someone who knew exactly what she was doing. 'Something tells me this isn't new to you,' he said thoughtfully.

Jessie gave a small smile. 'It isn't.'

'Her husband is Tommy McBride of the Tommy McBride Skiffle Band,' Phil interrupted. 'She and he collaborated in the past.'

'Ah!' Marco breathed.

One of the songs they collaborated on is number six in the charts,' Phil continued, ignoring the look on Jessie's face.

'Well I'll be. . .!' Oscar whistled. Neither Phil nor Jessie had let on to him or Len about her connection with Tommy, or even that she was married. She didn't wear a wedding ring; she'd thrown that out of the carriage window during the train journey down from Glasgow.

'So it's a pro I've got here,' Marco smiled.

' "Missing Totti" is extremely good, it has quality,' Caroline said.

Jessie blushed. If anyone at that table knew about quality it was the aristocratic Caroline. 'Thank you,' she mumbled.

'What day the week after next?' Phil asked Marco.

Marco shrugged. 'Do you have a preference?'

'The Monday would be best. It's Jessie's day off and it's only right that she's there at the recording,' Phil explained.

Marco again consulted his diary. 'At the moment, that date is fully booked, but there's a switch I can make, so the Monday it is. Shall we say two in the afternoon at our studios in Foubert's Place?'

'Two it is, then,' Phil replied quickly.

Marco was pleased with himself. He had a feeling about 'Missing Totti'. As Caroline said, it had quality, and, as he saw it, wide appeal.

When the girls had finished washing up and drying Julian bought another round, which included the staff drink, and Marco another after that. Julian was delighted to hear the news that The Light would be making a record, but also a bit worried about it. He could see himself losing this band that had done so much for his weekend takings, and which had made his pub the 'in' place in Islington.

Later Jessie went with Phil to St. Peter's Street, where they celebrated the forthcoming record with Carlsberg Specials they'd brought from the pub, lying naked in front of the blazing gas fire.

Foubert's Place was in Soho, an area Jessie hadn't been to before. Strolling along the narrow streets with Phil and Len its bohemian ambience now delighted her. It didn't even smell like a part of Britain, but the way she imagined the Continent must smell.

The majority of the shops were foreign, and filled with things she'd never seen before. One shop window was crammed with more types of cheeses than she would have thought existed in the entire world. The exotic smells were almost intoxicating.

On arriving in Foubert's Place they saw that Oscar and his van were there waiting for them, as they'd arranged.

They all went inside together.

The pretty receptionist made an internal telephone call and moments later Marco came bustling out to greet them personally. He asked Oscar for the van's keys, which Oscar handed over, saying they weren't to worry about their gear and equipment, he'd have his people unload and set it up for them in the studio.

Jessie was thrilled with everything. It was all so tremendously exciting, and she could tell from the gleam in Phil's eyes that she thought so, too.

The studio itself was something of a disappointment, smaller and more cramped than she'd expected. Sound technicians were fussing around, testing and making adjustments to the various mikes overhanging the performing area.

Marco ordered coffee, which appeared almost instantly, and they all repaired to the producer's booth which could only be entered from the corridor outside.

'How do you feel?' Marco smiled at Phil.

'Raring to go,' Phil replied.

'What's the second number you've got for me?' Marco asked Jessie, who handed him her score of 'Lamplighter Rock', a number in complete contrast to the sad, haunting 'Missing Totti'.

'They go well together,' Len said.

Marco didn't have to be told that, for he read music, and could see for himself that was the case.

The band drank coffee and chatted till the set up had been completed for them, they went through to the performing area for rehearsal. Jessie remained in the booth with Marco and four console operators.

The band played each number through twice, then announced they were ready whenever Marco was. Marco told them the operators said they'd go in a minute. They'd get a red light for warning, a green for the off.

It didn't start well. Phil was so nervous he fluffed his lyrics during the first two takes, and Len sounded as if he was playing with ten thumbs, all of them bandaged.

Marco assured Jessie in a whisper that he'd been expecting this. It wasn't at all uncommon when bands recorded for the first time and they'd settle down eventually. Sure enough, after a while they did.

It was twenty to five when they finally laid down a satisfactory tape of 'Missing Totti' and Marco called a break for coffee and cigarettes. Len asked for a proper drink, and was refused. No booze in studio time; house rules.

As the band trooped back into the performing area Caroline slipped into the booth. She gave Marco a peck on the cheek, then came to sit beside Jessie.

'How's it going?' she whispered.

Jessie grimaced, and Caroline gave a sympathetic smile.

Phil broke a guitar string, and everyone had to wait while he fixed a new one. There was a further hold-up while he retuned the guitar.

'You learn patience in this game,' Marco said to Jessie.

After twenty-seven takes, Marco glanced at the console operators in turn. Receiving a confirmatory nod from each, he flicked a switch and spoke directly to the band. 'That's it, lads. I'm satisfied. We've got two good masters. You can have that drink now, Len.'

Jessie had been watching Marco's face. He wasn't ecstatic about the final takes, but on the other hand he wasn't disappointed. She glanced through the glass panels. Phil had taken off his guitar, and was stretching. There were dark stains under his arms and at the small of his back.

Marco asked Caroline to take Jessie and the band to the hospitality room. He'd be along in a few minutes when he'd finished in the studio.

'How do you think it went?' Phil whispered to Jessie as they followed Caroline.

'It was fine,' she whispered in reply.

'Was Marco pleased?'

'Well, he wasn't jumping about shouting eureka! But he wasn't throwing up in the corner, either. I'd say he got what he wanted.'

Phil took a deep breath, he was absolutely shattered. He wouldn't have believed that recording could take so much out of you. It took up far more energy than playing before a live audience, for him at least.

The hospitality room was decorated in a soothing shade of green. Along one wall there was a trellis table with a white linen tablecloth over it. There were so many bottles on the table that it seemed strange that it wasn't sagging under the weight of them.

There were other people dotted round the largish room, all talking in low tones, as if confiding secrets to one another. They were all men, and they all wore expensive business suits.

Jessie gazed about her, taking everything in, just as she'd been taking everything in since entering the building. Vestal Records might be a small company, but it

281

certainly wasn't operating on a shoestring. There was money here, and a lot of it.

'Jesus Christ!' Phil exclaimed suddenly, his voice shrill with excitement.

She turned, startled. 'What is it?'

'Do you know who that is?' he asked, nodding in the direction of two of the business suits.

She'd never seen either man before. 'No, who is it?'

'The taller man is Larry Parnes, who handles Billy Fury, Joe Brown, Duffy Power and Georgie Fame, to mention but a few. He's a very big noise indeed!' Phil breathed.

Jessie studied the man in question. She knew of him by reputation, and Phil was right, he was a big noise, in pop music his name was about as big as it got.

Phil gripped Jessie by the arm. 'Seeing him makes me realize I'm really on my way. It won't be long now till I'm up there with Billy Fury and Joe Brown, as big a star as they are,' he said, his voice filled with longing and desire.

A star! What memories that word evoked. Star Gray – it seemed a lifetime ago.

What is love? It is the morning and the evening star.

She had to smile. How pretentious to call herself Star; she cringed now to think about it. Yet, then, she'd considered it the most sophisticated thing in the world.

She remembered the night in Tommy's bedroom, the first time she'd visited the house in Millbrae Crescent, when she'd explained her chosen name to him. She also remembered that it was because of him that, later, she'd dropped the name.

'What are you thinking about?' Phil asked, noticing the far away look in her eyes, as if she were watching something a long way off.

With an effort, she brought herself back to the present. 'I was just recalling a star I used to know when I was young, so very young,' she replied wistfully.

He wondered what she was talking about. A star, what star? But before he could get her to elaborate, Mick

Marco arrived and gestured him over to the drinks table. He promptly forgot about Jessie and her mysterious star.

Jessie was serving up a pint of Guinness when Phil came into the pub. Although it was nearly noon he'd just got up because the band had been playing a private function down in Godalming, Surrey, the night before.

If it hadn't been *the day*, he'd still be in bed. But it was *the day*, the day 'Missing Totti' was being released, so he'd forced himself to get up hours before he would have done otherwise.

Jessie served the Guinness, then went over to where Julian was chatting animatedly to a customer about rugby. Julian was a great rugby fan.

'Phil's here. Can I take my break now?' she asked.

'Is it straight to the record shop?' Julian smiled.

'That's the plan.'

'Then away you go.'

Emerging from behind the counter she slipped an arm through one of Phil's. 'Excited?' she asked.

'Can't remember when I was more excited,' he grinned. 'Not even when I was little.'

Jessie pulled herself closer to him. She'd been looking forward to this moment ever since the recording session. Marco had sent them free copies of the single, but they still wanted to go into a shop and actually buy it for themselves, to make the whole thing real.

The closest record shop was in Cross Street, just off Upper Street. Arriving there they stopped outside to stare in the window.

Norman Banks, the owner, and a Lonsdale Arms regular, hadn't let them down. Norman had made a display of 'Missing Totti' and 'Lamplighter Rock'. A hand-written card at the front of the display informed the public that The Light were a local band and that Jessie McBride, who'd written the numbers, was another local.

They entered the shop and Norman greeted them

effusively, gushing about what a fab disc he thought it was and how it was bound to sell a million. Then he asked them if they would autograph some copies for him, which could only help sales, and was a personal booster for the shop.

They ended up signing every copy there, with the exception of the two they bought for themselves and those in the window.

Outside again, and laughing with sheer joy, they collapsed in each other's arms. 'Come on,' said Jessie, 'I'm taking you back to the pub for a drink. A celebration is definitely in order.'

En route she stopped at a street kiosk and bought a copy of the *Glasgow Herald*, as she did two or three times a week, for she liked to keep abreast of the Glasgow news.

At the pub a surprise awaited them. Julian had set up a hi-fi on the bar, his own machine from upstairs. As they came in through the front door Julian switched off the music he'd been playing, and the entire pub broke into applause. Nor did Jessie have to buy that drink for Julian had already put double whiskies on the bar for them.

Julian called for silence. 'You are now going to hear the disc of a song that was first sung in this very pub,' he announced. 'And I'm expecting each and every one of you to go out and buy a copy of it.'

Julian then solemnly asked Phil for his copy of the record, which Phil, equally solemnly, handed over.

There was a collective hush as Julian placed the disc on the spindle, a hush that continued as he clicked the play switch, and the arm descended.

'I miss my baby,' Phil's voice sang in the silent room. 'I miss her, oh, Why, oh why, do I still love her so?'

It was quite impossible to honestly judge the record in these circumstances, Jessie thought, and anyway, for the moment she was too subjective by far. To her it sounded great.

Listening to the lyrics she couldn't help but think of Tommy. Every detail of him came back to her, as though she were flipping through the pages of a photograph album. When would the pain stop, she wondered for the millionth time. When would she be able to think about him without re-breaking her heart?

'Missing Totti' came to an end, and everyone clapped enthusiastically. Julian turned the disc over and played the flip side.

Phil's face was flushed with pride. He accepted another large whisky that was thrust on him, as did Jessie, telling herself that that would have to be the last if she was going to get back to work, which she'd have to do shortly.

'Missing Totti' was played again, and Pixie suddenly appeared from the rear of the pub, where she'd been cooking, to declare it the best thing she'd heard in years, a remark which raised a ragged cheer of approval.

The record was played non-stop for half an hour, then Jessie insisted they stop playing it before everyone was sick and tired of it and never wanted to hear it again.

Phil stayed on a little longer, then told Jessie he was going home to get some more sleep. She could see this was only partly true. His real reason for going home was to continue playing his record. 'You go get some rest,' she said understandingly. Having your first disc out was something very special she knew, particularly for someone like Phil who so hungered after success.

It developed into a pretty hectic lunch time session. When it was all over, the glasses washed and dried, and the floor swept, Jessie sat down with Julian and Pixie to have their own lunch. It wasn't until then, while Julian and Pixie were chatting about the children, that Jessie opened her *Glasgow Herald* and began to read.

Almost accidentally, she cast an eye over the obituary column. She had glanced over most of the list before she realized what she'd read. Slowly, she brought her gaze back to the name which now leapt off the page at her.

285

Alison Irene Scott Gray, nee Turnbull, beloved wife of the Reverend Kenneth Cranston Gray. . .

The words misted in front of Jessie's eyes. Her mother was dead. The funeral was in two days.

Tears trickled down her cheeks as the memories came back. They'd had some good times, she and her mother, before that last awful confrontation.

She remembered a picnic the two of them had once had at Fairlie on the Firth of Clyde, travelling there by red bus and picnicking amongst the dunes while the herring gulls screeched and squawked overhead. A fishing boat had sailed past while she was tucking into banana sandwiches and lemonade, a fishing boat with a single, beautiful, rust-coloured sail.

And the time her mother had gone out and bought her the bonnet she'd been longing for every time she passed the window of Miss Agnes's Millinery Shop for ages and ages, when, as a twelve-year-old, she'd read the lesson for the first time in church. She'd been petrified of getting up in front of the congregation, but had taken confidence from the bonnet, knowing how braw it made her look. As a result of that confidence, and her mother's thoughtfulness in buying her the bonnet, she'd got through the reading without any trouble.

And then there were the wee secrets they'd shared like the time Alison had connived and manipulated the minister into buying a Chinese style carpet she had wanted, which he had been adamant they couldn't afford. She could see Alison and herself standing side by side, laughing, the morning the carpet had been delivered.

Then, too, there was the patient, understanding way Alison had explained the workings of her body to her when she was old enough to need to know.

'What is it, Jessie?' Pixie demanded, having just that moment noticed Jessie's tears.

In a trembling voice Jessie told them about her mother's death. Julian immediately went up to the bar to get her a brandy.

She swallowed half of that, while Pixie made sympathetic noises and looked at her with anxious eyes. What should she do, if anything, she wondered. She decided to ring the manse.

When she said what she intended Julian replied she wasn't to bother with the pay phone, but to use the phone in their reception room upstairs. He added that if she wanted time off to go to the funeral then she could, of course, have it.

She went to her own room first to get a hanky, and put her copy of 'Missie Totti' beside the old wind-up gramophone. She then blew her nose, wiped her face and had a cigarette. Feeling somewhat better she went through to Julian and Pixie's reception room, heart pounding.

Her father answered the telephone. 'The Reverend Gray speaking,' he said in a quiet, distant voice.

'Father,' said Jessie nervously. 'Father, it's Jessie. I've just read about mother in the *Glasgow Herald*.'

There was a long silence. She began to think he'd hung up. 'She died of a heart attack, there was no pain,' he answered finally.

No pain, that was some consolation at least. 'Where did it happen?' she asked gently.

'At the Women's Guild. Alison was addressing them when she suddenly keeled over. The doctor said she was probably dead before she hit the floor.'

'I . . . I'm very sorry, you know,' Jessie whispered, her voice breaking. 'I . . .'

'Where are you speaking from?' her father interrupted, his voice sharp and impersonal.

'London. I live here now.'

If he was surprised to learn that she wasn't still in Glasgow he gave no sign. 'Oh, London,' was all he said.

'Do you want me to come to the funeral?' Jessie asked. His breathing suddenly became heavy and laboured, as if he were having trouble getting air into his lungs.

When he spoke again his voice was cold as ice, and hard

as Aberdeen granite. It didn't sound human at all. 'You're not welcome either in this house or at the funeral. Your mother and I disowned you years ago, I see no call to change that state of affairs because of what's happened.'

She felt as though she'd been punched in the stomach. 'I thought Jesus's creed was one of love and forgiveness,' she said. 'I think perhaps you should read the parable of the prodigal again, you seem to have forgotten its lesson.'

There was a click and then the disconnected tone buzzed in her ear. Her father had hung up.

Jessie shivered as she left the warmth of the pub. It was late November and the nights were now chilly and inhospitable. Hurrying round to St. Peter's Street, she rang Phil's bell impatiently.

When he answered the door she saw right away that he'd been boozing. Inside the flat she discovered that the floor round his chair strewn with empty beer bottles and cans.

He noticed her staring pointedly at the empties. 'Oscar and Len were round, they've just gone,' he explained, trying to appear more sober than he was.

He was clearly down and getting worse. 'How were the lads?' she asked casually.

Picking up *Melody Maker* from his bed, he thrust it into her hands. 'That's today's. After four weeks we're not even in the top fifty, let alone the top twenty,' he complained bitterly.

So that was it. She'd totally forgotten that *Melody Maker* came out that day, but Phil wouldn't forget. 'It's not the end of the world,' she replied cheerfully. He glared at her darkly – he obviously thought it was. 'Have you spoken to Marco about it?'

His lips thinned into a cynical smile. 'I've rung four times today, and each time I was told the same thing: out, out, out and out again. The message is crystal.'

He went into the kitchen, reappearing with two fresh bottles of beer.

'The message isn't at all crystal as you put it, Phil. Marco is a busy man, you know that,' she argued.

He repeated his cynical smile, and took a drink of his beer. The smile vanished as he slumped into the green moquette chair, which gave a squeak of protest. 'It was a good record, Jessie. It should have done better than it has, a damn sight better,' he complained.

She wished there were something comforting she could say. For some time now there had been something about the record that niggled her, something she hadn't been able to put her finger on. Over the past few days, however, she had listened to the record on her own and had figured it out. It was his voice. For some reason, it had a cold, alien quality about it. There was no emapthy or feeling in it. She realized then that when listening to the record she'd been hearing Phil's live voice in her mind, and not his recorded one. The two were as different as night and day. His live voice was rich and warm and haunting. Was Phil's coldness and lack of emotion on 'Missing Totti' and 'Lamplighter Rock' a fault of the sound engineers? Or was that simply the way his voice sounded on disc? It seemed to her, that there was only one way to discover the answer to that question, and that was to have a second record made.

'You must keep on at Marco, talk him into doing another record,' she said to Phil.

'Which means you now think this one's a bummer?' he replied quickly.

'Not at all, of course not. But if at first you don't succeed, try, try and try again.'

'Like your King Robert the Bruce's spider?' he asked, grinning suddenly.

'Precisely,' she grinned back, pleased to see she'd succeeded in snapping him out of his black mood.

'And *when* we get a second recording, it'll be one of your songs, I'll insist on that,'

He was lovely, she thought, if a little naive at times. 'You'll insist on nothing of the sort. If Marco wants you to record more of my songs, well and fine. If not, you'll record what he says, and not argue about it.'

He reached out and took her hand. 'You'll stay the night?' he asked in a new tone of voice.

She leaned her cheek against his hand. 'I'll stay the night,' she agreed.

Jessie was cleaning the St. Peter's Street flat. She was between pub sessions and waiting for Phil to get back from Soho where The Light was making a demo for Marco. Marco had insisted on it before he committed himself to a second record. The material being used wasn't Jessie's this time. Marco had shied away when Phil had broached the subject, and Phil, wisely heeding Jessie's advice, hadn't pursued the matter.

It was now seven weeks since 'Missing Totti' was released, and it had sunk without trace. Jessie didn't know if Vestal had pushed the record, but she suspected they hadn't. When she'd tried to quiz Marco about it he'd been evasive, muttering about the cost of promotion and the risks with new artists.

It was Jessie's guess, however, that other Vestal records coming out at the same time had been chosen to be pushed, and have money spent on them. If that was so, 'Missing Totti' had failed at the starter's gate.

She was in the kitchen, wiping down the soot ingrained Ascot, when Phil returned. 'How did it go?' she asked eagerly.

Phil took her in his arms and kissed her. 'I'm hopeful. Marco wouldn't give a decision there and then, he had to consult with other people before he did that, but I'm hopeful. It went well, I could feel it.' Phil was excited. It was the brightest he'd been in a long time.

She hugged him tightly. 'So how long before you hear?'

'Next couple of days, three at the most. Shouldn't be longer than that.'

'Then we'll just have to keep our fingers crossed,' she laughed and wished she was more hopeful for him.

In the event, Marco's verdict arrived by the next morning's post. It was only a few minutes past opening time when Phil, Oscar and Len trooped into The Lonsdale Arms, their gloomy expressions telling the whole sorry story.

'It's a bust with Marco and Vestal Records,' Phil said to Jessie, his face white as a sheet. Up until the arrival of the letter he'd been convinced Marco's decision would be in the affirmative.

'Three large navy rums, and a pistol if you have one,' Oscar ordered.

'Did Marco give you a reason?' Jessie asked as she poured the rums at the gantry.

Phil shook his head. 'Just that there wouldn't be a second recording with Vestel. But he wishes us all the very best for the future.'

If the demo session had gone as well as Phil had believed, then it had to be the way his voice came out on disc, Jessie thought. Later, when Phil played a copy of the demo record for her, this proved to be true. His voice was just as it had been on 'Missing Totti' and 'Lamplighter Rock'.

Jessie commiserated with the three downcast musicians, several times squeezing Phil's hand in sympathy. This was an awful blow to them all, but especially to him.

Len finished his rum and said they'd have another round. 'As we don't have a gig tonight,' he announced, 'I am going to get as drunk as the proverbial skunk.' Oscar and Phil cheered.

Julian appeared, and heard the news. Although secretly pleased, for he feared that a successful The Light would leave his pub, he kept a straight face as he condemned Marco's action, saying Marco had made a big mistake. He then announced that a further round of rums was to be on him.

A little later, Pixie, dressed for town, came down from upstairs. Julian had informed her what had happened. 'As far as I'm concerned,' she said loudly, 'Marco is a horse's backside. Why, The Light is fantastic! Everybody knows that.'

Pixie hung around for a few minutes, until Yvonne came on duty, wanting to make sure Yvonne turned up before leaving, then said goodbye to everyone, she was off to Oxford Street to do some Christmas shopping. Christmas was less than a fortnight away. As soon as she was gone the brief euphoria she'd generated vanished.

Julian reappeared to tell Jessie he'd decided to do a spirits stock-take, and Yvonne was going to assist him by restocking the two spirits cupboards under the bar which were nearly depleted.

Julian and Yvonne disappeared down into the cellar leaving Jessie in charge of the bar, and pouring yet another round of rums for The Light who were now well on the way to getting drunk.

Customers came and went, and The Light continued drinking heavily. Jessie began to wonder what was keeping Yvonne. She hadn't brought a single bottle up yet. Another round finished the navy rum on the gantry, nor was there any more in the two cupboards under the bar.

Minutes later, Len was demanding another round. 'You'll have to wait until Yvonne brings some up,' she told him shortly, too busy to be polite. She served more pints, shooed a tramp out the door who'd come into the pub in the hope of being able to cadge a wet, and answered the public phone, which turned out to be a wrong number.

'Where's that bloody rum!' Oscar complained.

Jessie slammed a pint on the counter. She'd have to give Yvonne a shout. She and Julian were probably yakking nineteen to the dozen and hadn't noticed how much time had slipped by.

Jessie called Phil up to the bar and asked him to keep an eye on the till while she popped down to the cellar to hurry up their rum. 'I'll not be a moment,' she promised.

The cellar was a large one, rectangular in shape and the spirits' store was located at the area of the cellar furthest away from the stairs. All the lights were on, and the hoppy tang of beer hung heavily in the air. There were numerous stacks of wooden barrels to be seen, and other stacks of the relatively new metal casks which, according to Julian, were revolutionizing the beer trade.

Jessie was about to stride in the direction of the store when she heard a groan that made her pause. Then there it was again, another groan. There was no mistaking what it meant. And then she distinguished Julian's voice, murmuring words of endearment, and Yvonne's soft moans.

Jessie went cold all over, beginning to tremble. It was as though she were back in Glasgow, back in that bedroom of so long ago.

She took a sideways step, and Julian and Yvonne came into view, both turned away from her.

Jessie stared at them, frozen in time. It wasn't Julian and Yvonne she saw, but Tommy and Eve. She wanted to be sick, or to cry out. How could Julian do this to Pixie in what amounted to their own house? For the pub wasn't only their place of business, it was where they lived – it was their home.

Her disgust and horror were so great that her trembling turned into actual shaking. How *could* Julian do this to Pixie? Why, a sweeter woman never lived!

In the awful seconds she stood rooted to the spot, Jessie heard enough to realize this wasn't something that had happened on the spur of the moment. It had been going on for quite some time.

As quietly as she was able, Jessie tip-toed back the way she'd come.

*   *   *

293

The rest of the day somehow passed. She managed to be civil to Julian and Yvonne, and also managed to avoid coming face to face with Pixie.

When the evening session was finally over, and the glasses washed and put away, she made her excuses and fled without having her staff drink. She'd never done that before, but they assumed she was upset because of Phil and the band.

She ran round to St. Peter's Street, where she found Phil nursing a sore head and drinking black coffee. He told her he'd only woken an hour since, having been asleep since staggering back at lunch time. He sat in the kitchen with her while she made some coffee for herself.

Jessie had come to a decision. She was going to leave The Lonsdale Arms, and the sooner the better. She just couldn't continue to work and live alongside Pixie and Julian knowing what she did. She was genuinely terrified, feeling as strongly as she did, that she might let slip something of what she'd witnessed in the cellar. If Pixie was ever to find out about Julian and Yvonne, she didn't want it coming from her.

'Do you know of any rooms or flat shares going locally?' she asked Phil suddenly.

'Somebody in the pub asked you to look out for them?' he asked, going over to the counter for more aspirin. His head was unbelievable.

'No, it's for me. I'm quitting The Lonsdale Arms,' she said shortly.

He turned round to stare at her in surprise. 'This is rather sudden, isn't it? Why?'

'I have my reasons.' She had no intention of disclosing to Phil what those reasons were.

He tried to probe, but got nowhere. All Jessie would say was that she intended leaving, and that was that. 'What about a job?' he demanded.

'There's a barmaid's position going at The York. I'll apply for it as soon as I can get round there. I know the governor, so if the job hasn't gone I should be all right there. The big drawback is it isn't live in.'

Phil listened thoughtfully. 'Can I ask you a question?' he asked somewhat nervously.

'Of course.'

'You do like me don't you? I mean *really* like me?'

'I wouldn't sleep with you if I didn't,' she replied gently.

'Then why don't you come and stay here?'

The thought had crossed her mind, but she wasn't at all sure about it. The trouble was that when she thought of herself living with a man it was always Tommy she imagined, and no one else.

'You don't fancy the idea?' Phil looked suddenly crestfallen.

There were occasions when Phil looked such a little boy that all she wanted to do was to take him in her arms, stroke his hair, and tell him it was all right, the nasty bogey man wouldn't get him, not while she was there.

But she also remembered why she had begun to sleep with Phil in the first place. Tommy was gone. He was the past, and she had the rest of her life to live, and live it to the full she would. There was no use clinging on to what had been. Phil was here and now, today and the future; Tommy was yesterday.

'I've never lived with a girl,' he said miserably. 'And to be honest, you're the first I've ever asked to live with me.'

It was embarrassing him to be so open with her. Jessie could see the discomfort and pain in his downcast eyes.

She went over and put her hands on his shoulders. 'You can help me move my bits and pieces round tomorrow,' she said softly.

Phil looked up at her, beaming. 'I'm not doing so well at the moment,' he said, 'but I'll make good yet. I'll be up there with the stars, I promise you.'

She wanted to say to him that his being a star didn't matter to her, except for the fact that he wanted it so badly. What did matter was the quality of their relationship, that they were happy together.

Instead, she announced that she was suddenly ravenous. 'What food have you got? Eggs? Milk? Onions? Mushrooms?'

'You haven't even moved in yet and already you're taking over,' he laughed.

'I am going to make you the best omelette you've ever had,' she laughed back. 'No flat mate of mine's going to go hungry.'

Busying herself preparing the omelette, Jessie began to sing.

Jessie came awake, her eyes still closed, and stretched languorously. She sought out Phil's naked body with her hand, and snuggled closer. She felt absolutely marvellous. Despite the narrowness of the bed, she'd slept extremely well. Twice during the night he'd made love to her, and as a result she was filled with well being.

'What is the meaning of this Philip?' a woman's voice suddenly demanded.

Jessie was so startled she nearly jumped out of her skin. She hadn't heard anyone come into the flat. Her eyes flew open, and she found herself staring at a heavily built woman whose small eyes bored disapprovingly into hers.

'Hello, mamma,' Phil said in a small voice.

So this was the redoubtable Mrs Jacobs, whom she'd heard so much about. She should have guessed.

Mrs Jacobs was in her late fifties. Her clothes were expensive, but flamboyant and the pudgy hands were loaded down with rings.

'Pleased to meet you,' Jessie said as evenly as she could, attempting a smile that came out more as a grimace.

'Who is this . . . this *person* Philip?' Mrs Jacobs asked in a tone as heavy as her build.

Phil cleared his throat. He hadn't been expecting his

296

mother for another couple of days yet, and had been going to phone and explain. At least that had been his intention. As ever, though, he had put it off and was too late. 'This is Jessie McBride, mother,' he said, trying to sit up. 'She and I are living together now.'

Mrs Jacobs eyes narrowed. 'You're not Jewish, are you?' she asked.

'No, I'm Scots,' Jessie replied.

Mrs Jacobs sniffed. 'You'll never get him for good, you know,' she said. 'He'll never marry you. He'll only marry one of his own kind.'

Jessie was taken aback by the woman's vehemence. If only she wasn't naked under the bedclothes, she could get up and stand her ground properly. 'That's fine with me,' she said sweetly. 'I'm already married anyway.'

Mrs Jacob's expression as she stared at Jessie was one of contempt. Things were clearly as bad as she'd thought.

Jessie stared defiantly back, she wasn't going to let Phil's mother browbeat her, no matter what.

Mrs Jacobs' gaze moved to the cringing Phil. 'So this is what you've sunk to, living in sin with a married shiksa. I weep for you, my son,' she wailed, though Jessie could see no tears. 'I weep for what you've become.'

'Mother, please . . .' Phil began.

'It's still not too late, you can still come home with me and take up again where you left off,' she interrupted.

Phil shook his head. 'I can never go back to that world,' he said in a voice he hadn't used before to his mother. 'I hate it. I'm a musician, that's what I want to do, and this is the life that makes me happy.'

There was a moment of silence and then, giving up on that argument, Mrs Jacobs brought her attention back to Jessie. She stared at her briefly, and then gave a dismissive snort. 'Get your washing together for me Philip,' she said to her son, continuing to look at Jessie as though she were in a cage.

'Mamma does my washing for me,' Phil explained to

Jessie in a small voice. 'That's why she has her own keys.'

'Well now I'm in residence she won't have to bother any more,' said Jessie sweetly. 'I'll be doing your washing from here on.'

Mrs Jacobs turned her eyes from Jessie to her son. 'Philip . . .'

Phil looked from one to the other. 'I don't know. . .'

'I can always find another place,' said Jessie quietly.

'Philip doesn't have a washing machine,' argued Mrs Jacobs. 'It's never the same done by hand.'

Jessie smiled. 'There's a launderette down the road.'

Mrs Jacobs glared at her for a second, then again decided to change the conversation. 'Your poppa and I want to speak to you at home. Come and see us as soon as you can,' she commanded Phil. Then, without waiting for a reply, she stormed off, banging the three doors from where she'd been standing to the outside behind her.

'She's really very nice,' said Phil weakly.

'Make sure you get those keys back when you go home,' Jessie replied, and got out of bed.

It was St. Valentine's day, 1960, and Jessie was pleased because when she'd got up in the morning she'd found a card on the kitchen table from Phil. He must have stuck it there the night before. It was sloppily romantic with lots of hearts and cupids on it, she was delighted with it. Phil had penned in many of the old favourite rhymes and legends – everything from 'Postie postie do not falter, this may lead me to the altar' to 'Roses are red, violets are blue, I'm full of love and it's all for you'. He had even written 'S.W.A.L.K.' (Sealed with a Loving Kiss) on the back flap.

She'd been thrilled, not only with the card but with the effort he'd gone to. It had put her into a good mood for the entire day.

Jessie was bottling up with Clive, the governor of the

new pub she was working at, when the telephone rang. Thinking it was his bookie, Clive answered it immediately.

'For you,' he said to Jessie, offering her the receiver.

Must be Phil, she thought, for he buzzed her at the pub occasionally. But it wasn't Phil. 'Hello?'

'Jessie this is Caroline, Mick Marco's friend. How are you?'

Jessie blinked in astonishment. She'd thought she'd seen the last of Caroline, and Mick Marco.

They exchanged pleasantries, and Caroline explained that she'd rung The Lonsdale Arms first and been told Jessie was now at The York. 'I was wondering if you could have dinner with me tomorrow night,' Caroline said at last.

Now why should Caroline want to invite her to dinner. 'I'm afraid I'm on duty,' Jessie said guardedly.

There was a slight pause. 'It's not exactly a social meeting I'm proposing. Dinner could be to your advantage, in fact it could be very much to your advantage,' Caroline said mysteriously.

'Can you be more specific?'

'Mick and I want you to meet someone. A rather special person whose name I don't particularly wish to mention over the telephone,' Caroline answered cagily.

Very mysterious, Jessie thought. Of course she'd have to go now, wild horses wouldn't keep her away. She was intrigued. 'Hang on a mo',' she said, and laying down the receiver went to check with Clive that she could get the night off. 'All right, it's on. Where and when?' Jessie said to Caroline.

'Eight o'clock at the Savoy. I'll be waiting for you in the foyer. And . . . the invitation is for you alone. Please don't turn up with Phil,' Caroline said.

'All right,' said Jessie even more puzzled.

Jessie cradled the receiver. How tantalizing! she thought.

Who was she going to be meeting?

★   ★   ★

Nervous and excited, Jessie arrived at the Savoy at exactly eight o'clock and found Caroline waiting for her as she had promised. Caroline, as always, looked absolutely stunning in a beige dress that had clearly been made for her.

Jessie was content with her own outfit, a beaded and sequinned black Victorian dress that she'd bought from a junk stall in Camden Passage for the princely sum of five bob.

'They're in the bar having a drink before dinner, shall we join them?' Caroline said after greeting Jessie.

'So who am I going to meet?' Jessie asked eagerly, consumed with curiosity. She hadn't been able to think of anything else since the telephone call.

'Wait and see,' Caroline teased.

Marco and the man with him were in a booth. The man was a small, handsome Negro dressed in flamingo pink suit, with shirt, tie and socks to match. There was something familiar about the man's face, Jessie thought, almost feeling as if she'd met him before. But if she had met him before she would certainly remember it.

Marco and the stranger climbed out of the booth. 'How nice to see you again, darling, I'm so glad you could make it,' Marco gushed, kissing Jessie on the cheek.

'Jessie,' Caroline said. 'I'd like you to meet Marvin Leroi.'

Marvin Leroi shook her hand warmly. 'It's a real pleasure to meet you, Miss McBride,' he declared in an accent straight out of *Gone with the Wind*.

Jessie stared at him in amazement, her good manners totally forgotten. Marvin Leroi! No wonder he looked familiar. On the American rock scene there was only one name bigger, and that was Elvis himself.

'How do you do Mr Leroi,' Jessie replied in a shaky voice, trying not to appear as star-struck as she felt.

He flashed her a brilliant smile. 'Hey, let's forget all this formal Miss and Mr jazz. I'm Marvin and you're Jessie, okay?'

Jessie laughed. 'Okay,' she agreed, feeling herself relax under his charm. He was obviously not only one of the most famous singers in the world, but one of the nicest as well.

They all sat, ordered drinks, and then chatted about London and the States for a while. It was Marvin's last night in Britain, he was flying home next morning.

There has to be a reason behind all this, Jessie told herself, as the talk went on, and tried to be patient.

Finally they left the bar and went to the Grill, where a table had been reserved for them. Jessie tried several times to catch Caroline's eye, wanting some sort of sign from her, but Caroline was obviously enjoying Jessie's suspense.

It wasn't until the they were in the middle of the first course that Marvin dropped his bombshell. 'I'm interested in your song "Missing Totti" Jessie,' he said. 'I like it very much.'

'Very much,' Marco echoed with a broad smile.

Jessie was too surprised to speak.

'I do think however that the lyrics could do with a. . . a little polishing here and there,' Marvin went on carefully, toying with his avocado.

Jessie was suddenly aware that the three of them were staring at her, waiting for her response.

'Lyrics have always been my weak point,' she admitted.

Marvin looked relieved. Reaching into his inside jacket pocket he pulled out a folded score. 'I took the liberty, Jessie, of making a few alterations as I saw them. I'd like you to tell me what you think.'

She took the score from him and read it through. To begin with, the song had a new title, it was now called 'Together'. The other changes he'd made, though minor, tightened the song and made quite a difference for the better.

'I'm really impressed,' Jessie said, looking up at Marvin. 'You've made a definite improvement.'

'In that case,' he said, smiling, 'how would you feel about me recording your song?'

Jessie could only stare at him in disbelief. Could it really be true that an artist of Leroi's reputation wanted to record a song of hers?

'In Nashville,' he explained.

Marvin Leroi record *her* song? In Nashville? She was asleep and dreaming, she had to be! But she wasn't. Caroline and Marco were still sitting at the table, looking at her expectantly. Around the room, the other diners continued to eat and talk while the waiters threaded their way amongst the tables. None of them seemed aware that the world had stopped turning. And those brown eyes gazing into hers couldn't have been more serious.

'Well,' she breathed, finding her voice at last. 'Marvin, you've got yourself a song.'

8

It was August 1961, eighteen months since Marvin Leroi had recorded 'Together', and seventeen since he'd been tragically killed in an air crash along with several members of his band and another singer.

It had been a copper-bottomed certainty before Marvin's death that 'Together' would be a success, all his records were, but as a result of his untimely death 'Together' had gone straight to the number one spot on the American charts, and had stayed there for an unprecedented thirteen weeks. Altogether, it had remained on the charts for twenty-seven weeks. The story in Britain had been similar: nine weeks at number one; twenty-two in the charts overall.

Marvin's death had transformed him into an instant legend. 'Together', his last single, had become his biggest, and many said, his greatest.

All this had meant an amazing amount of money for Jessie, and she was, in fact, just coming from a meeting with her bank manager, who acted as her financial advisor.

After the quiet and coolness of the bank, the street outside was hot and muggy. Jessie pondered on what to do with the rest of the afternoon, she'd long since stopped working at the pub, and decided she'd pay Harrod's Food Hall a visit.

She'd buy some haggis, Scotch mutton pies. Scotch rolls, and a ring of black pudding. She called it nostalgia food. More and more lately, her thoughts were turning to Glasgow. Although well settled in London, she was beginning to miss it dreadfully.

She stopped at a phone box to ring Phil and tell him what she intended doing. He was at home, in the Georgian house she'd bought in Islington. It was a beautiful house, and she loved it, but half of her wished that when she opened the door it was a Scottish street she would come out on, and not an English one.

Phil grumbled because she'd woken him up. The Light had a gig that night at a party being thrown by a group of Fleet Street journalists and so he'd been taking a kip.

The Light was continuing to play local gigs and private parties, and The Lonsdale Arms at weekends. Phil was becoming gloomier and gloomier, and he was afraid it was a pattern which was never going to be broken. His dreams were further away than ever from coming true. There was nothing she could say any more to cheer him up. Her own unexpected success didn't help.

Emerging from the phone box, Jessie crossed to the kerbside with the intention of hailing a passing taxi. She was still waiting minutes later when there was an ominous roll of thunder and the heavens opened.

She took refuge in a cheap cafe-cum-restaurant just around the corner. She was already soaked, and the rain didn't look as though it was going to stop in a hurry. At least there she could have a warming cup of tea.

The cafe was typical of many to be found in central London: there were no frills, the accent, first and foremost, was on economy. Economy for the management, economy for the customers.

Jessie sat at a plastic topped table. A man, you could hardly give him the title of waiter, came over reluctantly and took her order. There were several other people in the cafe, most of whom seemed to be escaping the downpour as well. She looked around at the yellowed walls and the counter with its display of rolls and pastries. And then her gaze stopped at a neck behind the counter. It belonged to the man cooking on the large gas stove fixed to the far wall of the room. For a second, she couldn't catch her breath. She knew that neck and she knew the back of the head above it. She rubbed her eyes and blinked. Maybe it was just her memory playing her tricks. She craned around, trying to see the man's face, but couldn't. Come on, turn, she commanded silently. She looked away, then looked back. No, it couldn't be, she told herself, she was definitely imagining things.

Suddenly, he turned, slapping a plate of food on the counter.

Jessie must have made an exclamation, for the people near her turned in her direction. There, behind the counter was Tommy McBride.

He hadn't been back in the charts after that initial hit, but she'd imagined that he must be back in Glasgow, working the clubs there. It had never occurred to her that he might be in the same city as she. That she might bump into him at any time.

She quickly looked away as he glanced in her direction, pretending to be engrossed in studying the rain as it lashed against the street outside.

There was a tight knot in her stomach, and her heart was pounding so loudly she was sure everyone in the room could hear it.

She didn't want to talk to him. She had to get out of there as quickly and quietly as she could. It didn't matter that it was pouring cats and dogs, she couldn't remain in this cafe a second longer. She glanced out of the corner of her eye and saw that he was facing the wall again.

She fumbled in her handbag, found a two shilling piece, and then she hurried to the counter, put the coin beside the till, and raced out through the door. 'Hey,' called the man at the till, 'You forgot your change.'

She ran through the rain, looking neither left nor right, only intent on putting as much distance between her and Tommy McBride as she could. She broke a heel outside of Charing Cross Station, but she also finally found a taxi.

She wept all the way to Islington. He'd looked the same, exactly as she remembered. If she'd imagined that with time her image of him had faded, she'd been wrong. Very, very wrong. And if she'd thought that the pain had lessened, she'd been even more wrong.

When she arrived home she told Phil she wasn't feeling too well, and went to bed. There she resumed crying, and hid under the bedclothes, till she finally realized it was herself she was hiding from.

She thought Phil might bring her a nice cup of tea, or just come up to see how she was. But he didn't.

Finally, still sobbing, she fell into an exhausted sleep.

Jessie sat at her piano and began playing 'Together'. She'd been playing it every day since seeing Tommy a fortnight ago. He hadn't been out of her thoughts since.

There was a commotion in the hallway, then Phil and Len lurched in. It was clear to her right away that they'd been smoking marijuana. Phil always got a supercilious expression on his face after he'd been 'smoking', it was an expression she'd come to know well of late.

'That old song again? What about something new and exciting, another international number one hit!' Phil mocked, coming across the room.

She regarded him warily. He resented the success she'd

had with 'Together', resented it and was jealous of it, as though it was her success that was holding him back. With each passing day he grew more and more bitter about his own static situation. There was nothing she could do any more that wasn't wrong.

She'd written several numbers since Marvin Leroi had recorded 'Together', but they hadn't done much, staying low on the charts for a few weeks before fizzling out completely. And that had been the British charts, none of them had made the American. It might have been different if Marvin had lived, possibly he would have written the lyrics himself while she supplied the tune, but there was no point in wishing for what might have been.

'Beautiful dreams,' a totally spaced out Len said to no one in particular.

'Come on, Jessie,' Phil went on. 'Lets have another million-seller.'

There are times when you can be such a bore,' Jessie said to Phil, sending him into a fit of giggles.

Jessie came to the end of 'Together', and reached for the whisky and lemonade she had sitting atop the piano. She stared at Phil over the rim of her glass. Only the other night he'd cried in her arms, making up excuses for his failure, begging her to stick with him, promising her the moon. Today, however, the chip was back on his shoulder and everything was her fault.

Maybe one day she'd write a song about Phil, she thought. If she ever did, she'd call it 'Lost Man's Rock'.

Phil and Len disappeared off upstairs where there was a second reception room, and soon the sweet smell of marijuana came wafting down the stairs.

Jessie started playing 'Together' again.

Jessie sat in the corner of the cafe, watching Tommy being busy at the stove. She'd been there for ten minutes and he hadn't noticed her yet. She wasn't sure what madness had driven her here, but it was too late to back

306

out now. She chose a moment when the cafe was the emptiest it had been since she'd arrived. Steeling herself, she rose, walked over and paid her bill. She had to steel herself further to walk along the counter until she was directly behind him.

'Hello Tommy,' she said in a voice that almost sounded normal.

He didn't take in whose voice it was, he thought it was just one of the regular customers. He turned, the standard smile on his face, already saying, 'How are you?' before he looked up to face her.

She had put on weight, and there was little of the girl she'd been left in her eyes, but he would have recognized her anywhere.

'You've aged,' he blurted out.

'Oh, that's nice,' she replied sarcastically, but couldn't manage to say anything else.

'Well,' he laughed nervously, 'long time no see.'

'Yes,' she whispered. 'A long time.'

They stared at each other in silence. Now that she was meeting him again she didn't know what to say. In one way she knew so much about this man in front of her, in another he was a total stranger.

'I dropped in for coffee, and here you were,' she said at last.

Embarrassment crept into his face. He was acutely conscious of his greasy hands, his soiled apron and the stupid wee hat stuck on his head. 'Um. Here I am.'

'I didn't know you could cook,' she said, her voice sounding shrill in her ears.

He shrugged. 'The job was going, so I learned.'

Oh, Tommy! a voice inside her wailed.

'You look grand,' he said shyly.

'Grand but old,' she smiled 'You're not looking so bad yourself,' she went on. 'You're just as I remember you.'

'My hair's different,' he replied ruefully. 'And the clothes are less stylish,' indicating the apron and hat.

307

'Oh, but just as dashing,' she said instantly, trying to control her voice.

He cleared his throat. 'You didn't know I worked here then?'

'No, no. It was sheer chance that I came in.'

He cleared his throat again. He was finding this difficult. It would have been hard enough to know what to do if they'd been alone, but here it was impossible. After all these years, she was actually standing in front of him and he was making a fool of himself again. 'Are you living in London now?'

'I have been ever since . . . ever since . . . Yes, for some time.'

'I see,' he said, nodding. 'I see.'

She took a deep breath and decided to say what she'd come to say. 'Look we should talk, and we can't do that properly here. How about we meet?' she said in a rush.

He tried not to let his enthusiasm show. 'All right,' he replied casually.

Relief made her smile. 'When suits you? I can manage almost any time.'

He wanted to propose that night, but his pride restrained him. The last thing he wanted was to appear over eager. 'How about the evening after next? I knock off here at six and usually have a pint in the Globe across from the opera house before going home.'

'I'll be there just after six, then,' she said. 'Day after tomorrow.'

She smiled, and he smiled in return.

'Till then,' she said.

'Till then,' he repeated.

As she walked away from the cafe, she felt like a young lassie looking forward to her first date, and wasn't sure whether she was glad she felt so glad or not.

Jessie arrived outside the Globe at quarter to six; she'd been so anxious to get there that she'd left home far too early. She decided to go for a walk round about, she wanted Tommy to be waiting for her, not the other way around.

She'd been through Covent Garden a number of times, and always enjoyed it, for it was an interesting and colourful place. This time, though, it was completely wasted on her. All she could think of was that the minutes till her rendezvous with Tommy were crawling by so slowly each seemed like an hour. At eight minutes past, feverish with impatience, she decided to chance it. She charged through the doors of the Globe, relieved to discover him there, ordering at the bar.

She was nervous, but certain it didn't show. Tommy was thinking exactly the same thing about himself. He ordered their drinks and carried them to a table.

They sat, and looked at one another. 'How are Jack, Sammy and Jake "The Rake"?' she asked finally.

'Dandy, last I heard. Back in Glasgow, of course. The three of them caught the same train up when the band folded. Sammy's married now, to Cass McNulty. She used to go jigging at the Cameo.'

Jessie searched her memory. 'I remember her, she was very wee, and had ginger hair.'

'That's Cass,' Tommy grinned.

She pulled out her fags and he expressed surprise that she now smoked. A far cry from the upright minister's daughter he'd first met at Queen's Park School, she replied; and thought to herself, aye, a helluva far cry. He accepted a cigarette when she offered the packet.

'How come the band folded?' she asked when they were settled again.

Tommy made a face. 'After we won that talent show we landed a contract with M.M.T., and for a while things looked good. Then the skiffle fad began to wane, and M.M.T. lost interest in us. One morning, when it was three weeks since our last gig, Jack announced that he'd had enough and that he was off home to Glasgow.

309

And that was that – the end of the Tommy McBride Skiffle Band.'

He should have gone solo then, she thought. That had always been her plan for him. 'I'm sorry,' she murmured.

He drew savagely on his cigarette. The palms of his hands were sweating, and when he next spoke his voice had gone tight and husky. 'I can explain that afternoon in Allison Street,' he nearly whispered.

Jessie gave a dismissive shrug. 'There's nothing to explain. Eve was always attractive.' She had known this wouldn't be easy, but it was worse than she'd imagined. In a minute she'd be in tears.

'Oh, aye, she was attractive enough, I can't deny that. But that wasn't the reason why I was sleeping with her.' He paused his hand reaching for hers across the table. 'You've got to believe me, Jessie she was blackmailing me.'

Jessie looked at him sharply. 'Blackmail. Don't be ridiculous, Tommy McBride. I've heard it called a lot of things in my time, but blackmail's a new one.'

Slowly, and haltingly, he told her the whole story from start to finish. Eve propositioning him, her promise that the band would win the show, Sally Grierson and M.M.T., everything.

'You didn't *have* to be blackmailed, you could have said no,' Jessie said softly when he'd finished.

Tommy dropped his eyes to stare at the table. 'I won't try and excuse myself, I suppose all I can say is that the temptation was too great. Eve offered me an exit from Glasgow, to be able to break with the Ted scene once and for all, and so I went along with her proposition. And if I hadn't slept with her she'd have put the mockers on my singing career, and I'd never have broken away from the fix I was in.'

He looked up at Jessie, his eyes pleading. 'But I swear to God, if I'd known that sleeping with Eve was going to lose me you I'd never have agreed to it in a million years.

No opportunity, no big break, nothing was worth losing you. You've got to believe me. I've been living in hell since you left.'

There was a lump in her throat. He *had* loved her after all, that hadn't been a lie. That knowledge meant more than a lot to her – it meant the world.

'Me and the Boyd Street Boys scoured Glasgow for you after you'd run off, we tramped the streets for a week. I kept praying that one of us would stumble onto you, but, of course, you weren't there.'

Jessie wiped a tear from her eye. 'What happened to you and Eve?'

'I made her keep her side of the bargain. I promised her that if she didn't I'd razor her face so badly she'd be a monster for the rest of her natural if she didn't.' Tommy paused, then said quietly 'I never laid a finger on her again after you found us together. I swear that.'

Jessie took a deep breath. 'What a mess,' she whispered.

'If only I'd had the chance to talk to you after. If only you hadn't disappeared the way you did,' he said wretchedly.

How could she explain what had gone on in her mind, the profound sense of betrayal she'd felt? Life had been a bubble of love and happiness, then she'd walked into that room and the bubble had burst in her face.

'I didn't see how you could do what you were doing to her in our bed . . . and still care for me,' she said in a sob.

Tommy gazed into his pint. 'It was dreadful after you left. I did all manner of things I'm not proud of. In fact, I think it's fair to say that for a while I went a wee bit daft.'

She'd gone a wee bit daft herself, she thought. 'So why didn't you go back to Glasgow with the lads then?'

'If I'd done that I'd have had to have taken up where I left off, King of the Glasgow Teds and all that horror. By staying in London I was able to just be myself.'

He drank off what remained of his pint, and she went up to the bar where she ordered two more, and a couple of large drams.

He grinned when she placed his beer and whisky before him. 'The old Glasgow combination, heavy and 'the cratur', Rangers and Celtic, Protestants and Catholics,' he said.

'And what are you up to nowadays?' he asked after she'd sat back down. 'You look like you're doing all right.'

She'd wondered if he knew about her success, he clearly didn't.

'Remember Marvin Leroi's hit "Together"?'

Tommy nodded.

'I wrote it.'

He stared at her in astonishment. 'You?'

She nodded, laughing. 'It was recorded originally by a band called The Light, but that version flopped. Then Marvin heard it while he was over here on a trip, decided he wanted it for himself, recorded it in Nashville, and bingo!'

'That was one of the biggest hits ever,' Tommy whispered.

'An "all time great" it's been called,' she agreed. To hell with being modest. She wanted to impress Tommy, and maybe even rub salt in a bit.

Tommy was shaken. He didn't know what he'd been expecting her to tell him she'd been doing, but not that. 'I don't know why, but I never thought of you continuing to write songs,' he said at last.

'I hadn't planned to, I just sort of got caught up in it again.'

He looked at her sharply. 'How was that?'

She picked up her whisky and swirled it round in her glass. Did she tell him about Phil or didn't she? She decided she would. 'My chap is the singer with The Light, the band that recorded the song in the first place. It was he who asked me to write something for them. The old thing, desperate for new material,' she said quickly.

Tommy had gone very pale. 'Déjà vu,' he replied, giving a feeble grin.

'Déjà vu,' she agreed.

'You and this chap, is it serious?'

'We live together,' she replied, which didn't answer his question, but gave the impression it did.

'I see,' Tommy said.

'I've bought this house in Islington.'

He pretended to whistle. 'You must have made a fortune out of "Together".'

'A modest fortune.'

Rich and in love! Tommy was pleased for her, but at the same time he was madly jealous of this other man, whoever the man was. He reminded himself he had no right to be jealous, he had no claim on Jessie anymore. But claim or not, he was still jealous.

Then he had another thought. It would be dreadful if she went away from this meeting feeling *sorry* for him, he didn't want that at all. His pride couldn't take the humiliation. 'I'm over in Clapham, I live there with a friend,' he said casually, though it was clear from his voice that the friend was a woman.

'I don't know south of the river, it's a complete mystery to me,' was the only thing she could think of in reply to that.

Tommy grinned. 'And the north side, outside of central London, is a mystery to me.'

Jessie's emotions were in a turmoil, but the predominant one was jealousy. Another was anger, anger with herself at being jealous of this unknown woman Tommy had taken up with. 'What does your friend do?' she asked, trying to match Tommy's casual tone.

'Ania's on social security. She can't work because of the children.'

Jessie's heart skipped a beat. 'Yours?'

'No, their father was booted out by Ania shortly before I met her.'

'Ania's a pretty name,' Jessie said.

313

'She's a very pretty woman. She's got those high cheekbones that many Poles and Hungarians have. Her parents came over here from Cracow just before the war.'

Very pretty woman indeed, she was probably a bloody ravishing beauty! Jessie fought to control her features so that her jealousy didn't show. Or the black despair she felt to think how unattractive she'd become.

Tommy didn't want to say what he said next, but it seemed to him that with Jessie doing so well, and having fallen in love again, he was almost obliged to. 'I suppose we should talk about the divorce,' he said hesitantly.

She felt as though she'd been hit in the stomach. This wasn't at all how she'd planned their drink should go. It had started off so pleasantly, and now they were talking about divorce!

'I know you have to be separated for seven years in Scotland before you can file for one, but of course English law is different. We can probably go ahead and file right away down here,' Tommy rolled on.

'I imagine so,' Jessie replied reluctantly.

'Do you want me to initiate proceedings, or will you?'

She had the sudden urge to slap him silly. 'I'll file. If it turns out I have to cite someone do you want me to cite Ania or Eve?' she answered.

'Eve.' He wished he had kept his mouth shut. How had they gotten this far so quickly?

Protecting his lady, just like Tommy, he'd always been gallant, Jessie thought miserably. 'Right then,' she replied brightly.

'Right then,' Tommy echoed

Their conversation became static. They drank quickly and were soon on their way out of the pub.

'Can I give you a lift home, my car's parked nearby?' Jessie asked.

That was the last thing he wanted. Where he lived wasn't exactly a slum, but he was sure it would compare unfavourably with Jessie's home. 'That would be nonsense. I'm the other way from you entirely,' he said quickly.

She fumbled in her handbag to produce her card. 'That's my address and phone number, we'll have to keep in touch about the divorce,' she said.

'I'm afraid I don't have a card,' he admitted.

Jessie dived back into her handbag to bring out a small notepad and a pencil. 'Write it down,' she said, handing them to him.

When that was over neither of them was sure how to say goodbye, Jessie was about to kiss him on the cheek when he stuck out his hand. They shook as though mere acquaintances parting from each other after a night out.

Hands in pockets, and shoulders hunched, Tommy walked off down the street.

Jessie, feeling wretched and sick inside, watched him go. She'd been looking forward so much to their rendezvous. And now they were practically divorced!

Mick Marco switched off the hi-fi system he had in his office, at Jessie's request he'd been listening to the record the Tommy McBride Skiffle Band had got into the charts shortly after Jessie's arrival in London.

'You're right, McBride has got a good voice,' Marco nodded.

Jessie had come to Marco after a great deal of thought. She hated the idea of Tommy ending up as a short order cook, and had decided, if he was agreeable, to see if she couldn't give him a helping hand. Before speaking to Tommy, however, she'd come to Marco. She wanted him behind her before putting her proposal to Tommy.

'I always thought that he should go solo, eventually' she explained. 'The band was only a device to launch his career.'

Marco looked at her thoughtfully. 'What do you see him singing, rock or ballad?'

315

'He can sing either, but I'd prefer him to do rock. That's the market of the immediate future, and it's also what he identifies with the most.'

Marco nodded, she was quite right, of course. This boy wasn't just a good singer – when he sang you believed him. 'What about material? Would you like me to try and find something suitable, or are you intending to write for him yourself?'

'If he does want to make a comeback, then we'll team up as before. I'll write the tune, Tommy the lyrics.'

'Okay, then if he wants to go ahead, the pair of you get together and come back to me when you've got an A and B side. We'll make a demo and see what the reaction is within the company.'

That was precisely what Jessie had wanted to hear. 'If you do decide to cut a disc with him I want him promoted, the last thing I want is a repetition of what happened to "Missing Totti",' she said immediately.

'Promotion costs money,' Marco replied slowly.

'Money makes money, as you well know. I'll have Tommy and the record promoted even if I have to fund the campaign myself. But if I do that it's a completely different percentage deal. I want that clearly understood right from the word go.'

'Let's not cross bridges before we get to them. Let's just concentrate on the demo for now, and worry about promotion afterwards.'

She could see he was impressed she was willing to put her own money up front, which was what she'd intended. She wanted Marco to appreciate just how serious she was about this one.

The next night found Jessie and Tommy back in the Globe. She had rung him at home the previous evening. She hadn't specified why she wanted them to meet again other than it was imperative they do. He'd assumed it concerned the divorce – only he'd been wrong.

'A comeback?' Tommy repeated, quite stunned by her proposal.

'With us collaborating on the material.'

He drank some whisky, trying to collect his thoughts. He'd thought she was going to say everything was set for the divorce and they'd never have to see each other again, and she was offering a partnership!

'Are you suggesting this because you've taken pity on me?' he asked angrily. 'Because if you are, forget it, I don't want to know.'

The same old Tommy with his stubborn pride. 'You've got a damned fine singing voice, I've always said that, and Mick Marco of Vestal Records agrees with me.'

'Oh, yes?'

'For heaven's sake, Tommy, what future is there in being a short order cook?'

Tommy winced. 'That's exactly what I mean. You feel sorry for me.'

'What I'm feeling for you at this moment is not sorry,' she cried, exasperated. 'You've got nothing to lose Tommy, and everything to gain. So what do you say?'

He remained unconvinced. 'I don't need anybody's charity.'

She offered him a cigarette, and he snapped he'd have one of his own. 'Okay,' she snapped back, 'I'll have one of yours, too.'

'Look, Tommy, I'll be getting something out of this as well,' she said when she was calm again.

'What?' he demanded.

'Sure I had enormous success with "Together", but the finished version of the lyrics owed a great deal to Marvin Leroi. The tunes I've composed since have been just as good, but the lyrics haven't. I need a lyricist, and you're the natural choice. Your lyrics fit my tunes. If you agree to join forces with me you'll be helping me just as much as I'll be helping you.'

Tommy looked thoughtful. 'And this Mick Marco is definitely interested in me as a singer?'

Jessie nodded.

He thought of the cafe where he worked now, it was a dead end job if ever there was one. Jessie was right, so what did he have to lose? The answer was sod all. And she needed him, that was the clincher. She wasn't feeling sorry for him, or patronizing him. She *needed* him – him and his lyrics.

'You're on,' he said at last.

Jessie beamed. 'I'll get another round in to celebrate.'

'I'll get it in.' he said, already on his feet.

She watched him saunter up to the bar in that gallus way Glaswegian men have when they consider themselves cock of the walk. Tomorrow she was definitely going to start slimming she decided. And maybe see about having something done to her hair.

.

'But why do I have to go out? It's my home as well, you know,' Phil said angrily.

Jessie glanced at her watch. Tommy would be here at any moment to start their first session together as collaborators.

Tommy hadn't wanted to come to her house to work, but hadn't wanted her to go to his either. In the end, after some heated argument, he'd capitulated, although with bad grace.

Jessie had thought the reason he didn't want to come was because he didn't want to meet Phil. But that was only partly true. He didn't want to come because it was where she stayed with Phil, where she *slept* with Phil.

'I've already explained to you, I don't want him being inhibited by your presence. Say hello, give him a drink, then scoot off so he can relax and we can get some work done together.

'If anyone should be inhibited it's me, he's your husband after all, and I'm just the guy you're living in sin with.'

Jessie laughed.

318

'Anyway, I don't like the idea of you writing for him. If you have to write for someone write for me.' Phil continued petulantly.

Jessie sighed. 'First of all, I'm not writing for him, we'll be collaborating. And secondly I do write songs for you.'

'None I can ever get recorded,' he complained.

She'd been in a lighthearted mood up until then, now she began to get cross with him. 'Don't blame my songs for that,' she shapped.

If the bell hadn't rung then it would have developed into a blistering fight, of which they'd had so many of late. They seemed to be forever at one another's throats.

'Now you be pleasant,' she warned.

He raised his arm in the Nazi salute. 'Jawohl, Mein Führeress!' he barked out.

Phil was smiling, and the epitome of charm itself, when Jessie showed Tommy in. She introduced them, and they shook hands. Tommy replied he'd have a whisky when Phil asked him what he'd have to drink.

Tommy took in Phil's tall, slim figure as Phil poured the drinks. A good looking bugger, he thought. He glanced round the room, Jessie certainly hadn't stinted herself in the furnishings. The house and its contents must have cost a bomb!

The three of them chatted for a couple of minutes, then Phil announced he had to go out. Wishing them well with their work session, he took his leave of them.

Jessie was relieved to see him go, having feared he might say something snide or nasty to Tommy.

'Lovely place,' said Tommy, making a gesture that encompassed the entire house.

Jessie was about to remark on how different it was to Allison Street, but stopped herself, thinking Tommy might consider that to be a dig.

She refilled his glass, and suggested they go through to the music room, a room at the rear where she'd had the piano installed.

Tommy raised an eyebrow on seeing the piano was a Steinway Grand. Nothing but the very best for our Jessie now, he thought.

She sat at the piano, and he took off his jacket and placed it to one side.

They set to work.

Somewhere in the house a clock chimed midnight. Jessie was drained, and Tommy was the same. So far they'd failed to come up with anything that could be considered even half decent.

The outside door clicked shut, and a few minutes later Phil poked his head into the room. 'Still at it?' he said.

Jessie found his cheerful tone irritating, what was there to be so cheerful about! In the old days it had always been so easy for her and Tommy, but not now it seemed.

'Yes,' she replied balefully, 'we're still at it.'

'I'll away up to bed then,' Phil said to Jessie, rather pleased that it wasn't going well for them.

The word bed was like a shower of cold water to Tommy. The bed in question must be the one where Jessie would later be joining Phil. Where they made love together. 'I think we need a break, and another drink,' Tommy said, his voice suddenly husky.

Jessie agreed, they were batting their heads against a brick wall at the moment.

They returned to the lounge, and Tommy sank into a chesterfield while she poured out hefty drams for the pair of them.

'Do you want to ring Ania?' Jessie asked.

Tommy shook his head. 'She'll be in her pit long since. If I was to buzz her now I'd only wake her up,' he replied.

Tommy spied a framed blown up photo on the wall nearest him that he hadn't noticed before. The scene was a city street, the architecture unmistakable. Smiling in recognition, he went over to study the photo. The street was in Springburn, the horse drawn tram in it belonged to the now defunct Glasgow Tramway & Omnibus Company. A date in the corner said the photo had been taken in 1890.

'When I came across it in a local antique market I just had to buy it,' Jessie explained.

Springburn had changed a lot since then, Tommy thought, and pictured Springburn in his mind as he'd last seen it. 'Do you miss Glasgow?' he asked softly.

'I didn't all that much to begin with, but I do more and more as time goes past.'

'I miss it, too. London's all right, but it's just not the same mind.'

She knew exactly what he meant. 'It's funny, mostly it's dirty and horrible, with so many problems, but I've never known a Glaswegian yet who didn't love the grey city, and if it came to the crunch wouldn't give his or her right arm for it,' she said.

'Aye, that's a fact sure enough,' Tommy agreed quietly. 'I'll never forget the Linn Park, my magic place.

'How about Lover's Lane, that bit of the Cart riverbank where you used to walk?'

'I'll never forget there, either.'

Her face clouded. 'Do you remember . . . that time when I thought I was . . . and you . . .'

'Aye,' he cut in. 'I remember.'

'Star Gray, what a silly name.' She laughed, dispelling the sombre mood of the past few seconds.

'I thought it was great. It made you different, not that you needed a name to be that.'

Glasgow, once born there it was with you for life, she thought. She wouldn't have been at all surprised if when dead Glaswegians were cut open they were found to have the word Glasgow running through their insides as though they were sticks of rock.

'Will you ever go back?' she asked.

'Will you?'

Neither replied because it was a question they didn't

know the answer to. If the question had been, would you like to go back, they'd have answered yes without hesitation.

'Maybe that's where I'm going wrong,' Tommy mused.

'Wrong about what?'

'The lyrics I've been trying to write this evening. When I wrote before it was always about Glasgow, and the Glasgow situation, real things that I know inside out, and which are important to me.'

Jessie's interest quickened, he could well have put his finger on the problem.

'What I've been doing tonight is to write mid-Atlantic pap, froth and candy floss with nae guts or reality to it,' Tommy said slowly, thinking aloud.

'I'm not against you writing about Glasgow, but isn't it going to be limited in its appeal?' Jessie argued.

'Why should it be? Poverty, slums, hardship, hunger – they aren't just unique to Glasgow. They know all about them in Liverpool, Newcastle, London's East End, not to mention, New York City for example.' He paused, frowning in thought.

'Defiance, that's what I should make this song about. An individual's defiance against the terrible conditions he's been born into. It should be a great shout of fury, resolve to break free, to come out the dark into the light.

'It'll be pure Glasgow through and through, but folk the world over will understand, and I mean *understand*, what it's about.'

As Jessie had been listening to Tommy speak a tune had begun forming in her mind, a strident tune that matched the sort of lyrics he was talking about.

'Well?' he demanded.

'Let's get to it,' she replied, and led the way, almost at a run, she was so eager, back to the music room.

Dawn was tinting the sky outside when Jessie let herself into her bedroom having just seen Tommy off in a taxi.

She was filled with elation at what she and Tommy had achieved that evening. Both of them were happy with the song they'd finally produced.

She was slipping out of her dress when the bedside light suddenly snapped on, causing her to gasp in surprise.

'Sorry if I woke you,' she said to Phil who was leaning on an elbow staring coldly at her.

'You're like a bloody elephant the way you blunder round at times,' he grumbled.

Typical Phil comment of late, she thought. How loathsome he could be when he had a mind. She continued to undress.

'I wish I could say I liked him, but I didn't. To tell you the truth he struck me as a right yob,' Phil went on, and smiled.

She ignored that, at the same time feeling the elation begin to seep out of her. Trust Phil to spoil what had been a marvellous evening.

'But I was nice to him, wasn't I?'

She didn't reply.

'But then I had to be, those were your orders.'

Naked, she hurriedly reached for her nightie. She didn't want to be naked in front of him a second longer than she had to. He completely repulsed her when he was like this.

'And when you crack the whip I jump. I have to,' he continued, lighting a cigarette.

'You don't have to do any such thing,' she replied.

'Oh, but I do, my darling. And you know why? Because you pay all the bills round here.'

So that was it. Her paying all the bills was a subject he brought up periodically lately.

'I've told you before not to worry about that. It certainly doesn't bother me,' she said coolly.

He ground out his cigarette as she got into bed beside him. Reaching over to take hold of her.

'Not tonight, I'm far too tired,' she pleaded.

His hand moved under her nightie, seeking out a breast.

'A right yob,' Phil repeated, and gave a derisory laugh.

Jessie sipped her glass of Buck's Fizz and glanced about her. She and Phil were at Mick Marco's birthday party, which was being held in Marco's house off the King's Road in Chelsea.

There were about fifty people at the party, nearly all of them in some way connected with the music business. It was a very chic affair, and fascinating to observe as Jessie had been doing.

She looked over to where Phil was chatting up a pretty blonde, and recognized the girl as working for Vestal Records. She wondered idly if Phil was chatting the girl up because she was pretty, or because she worked for Vestal.

'You all right?' Caroline asked Jessie, joining her.

'Fine. Has Tommy arrived yet?'

'I haven't seen him. But that doesn't mean he's not in the house somewhere.'

Jessie glanced at her watch. He wasn't really late it was just that she was impatient for his company.

After a few minutes Caroline excused herself and moved on. An executive from H.M.V. came over to talk to Jessie, saying he understood she had written 'Together', the Marvin Leroi hit and how pleased he was to meet her.

Tommy arrived five minutes later, and Jessie's smile of greeting as he walked into the room died on her face when she realized he wasn't alone. A stunning brunette had hurried through the door after him, and slipped an arm through his. She had a sylphlike figure, and long, shapely legs. The eyes were wide, and vulnerable, the mouth a sensuous slash of red. She was Ania of course, the high cheekbones Tommy hd spoken of gave that away.

Jessie was glad the H.M.V. executive was still talking

to her, it would have been most embarrassing to have been seen by the pair of them to be standing on her own.

Out of the corner of her eye she saw Tommy steering Ania in her direction. Now what was the H.M.V. executive's name again? She was going to have to introduce him.

'Hello, Jessie,' Tommy said, giving her a shy, hesitant smile.

'Hello?' she smiled back.

'This is Ania Zumbach, Ania, this is Jessie.'

The hand that shook Jessie's was cool and delicate. Jessie could feel the bones under the skin.

'This is Clifford Grout who works for H.M.V.,' Jessie said, and Clifford shook hands with Ania and Tommy.

'I feel that I already know you, Tommy has told me so much about you,' Ania said to Jessie.

Jessie looked into Ania's face, searching for hidden dislike, contempt, amusement even, but all she saw was a genuine friendliness. The woman hadn't come to crow over a long fallen rival. What a relief. Jessie found herself, though jealous of her, warming to Ania Zumbach.

They chatted about records, and the music business in general, with Clifford Grout doing most of the talking. Then Clifford's wife joined them to say that Marco was going to make a speech shortly.

'Where's Phil?' Tommy asked Jessie.

'Oh, about somewhere,' she answered vaguely, hoping that Phil would come back soon and pay some attention to her so that Tommy could see him doing so. But Phil was no longer in the room, Jessie had already ascertained that, nor was the blonde he'd been chatting up. She hadn't noticed either of them leave.

Several minutes later Caroline appeared and in a loud voice, requested everyone to go upstairs to the lounge where Marco wanted to address them.

Caroline then came over to Jessie and Tommy, and said they were to stick with her, Marco wanted them close to him when he spoke.

'Why?' Tommy asked.

Caroline gave a conspiratorial wink. 'You'll soon find out,' she smiled.

Tommy glanced at Jessie, who shrugged. 'I don't know,' Jessie said. She was just as much in the dark as he was.

When everyone had crowded into the upstairs lounge Marco held his hands up and called for quiet.

He thanked all those present for coming to his party, and hoped they were enjoying themselves, for he certainly was. 'And now I'd like you to meet two people from Glasgow, Scotland, who've become friends of mine, and who are here tonight. The first is Tommy McBride whose brand new disc Vestal will be releasing in a few weeks time. Folks, Tommy McBride!'

Caroline propelled a startled, and momentarily nonplussed, Tommy forward to stand beside Marco who was leading the applause.

'Every so often a singer emerges whom you just know is going to make it to the top, and I, and Vestal, think that of Tommy,' Marco enthused.

Jessie saw that Phil had appeared at the back of the room. His features were contorted with jealousy as he glared at Tommy.

'Tommy's new single is called "Big City Shout", and was written by him in collaboration with that other Glaswegian I mentioned, the woman who wrote the all-time chart buster "Together", Jessie McBride!' Marco went on.

Jessie didn't wait for Caroline to give her a push, she knew what was expected of her. She went to stand at Marco's other side.

'Folks, I give you Vestal's next number one hit, "Big City Shout"!' proclaimed Marco, and punched the air with his fist, the cue for a copy of the demo to be played.

Everyone listened as the number thundered out, but none more intently than Jessie who was staring at the floor, not wanting the others to see her face in what was for her an highly intimate moment.

It was every bit as good as she'd thought at the recording session, she told herself. Slowly, she let her gaze wander to the room. Those present were responding positively, and with enthusiasm. Any lingering doubts were blown away: she and Tommy were on a winner.

Then the number was over and everyone was clapping again. Jessie glanced up to see Ania staring at Tommy in open admiration. He stared back proudly at her.

Marco said a few more words about 'Big City Shout', then concluded his speech by announcing that a buffet supper was now available in the adjoining room.

'You might have given us some warning about that,' Tommy said to Marco when Marco's speech was over, and the crowd had begun to disperse.

'I thought it'd be far more fun to spring it on you,' Marco laughed. 'You should have seen your face.'

'When did Vestal finally decide to go ahead?' Jessie asked; she and Tommy had been waiting anxiously for the decision since the demo had been cut.

'Just this morning,' Marco grinned.

'When do we do the actual recording?' demanded Tommy.

'Monday next.'

'And what about promotion?' Jessie asked softly.

'Vestal will be pushing the record hard, you have my word on that. Okay?'

'Okay,' Jessie nodded.

Ania joined Tommy as Caroline came over with fresh glasses of Buck's Fizz. The toast, proposed by Marco was to 'Big City Shout'.

After drinking Jessie glanced round the room, looking for Phil. But he had disappeared again.

Jessie picked up a sample of fabric and studied it. She and Tommy were in Gruman's Tailor Shop in Soho's Bridle

327

Lane. Solly Gruman specialized in show clothes which Tommy, at her insistence, was being kitted out with, and for which Vestal Records would be picking up the tab.

Solly Gruman was an old gentleman who still spoke with a heavy Russian accent, even though he'd been in Britain for sixty-eight years, having arrived from Russia at the age of nine. In show business circles his clothes were legendary.

Solly was in the middle of measuring Tommy when the telephone rang. An assistant informed Solly it was someone who wished to speak to him personally. Solly apologized to Tommy, and said he wouldn't be a moment, but he didn't ask the assistant to continue with the measuring. Solly always did that himself.

Jessie was bending over a box to pick up some more fabric samples when she happned to catch Tommy's reflection in a nearby full length mirror.

He, unaware she could see him, was watching her, his expression one she remembered only too well from the days when they'd been together. She called it his randy look. In the past when it had appeared they'd always ended up in bed shortly afterwards.

Seeing that look again, and directed at her, made her flustered. She could feel herself blush, for all the world like some virginal lassie.

Could he still fancy her, even though she'd become so unattractive? Then she thought of the beautiful Ania, and her spirits, which had soared, dropped again. She had no chance against Ania, not the chance of a snowball in hell. Whatever she thought she saw in his eyes was not for her.

As they were walking away from Gruman's, Tommy said he wanted to stop at the first newsagent they came to, he needed to buy a packet of cigarettes. The newsagent they went into had a large magazine rack, and Tommy surprised Jessie by not only buying cigarettes but a copy of *Town and Country* as well.

'I would hardly have thought that *Town and Country*

328

would have interested you,' Jessie teased when they were back outside again.

'If I'm going to be rich and famous I'll need a house to reflect my status,' he said in a posh voice. 'And *Town and Country* has an excellent real estate section.'

Jessie could see that, despite the joke voice, he was in deadly earnest. 'What's this, delusions of grandeur already?' she mocked, speaking in broad Glasgow, which made it sound even more mocking.

'And why the hell not!' he answered in a voice just as broad as hers.

They both burst out laughing.

'Big City Shout' was launched at Vestal Records with a drinks reception. A great many people in key positions crucial to the sales of records were invited, and most of them had turned up to be plied with as much liquor as they could drink and a free copy of 'Big City Shout'.

It was hard work for Jessie and Tommy who'd been primed by Marco that they were to continually circulate, and generally make themselves available.

'How are we doing?' Jessie asked Caroline, having taken Caroline to one side so the pair of them could have a moment's breather. She'd just been talking to an intellectual type whose conversation, thanks to the more obscure words in the English language he'd persisted in using, had been mainly way over her head. She'd just kept muttering yes, and no, and hoping she was saying the right thing at the right time.

'It's going great guns, Mick's pleased,' Caroline replied.

Jessie glanced over to where Tommy was standing. He was wearing one of Solly Gruman's suits, and looked extremely handsome. Very handsome indeed. It pleased her enormously to think she'd rescued him for that dreadful job. What a waste it would have been if he'd never gone back to music.

He suddenly gazed across at her, and their eyes met. She felt herself turn to jelly inside. She tore her gaze away from Tommy, and tried to concentrate again on what Caroline was saying.

'Jessie, I'd like you to meet Ron Bishop who handles our account at J. Walter Thompson,' said Marco, appearing beside Jessie and Caroline in the company of a small, smiling man.

Jessie shook hands, and plunged into yet another conversation about herself, Tommy and 'Big City Shout'.

Jessie sat on the edge of her bed staring at that day's edition of *Melody Maker* which had just been delivered to the house. 'Big City Shout' was at number twenty-five in the charts, only two places up on the previous week, and four on the week before that. It was now coming up to a month since the record had been released, and so far its performance in the shops had been unspectacular to say the very least.

Jessie worried a nail. Why wasn't it doing better? That's what she wanted to know. Marco had promised Vestal would push it, so why was it languishing so low down in the charts?

She decided to telephone Marco and demand an explanation. It was too early to ring him at Vestal, he wouldn't be there yet, so she'd contact him at home.

Caroline answered to say that Mick had just that minute left, then listened sympathetically while Jessie gave vent to her worries.

'It's a complete mystery to everybody at Vestal why 'Big City Shout' isn't doing better, no one can figure it out,' Caroline said.

'Are Vestal pushing it as they promised?' Jessie demanded.

'I can assure you they have been, Jessie. Really.'

'Hmmh!' said Jessie in disbelief.

'Vestal are doing all they can. But if it's one of those records that's just not going to go, then it's not going to go,' Caroline said bluntly.

Oh God, was it another 'Missing Totti'? And she'd come to be so sure about this song, a hundred percent certain. It was good, *it was*, she told herself. The only trouble was the buying public didn't seem to agree.

'There's still time yet for it to happen, and meanwhile everyone at Vestal will be doing their best to try and make it work,' Caroline reassured her.

Jessie eased off at that point, realizing that a slanging match with Caroline or Marco wasn't going to help matters. She spoke for a few more minutes to Caroline, then hung up, and got dressed.

She swithered about telephoning Tommy, decided not to, then changed her mind. Ania answered.

'Yes, he's seen *Melody Maker*,' she said with a sigh. 'You can imagine how depressed about it he is.'

'Maybe I can try and buck him up. Can I have a word with him?' Jessie asked.

'Of course.'

There was a pause during which Jessie knew Ania was still on the line.

'Jessie. . .' Ania said haltingly.

'Yes?'

There was a second pause, and Jessie got the distinct impression that Ania was debating with herself about whether or not to say something.

'Nothing, he'll tell you himself when he's ready. I'll get him,' Ania said in a rush, and laid down the phone.

Now what was that all about? *What* would Tommy tell her when he was ready, Jessie wondered, her curiosity aroused.

Although he tried to hide it Jessie could hear the disappointment in Tommy's voice when he came on the line. She did her best to cheer him up, but failed. When she finally rang off she was depressed as he.

331

Going downstairs, she found Phil sitting in the kitchen with a silly grin plastered all over his face and the cloying smell of grass hanging heavily in the air.

'I'm going out for a while,' she said, having decided to go to the shops and buy a new pair of shoes. Buying new shoes never failed to make her feel better.

Phil's eyes slowly focused on her, and the silly grin became a wide smile.

'You all right?' she asked.

'Oh, yes,' he whispered in reply. Then he laughed, a high pitched laugh that might have been a girl's.

Jessie was halfway down the street before it dawned on her why she'd been treated to the silly grin, wide smile, and funny laugh, as opposed to the supercilious expression that normally accompanied his pot smoking.

He'd brought *Melody Maker* up to her in the bedroom, but had looked up the charts before doing so.

He'd been celebrating the fact 'Big City Shout' was continuing to do badly.

'Bastard!' she hissed as she marched down the street.

The following day, a little after noon, Jessie was preparing a light lunch for herself – she'd taken off over a stone since starting on her diet – when the telephone rang. It was an ecstatic Tommy.

'Guess who's appearing on this week's 'Saturday Night Out'!' he cried jubilantly.

'Oh, Tommy!' she exclaimed. 'Saturday Night Out' was Britain's most popular television programme. There were millions who considered it an absolute must for weekend viewing.

'Marco buzzed just a few minutes ago. Apparently Stormy Waters was to top the bill on Saturday, but has had to drop out on account of laryngitis. Marco has persuaded them to book me in his place, although I won't get his top billing,' Tommy explained, having difficulty in keeping the excitement out of his voice.

Jessie felt almost as elated as he sounded 'That's absolutely marvellous news!'

'Will you watch me?'

'Of course I will. I wouldn't miss it for the world.'

'I'm totally bowled over, so's Ania. It's her favourite programme.'

Jessie's heart sank on hearing Ania's name mentioned. It had been on the tip of her tongue to suggest that she come to the studios with him, and sit in the live audience for the performance, but that was a suggestion she wouldn't make now. If he wanted anyone to go with him it would be Ania.

'Which of my suits should I wear?' he asked, sounding like a boy.

'I think you should let Ania choose. From the way she was dressed at Marco's party I'd guess she has excellent taste,' Jessie replied with no trace of the hurt she was feeling in her voice.

She'd also been contemplating asking Tommy and Ania over for a meal one night soon, but perversely decided that she wouldn't do that now.

'This might be just the boost the record needs,' Tommy said, unnecessarily, as that was obviously the reason Marco had fought so hard to get him booked as Stormy Waters' replacement.

'I'll have to go, I've got something in the oven and it smells like it's starting to burn,' Jessie lied.

'Oh, all right,' he replied somewhat put out by her abruptness. He'd wanted to talk with her longer.

'Good luck for Saturday, Tommy.'

'Thanks.'

She hung up. Frowning, she stared at the phone for some seconds. Maybe she should initiate the divorce proceedings, after all there was no point in being married to Tommy in name only.

Ania Zumbach.

She had nothing personally against the woman, in fact she liked her.

She just wished her parents had never bloody well left Cracow.

When 'Saturday Night Out' started she was so nervous for Tommy she poured most of a large whisky down the front of her dress rather than into her mouth.

'Buggeration!' she muttered, and refilled her glass. She would worry about the dress later, when the programme, or Tommy's part in it, was over.

The Light were playing The Lonsdale Arms, which meant she had the house to herself. She was pleased about that, the last thing she'd wanted was to watch Tommy in Phil's company. She had no doubt that Phil would have had something nasty and cutting to say no matter what Tommy's performance was like.

The master of ceremonies was a comedian called Dick Jones who told gags between the acts. He was a very funny man, and normally Jessie roared with laughter when he was on, but not tonight. Tonight she was far too wound up to pay attention to anything but Tommy.

The acts that came and went were all top class, for only the very best were booked for 'Saturday Night Out'. Then Dick Jones was introducing Tommy, and a curtain gauze flew away to reveal Tommy, holding a hand mike, picked out in spotlight.

Jessie crossed two fingers, and held her breath. She noticed that Ania had chosen the same suit for him that she would have chosen.

Tommy was in fine voice as he belted out 'Big City Shout'. More than the good voice, however, was his stage presence. There was not a second of his performance when he wasn't in control. When he was through, he got a terrific round of applause, louder and more intense than any of the other acts had received.

Jessie switched off her set, and poured a last large whisky. She'd already well broken her diet quota for the night, but it had been a special occasion after all.

She considered trying to ring Tommy at the studio, and decided not to. She'd ring him at home next morning.

Her own phone then rang and it was Marco asking her what she'd thought. She said that in her opinion Tommy and the song had come over very well indeed. Marco said that he and Caroline thought so, too.

She had a long bath which was so soothing and soporific she nearly nodded off. Coming out of it, she got ready for bed. She had no sooner turned off the bedside light than she fell instantly asleep, to dream of Tommy.

She awoke to find her shoulder being shaken by a flushed Phil, smelling of beer.

'We're on our way again,' he said excitedly.

She blinked in the sudden light. 'On our way where?'

'Not you and me, the lads and myself. The Light. There was a record producer in the pub tonight from Parlophone who was so knocked out by us he's invited us to make a demo for him.'

'That's smashing Phil, it really is,' she said, trying to come fully awake.

Phil jumped to his feet and began undressing. 'He thought "Why Fucking Not" was out of this world, but of course he can't record it for the same reasons Vestal couldn't.'

'So what are you going to record?' she asked, hoping it wasn't going to be one of the one's she'd written for him.

'He says he has a couple of numbers which are just right for us. He's sending them around by courier tomorrow morning.'

Naked now, Phil slid into bed alongside Jessie, his hand going straight to the hem of her nightie and pulling it up. 'Tommy McBride isn't the only one's who's going to get to the top, you wait and see,' he said.

She closed her eyes as he penetrated her, and conjured up in her mind a picture of Tommy as Tommy had been on television earlier.

She groaned as, still picturing Tommy, she had the first orgasm she'd had with Phil in ages.

As everyone connected with 'Big City Shout' had hoped, Tommy's appearance on 'Saturday Night Out' was a watershed for the song. Within days it had begun to sell in real quantity, and when the next charts came out it had risen to number nine. The following week it was at number three.

Jessie was in the process of painting her toenails blood red when she received a phone call from Caroline saying that Marco wanted to see her in his office that afternoon. When Jessie asked why Caroline said that she didn't know.

She's lying, Jessie thought as she hung up. But why would Caroline do that? It was all very mysterious.

Jessie arrived promptly at Vestal at the appointed time, to find Tommy waiting in reception. He said he didn't have a clue what this was all about, either.

Caroline took them up to Marco's office, and asked them to wait outside for a moment or two. When she reappeared, she was smiling. 'After you,' she grinned.

Marco and a number of other Vestal employees were grouped around Marco's desk. On the desk was a large cake with 'Big City Shout', Number 1 On The Hit Parade inscribed on it in pink icing.

'When the next charts come out "Big City Shout" is going to be Number 1, we have that on the q.t. from the very highest authority,' Marco beamed.

Jessie could only stare in amazement and joy. If a good fairy had granted her a wish, this would have been it. Well, one of two wishes, that is.

Champagne corks popped. The toast, proposed by Marco, was to Tommy, Jessie and 'Big City Shout'. "Long may it stay at Number 1,' he laughed.

'Let's hope it sells a million,' Tommy said after the toast had been drunk.

Marco raised a laugh all round by instantly replying he'd *certainly* drink to that.

Jessie was tipsy when she left Vestal Records, but quite sober again when she got back home. In the kitchen she found a letter from Phil.

He said he'd finally heard from Parlophone, the demo The Light had made for them had been rejected. This was the last straw, as far as he was concerned. He knew now he wasn't going to make it in the music business, at least not in the way he wanted.

He was getting out. Playing 'Why Fucking Not' at The Lonsdale Arms and other gigs had been great fun while it lasted, but he wasn't prepared to spend the rest of his life as a pub entertainer.

He was leaving her, and going back home to be a stockbroker. His mother had been right all along, that was where his future lay.

He was sorry, but goodbye.

Jessie put the letter down, and stared out the window. His leaving the music business, as a singer anyway, was undoubtedly the right decision. And as for leaving her. . .

Well they'd been all washed up for some time now, she'd known it, and he must have as well. She was pleased, and relieved, he'd gone before the situation had become any worse.

Now he would marry a good little Jewish girl, and keep regular nine to five working hours, just as his mother had wanted.

Throwing her head back Jessie laughed.

And laughed.

And laughed.

Then she went into the toilet and threw up.

'That's it, finished,' Jessie said.

She and Tommy, on Marco's instructions, had been

working all morning on a follow up to 'Big City Shout', which was now in its third week at the Number 1 spot. Tommy had titled the new number, 'Lonely Street Walk'.

Tommy picked the score off the piano, gave it a final glance through, then replaced it. 'I'll give Marco a ring, as he asked us to, to say we're done,' Tommy said, and stretched, yawning as he pushed his arms high above his head.

Jessie played the tune through again while Tommy was on the telephone. Her new tune was every bit as good as 'Big City Shout'; Tommy's lyrics were even better.

Tommy returned looking shaken. 'I'm off on tour, we open Norwich a week on Monday,' he announced.

'How long for?'

'Two months. Marco wants "Lonely Street Walk" recorded before I leave. And oh . . . I'm top of the bill.' His grin was as bright as the sun.

Two months without seeing him, it was a long time. 'That's marvellous. Congratulations,' she replied, doing her best to sound enthusiastic.

Tommy ran a hand through his hair. 'I've to close the first half, and the show itself. Marco says I'll need six numbers in all.'

'Don't worry about that, we'll do a song a day for the next four. You'll have your material.'

'Top of the hit parade, and a show in which I'm top of the bill, I couldn't ask for anything more, eh?' But to himself he thought that was a lie, there was something he wanted far more than either of those, something he would give his right arm for.

'This calls for a drink,' Jessie said, and led the way through to the front lounge where the spirits were kept.

'Slainthe!' Tommy said when she handed him a whisky.

'To the show!' she responded.

He sipped, and then sipped again, thinking for propriety's sake he'd have to ask Phil along as well. He's suggest a foursome. 'Listen, I've had an idea, why don't we all go out tonight and have a slap up nosh to celebrate? You and Phil, and Ania and I. If I give her a buzz now it'll give her time to arrange for one of the neighbours to come in and baby sit,' he said.

Jessie's face froze, and she dropped her eyes to stare into her glass.

'What's the matter, has Phil got a gig this evening?'

She swirled her whisky round and round till it made a miniature whirlpool. She hadn't told Tommy about Phil yet, she'd never volunteered the information, nor had the opportunity naturally presented itself to mention what had happened. Until now.

'Phil doesn't have a gig, he's not in the music business anymore. He's given it up,' she said.

'Since when?'

'The day Marco invited us to Vestal for cake and champagne. The Light had done a demo for Parlophone, and Parlophone gave it the elbow. That finished him. He went home to mummy and became a stockbroker again.'

For the space of about ten seconds the full import of what she'd said didn't sink in, then Tommy's eyes widened in surprise.

'You mean he's left you?'

Jessie nodded.

'For good?'

She nodded a second time.

Tommy mouthed a crude obscenity, and threw what remained of his whisky down his throat. 'Can I have another?'

'Help yourself.'

He poured himself a huge whisky while he tried to collect his thoughts. This was so unexpected . . . 'I got the impression it was all sweetness and light between you two,' he said at last.

'Not quite.'

'Are you sorry he's gone?'

'No,' she whispered.

Tommy took a deep breath, then another. 'Can we go out for that nosh up together? Just the two of us?' he asked quietly.

'Won't Ania object?'

He gave a laugh. 'There's something I've got to tell you about us.'

Jessie remembered Ania saying on the telephone that Tommy had something to tell her, which he would do when he was ready. This must be it she thought. He was going to tell her they were getting married.

'Ania's not my girlfriend, and never has been,' Tommy said in a rush.

Jessie stared at him blankly. What on earth was he havering on about? Of course Ania was his girlfriend!

'Are you trying to tell me you and Ania don't live together?' Jessie asked in disbelief.

'Oh, we do, but not as I've been pretending to you.'

Jessie stared at Tommy who looked like a wee boy who'd just been caught out in a lie. 'So in what fashion *do* you live together?'

'We're not lovers, and never have been. She's exactly as I first described her to you, a *friend*. She's also my landlady, I'm her lodger,' Tommy explained.

Jessie fought back the hysteria she felt mounting within her, Ania's lodger!

'When she kicked her husband out it left her very short of money, as you can well imagine. She put a card in a local newsagent's window. I was looking for digs at the time, and I answered her advert,' he went on.

'But why did you let me believe you were lovers? And why did she go along with it?'

Tommy returned to the decanter and refilled his glass. He wasn't enjoying this confession one little bit. He felt such a fool. What had seemed logical at the time now seemed only stupid.

'That first night in the Globe pub when I discovered you were rich, and successful, and living with a chap, I

. . . well, I didn't want my life to appear a complete failure compared to yours. And I was jealous. It was a case of, if you've got someone then I've got someone too,' he admitted reluctantly.

Jessie gave a high, brittle laugh. She understood perfectly now, and, knowing herself, realized that if the positions had been reversed, she'd probably have done the same thing. What a couple of prize chumps they were.

'Ania went along with the charade, against her better judgment, because I pleaded with her to.'

Jessie could feel that her hands were trembling. She felt curiously lightheaded, that strange, ethereal sensation that often follows the breaking of a fever. When she spoke, her voice sounded far away. 'When Phil asked me out I went because I told myself that even though I'd lost you my life wasn't over, and that I had to keep going and live what remained of it as best I could. I never loved Phil, although to begin with I did like him a great deal. Lately, though, I stopped liking him.' She paused for a brief second, then continued. 'I think, in truth, because he so resented my success with "Together", he stopped liking me before I stopped liking him.'

Tommy gazed fondly at Jessie, thinking how much they'd been through together – the spell at Queen's Park Senior Secondary which had terminated so abruptly when his father had been killed, their meeting up again, Ken Young and Linton Street, his period in Barlinne Prison, their marriage and being King and Queen of the Glasgow Teds, The Tommy McBride Skiffle Band, Allison Street. . .

'What I've never stopped doing is loving you, I want you to know that,' he whispered.

'Nor I you.'

Jessie read in his face what was coming next, and it was what she wanted also. For the first time since running away from Allison Street she felt whole again, complete.

'Ania's going to have to get herself another lodger,' she said as he came over and took her in his arms.

Tommy's tour had seemed interminable to Jessie. Each day might have been a week, each week a month, a month a year. But now the end was in sight. It was Tuesday of the last week.

Tommy had just been on the telephone proposing she drive up on Saturday and join him in Newcastle. She would see the final performance, and stay the night.

And on Sunday, well he had a surprise for her then, a real humdinger of a surprise that was going to take her breath away.

She'd done her best to winkle out of him what the surprise was, but he'd refused to tell her, saying adamantly that it would hardly be a surprise if he did.

Jessie then had a thought which brought a smile to her face. Two could play at this surprise business, why wait till Saturday to go to Newcastle, why not go tomorrow! There was nothing to keep her in London after all, nothing whatever.

Jessie had thoroughly enjoyed her drive north, the July weather had been balmy, perfect for motoring, and she'd had an absolutely splendid lunch in Chester-Le-Street where she'd stopped off for a leg stretch and leisurely meal.

Tommy was staying at the Royal Turks Head Hotel in Newcastle, but she had no intentions of going there directly. She'd see the show first, then surprise him after.

The Theatre Royal, where Tommy was playing, was directly opposite the hotel, so she parked the car round the corner, away from the stage door, and sneaked into the foyer where she ran into an unexpected problem in that the show was booked out.

She didn't want to contact Tommy and, as she saw it,

spoil her surprise, so, reluctantly, she asked for the Front of House Manager.

When Mr Inglis appeared she explained who she was, that she wanted to surprise Tommy after the show, and could he please find her a seat, and *not* let on to Tommy.

Mr Inglis was happy to oblige, and swore that no one would know from him that she was going to be at that evening's performance. Several house seats were always kept in reserve, and she could have one of those.

She had a couple of hours to kill before showtime, so she walked round the centre of Newcastle doing some sightseeing and window shopping, rounding that off with a drink in a pub snug.

Inside the theatre, and in a rapidly filling auditorium, she bought a programme, and sat back to enjoy herself.

And enjoy herself she most certainly did. The show was terrific. Tommy was better than she'd ever imagined.

Finally it was all over, the curtain ringing down for the last time to thunderous applause.

She went round to the stage door, where she expected to find a stage doorkeeper, but didn't. The man's cubby-hole was empty, of the man himself there was no sign. She asked a passing showgirl where Number 1 dressing room was, and was directed along an adjacent corridor. The first door she came to in the corridor had the figure 1 painted on it in gold, and beneath that a large gold star.

She tapped the door, and heard a muffled response. 'Surprise!' she cried as she stepped inside.

The scene that greeted her instantly transported her back in time to another door she'd stepped through to discover Tommy with Eve Baxter. This time, however, he was with a girl completely unknown to her, a girl stripped to the waist who was all over him like a rash.

Tommy's head jerked round to stare at Jessie in horror. 'Jesus!' he whispered.

Jessie reacted in the same way she'd done before. Turning tail she ran, the heels of her shoes rat-tat-tatting on the stone floor as she raced back up the corridor.

Tommy pushed the girl from him, and went after Jessie. This time, at least, he was fully dressed and didn't have to stop when he reached the street.

He caught her about two hundred yards from the theatre, grabbing hold of her arm and forcing her to stop.

'Go away! Just leave me alone!' Jessie spat, her face awash with scalding tears. She was mortified at this second betrayal of her love. And if there had been this girl how many others had there been while she'd been counting the long days to their being reunited!

'It's not what you think you've got it all wrong,' he shouted, holding her tightly.

'You had a half naked woman in your arms, are you now going to try and tell me you were teaching her to dance?' Jessie choked.

'I swear to you on all that's holy I've never seen that girl before. I came off stage, went into my dressing room, then there was a knock and it was her asking for my autograph. I thought she must be known to one of the other performers, how else would she get backstage? I bent over my dressing table to sign her book, and the next thing I know she's whipped off the top part of her clothes and is assaulting me.'

Jessie used the coat sleeve of the arm he wasn't holding fast to wipe wet from her face.

'If she's just a crazy fan I've no idea how she got past the stage doorkeeper, fans are usually kept waiting outside,' he went on.

Jessie remembered then that the stage doorkeeper hadn't been in his cubbyhole when she'd presented herself at the stage door. He hadn't been in evidence at all which had allowed her unchallenged access to the theatre. Was Tommy's explanation the truth then?

'The bird threw herself at me, and I was standing there wondering what the hell to do when you walked in.' Tommy paused, looked Jessie straight in the eyes, and added. 'What I'm telling you is the God's honest. May he strike me down dead here and now if it's not.'

Jessie sniffed. 'Just whipped half her clothes off?'

'While I was signing her autograph book.'

'No indication she was going to do it?'

'None at all.'

'And you'd never seen her before?'

'Never.'

Jessie sniffed again. 'You can let go now,' she said.

'I love you Jessie,' he told her, and kissed her. Then he let her go.

As they walked back to the theatre, she dabbed at her face with a hanky. She told Tommy about the stage doorkeeper's absence from his post, and he replied grimly the man would get a right telling off unless he had a damn good reason for not being there.

At the stage door they found the stage doorkeeper and several stage hands manhandling a group of shrieking girls, one of whom had been the lassie in Tommy's dressing room, out the door.

'Come on!' Tommy hissed to Jessie, and together they forced their way through the throng and into the theatre.

More stage hands came running to assist their mates and the aged, sweating, doorkeeper broke away to come over to Tommy and Jessie.

'I'm awful sorry Mr McBride, but that entire gang just burst past me and there was nothing I could do to stop them. They scattered in all directions trying to find you, and I did my best to go after them – but I'm afraid I'm only one man,' he explained.

So that was it, the poor old man had been backstage chasing the girls when she'd presented herself, Jessie thought.

'Some of these fans can be a proper menace,' the stage doorkeeper added sourly.

'All right?' Tommy asked Jessie.

She nodded.

They returned then to his dressing room where he changed out of his stage suit, and Jessie washed her face, and put on some fresh make-up.

'I'm sorry for jumping to conclusions,' she said.

'Considering what you saw when you walked in on Eve and me, I can't blame you,' Tommy replied, and kissed her again.

Jessie explained that her coming early to Newcastle was to surprise him, and he laughed, saying her turning up at the moment she had had certainly done that.

'So much for my surprise, now what about your surprise for me?' she asked.

Tommy's brow furrowed in thought. He'd planned this for Sunday, but he supposed he could advance the date. She could sleep going, he coming back, that way he shouldn't be too tired for tomorrow night's performance.

'You did drive up as I suggested?' he asked.

'Yes, of course.'

'Then come on.'

They left the theatre by the front entrance, just to be on the safe side in case any of those girls were still lurking round the stage door.

Tommy instructed Jessie to take them to where the car was parked, and on arriving at it asked her for the keys. After she'd given them to him he opened the driver's door and climbed into the driving seat. Leaning over, he opened the other door.

Jessie got in, an stared at him in astonishment. 'But you can't drive!' she exclaimed.

He grinned at her. 'I couldn't drive when I left London, but I can now. I've been going out every day with a chap from one of the acts who says I should now pass my test no bother.'

'Is *that* the surprise?'

He switched on the engine. 'A surprise, but not *the* surprise,' he said, and took the car smoothly away from the kerb.

He knew how to get where he wanted to go, having already mapped it out for that coming Sunday. On the outskirts of Newcastle he brought the car on to the Gosforth road, heading northwest.

'Where are we going?' Jessie demanded.

'Ask no questions, get no lies. Shut your mouth, and you'll catch no flies,' he replied.

'Be that way then,' she retorted, and pretended to be in the huff.

He was really looking forward to this, he thought, smiling in anticipation.

Jessie came awake to the chatter of birds. 'We've just this minute arrived,' Tommy said, and handed her a lit cigarette. Dawn had been half an hour previously.

She accepted the cigarette, took a drag, coughed, then glanced around, wondering where they were.

'It was with a shock that she recognized the street. 'Old Castle Road!' she breathed. They were back in Glasgow.

Tommy got out the car, then coming to her side helped her out.

Jessie stared ahead of them at the Linn Park which had meant so much to Tommy when he was at Queen's Park School, his magic place he'd called it. And there was the Snuffmill Bridge, she could hear the water rumbling below it.

Tommy led her over to a grey granite house that was somewhat smaller than the rest, though still a fair size all the same. A plate on the left hand pillar of the wrought iron gate bore the name GREENDAYS.

'This was the house you thought of as being special,' Jessie said, that conversation coming back to her suddenly.

'And this street way and far my most favourite in all Glasgow, and where I said I'd choose to live if I ever did make big money.' Tommy paused, savouring what he was going to say next. 'It's not finalized yet, but I'm in the process of buying GREENDAYS. For *us*,' he announced quietly.

Jessie caught her breath. 'But . . . how on earth did you know it was for sale?'

347

'Remember, looking for a suitable property, I started reading *Town and Country*?'

She nodded.

'Well I opened last month's issue and there was GREENDAYS on the market. I had already been swithering about my singing career, and as far as I was concerned that clinched it. Fate had intervened, and pointed the way.'

'I don't follow the bit about your singing career?' she said.

'Why did you get me to start singing in the first place? Because I didn't have a job. And in the second? To take me out of that rotten cafe. But from now on that's all over and done with, it's the quiet life for me. For us.'

'Are you saying what I think you are?' she prompted, wanting it spelled out.

'If you agree, we'll live in GREENDAYS and concentrate solely on writing songs together. No more recording or performing for me,' he answered.

'Oh Tommy!' she whispered, thrilled at the prospect.

'So what do you say, Mrs McBride?'

She threw her arms round his neck, and kissed him deeply. It had all come right at last. She had Tommy, a dream house in a part of Glasgow so loved by both of them, the rest was jam on the cake.

'It'll be heaven on earth, Tommy, I couldn't ask for anything more.'

He swelled with pleasure, and pride. There had been bad years, for each of them, but they were over now. In Jessie, and the house, he had everything he'd ever wanted and more.

'I love you, Mrs McBride,' he told her softly.

'And I love you, Mr McBride.'

He opened the wrought iron gate and they went into the garden. He didn't have the front door key, but that didn't stop them looking around the outside of the house.

As they strolled over the lush lawn, Jessie remembered something. 'If we're going to be writing for singers other than you, would we be interested in a telephone call I had the other day from a chap in Liverpool asking if we'd write a song for a new group?'

'Oh aye?'

'They're called the . . .' She racked her memory for the name, it had been a funny one. Then it came back. 'The Beatles.'

Tommy paused to ponder the name. 'Never heard of them,' he replied eventually, and led Jessie over to some tall sunflowers which he proceeded to enthuse about at length.

THE PRINCESS OF
<u>POOR STREET</u>
Emma Blair

An enthralling saga of love, courage and
defiance . . .

They called it Black Friday in Parr Street when
the factory closed. Glasgow's slums were caught in
the depths of the Depression and whole families
felt the cruel sting of despair. Vicky Devine's
father, George, was devastated, but young Ken
Blacklaws had steel in his veins: 'I'm going to
make something of my life,' he would tell her with
passion and a dangerous fire in his eyes. Maybe
that's why Vicky loved him so much.

Beautiful Vicky, her love gained strength and
defiance in the midst of bleakness and hardship.
But as Ken ruthlessly fought his way out of
poverty, his ambition knew no bounds. In his
lifetime, he would break the law and Vicky's heart,
but he could never break her spirit . . .

'Emma Blair is a dab hand at pulling heart strings'
Today

NELLIE WILDCHILD
Emma Blair

The Glasgow Nellie Thompson had been born to was a city bled colourless by poverty and despair, and divided against itself by religion and class. A city where appearances meant more than the truth that might lie in a person's heart . . .

Nellie knew what it was like to be hungry and hopeless; to live a bitter lie with a man she hated. But still she held on to her dreams. Somehow she would leave those grey and violent streets behind. Somehow she would make her own life and her own world — even if she were forever denied the comfort of love.

Time Warner Paperback titles available by post:

☐ The Blackbird's Tale	Emma Blair	£6.99
☐ A Most Determined Woman	Emma Blair	£6.99
☐ Street Song	Emma Blair	£5.99
☐ When Dreams Come True	Emma Blair	£6.99
☐ The Princess of Poor Street	Emma Blair	£5.99
☐ Nellie Wildchild	Emma Blair	£6.99
☐ Hester Dark	Emma Blair	£5.99
☐ Half Hidden	Emma Blair	£6.99
☐ This Side of Heaven	Emma Blair	£5.99
☐ Where No Man Cries	Emma Blair	£5.99

The prices shown above are correct at time of going to press. However, the publishers reserve the right to increase prices on covers from those previously advertised without prior notice.

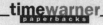

TIME WARNER PAPERBACKS
P.O. Box 121, Kettering, Northants NN14 4ZQ
Tel: 01832 737525, Fax: 01832 733076
Email: aspenhouse@FSBDial.co.uk

POST AND PACKING:
Payments can be made as follows: cheque, postal order (payable to Time Warner Books) or by credit cards. Do not send cash or currency.

All U.K. Orders	**FREE OF CHARGE**
E.E.C. & Overseas	25% of order value

Name (Block Letters) _____

Address_____

_____

Post/zip code:_____

☐ Please keep me in touch with future Time Warner publications

☐ I enclose my remittance £_____

☐ I wish to pay by Visa/Access/Mastercard/Eurocard

Card Expiry Date

_____